Tess Woods
Perth, Austr
one dog and
Love at First
and received worldwide critical acclaim. It hit
the bestseller charts in Australia and was voted
Book of the Year in the AusRom Today Reader's
Choice Awards 2015 where Tess was also
nominated in the top ten as Best New Author.

When she isn't working or being a personal assistant to her kids, Tess enjoys reading and all kinds of grannyish pleasures like knitting, baking, drinking tea, watching *Downton Abbey* and tending to the veggie patch.

www.tesswoods.com.au
www.facebook.com/Tesswoods.harpercollins
@TessWoodsAuthor

Praise for *Love at First Flight*

'An entertaining read … The main characters are believable and well-rounded and the plot both entertaining and engaging' – *Weekly Times*

'Every once in a while a book comes along to completely captivate you – *Love at First Flight* is that book' – Jersey Girl Book Reviews

'Unforgettable, compelling, powerful, heartbreaking' – A Tattered Copy

'Beautiful, real, relatable, wonderful' – Book Muster Down Under

'A powerful story that will stir your emotions – a fantastic read' – Sharon's Booknook

'It's been a very long time since a book had me hooked this much' – Books, Chocolate and Wine

'A powerful story of love and lust, agony and ecstasy. The characters are real and complicated and a little foolish. The storyline smart, brave, believable and a little tragic' – Jenn J McLeod, author of *A House for All Seasons*

LOVE AT FIRST FLIGHT

TESS WOODS

HarperCollins*Publishers*

HarperCollins_Publishers_

First published in Australia in 2015
This edition published in 2017
by HarperCollins_Publishers_ Australia Pty Limited
ABN 36 009 913 517
harpercollins.com.au

Copyright © Tess Woods 2015, 2017

HarperCollins_Publishers_
Level 13, 201 Elizabeth Street, Sydney NSW 2000 Australia
Unit D1, 63 Apollo Drive Rosedale, Auckland 0632
A 53, Sector 57, Noida, UP, India
1 London Bridge Road, London SE1 9GF United Kingdom
2 Bloor Street East, 20th floor, Toronto, Ontario M4W 1A8, Canada
195 Broadway, New York NY 10007, USA

National Library of Australia Cataloguing-in-Publication entry:

Woods, Tess, author.
  Love at first flight / Tess Woods.
  ISBN: 978 1 4607 5455 9 (paperback)
  ISBN: 978 1 4607 0541 4 (ebook)
  Love stories, Australian.
  Man-woman relationships – Australia – Fiction.
A823.4

Cover design by Hazel Lam, HarperCollins Design Studio
Cover image by Marta Syrko / Trevillion Images
Back cover image by shutterstock.com
Author photograph by Heidi Lauri
Typeset in Bembo Std by Kirby Jones
Printed and bound by CPI Group (UK) Ltd, Croydon CR0 4YY

For Paul, Tommy and Lara – my sun, moon and stars.

And for Lachy and Julesy – I hope you found each other and that you are flying together above the clouds.

PROLOGUE

MEL

Looking back on it now, I can see it was instant. No question about it. The second we locked eyes. Boom. Just like that. The me I had spent a lifetime perfecting began its disintegration from that moment. I had no idea at the time of course, I was simply relieved to be on the plane and sitting down. But it was definitely instant. And despite the carnage it brought to all our lives, I still don't regret it. Because by losing everything I was introduced to myself for the first time. Would I wish away what happened, given hindsight? No way. Would I go down the same road again given the opportunity? Not a chance.

THE DEPARTURE LOUNGE

MEL

Maybe Adam sensed what was coming. He'd shifted irritably in his sleep throughout the night as I lay wide awake, watching the fluorescent green numbers flick over on the alarm clock. Occasionally he threw a heavy leg across my thigh and I gently lifted it off. It was too hot a night for any kind of body contact.

At four-thirty I got up, fumbled with my bra strap in the dark, then tip-toed down to the kitchen, being careful not to wake the children. The coffee machine kicked into life grinding the beans and I sipped a double espresso to shake off the fatigue. The empty coffee cup echoed when it made contact with the sink. Everything echoed in this house. I looked around at the granite benchtop, the stone floor, the high ceilings, the generous open-plan living areas. What did it all amount to? A house that echoed.

I wished for a second I was back in our old cosy home but quickly admonished myself. Other people, some of our friends included, would have given anything to live in a house this extravagant. It was the biggest house, in the best street, in Perth's exclusive Mosman Park.

I really should have felt more grateful. Instead I just felt homesick.

The caffeine kicked in. I tended to my hair and face, making the dark circles under my eyes disappear, and then dabbed at my neck with a few drops of Dior. I zipped up the suitcase, parked it in the hallway and crept into the bedrooms, one by one, to kiss my sleeping family goodbye. Neither Nick nor Lily stirred.

Adam sat up, bleary-eyed, and slid an arm around my waist as I sat on the edge of our bed.

'Hey, mate.' He had that husky voice men have when they first wake up. 'Try not to bankrupt me this weekend, would you?'

'You know I'm not the type of girl to make promises she can't keep.'

He chuckled. 'I love you.'

'I love you too, Adam.'

And then I left.

I stepped outside and breathed in the hot dry air. The weather man had predicted another scorching day, as expected for February in Perth. Doubtlessly, Nick and Lily would be in the pool straight after breakfast and remain there for most of the day.

I avoided the footballs, hand weights and skipping rope littering the backyard on my way to the garage. The Mercedes was sparkling clean. It had been badly in need of a wash when I'd parked it there yesterday. Adam, I smiled.

As I reversed out of the driveway and onto the wide tree-lined street I glanced back up at the house. Its size and elegance was a tangible daily reminder of Adam's success. The house that echoed.

It was silent in the car with the radio off and nobody in the backseat, a welcome silence. I wondered whether the children would remember I was away for the weekend when they woke up. Would Lily cry? She'd given Adam a hellish time with her adolescent theatrics at being left behind last year. Perhaps this year it would be easier for her to accept my desire to go alone.

I drove along the deserted highway, heading for the domestic airport. I was flying to Melbourne to spend the weekend with Sarah, my best friend, and one of the very few people I was still in touch with from Sydney. We spoke on the phone most days. Last year, for the first time, we left our families behind and met up in Melbourne for a girls-only weekend. The euphoria at forty-eight hours of freedom from parenting had us making it an annual event.

I turned into the airport car park and of course I didn't pull in close enough to the ticket dispenser, so I had to madly jump out, grab the ticket, hop back in and take off before the boom gate came down. Was I the only person this always happened to?

I parked in one of the few spaces left, a long walk away from the terminal. By the time I entered through its large automatic doors, blisters were already forming on the balls of my feet, thanks to my way-too-high heels. On the phone yesterday, Sarah had reminded me of our plan to dress to impress. No 'mumsy' get-up allowed. For one weekend we'd be fabulous and sexy and dress boldly and feel confident for a change. So here I was, in new clothes I'd bought in a frantic rush yesterday afternoon between finishing work and picking up the children from school: a black fitted T-shirt with a deep V neck that made me feel extremely awkward about how enormous my breasts looked. This was paired with dark skinny-leg jeans that were so tight I literally had to jump around the room for two minutes to get them all the way up, and the skyscraper strappy black heels I now regretted choosing, thanks to the searing pain shooting up both feet with each step.

After spending hours at the hairdresser yesterday evening, my long crazy curls were straightened and the grey roots were brown once more. My fingernails and toenails were painted fire engine red. I wore my best silver hooped earrings and thick silver bangles that jingled against each other.

I caught sight of myself walking past a window and gasped. I was far too curvy and way too past my twenties to pull off this look. What had I been thinking yesterday? I didn't feel at all fabulous or glamorous, I felt like a silly, mutton/lamb try-hard. Hopefully Sarah would be impressed by the effort at least.

It was liberating not having any luggage to check in. Last time I was here it had been a logistical nightmare involving oversized suitcases, two bicycles and a surfboard. This time it was just me and my one little carry-on case!

After passing through security, I removed the case and my black leather handbag from the conveyor belt and was just about to go to the departure gate when a small bright yellow piece of paper on the floor caught my eye. Like a true sticky-beak, I bent down to examine it. It was a handwritten note.

Lara
Just in case, here's my number.
Jack

Just in case of what? I imagined poor Lara, whoever she was, deciding to call this Jack she'd met in Perth. She'd frantically look for the note and realise with a crushing blow it was gone. How tragic. With a pang I left it where it was and followed the signs to the departure lounge. All the seats were occupied, so I leaned against a pillar. I rubbed at the goose pimples on my arms and thought wistfully of the cardigan I'd accidentally left in the car.

I stood there people-watching. Ever since *Love Actually* I'd been fascinated by people at airports.

But I didn't notice him. How, I don't know.

Then the announcement came that the plane was ready to board. I followed the long line of travellers down the gangway, thrilled at the prospect of close to four hours with Marian Keyes and the chance to escape into another one of her funny romantic stories. I never had the time to read at home.

Once on board, I smiled at the beaming young flight attendant with the shiny blonde ponytail and shiny white teeth. I made my way along the narrow aisle, stopping every few feet as people found their seats and put away their luggage. It was no warmer here than inside the airport. Guess I was going to freeze for the next three and a half hours.

As I approached the back of the plane I noticed a man, head down, in the window seat in my row. I'd reserved an aisle seat. Please let nobody fill the middle seat, please let me be lucky enough to score a bit of extra room.

I popped my bag in the overhead compartment and sat down, relieved to finally get off my feet. I smoothed my hair and my top and turned to say hello to my neighbour. His eyes were already on me. It's those eyes that I'll always hold responsible.

'Hi.' He smiled at me and I lost my mind.

MATT

My eyes snapped open and my right hand slapped around on the bedside table until I felt the vibrating phone. I slid my finger across the screen and the shrilling stopped, thank Christ.

'Hello?' I mumbled, disorientated, my voice thick with sleep. 'Hello?'

No answer.

I sat up and rubbed the crust from my eyes as they adjusted to the dark. Where the hell was I? The bar fridge hummed loudly. Oh yeah, I was in Perth, at the Rendezvous Hotel. It was just the alarm I'd set for myself. I stared at the phone screen. 4.31 am. Ugh.

I yawned, stretched and staggered reluctantly out of bed, reaching for the light switch. I pulled open the heavy curtains and unlocked the glass sliding door that opened out onto the balcony. The temperature was mild with the slightest of sea breezes.

I rested my forearms on the railing and looked down at the frothy white waves along Scarborough Beach, still visible in the dark. The crash as each wave hit the shore broke the early morning silence. I loved that sound.

I walked back inside and found the room service menu. I rang through my order, and then packed the few things I had lying around the room. If I was quick I could sneak in a shower before breakfast came.

The warm water poured from the shower head onto my face, waking me up properly. Once dry, I threw on a faded grey T-shirt and some old board shorts and sneakers. I really should have packed more clothes; these weren't even clean. Lydia would be unimpressed when I showed up in Melbourne in this get-up. She also hated it whenever I had stubble, she said it was 'icky' to kiss me with facial hair but I had enjoyed this break from my razor. I made a mental note to hunt around for a present for her at the airport that would hopefully take her attention away from how grotty I looked.

There was a loud knock at the door. Room service. I took the tray out onto the balcony. The sky was just beginning to lighten as I drank my coffee and lifted the lid to find breakfast. Bacon, eggs, beans, hash browns. Why the hell did I order all of that at this hour? With guilt at the waste, I picked at a piece of bacon, found that I wasn't hungry at all, put the lid back on the plate and poured myself another coffee. I'd just eat something later on the flight.

The colours changed around me as I sat there on the balcony waiting for the taxi. I took a deep breath in and tasted sea salt. I could just make out Rottnest Island on the horizon.

'I could easily live here,' I thought out loud. Where in Victoria could you sit sixteen floors up and watch endless ocean like this?

It was an undisputed fact, however, that I'd never live anywhere but in Melbourne's inner suburbs. Even though I'd been here investigating a potential career, Melbourne was the only town I'd ever call home. Lydia was umbilically tied to her parents there. In any case, I'd said no to the job.

I'd been dumped back at the hotel yesterday evening by the sulking executive whose offer I'd rejected. But I'd discovered Western Australia, and that had made the trip worth it. I would definitely bring Lydia back for a holiday one day.

I checked my watch, scooped up my backpack, and took one last glimpse at the sea below. I caught the lift down to the lobby and walked out of the hotel just as the taxi pulled into the driveway. After a fleeting 'front seat versus back seat' debate in my head, I opened the front passenger door.

The taxi driver gave me a toothy grin and stroked his goatee with long curly fingernails. 'Welcome, my friend, welcome!'

Bad decision.

We took off for the airport at an alarming speed. I grabbed for the seatbelt. The cab reeked of onion and the radio was spectacularly loud, tuned into a talkback station. I stared out the window to avoid having to make conversation, but the driver had other ideas.

'What are we going to do about all the terrorists in the world, man?'

Excellent. Five-thirty in the morning and I had to help him solve the world's problems.

The trip was mercifully quick thanks to the death-defying speed undertaken by my new mate. Relieved to be out of the taxi in one piece, I walked into the domestic terminal and headed for the departure gates.

I passed through airport security with dread as I always do, and with good reason. Every single time, I am chosen for the random bag search. Literally, every time. And sure enough, as I passed through the metal detector a beady-eyed security officer with his fly half undone, beckoned me over. Finding nothing but dirty clothes in my bag he let me go, but not without giving me a 'We're watching you, mate' look.

As I walked off with my now ransacked backpack, I noticed a small slip of yellow paper on the carpet at my feet. I'm not sure what made me do it, but I squatted down to take a closer look at it. That poor bastard, Jack. He'd be waiting for the 'just in case' call that Lara would never make.

I continued on to the departure gate and took one of the few seats left in the lounge. Almost immediately I found myself snugly nestled in between two old ladies who came to sit on either side of me. So snug that I couldn't reach into my pocket and pull out my

phone to while away the time. We all silently waited for boarding
and I stared vaguely around the place.

Moments later, any trace of vagueness was sucked out of me
as adrenaline pumped through my veins. She was impossibly
beautiful. The sexy high-heel shoes, the way her body curved as
she leaned against the pillar, the jeans that hugged her hips and
thighs as if they were painted on, and the waves of honey brown
hair that fell over her shoulders and onto her gorgeous breasts,
squeezed into a black slinky T-shirt.

Who dressed like that at six in the morning? I watched her
watching others. She smiled faintly and raised her eyebrows when
a young mother with a baby in her arms walked past. Her eyes
were soft and vulnerable, a sharp contrast to her smoking body in
those jeans. I imagined myself walking over to her and striking up
a conversation. Making her laugh.

She bent down and fiddled with the strap of her shoe and
I felt major stirrings where I shouldn't. What was wrong with
me – in the middle of a departure lounge, for Christ's sake? I
crossed my legs and looked away. But a second later I looked
back, zoning in on her hips. They moved a little. Oh Jesus. I
tried thinking of Lydia but it was no good. There was no space
at all for Lydia in my brain right now. I forced an image of my
mum into my mind. Mum doing the ironing in her nightie with
her hair in rollers and her swollen feet in moccasins. That did
the trick.

When I was positive it was safe to do so without the bulge at
the front of my shorts giving me away, I stood and walked in the
opposite direction to her.

Bloody idiot! Acting like a sixteen-year-old watching his first
porno.

I stopped at the newsagency and picked up a novel from the bestseller stand at the front of the store. It had a purple cover with sparkles on it and a catchy title. Marian Keyes' latest. I remembered Lydia liked the author, so I bought it.

It did nothing to help ease my guilt about the woman. It wasn't as if I'd stopped noticing women once I'd committed to Lydia, but imagining hard and fast sex with a stranger against a pillar in the middle of a crowded airport? That was a bit much.

I heard the boarding announcement and headed back through the maze of people to the departure gate. She was still standing there. I walked past quickly, avoiding any possible eye contact.

I took my window seat towards the back of the plane and discreetly looked out for her. Had she been waiting for somebody? Was she still alone?

The plane slowly filled up, tinny reggae music coming from its speakers. A massive middle-aged guy in a bright orange T-shirt blocked my view as he struggled to fit his luggage into an overhead locker. I became agitated, worried I'd missed her taking her seat.

Then I saw her.

FLIGHT

MATT

God, she was beautiful!

She lifted her small suitcase up into the overhead locker which caused her top to hitch up and expose her bare midriff. I stared at the outline of her breasts in the T-shirt and then quickly looked down before she caught me. The fact that I wasn't watching her didn't stop her perfume from saturating the air I breathed. She even *smelled* sexy, for the love of God. I looked up to see her taking the aisle seat in my row and I almost stopped breathing.

What was this? Some kind of cruel joke? Then she turned to face me with the most amazing smile.

'Hi.' My voice came out far more hoarse than usual.

'Hi there. How's it going?' she said brightly.

Her mouth! Blood-red lipstick on Angelina Jolie lips.

'Yeah, um, I'm, yeah, really good, thanks. And you?'

'Tired!' She laughed. 'It looks like we might have nobody in this middle seat, doesn't it? Some extra elbow room would be nice.'

She smiled again. I felt stirrings again. Her light green eyes had me mesmerised. I had to stop staring at her.

The bustle around us died down as most people were now seated. She bent down and grabbed a book from her handbag as the plane began to reverse away from the terminal and taxi towards the runway.

'Hey, I just bought that book today!' I said, happy I had an excuse to talk to her.

She looked amused. 'You're into Marian Keyes, are you?'

'No, no, not at all. It's a present for my fiancée.'

'Oh, so sweet. Getting married soon?'

'Yeah, pretty soon. We're, um ...' That smile. Those eyes. That hair ...

'Hello? You still here?' She was waving a hand in front of my face.

'Oh, sorry,' I said suddenly. 'I zoned out there. It's just ... you're just so beautiful.'

Did I just say that? What the fuck? I mentioned my wedding and then *hit* on her? Brilliant.

She gave me an incredulous smile. 'Oh, right ... okay ... thanks. Your fiancée should look out for you.'

'I'm so sorry. Shit, I can't believe I just said that. I just looked at you and thought you were beautiful and blurted it out. Bloody embarrassing. Sorry.' I stared out the window as the plane took off. 'Good job, Matt. Well done, mate,' I said under my breath.

I had this gorgeous woman to myself for hours and I'd screwed it up in the first sixty seconds. What an achievement.

After the plane had gone through the clouds, I turned back to apologise again. She was looking at me.

'You don't need to be embarrassed.' She took a deep breath. 'I've been married a long time, but what you said just then ... well, nobody's ever said anything like that to me before. I'm very flattered actually. Thank you. And you're not so bad yourself.' She giggled nervously and tugged at her T-shirt. 'Oh God, now I wish there was someone in this middle seat.'

So she wasn't disgusted by me!

'You're joking, aren't you,' I said to her, 'that nobody's ever called you beautiful? I mean, look at you.'

She blushed deeply and bit her lip. 'I'm seeing red flags everywhere here, and it's barely a minute that we've been talking … so I'm going to stop now and read my book, you know – the same one your *fiancée* will probably be reading tonight.' She raised an eyebrow.

'Understood.' I wasn't smiling any more. I was imagining pulling her on top of me right now on this seat. 'I'm Matt, by the way.'

'Hi, Matt. I'm Mel.' She paused, and then continued slowly and deliberately. 'Matt, I'm married. So you need to stop staring at me like that. Please.' She had stopped smiling too.

'I'm really sorry.' I snapped out of the daydream. 'I swear to you this isn't how I usually behave. I'm a normal person any other day. I don't know why I'm being such a dickhead around you.'

She looked down at her lap and shook her head. 'I'm married,' she repeated and then she opened her book.

There was nothing else to say. I sat there, eyes focused on my shoes. Now I'd gone and humiliated myself and made her extremely uncomfortable. It was up to me to fix it so we could both get through the next few hours.

I had an idea. Fumbling through my backpack, I dug out the book I'd bought for Lydia and started reading.

Mel glanced across and snorted a laugh.

'Don't distract me, please, Mel. I need to concentrate, this is heavy stuff.' I buried my nose further into the book.

She laughed once more and I breathed again. We would survive the flight.

I gave her my best smile. 'Let me start again. My name's Matt. It's a pleasure to meet you.'

She assessed me for a moment, before closing her book. 'Hi, Matt. My name's Mel.'

'Are you going home to Melbourne or just visiting?' I asked.

'I'm only visiting for the weekend. How about you?'

'I'm a Melbourne boy. You know what, Mel? I'm glad I'm sitting next to you. I was worried I'd land next to some psycho who'd try to come on to me.'

Her laugh was infectious as she shook her head.

'Listen, I really am sorry for making you uncomfortable,' I said.

'I wasn't uncomfortable, Matt, just surprised.' She smiled. 'It's not a regular thing for me to sit on a plane and have someone like you tell me I'm beautiful. But there are worse things that can happen to a woman.'

Someone like me?

She shivered and rubbed her arms. 'I left my cardigan in the car and now I'm freezing.'

I reached into my backpack and pulled out a hoodie. 'You can wear this. And I don't say that lightly to anybody. This is official Manchester United merchandise, bought at Old Trafford, the holy grail of football. This hoodie is blessed, Mel. Take it.'

She hesitated. 'No, I shouldn't. Thank you, Matt, that's sweet of you, though.'

'You're cold.' I held the hoodie out closer to her.

She shook her head.

'Now that you know it's a Man U hoodie, you don't trust yourself to give it back, am I right?'

'Something like that.' The way she arched her left eyebrow sent a rush of pins and needles between my shoulder blades.

She dimmed her TV screen and refused a set of headphones offered by a flight attendant. I promptly did the same.

'So you've put away your book and you're not watching a movie. Are you going to try to sleep? Or do you want to give me another go at making an idiot of myself?' I rested the hoodie on the seat between us and gave it a pat, hoping she'd be tempted if it sat there long enough. The thought of her skin against my clothes was a turn on.

'I'd rather talk to you some more than watch a movie.' Her eyes danced. 'You're far more entertaining.'

'And are we going to keep flirting with each other and pretending we're not?' I asked with a tilt of my head.

'Absolutely not!' She laughed. 'Let's try talking like normal people. What brought you to Perth?'

I told her about the position with the large mining company that I'd rejected. One of the directors had dragged me around for two days on an exhausting series of meet and greets, and tours of the facilities. They were desperate for an experienced physiotherapist for their two thousand–plus employees and had advertised Australia-wide. So far I was the third physio who had flown over there and then said, 'Thanks, but no thanks.'

'Why did you knock it back?' Mel asked with genuine interest.

'Never really planned on taking it in the first place,' I said. 'The money's awesome, but the conditions are just stupid. It's ten hours a day, twenty-one days straight, and then you get fifteen days off. And I'd be flying to and from Melbourne as well, not Perth. I mean, that'd just suck more and more as time went on.'

'What I don't understand,' she said, tilting her head, 'is why you flew to WA in the first place if you weren't interested in the job.'

I sighed. 'Lydia, my fiancée, she kind of pushed me into it.'

'Oh?'

'Yeah. She's desperate to move into one of those fancy Federation houses in Malvern. There's just no way I can afford that on the money I make now. So she found out about the huge salaries the mining companies are paying, and nagged and nagged me about going to check it out. She refuses to consider moving to WA herself, so the whole thing seemed pointless to me. But hey, I can tell her I checked it out now, can't I?'

Mel's eyes widened. 'But you'll be newlyweds, and she's not prepared to move there with you? Wouldn't you guys miss each other?' She stopped and grimaced. 'Sorry, that was harsh. It's none of my business.'

I shrugged. 'No worries. She just thinks it'd be exciting to reunite each time, "like new lovers".' I made quotation marks with my fingers, rolling my eyes. 'Anyway, I'm a smart man if I give Lydia what she wants, so I'll have to come up with a way to earn more.'

'That's a lot of pressure, isn't it, Matt?'

'Yep.'

'Have you thought about how you'll do it? Make more money, I mean.'

'Not yet,' I said with a heavy voice. 'Not yet.'

Mel picked up an edge of the hoodie and fidgeted with it. 'When my husband and I first started out, we could barely make rent on a tiny unit. Know something funny though? I was happier there than in the huge house we've got now.'

I nodded. She was easy to talk to, but my stomach was in knots and my heart pounded. And her fingers hypnotised me as she gave the hoodie a massage.

'So how did you and Lydia meet?'

The last thing I wanted to do was talk about Lydia. But I was desperate to keep the momentum going. 'She was a student on placement at the clinic I own with my friend Tom.'

'Oh, you own your own clinic? Tell me about it.' She leaned in.

I described the small but busy clinic in the heart of the city that Tom and I had taken over four years ago. 'Being on Little Collins Street, the rent's astronomical. But we've built a decent practice, 'cause it's so convenient for all the office and retail workers around us.'

'Do you love your job, Matt?'

'Nah, not really. But it's good enough, I suppose. I like not having to answer to anyone, and the work's all right, most of the time. It's hardly living the dream though.'

'What would living the dream be then?'

'Not working.' I laughed.

'I bet you've got hordes of female fans coming in for treatments they don't need.' She smiled, spinning the bangles around her wrist.

'Yeah, in my dreams.' I sensed the heat in my cheeks. Oh fuck, was I blushing?

She was right though, I did have patients like that. Lonely women who came to have the undivided attention of a man for half an hour; a man who listened to their problems with empathy and more often than not rubbed their backs. Tom and I often joked about who was given more home-made cupcakes out of the two of us. It was usually him.

'So what made you go into physiotherapy in the first place?' Mel tucked her hair behind her ears and turned herself around so she was fully facing me.

I couldn't remember a time when anybody had shown so much interest in me, Lydia included.

'Sport,' I replied. 'I'd played soccer since I was a kid, and then right up until I finished uni. I got injured heaps and spent a lot of time at the physio. It seemed like an okay job that wasn't too hard. I started out thinking I'd go on to specialise in sports, but by the time I graduated I'd had a gutful of studying. So here I am, treating a few sports injuries in among hundreds of backs and necks.'

'Would you consider going back to uni to specialise?'

I laughed. 'Lydia would kick my arse if I even suggested it.'

'Ah, of course. You have to go and make your millions now.' She smiled sympathetically.

While we were talking the flight attendants had been slowly making their way down the aisle towards us, pushing the refreshments trolley. They stopped at our row and one of the flight attendants smiled expectantly at us. I read her name tag. Lara. Now that wasn't a common name. I wondered if I should tell her about the note I saw at the airport. No, I'd look like a weirdo to both her and Mel so I said nothing.

'Black coffee, thanks,' Mel requested.

'The same for me, thank you.'

'The breakfast service will be here shortly.' Lara handed me the cup.

My stomach had been audibly growling when I got on the plane but I wasn't sure I'd be able to tuck into breakfast with a chest this tight.

'So what do you do for a living, Mel?' I asked.

'I'm a GP.'

My jaw dropped. Holy shit! Since when did doctors look like that? 'You're a GP?'

Luckily she didn't seem to notice my shock.

'I am, I work in a family practice.'

'Is it your practice?'

'Partly. The other two partners are really old, as in *really* old, so they just hobble on in and treat their longstanding patients, and I get to run the place how I want, so it works well.'

'So do you love your job?' It was my turn to ask.

'I really do. I love it. It's the only thing I've ever wanted to do.'

I'd never known anybody who said they had their dream job. 'Why do you love it so much?'

'I know this is going to sound really clichéd, but it feels like my calling.' She shrugged.

'Doesn't sound clichéd at all. I wish I had that feeling. You're living the dream.'

'Yeah I guess I am.'

She grew quiet, and I wondered what she was thinking.

'What do you like the best about it, Mel?'

'That's easy.' She smiled widely. 'It's putting my patients' minds at ease. Like reassuring mums their kids will be okay, telling patients their tests are clear, that kind of stuff. I get a huge buzz from that every time. Of course, it's not always good news, I have to give out some pretty dreadful news too, and … Matt? *Matt*?'

'Sorry what?' I'd gone off on a tangent in my head.

'Matt!' She laughed. 'You did it again!'

'Sorry, I was just thinking about how unfair it is that I never had a doctor that looked like you.'

She blushed.

'Seriously, if you were my doctor while I was growing up, I would've been faking sick every week. Actually, I'd probably still be doing that now.'

She groaned. 'Argh, don't even joke about it, I get enough fakers already. There's nothing worse than when I'm knocking patients back because my appointments are taken up by malingerers. Do you know what I do with the ones I can't get rid of?'

I shook my head.

'Send them to the physio!' She laughed.

I laughed too. 'Excellent. The more the merrier. Who needs sports injuries when I can spend my days working on fake compo patients defrauding insurance companies? Makes me jump out of bed every morning.'

'Hey, come on, isn't that what you physios love? Patients you can keep on your books forever while you treat them with hot packs?' She was animated now, smiling, and sat up tall, enjoying the stir.

But she'd hit me where it hurt. Right in the guts. I scratched my stubble. 'No, funnily enough we actually like to help people get better.' Nothing pissed me off more than doctors who had no idea what we did or how much we knew, but felt free to pass judgement regardless. Suddenly she was a little less appealing to me.

'Oh gosh, I didn't mean to offend you. Sorry, I just genuinely thought those were the kind of patients you people liked. Because they're big money earners. I'm sorry.'

'You people?'

She flicked her hair and sat even taller. 'Matt, I'm sure you're really committed to your job, but I personally know lots of physios who aren't. Honestly, I tell my patients to take anti-inflammatories and rest up for a few days, and most of the time that's all they need to get better. But whenever I've sent them off to a physio, they end up spending hundreds of dollars being treated for weeks or months, or even years on end, for basically the same results. I'm afraid it's made me cynical about physiotherapy, and a lot of my colleagues agree with me. But I am sorry for offending you. I'm sure that you believe what you're doing is worthwhile.'

I took a minute to answer. My jaw hurt from clenching. 'That is so patronising. You're basically saying my job is rubbish but it's good that I believe in it, even though nobody else does. You might think it's pointless but I know that I'm really, really good at what I do. I diagnose accurately and I treat effectively, and then I make sure my patients can self-manage to prevent future injuries.'

Mel looked crestfallen. 'Matt, I'm really and truly sorry I offended you. That was an awful thing I said. I had no right to diss your profession like that. I've had a bad run with other physios and I guess that's why I made an unfair call on you. I'm so sorry. Forgive me?' she asked with genuine warmth.

I realised I was glaring at her and tried to relax my shoulders. 'Sure. I'm sorry too. I get fired up easily.'

'I'm sure you're a fantastic physio, Matt. I would totally send patients to you after listening to you talk so passionately.' She seemed very keen to convince me she was genuine.

'Thanks.'

We sat in silence for a while.

'I'm very sorry, Matt, truly.'

'It's really okay,' I said, meaning it.

She still looked anxious. 'I hate that I upset you with my big mouth.'

'Hey, don't worry. Really. I've got thicker skin than that.' I gave her a big smile to prove my point.

'No, you don't,' she said seriously. 'You're obviously sensitive and I hurt you.'

I felt my cheeks redden. 'Ah, you clearly don't know me if you think that.'

'I can tell that about you,' she said quite certainly.

I looked into her eyes, and felt a connection between us in that moment that went through me like a hot poker.

I didn't really know what to say next.

Mel crossed and uncrossed her legs and twirled her foot around, pointing it in my direction. Was she being seductive? Was she using her appeal to get back into my good books? Or was I deluding myself? She flicked her hair and smiled at me. Not a normal smile. A smile you smiled when you wanted someone.

'Did we just have our first fight?' I asked her with a laugh, to dispel the pornographic thoughts I was having.

'I believe we did,' she said. 'But we got through it. We did good.' She gave me a thumbs up.

'Can we make up now?' I grinned.

'I think we already have.'

'Not properly.'

'We made up enough.' She laughed.

'So, doctor who knows nothing about physios,' I teased, 'what kind of area are you most into then?'

She sighed dreamily. 'I love babies.'

'Sounds nice. I love babies too. Not sure about the birthing part, though.'

'I love all of it, but it's too hard for me to specialise in obstetrics at the moment. I tag along to the births of most of my pregnant patients, and at least then I get to help with deliveries. And cuddle the new babies.'

Watching her now, my anger was totally replaced by desire. As she spoke, I tried not to stare too much at her lips, or at the sexy lipstick mark she'd left on the coffee cup, or at the way she made little circles with her index finger on the arm of her seat. Everything was a turn on. Every little thing.

'Oh, and I love working in mental health as well,' she added with a bright smile.

'Wait. What?'

She laughed. 'Bring on the dramas and I'm there.'

'Really? Mental illness rocks your socks?'

'Really.' She wasn't joking.

'Why?' I was dumbfounded.

'Because I love seeing my patients beat their demons. I like helping them come out the other side when they think there is no other side.' She looked down at her drink and added softly, 'When they're feeling caged.'

Hmm, feeling caged? Interesting.

'Anyway, enough about my work, Matt. I must be boring you to tears.'

'No way! I find issues around mental health really interesting. I bet it gets heavy going though?'

She told me about a patient of hers who had recently committed suicide – a young woman in her twenties with two small children. 'Not many things worse than losing a patient when you could've prevented it.'

'Surely you don't blame yourself?'

'Yes, I do. I completely blame myself.' She sighed. 'You see, she stopped taking her medication, and I saw her only a couple of days before she died. Looking back, there were signs I should've picked up that all was not well. She was under my care and she died. My husband keeps telling me to ease up, but then he has this uncanny ability to shut out work the second he gets home. Me, I just torture myself.'

'What does your husband do?' I asked, unable to help myself.

'Adam's an anaesthetist.'

'Oh. You been married long?'

'Fourteen years.' She bit on her lower lip.

'Is he a good guy, this specialist who never tells his wife she's beautiful?' I smiled.

I expected her to laugh, but she didn't.

'He is a good guy. He's a really great guy, actually.' She looked at me for a second. 'I do love him.' She hesitated. 'But ...' She stopped and shook her head.

'But what, Mel?'

'Nothing,' she whispered but her eyes told a different story.

'What are you afraid to say?'

'It's more what I'm afraid to admit to myself.'

'And what's that?' My gut clenched. She hung her head.

'That he doesn't make my belly flip.'

That's the moment when everything changed. When she said that.

'Belly flips are important.' I managed to get the words out after a long silence. 'That's a big thing to be missing in a relationship.'

When her eyes met mine again, a long look passed between us before she turned her head away. 'We need to change the subject, Matt. Red flags again for me. Huge, giant red flags.' She squirmed in her seat.

The last thing I wanted was to make her squirm.

'Yeah, okay. So, I hear that Melbourne's going to turn some sun on for you this weekend.'

'Talking about the weather, excellent move. Thank you, Matt.' She sighed and picked at the ends of her hair.

'What's wrong?'

'I don't know. Nothing, everything. Matt, I don't what's happening to me on this flight. I'm losing it completely, I can't think straight.'

'I'm glad it's not just me.' It was such a relief to hear her admit that out loud.

'This isn't right, Matt. It just isn't. I shouldn't even be talking to you any more.'

'I know that.' I took a swig of my coffee that had gone cold. 'What about what feels right, though, even when the brain tells you it's not? What about following your gut?'

'Do you know what my gut's telling me, Matt? That there are red flags I should be paying attention to.'

'Is that all your gut's telling you?' I knew there was more, there had to be more.

She took her time to answer. 'No … no, it isn't all my gut's telling me. But I know which part I'm going to listen to.'

I nodded and smiled. 'I know it's selfish, but I'm glad there's an inner battle going on in you. At least I feel a little less ridiculous with this pull I'm feeling towards you.'

She smiled back at me. 'Anyway, even without the inner battle, you're too young for me regardless.'

Was she serious? 'And *that's* what you think the problem is here, Mel, my age?'

She frowned. 'How old are you, anyway?'

'I'm twenty-eight.'

'I'm thirty-seven,' she announced, emphasising each syllable.

'That's got absolutely no bearing on what's going on here, Mel.'

'Subject change, please. Please?'

Yes, I wanted her. I wanted nothing more than to further explore this thing developing between us. But I wanted her to be comfortable and she was obviously very, very uncomfortable. 'Okay, then have you got any kids?'

'Two.' She smiled broadly and there was a gleam in her eye. Here was a topic she was clearly happy to talk about.

'Tell me about them.'

Her shoulders relaxed. 'Well my son, Nick, he's fourteen. He's really quiet, and he reminds me a lot of me, actually. And Lily, she's my little fireball, she's thirteen.' She looked every bit the proud mum.

'Lily's not so quiet then?'

'Uh-uh.' Mel shook her head. 'She's her dad all over.'

'Fourteen and thirteen – that's a small age gap. Is that how you planned it?'

She laughed. 'Ah, no! Nobody sane would plan that. But you know what? It actually worked out perfectly, once I got past those first few years. They've grown up being best friends which might not have happened with a bigger age gap.'

'That's great that they're close.'

'Mmm, it really is. We're lucky like that. Mind you, they have completely different interests. Nick lives and breathes football and Lily's a little bookworm. But they're great kids. I'm tempted to whip my phone out and show you photos but I know how annoying that is.' She smiled.

I definitely did not want to see any photos of her kids. I knew that would just make me feel like a huge creep, sitting here chatting up their mum. We needed to move off the topic of kids. 'You're obviously really proud of them. So what's taking you away from them this weekend?'

'I'm catching up with an old friend.'

'From Melbourne?'

'No, she's from Sydney. I'm originally from Sydney.'

'What made you move to Perth?'

'We couldn't afford the rent in Sydney. Adam was working at the Prince of Wales Hospital and the prices around there were way out of our price range so he was doing a really long commute every day. He'd been to Perth before and he thought it'd be a perfect place to raise a family where we could also afford to rent somewhere close to town. Back then the housing prices were low, it was before the mining boom. So we moved when Nick was two and Lily was one.' She paused. 'And here we still are.'

'That couldn't have been easy, hey?' I asked. 'Moving across the country with toddlers.'

'No, it wasn't. But we settled in and we're happy now. So it's all good.' She met my eyes.

I gulped. Couldn't be that good. I wondered what to ask next to keep the conversation flowing. 'Do you live on the coast there?'

'We did, but not any more. We recently moved house, and it just feels like a big mistake for us to have moved away from the ocean. All four of us live and breathe the beach. I wish we hadn't moved.' She had a wistful look in her eyes.

There was a lot of 'us' and 'we' in her language. This was a family. An established family. I had no place in it. And yet I couldn't make myself stop thinking about being with her.

I banished the thought with another question. 'Do your family from Sydney visit much?'

'We don't have any family. Some of our friends visit though.'

'What, you mean literally no family at all? For either of you?' Surely not.

'Nope, none at all. Adam and I don't have siblings and his parents and my dad all died before we moved. My mum moved across soon after us though, so we had her for quite a while.' She had a faraway look. 'Not that long ago, Mum had a pulmonary embolism from a DVT after a total knee replacement. So Adam and I are both orphans now.'

'Oh, that's no good, Mel. I'm sorry to hear that.'

'Yeah, I miss Mum like crazy.' She smiled sadly. 'We were really close. My dad left her for someone else when I was two, so it was just me and her while I was growing up.'

'That sounds lonely.' I wanted so much to reach for her hand just then. But I didn't dare. She seemed much more relaxed now and I didn't want to ruin that.

'It was lonely,' she admitted. 'I had a couple of older cousins but we didn't see them all that often.'

'Did you stay in touch with your dad?'

'Yes, I spent every second weekend with him and my step-mum. They never had their own kids so I was lonely there too. I was one of those pathetic kids with heaps of imaginary friends.' She smiled self-consciously.

'Doesn't sound like the happiest of childhoods.'

'Hey, it wasn't that bad. And then I got to make my own family.' After a long pause, she continued, 'So were you a "lonely only" like me, Matt, or are you from a big family?'

'I've got an older sister, Holly. She's thirty.' I hesitated. 'And I had a brother, Rob. He died in a car accident when I was twelve.'

Mel gasped. 'Oh, Matt, that's just awful. I'm so sorry.'

'It's okay.'

'How do you ever get over something like that?'

'You don't.' I felt the familiar heaviness weigh down on my chest.

'That would've made your teenage years so hard, you poor thing.' Her tone was sympathetic and genuine. No doubt her patients loved her.

'Well, I was a pretty mellow teenager – couldn't give my folks anything else to stress about. But when I left home to start uni, I let rip. I partied hard, failed my first year. I had to get my act together if I didn't want to get myself kicked out of the course.'

She nodded. 'How did your parents cope with your brother's death?'

'They didn't really,' I sighed. 'They've never been the same since. We moved soon afterwards, out to the country. They didn't want any reminders of our old life. I wasn't too fussed with the move, to be honest, but moving Holly away from all her friends, that was such a stupid thing to do. She was out of control, just diabolical. And then Mum threw herself into the church, started Bible-bashing us, big time. It was nuts.'

Mel was now sitting with her chin resting on her open palm and her eyes wide, facing me. 'And did you find comfort in the church, like your mum did?'

'Nah,' I scoffed. 'I was too bloody angry that my brother was dead! I couldn't believe in a god that would sit back and let that happen. No, I've turned my back on religion altogether. It kills my mum that I have.'

Lara reappeared with the breakfast trolley but we both declined the offer of food.

'So you weren't a religious family before Rob died?' Mel asked me.

I shook my head. 'In name only. Rob thought the whole idea of religion was a joke, so it's kind of ironic that him dying led Mum to God. I sometimes wonder if she actually isn't as religious as she makes out to be but it gives her the crutch that she needs.'

'What does your fiancée think about your mum's beliefs?'

'We've never talked about it so I have no idea what she thinks,' I said quietly.

'Oh. You don't talk to her about that stuff?'

'No, I don't talk about it to anyone. Until now.'

'Oh.'

Silence.

'Anyway, what about you? Are you religious, Mel?'

'Well …' She raised an eyebrow. 'I'll tell you a secret. I'm not religious at all. I mean, deep down maybe I do have some kind of faith. But I don't buy into organised religion, which is hilarious because I go to church every Sunday.'

'Do you really? Why?'

'Adam's always been right into it, so I started going with him when we got married. He's on the church board and the kids are in youth group. I just go along with it all and use the time on Sunday mornings to think and daydream and make to-do lists in my head.' She gave me a guilty smile.

'So does your husband know how you feel?'

'No,' she said. 'I've never told anybody. Until now.'

Some marriage she had going on there. The guy never told her she was beautiful and she'd been lying to him for fourteen years about her basic religious beliefs. But, hey, who was I to judge? It's not like Lydia and I had deep and meaningful conversations about religion either.

'I should tell him,' she murmured. Then she clapped her hands together. 'Well, we've covered religion, Matt, shall we move onto politics next?'

'You really don't want to go there with me.' I shook my head, grinning, while I leaned back in my seat.

'Ooh, now I'm fascinated. Why not?' she asked conspiratorially.

'Because I'm way too opinionated, that's why.' I laughed. 'See, my sister Holly's a human rights lawyer. She's one of the head honchos here with Amnesty International. She sold me on the whole thing, so now I'm knee-deep in it too. There isn't much I'm more passionate about.'

'Is that right?' Mel's eyebrows shot up. 'But why does you being passionate about human rights mean I wouldn't want to talk politics with you?'

'I have some pretty solid opinions, Mel, and I'm afraid I'm not all that diplomatic if people come across as bigoted, which kind of lands me in hot water a fair bit. It's a big character flaw I guess, I'm very one-eyed.'

'I can understand that.' Mel looked at me with a tilt of her head. 'Sometimes there's just a right and a wrong, isn't there, and it's not a matter of opinion? It just *is* right or wrong. Like, the way our government treats asylum seekers is just plain wrong.'

'Exactly! Holly and I do advocacy work for asylum seekers so I'm always getting into arguments with the haters. I'm glad you're not one.'

'God, no. I'm horrified by that situation. But, to be honest, I don't really do much about it except for being horrified. I've never looked for a way to get involved. Lazy and selfish, I guess.' She dropped her gaze.

'Life's busy, don't be too hard on yourself. You're a working mum. I'm a single guy. I'd have a lot more time on my hands than you would.'

'Hmm, you're not exactly single,' Mel said, raising that left eyebrow again.

'Well, no.' The heat crept up behind my ears again and I was lost for what to say next.

'So is it mostly working with asylum seekers?' she asked, rescuing me. 'Is that what you do for Amnesty International?'

'No, it's a mixed bag. There's a lot of work with asylum seekers, for sure, but we also do research and we advocate for people detained unfairly overseas. We try to locate people who are missing and suspected held by governments. You wouldn't believe how many people are held in detention overseas with no access to legal representation. Journalists disappear after writing articles that criticise the governments. And when they do disappear like that you can bet they aren't going to be treated kindly in detention, so we campaign hard against torture of prisoners of conscience. There's lots more but that kind of gives you an idea of what we do.'

'That's intense. Do you get paid or volunteer?'

'No, I volunteer. Holly's paid.'

'That sounds like a big commitment from you, Matt. It's very impressive. It must take up heaps of your spare time.'

'I put in a few hours a week, it's not too bad at all. And when I see some of the cases, I can't not help out. I mean, the fact that Amnesty International is even needed says a lot about the state of the world … I don't know how people can treat other people like that. I can't believe we live in the twenty-first century and they're still crucifying people on crosses, young innocent boys who just happen to belong to the wrong religion, that it's still allowed to happen. And the girls, the things some governments allow to happen to girls …' I remembered the terrified expression frozen on the face of a sixteen-year-old Iranian girl whose government-sanctioned death we were currently investigating, and I blinked hard before looking back at Mel. She was watching my hands. Looking down, I realised I'd snapped the rim of the coffee cup.

Great. Now she thought I was a lunatic.

'Sorry,' I said quietly, scratching my head. 'I'll shut up now.'

'Are you kidding me, Matt? Most men I know don't get passionate about anything but footy. Why on earth would you think I'd want you to shut up? I'd love to hear more.' Her stare was intense.

I pushed the awful picture of the girl out of my head. This wasn't the time or the place to go down that road. 'No, no, I need to stop. I'll get too worked up if I keep talking about it. It makes me so angry when I think about what men do to women and get away with and how much work we've got ahead of us before it changes. I'll start ranting in a minute if I keep going and you don't want to hear that.'

'Well, I think it's beautiful that the plight of others moves you this way. It's rare for me to see a man be this passionate about the rights of women. You're amazing, Matt.' Her eyes locked on mine.

'Stop it, you'll give me a big head.' Shit, I was blushing again.

She was looking at me as if she was trying to see further inside me.

'Red flag?' I joked, feeling self-conscious under her gaze.

She nodded slowly.

'Why are we talking about bloody politics at this time of the morning anyway?' I laughed nervously and cleared my throat.

Mel interrupted my confused thoughts. 'I wish one of those flight attendants would come past and offer us another coffee. I might call her, do you want one?'

'No thanks. I'll put a hole in my empty stomach if I have any more caffeine. I skipped breakfast.'

'Why didn't you have something when they came around earlier?'

'I was too nervous to eat,' I said honestly.

'I didn't have any breakfast either, Matt. And I'm usually all about filling my belly.' She patted her stomach. 'But then again, nothing about this flight is normal in any way, so I shouldn't be surprised that I'm not hungry.' She broke eye contact and looked out into the aisle.

The pilot announced that the descent into Melbourne was about to begin.

Mel stood up. 'Well if we're landing soon, I guess that coffee can wait until Melbourne. Excuse me, Matt, I need to pop into the ladies.'

I'd tried hard up until now to resist the temptation to look at her body too much, and to keep my eyes fixed on her face, but as she stood before me I couldn't help myself. I felt an undeniable connection to her. I'd talked more openly with her than with anyone I could remember. And oh my God, just the thought of the sex. What I would give to have sex with her. I knew the situation between us was impossible and that no good could come of it. I knew that. And yet I had to give it one last shot. Just one more shot.

'Want some company in there?' I grinned at her.

'Matt, *I'm married.*'

'That wasn't a no.'

'No,' she said. 'Red flag!'

'Okay, okay!' I held my arms up in surrender and grinned more broadly. 'But would you consider going out for dinner with me tonight in Melbourne? I know a place.'

She arched her eyebrows and ducked back down into her seat, lowering her voice. 'Matt, the idea of this weekend in Melbourne is to spend time with my best friend, not to do things I'll regret with you.'

'What if never seeing each other again is the thing we'll regret?' I stopped smiling and looked at her in a way that made it clear I wasn't kidding around any more. 'What if we regret not being honest right now?'

'Matt, we've only just met. We don't really know each other,' she said with a strained look.

'I know we just met. I'm acting like an idiot, I know that too. But this connection feels real. I know it's real. Please tell me it's not just me.'

'Of course it's not just you.'

'All I want is for us to see where that connection would take us if we let it.'

'I already know where it would take us, Matt. I've got absolutely no doubt where it would take us.' She gave me a sideways glance.

This time the 'us' she was talking about was me and her.

'Yeah, and it would be amazing, Mel. Imagine it.'

She looked down at her feet. 'I really do need to go to the ladies, Matt. Excuse me.' She slid out of her seat and into the aisle, but then she stopped and turned to face me. She said nothing for a minute as we stared at each other. Then she took a deep breath. 'You're not an idiot. You're just a little late.' She turned and walked off down the aisle.

I stared out the window. I could make out the farmland in Victoria's outer suburbs. In about twenty minutes we'd land at the airport, where Lydia would be waiting to drive me home.

I wondered what Mel must be thinking about. Her husband probably. I pictured a boring rich guy completely distanced from her. Regardless, he was still her husband.

'She's married,' I said out loud. 'She's married. She has kids. And she lives in Perth. It's not going to happen.'

And, fuck, I was engaged! About to be married.

But none of that was enough to make me feel better about getting off this flight and never seeing Mel again.

I scrambled around in my backpack for a pen, and quickly scrawled my name and number on a paper sick bag. Then I shoved it inside the front cover of her book. I knew there was a slim to no chance of that achieving anything, but at least it would give her the opportunity to reconsider things.

Mel returned to her seat a few minutes later, looking more uptight than she had before, and we smiled awkwardly at each other. The plane started on its final descent. We continued to make small talk, which was a little stilted now.

She leaned towards me after the smooth landing at Tullamarine. 'Matt, I had such a great time with you, I feel like I've cheated on my husband. You're lovely.' She spun her bangles around extra fast. 'You've made me feel beautiful and desirable, and I haven't felt that way for a really, really long time, believe me. Thank you. I'm not going to forget this flight.'

'But you *are* beautiful,' I said, 'and if you haven't been made to feel that way, then your husband's a moron. He's a lucky bastard too. And you don't have to feel guilty, your behaviour was completely above board.' I stopped and looked down. 'Mel, I wish we didn't have to say goodbye.'

The plane was nearly empty now.

She sighed. 'Me neither, Matt, me neither. But we do. For it to stay above board, we have to.' She stood up and grabbed her bag from the overhead locker. 'Take care. Good luck with the wedding and with everything. I'd better go,' she said in a rush and she walked away quickly, dragging her roll-along luggage behind her.

I didn't get the chance to touch her, even just to shake her hand. As I stood up to follow her, that same enormous orange T-shirt guy with sweaty armpits barged in front of me and blocked her from my view. Arsehole.

When I walked into the arrivals area, Lydia came bounding towards me with a big wave and a bright smile. I caught sight of Mel and her friend squealing as they hugged a few metres away.

A wave of nausea swept through me.

'Hey, Lyds, look what I bought you.' I hugged Lydia and held out the book.

MELBOURNE

MEL

I knew within minutes of meeting him I was in deep, deep trouble. The power of my attraction to him blindsided me.

It was his eyes that undid me. Nobody had ever stared into me the way he did, as if he was hungry for me. And I craved him in return. There was a raw masculine edge to him with his tall taut body, the stubble that covered his jaw, and the wild curly brown hair that fell over his caramel eyes. Even his voice was sexy. It was low and husky, bordering on raspy and made him sound as though he'd either been partying too hard or smoking too many cigarettes.

I'd never felt this physical about a man before, including Adam. And Adam was no bridge troll. He was built like a Greek god, thanks to his rigorous daily routine of running, surfing and weight training. His perpetual tan contrasted with his sparkling light blue eyes, his smile was always wide and welcoming, and his wavy blond hair was only just beginning to be speckled with grey.

Adam was the object of much swooning from the staff at the hospital where he worked, from mothers at our children's schools, and even from our friends. His charming personality didn't hurt either.

I was considered lucky to have landed him. And I definitely thought he was great looking, especially compared to some of my friends' husbands who'd succumbed to middle age with their balding heads and beer bellies. Occasionally, Adam would step out of the shower and it would make me mildly excited, but those moments were becoming few and far between. Although I was married to an Adonis, Greek gods had never been my type.

It wasn't just about the physical though. Matt was intense, and I loved that. It made me wish Adam was that intense. It never ceased to amaze me how serious Adam was when it came to work and sport, because at home his constantly relaxed attitude infuriated me no end. His easy jokey manner was something I'd initially found charming about him – he could always make me laugh. But for a long, long time I'd been fighting the feeling that I wanted a side serve of passion with the pleasant.

I'd been struggling more and more over the years to be satisfied with Adam's perennial cheerfulness. A few times I'd complained to him about how unnatural it was, this perfect happy bubble he lived in, but he told me to be grateful I wasn't married to an old whingeing bastard. *He's right*, I would think to myself and I'd try as hard as I could to let his happiness bring out mine. And I was lost as to why it just didn't. Why it drove me up the wall instead.

Matt's vulnerability when he talked about the loss of his brother, and his zeal for his humanitarian work turned me on more than anything physical about him. That a man so dramatically different from my husband elicited such desire from me was wrong. Of course I knew that. But somewhere mid-air between Perth and Melbourne I was honest with myself about my feelings for Adam for the first time. I had experienced niggles of doubt through the years, and sometimes those niggles were annoyingly loud, but I'd successfully shut them down. Adam's perfect, I would tell myself. He's perfect. You're so lucky. Be grateful. And that had worked – until I met Matt.

My attraction to Matt was primitive and visceral. There was a palpable electric current between us that I'd desperately wanted to act on. When I was in the bathroom after he'd offered to accompany me there, my entire body tingled as I held myself up against the steel sink, eyes shut, my breath fast and shallow, imagining the scenario if I had said yes.

And so I'd hurried away off the plane before I could do anything so stupid as to give him my phone number. How I managed to get down the stairs and all the way to the arrivals lounge at Tullamarine without my knees buckling beneath me was nothing short of a miracle.

I found Sarah, whose flight had come in earlier, and we raced into each other's arms. Here was my security blanket, safe and familiar after the insanity of the flight. I hugged her fiercely as I closed my eyes and felt her warmth.

She looked sun-kissed, as she always did. Her wavy strawberry-blonde hair was loosely held off her face with a silver slide. She seemed to me to look years younger than I did, when in fact there was only three months separating us.

She held me at arm's length and her pale blue eyes danced. 'What happened to my friend, Mel? Who's this vixen that's invaded her body? And hello – how tight are those jeans? You're scorching hot, woman!'

I laughed a little too hysterically. 'I'm not hot! And I can't breathe in these stupid jeans. I need to get changed, I look like a middle-aged hooker. But look at you! See,' I pulled back, 'that's how you do fabulous. You look gorgeous, honey.' And she did –

sleek and sophisticated in a pale pink mini-dress that hugged her slender frame.

Over Sarah's shoulder I noticed Matt with his fiancée. She was clutching the book he'd bought her. He had his arm draped over her shoulder, smiling widely at her. I was insanely jealous.

How could he have been even remotely interested in me? Lydia was effortlessly stunning. She was almost Matt's height, her long brown legs and toned body shown off in a teeny tiny strapless yellow summer dress. Her cropped shiny blonde hair framed her naturally pretty face and her smile was captivating. She looked young enough to be my daughter. I felt ashamed and foolish.

In the presence of all that beauty, Matt would've already forgotten me. If I was sensible, I'd do the same about him.

'Mel? You okay, darling?'

'Hmm? Oh sorry, Sare. Yeah, I'm fine.'

Matt and Lydia were walking off around a corner, her hand tucked in the back pocket of his shorts. My heart clenched as I lost sight of him, and I turned my attention back to Sarah. 'I'm just sleep-deprived as usual.'

'I still don't get why you refuse to fly business,' said Sarah. 'You could've slept on the plane.'

'Only people who are full of themselves fly business on domestic when it's a personal trip not a work one.' I winked at her, knowing that's what she'd done, and she laughed. Maybe I should have travelled business class, like Adam had strongly suggested. Maybe then I wouldn't be standing here, pining for another woman's fiancé.

'Well, sleep-deprived or not, you'd better still be firing for a big one tonight!' Sarah smiled, mimicking a drinking action. 'Let's dump this stuff and go get lunch. I've had nothing to eat and it's late. I'm so hungry the luggage looks appetising.'

'Sounds perfect. I'm beside myself with hunger too.'

I did a quick scan of the street when we walked out of the terminal. He was gone.

Sarah hailed a taxi that was pulling up to the empty rank. As we hopped into the backseat, she asked the driver to take us to Flinders Street, right in the centre of town. Less than half an hour later, we checked into the same hotel where we'd stayed last year. It was one of Melbourne's finest, whose homepage boasted it had a *'charming old world feel'*.

'Welcome back to the Old Colonial, Dr Michaelson, Dr Harding. What an *honour* for us that you've chosen to stay with us again. A *true* honour.' The desk manager smiled, baring all his teeth. 'I trust you'll find everything in order. Please, *please* let me know if there's *anything at all* I can help you with. *Absolutely anything*, doctors. It would be of my utmost pleasure to be of *any service* to you.'

I couldn't peel my eyes away from his ill-fitting toupee.

I punched Sarah lightly in the arm when we entered the mirror-walled lift on the way up to our suite. 'Why did you have to go and say we were doctors? For God's sake, Sare, it's so pretentious.'

She smirked. 'I only did it because Adam told me to when he answered the phone the other day. I specifically said I wanted us to be referred to as doctors at all times by all hotel staff when I made the booking. Adam said it would get a good reaction from you. He knows you so well.'

I grunted. 'Next year we're staying somewhere else. This place is stuffy and pompous. I can't handle that wheat-bag at reception.'

'Oh, stop your whingeing. Where's the key card?'

I unlocked the door to our room, and as we stepped inside I immediately forgot any misgivings I had about the hotel and silently marvelled at its luxury.

'It's shithouse, isn't it, Mel?' Sarah said, picking up a fluffy white bathrobe and holding it to her face. 'Can't believe we're stuck in this hole. We'll find a nice clean backpackers next year.'

I rolled my eyes as I kicked off the horrible heels and slid my feet into a pair of warm and fuzzy pink slippers sitting by the bed. 'Okay, Sare. You were right, I was wrong. Happy?'

'Yes, thank you,' she replied, tossing her hair with flair. 'Now, what goodies have they got here?'

Without further hesitation we raided the mini bar, indiscriminately tearing open chocolate wrappers and chip packets. I released my pent-up feelings from the flight and barely chewed what I swallowed.

'I hope this doesn't ruin our appetites,' I said with a mouth full of chocolate chip biscuit, feeling instantly comforted from the sugar.

'As if. This is us you're talking about. Now hand over that biscuit and let's go get some real food.'

'I just need to change out of these jeans.' I unzipped my suitcase.

Sarah put her hand down on top of the case. 'No way are you getting into your boring mum clothes when you look this gorgeous. Let's go!'

We were as giddy as schoolgirls as we set off in search of lunch, me in black ballet flats now, but both of us otherwise unchanged. Trams clattered along with people crammed inside. Cars lined up bumper to bumper along the street and people scurried around like ants in their hundreds. Sarah and I were separated twice by the human traffic around us.

When we turned onto Swanston Street, we caught sight of a man in a wheelchair. He had waist-length wavy brown hair and a full beard and he was draped in a threadbare blue caftan.

'Oh my God, it's Bagpipe Jesus!' Sarah whispered in my ear, pointing.

He was playing the bagpipes ear-splittingly badly. There was a handwritten torn cardboard sign leaning against his open instrument case, thanking the people who were kind enough to donate money towards his escalating medical costs.

We collapsed with laughter as we remembered how we'd emptied our wallets out for him last year, only to have him thank us and blow kisses as he stood up, stuffed our wad of notes in his pocket and sauntered off whistling, carrying his bagpipes under one arm, his folded wheelchair under the other.

Now people stared as we leaned against each other for support, doubled over in hysterics.

'Shall we go back to that little Vietnamese place in the laneway?' Sarah linked her arm through mine as we walked along. 'Or how about Japanese? The world is our restaurant, Meliboots!'

I stopped cold when we came to another crossing and looked up at the street sign. Little Collins Street. Where Matt had said his clinic was. I had to see it. There was no logic behind it, I just had to see it. The street stretched off in both directions. I made a snap decision to head left and grabbed Sarah's hand to stop her from crossing the road.

'Hey! Where are we going?' she asked as I dragged her behind me down the street.

'A friend of mine recommended a fantastic little cafe strip down here. Heaps of choices apparently,' I said, looking straight ahead and avoiding her eyes.

And so the lying began. I had no idea then how good I would get at it.

'Why Little Collins? There are great cafes in every street here.'

'Yes but I think Little Collins is the best known street for great places to eat.' I replied as my eyes scanned the shopfronts for a physiotherapy sign.

'Huh, okay. I never knew that.'

We walked the length of two blocks and there was still no indication of the clinic. I forged on for another two blocks before heading back in the opposite direction. I was highly charged and wide-eyed.

Sarah chatted amicably as we walked. 'Hey, check me out, Mel, no double pram with shrieking toddlers, no six-year-old pulling on my sleeve. How cool is this? Watch! My arms actually swing freely when I walk – who would've thunk it?'

Smiling briefly at her, I stopped and looked around, a little annoyed. 'It must be at the other end of the street.' We hadn't come across the clinic despite walking for over ten minutes. So we turned around and started back the way we came. When we reached the original intersection once again, I went to cross over and continue in the opposite direction along Little Collins Street.

Sarah held tightly on to my arm. 'No more, Mel. Please! Let's just go to the laneway now I'm starving.'

'Sare, my friend swore it was the best little cafe strip *in all of Melbourne*. And we already ate at that Vietnamese place in the laneway last year. Wouldn't it be fun to go somewhere new? Come on, let's just try another couple of blocks.'

Matt had said his clinic was smack-bang in the middle of the central business district, so it had to be nearby. Finally, three blocks along on the opposite side of the road, I saw the big blue sign in bold white letters: PHYSIOTHERAPY AND SPORTS INJURIES CLINIC.

'Oh look, a physio clinic.' I reached for Sarah's hand and ran across the road.

'So what?'

'Let's see what it's like.' I pressed my face up against the window and peered inside the empty clinic. My heart raced. This was where other lucky women got to spend time with Matt, and feel his touch on their skin, and hear his husky voice, and see his lopsided smile.

The clinic was closed but the lights were on, revealing a modern and spacious waiting room. It was uncannily similar to my own waiting room back home in Perth. A striking ocean print graced the wall behind a slim white reception desk, and a row of red leather chairs and a black three-seater couch lined the remaining walls.

I was committing it all to memory when Sarah sighed loudly. 'Mel, can you please tell me why we're standing here spying on the inside of a closed physiotherapy clinic?'

I was preparing some implausible explanation, when a male voice behind us scared me half to death.

'Hello, ladies. Can I help you?'

Sarah and I both yelped and turned to face him.

'Sorry,' he said with a grin. 'Didn't mean to scare you there.'

'S'okay,' I gasped. 'We were only walking past.'

He unlocked the door to the clinic and held it open, smiling at us.

So this must be Tom. He had a mop of black wavy hair. Wire-rimmed glasses sat on his oval face and his smile was warm. 'Would you like to make an appointment or take a card?'

'Um, no thanks. We were just, um, admiring your furniture.' I was sure my face turned a deep shade of crimson as I stumbled over my words.

'Oh right, thanks.' Tom raised his eyebrows as I stood there gaping at him. 'Ah, we're closed for the day now, but if you'd like to have a look inside you're welcome to. We just redecorated a few months ago actually. My partner's fiancée did it all. She's done an awesome job.'

Of course she had.

Sarah had her hands on her hips. 'Well? Are we going in? To *admire the furniture* some more?'

'No, no, we're not. Thanks anyway, Tom. Sorry. Bye.' I dashed off across the road paying no heed to the traffic, running as quickly as I could back in the direction from which we had come. Car horns blared angrily, and a man yelled abuse from his window as he drove past. Sarah was following, but she couldn't keep up.

'Mel … *Mel*!'

I turned, breathless, to be confronted by her bewildered expression.

'What … what the hell was that all about? What's going on?'

I panted, trying to regain my breath and slow down my heart rate. 'Sare, trust me, you really, truly, don't want to know.'

'Yes, I really, truly *do* want to know. Tell me. Who was that guy? How did you know his name?'

I shook my head. 'Please don't make me tell you. I just can't, I'm sorry. Can we try to forget that happened? Please?' I tried to make my voice light. 'Let's go and get something to eat. I'm about to faint with hunger.'

She eyed me for a few seconds, and then her face softened. 'Will you tell me later?'

'If you get me rolling drunk, then maybe.'

'Excellent, I'll definitely find out then. All right, come on, crazy woman, let's go.'

We walked in silence for several minutes. My skin prickled. I was disgusted by my compulsion to hunt down Matt's workplace, but at the same time I was thrilled I now had this little insight into his life. And I was shocked by the intensity of my dislike for Lydia. Who was she to me anyway? Why was I so put out that she'd decorated Matt's clinic? Who was Matt to me, for that matter?

Sarah broke my train of thought by putting her arm around me and sighing. 'I think you need to move back to Sydney, sweetie. Living in that backward state over there in the west all these years has turned you soft in the head.'

'No, it's healthier I stay away from Sydney, Sare. You've just seen how I cross roads. I'd be run over in a week.'

As we walked along I silently berated myself for being such an imbecile. I had to put a stop to it. I couldn't let a flirtation with a stranger sabotage my one weekend a year with Sarah. I deserved to have fun today and so did she.

Matt was nothing to me.

I was a happily married woman.

If only I wasn't so drawn to him.

My head spinning had drained my energy by the time we reached Bourke Street Mall. I needed some solid food. We chose an alfresco Italian cafe at the western end of the mall, and it buzzed with chatter and the sounds coming from the busy kitchen inside. We sat at a wobbly round table under the shade of a rusted umbrella. Time to be normal now.

Our mouths watered from the delectable smell of garlic and basil emanating from the kitchen. We weren't kept waiting long.

'How's the detective?' I asked her.

'I wouldn't know, he's never home. We've had dinner together once in the past ten nights. I'm so over it, Mel. We've both got a week off in a fortnight, thank God. I miss him so much.'

Sarah was a rare example of a woman still completely besotted with her husband after twelve years of marriage. I smiled when I remembered that their blessed union had begun with drunken sex in the main bedroom at a mutual friend's housewarming party, almost fifteen years ago. From that unlikely beginning, the otherwise shy medical student and the normally reserved burly young police officer found themselves in a relationship so intense they were often the cause of their fed-up friends' cries of 'Get a room!'

'Does he have to paw at her like that all the time?' Adam had complained one evening when they'd left our apartment.

'They're in love, Adam.'

'Big deal. So are we, but we've never carried on like that. It makes it bloody uncomfortable for everyone around them. In front of the baby too, mind you.'

'For heaven's sake, as if Nick would notice,' I'd said, exasperated.

'Don't you find their behaviour weird at all?'

'No, I don't,' I'd snapped. 'As a matter of fact, I think it's sweet and romantic. It wouldn't hurt you to show a little more affection when we're around people.'

Adam snorted. 'I don't need to prove to anyone how I feel about you. That stuff's for the bedroom.'

Sarah and Ryan's wedding day was an elaborate affair that took place a fortnight before Adam and I moved to Perth. The marriage had produced a now-precocious six-year-old daughter named Paris, in honour of their honeymoon destination, followed by now three-year-old twin boys, Alvin and Oscar, who were as adorable as they were a handful.

Over the years Sarah had applied herself to her studies with as much commitment as she showed towards her relationship, and she was now run off her feet as a consulting paediatrician at the Sydney Children's Hospital. Ryan had gone through the ranks and now had the dubious honour of being a senior detective on the city's drug squad. They lived life at a frantic pace, juggling children, live-in nannies, careers and their marriage, but they'd somehow found a way to make it all work and still remain crazy about each other.

I'd always wished that Adam and I had more of what they had. On one visit to their place in Sydney a few years back, as we'd all sat around their dining table, I'd seen Sarah slip Ryan a sultry look. He had responded by gazing intently at her as he slid his arm inside the back of her top.

'These two are going to have amazing sex later,' I'd thought to myself.

When we got home to Perth, I tried to recreate 'the look' for Adam.

'What's that weird look on your face, Mel?' he'd asked, bursting into laughter. 'You holding in a fart?'

'I'm trying to seduce you!' I cried.

'But, mate, you've already got me. Come here, you silly bugger.' And he'd crushed me in a bear hug before going off in search of his tennis racquet.

The niggles of doubt were extra loud that day.

Now as I listened to Sarah pining for Ryan, I felt the familiar envy surface, which I hid behind a sympathetic smile.

After the plates were cleared, Sarah leaned towards me across the table. 'Enough about us, tell me about Adam. How's he going?'

Even though she was my closest friend, I'd never once complained to Sarah about the things that frustrated me about

Adam. Part of it was out of shame – I didn't want her to know my marriage wasn't as intimate as hers. But also, it felt disloyal. Adam didn't deserve to have me whingeing about him. So Sarah, along with the rest of the world, happily believed what I put out there – that my life with Adam was nothing short of a dream. And I'd done such a great job of putting that out there that I'd even convinced myself.

But something had changed. I didn't want to say he was great/ we were great/everything was great. Up until yesterday I would have absolutely said that to anyone who asked. But not today.

'He's just the same as always,' I moaned. 'Same, same. Always happy. Nothing ever changes.'

She laughed. 'Did you just complain that you guys are always happy? Geez-Louise, bring out the violins. Poor you, suffering through a life of happiness. How do you bear it?'

I rolled my eyes and Sarah sat up a little taller. 'Hello … Is something going on here?'

I certainly wasn't going to tell her about Matt and the flight, but I did need to vent.

'Adam's been annoying me. I think his obsession with his health is getting worse,' I told her, which was true. It just wasn't particularly relevant to why I felt the way I felt today. 'He's making us buy all organic food now, Sare, and no bloody gluten. He's not even gluten intolerant! He's into that stupid clean-eating nonsense. He's planning to do the swim to Rottnest Island again this year too, the lunatic. I mean he's pushing fifty and he's up training every single morning. Who does that?'

'Guys who look as hot as Adam do,' she said. 'Mel, he bought you a bloody mansion for your birthday and you don't want to buy organic food for him?' Sarah started laughing again. 'I thought for a second there was something actually wrong between you, like a real problem.'

Her words made me blush. The house had come complete with a pink ribbon wrapped all the way around its cream rendered walls, and a huge banner hung from the roof that read 'Welcome Home Mel!'. I'd once casually pointed out the house to Adam when we drove past it and said it was my dream home. Unbeknownst to me, he never forgot, and a year later when it went up for sale, he approached the owner with an offer well above the asking price. He wasn't going to risk it going to auction.

'I'm an ungrateful cow, aren't I?' I said, twirling the ice in my glass around with a straw.

'Yep!' She smiled. 'I'd be rushing out to buy gluten-free pasta or anything else he asked for. Don't you dare complain about him, Mel. Do you know, I haven't seen good old Hercules for two whole years,' she sighed, as she polished off the last of the tiramisu we were sharing. 'Maybe we'll all come and visit you guys for a week in the July school holidays.'

I smiled and said nothing.

Sarah touched my hand. 'Meliboots, what is it? You're being weird. Is something wrong between you and Adam? You know you can tell me, right?'

After a pause I said, 'There's nothing wrong between us. But there's something wrong with me. I think I'm bored with him.'

'With Adam?' she asked incredulously. 'How is that even possible? He's one of the most interesting people I know. And he's hilarious! What are you on about, woman?'

I should have known that's what she'd say.

'I want a bit of drama, Sare,' I tried to make her understand. 'I want passion. I want us to have an argument and then rip each other's clothes off when we make up. I want to have deep meaningful talks with him and really get inside his head, but I don't have any of that.'

It felt good to say these things out loud for the first time – things I hadn't even admitted to myself before now.

Sarah looked confused. 'I thought you were really happy. Since when have you felt like this?'

'I've wanted more from Adam from pretty much the beginning, but he isn't interested in getting deep or passionate about anything. The boredom's been there for a long time too, I think, but I just hadn't realised it until recently.' As in a few hours ago. 'Sare, it's always the same temperature with Adam, sunny and warm, but not too warm, with a comfortable sea breeze. Every day. Every single day. Sometimes I want thunderstorms or extreme heat!'

'See, that doesn't actually sound bad to me, Mel. Sunny and warm every day is nice. You obviously want more though. Do you guys still – you know, do stuff?' she asked with a strained expression.

'Yes.' I nodded. 'We do stuff. And it's always pretty good when we're actually doing it. Adam certainly knows what he's doing in the bedroom. But unless we're having sex, we don't have any sexual chemistry. Literally none. And the sex is just part of our routine, the weekly shag. We never get caught up in the heat of a moment and have one thing lead to another.' It saddened me to admit this to her. I'd given her such a different impression for so many years.

Sarah's eyes widened. 'What do you mean by no chemistry? Do you not think he's hot? Are you serious? We are talking about the same Adam, aren't we?'

'Of course he's hot, Sare, I mean, come on, I'm not demented. It's just that I don't get that turned on by him. I don't *want* him.'

The waiter stopped at our table to asked if we'd like anything else. I used the interruption as an opportunity to end the conversation. I was beginning to depress myself, and that was not what this weekend was about.

'I just need a good romp with a random stranger!' I laughed, half joking, half wishful thinking. 'That'll sort me out.'

Sarah was nobody's fool. 'That good romp wouldn't have anything to do with scouring random physiotherapy clinics inspecting furniture, would it?'

I snorted into my coffee. 'You're terrible, Muriel!'

She tapped her nose with her index finger. 'I'm onto you, Meliboots. Spit it out!'

I shook my head vigorously. 'End of conversation.'

Thankfully Sarah dropped it, but she did squeeze my hand as we were getting up to leave. 'I don't really know anything wise to say to make you feel better. But I do think you need to go home after this weekend and pour your heart out to Adam. Tell him everything you just told me. Mel, he loves you so much and you love him too. For all you know, he may be feeling just as bored as you are. You can work it out together. But don't go and do anything stupid that you'll regret. No random stranger-ing, okay?'

'Thanks, honey. Okay, good idea, I'll talk to Adam,' I said, knowing I wouldn't. He'd hate a conversation like that, it'd be far too awkward. Perhaps now that I'd let it out though, I wouldn't be bothered by it as much any more. Who knew? But for now, I wanted to enjoy my time with Sarah. So I told Adam and Matt to please leave my brain and make way for my girly weekend with my best friend. Adam listened and obliged. Matt didn't.

As Sarah and I linked arms again, I found myself wondering whether Matt had a hairy chest under that fitted T-shirt. I hoped so.

Stop! You're married, you idiot. Why are you even thinking about his chest?

'Let's start the mega shopping spree, hey, Sare? I might just be able to squeeze into a good pair of elastic pants after that meal!' I forced myself to smile.

Twenty minutes and a heart-stopping taxi ride later, we were strutting along Chapel Street in the swanky suburb of South Yarra, delighted to be living the moment we'd fantasised about over the last few months in our phone calls to each other. We both loved the Rodeo Drive vibe of this part of Melbourne, with its beautifully groomed people, top designer stores and exclusive boutiques. The prices inside the impossibly small shops were not for the faint-hearted.

We shopped mercilessly for three hours, complimenting ourselves on our impeccable taste, assuring each other our bums looked small in everything, and convincing ourselves we worked hard and deserved the outrageously priced flimsy dresses and chunky costume jewellery we salivated over. We rationalised that the shoes that cost more than a week's wages were in fact quite a steal, when one considered the workmanship that had gone into making them. And God love them, they had my two favourite words in the universe written on their soles: *Jimmy Choo*.

As the afternoon wore on, our conversation dwindled and we narrowed our focus on the shopping task at hand. I tried on clothes wondering what Matt would think of me in them. I bought things that were more feminine, clingy and revealing than anything I owned. I desperately wanted to hang on to that feeling of sexiness I'd had when I was with him.

I studied my naked body under the unforgiving neon lights in a dressing room. I'd been on a *very* loose diet for the best part of twenty years and I struggled to remain a size ten. Whenever my pants tightened around my thighs, I punished myself with a miserable lemon detox. I'd just finished one such cleanse the week before, in anticipation of the weekend in Melbourne.

I looked at my breasts. They were once my claim to fame, but that was before having babies took away the va-va and just left me with a southbound voom. Still, the illusion created by the push-up bras I wore was pure magic. I dropped my gaze downwards and despaired at my belly, which was soft and rounded. Despite the thousands of sit-ups I'd done over the years, it still bore witness to my pregnancies. I had a small waist but quite sizeable hips which made shopping for clothes rather awkward, and I was on a first-name basis with a local seamstress in South Perth as a result. My legs, although not as long as I would have liked, were slim enough, but my eyes were drawn to the silvery stretch marks near my hips, another lasting legacy of pregnancy. And of course the cellulite – the bane of my existence. Cellulite, cellulite, everywhere!

I shut my eyes and pictured Lydia, whose perfect body with legs that went all the way to heaven was surely free from stretch marks and cellulite, and whose stomach was undoubtedly washboard flat. There was no chance I could ever compete with someone like her. But then again, Matt had wanted me. I had no doubt about that. If I'd accepted his proposition then I would have been with him in the bathroom on the plane. I shivered with pleasure at the thought and squeezed back into my jeans.

By five-thirty in the afternoon, the shutters were drawn on most of the shops and Chapel Street began its transformation from exclusive shopping precinct to up-market dinner destination. Laden with an excessive number of oversized carry bags, Sarah and I hailed another taxi.

Back in the luxury of our suite we collapsed onto the beds.

'Let's just lie here for a bit before we get changed,' Sarah whispered.

'Good idea. Just for a tiny bit,' I murmured, already half asleep, hugging a giant pillow.

With my eyes closed, I replayed my favourite parts of the flight in my head. I smiled as I remembered delicious details about Matt – the way he ran his fingers through his hair so his curls stood up, the adorable way he'd muttered abuse at himself at the start of the flight, the look in his eyes when he asked me out at the end of the flight.

Even though I knew he'd feature in my fantasies, I was dissatisfied that no more had happened between us for me to draw on. We hadn't even touched once. It wouldn't have caused me too much guilt if he'd brushed past me and our legs had lightly touched or if I'd leaned over and picked some imaginary lint off him, would it? And I should have accepted his offer of the hoodie when I was cold. In saying no, I had missed the chance to have something that smelled of him wrapped around me. Maybe he would have let me keep it …

Sarah pulled me out of my reverie by dragging herself off her bed with a loud groan and reaching across for my hand to help me up. As tired as we both were, we didn't want to regret not going out and enjoying our only night together.

I slipped on the expensive lacy black bra and knickers set I'd bought earlier in the day, with Matt in mind. Over this I wore an old favourite – a simple red cocktail dress that I adored for its miraculous ability to instantly shave five kilograms off my frame. I held my hair up in a loose comb and gave a new pair of high heels their first opportunity to inflict torture on me.

In the bathroom, I applied makeup a little heavier than usual, including the dark red lip colour I'd bought just for this weekend. I was feeling quite pleased with my glamorous new self and applying a second coat of mascara, when my mobile phone rang. The mascara smeared across my eyelid. I raced out to the bedroom, and pulled my phone out of my handbag. I read the caller ID on the display.

Home.

'Hi, love,' I said extra brightly.

Could he hear the strain in my voice?

'Hi, Mel. How's my fashionista? Have you maxed out the AMEX yet?' Adam's voice was tinged with laughter.

Of course he couldn't hear the strain. When did he ever notice these things? When did he ever notice anything?

'I think it's best you don't ask, darling,' I said. 'How are the kids?'

'They've both gone next door for a sleepover. Tomorrow after church we're going kayaking, and then Lil wants to have lunch at that new noodle place in Subiaco. I miss you, mate. Gotta find stuff to make those lonely hours with no wife tick by somehow.'

My heart squeezed as I listened to him. *I love him*, I thought with a tug. *I love this man. What's wrong with me?*

'I miss you too,' I replied. 'That all sounds great, love. Are you doing anything tonight, now that the kids are off your hands?'

'Don't know. I might go up to the hospital and get myself a couple of horny young medical students to warm the bed. Maybe a nurse or two as well. What do you reckon?'

'Get some footage for me,' I replied deadpan and he laughed.

'What about you, mate?' he asked. 'Are you and that wild woman of Borneo planning to make disgraces of yourselves again?'

'Um, yes,' I freely admitted.

'That's my girl! Okay, matey, I'll let you go. I'm going to get stuck into that pumpkin soup. Don't know why but I'm wrecked tonight. Think I'll have an early one.'

'All right, love, have a good night.'

'You too, hey? Be safe. Don't talk to strangers. See you tomorrow. Love you.'

His voice was warm. No suspicion there whatsoever. Of course there wasn't, Adam trusted me. I'd never given him reason to be suspicious before.

'Love you too, Adam. See you tomorrow, darling,' I croaked.

I dropped the phone into my bag and walked back into the bathroom, with a sudden sharp headache behind my left eye.

'How's Hercules?' Sarah looked up from painting her toenails.

'He's fine,' I said flatly. 'He says hi. He's having an early night.'

'God bless him, like he needs the beauty sleep,' she laughed.

I regarded myself coolly in the bathroom mirror. 'You are a stupid, stupid woman,' I hissed at the reflection.

I shook Matt from my head, wiped off the red lipstick, replaced it with a clear gloss, and sent a mental kiss to my unsuspecting husband who was missing me back at home.

No more nonsense.

Finished.

It was still warm outside as Sarah and I walked the two blocks to Collins Street. When we reached the corner, she looked at me with a grin.

'Now, Meliboots, are you absolutely sure you don't feel like going up an extra block and taking me for a quick run up and down Little Collins before dinner?'

I bumped her shoulder with mine as I soaked in the atmosphere created by the thousands of fairy lights embedded in the branches of the trees that lined the street. It was spectacular.

We walked to a little Indian restaurant that Sarah had chosen after reading a great review about it. As we ploughed through a delicious and spicy dinner, we were entertained by an elderly musician with a startlingly long white moustache. He was flogging a sitar with impressive gusto and singing passionately, inviting 'everybody now' to join in with the Hindu lyrics. Sarah, to my embarrassment, did so quite loudly with a sequence of 'hummenna hummennas'. The man beamed at her and strummed a little louder, encouraged by her enthusiasm.

Following dinner, we strolled back to the hotel and took up residency at the crowded nightclub on the first floor, where we were lucky enough to find seats. The two smirking men who sidled up to us offering to buy our drinks were shooed away, and we proceeded to down Cosmopolitans that were dangerously easy to drink, lining up our empty glasses in a row along the table between us.

Later in the evening, a fantastic cover band took over the small stage and we sang along – not caring how out of tune we sounded – to all the songs we recognised from our youth. We joined the other patrons in a particularly rousing version of Cold Chisel's 'Khe Sanh'.

We were too afraid of losing our prized seats to risk getting up for a twirl on the dance floor, so we compensated with exaggerated upper body moves while we stayed seated. The vibration of the music pumped through the stool and up into my body. It was hot, sweaty and so noisy that we had to shout in each other's ears to be heard. It was perfect.

With our voices escalating and our drinks taking effect, Sarah lost her balance and fell off her bar stool with a resounding thump. She stood herself up happily, claiming she didn't feel a thing, despite a rather large bruise immediately appearing on her upper arm.

Several times over the course of the evening she tried to coax information out of me. 'So are you drunk enough to tell me about that hot physio, Tom?' she asked, wiggling her eyebrows each time.

'Nowhere near drunk enough, I'm afraid. It's going to take another Cosmo, I think,' I replied every time with a sigh.

Soon after midnight, we held onto each other as we stumbled to the lift and back up into our suite. We were more than a little drunk.

'Mel, I need drink!' Sarah announced as she shoved her head deep inside the bar fridge.

I cheered as she emerged with a bottle of champagne.

'Ya wanna join me for a nightcap, Melibootsh?'

'I'd love to, darling.'

'Eggshellent! Lemme jus lie down 'ere for a shec and then we'll toasht ourshelves, becosh my darlin' girl, *we* are fabuloush women!' She dropped the full bottle onto the carpeted floor and staggered to bed. Less than a minute later, she was unconscious and snoring deeply.

I struggled to take off her stilettos and then covered her with a bathrobe. I congratulated myself out loud for being so considerate. Then I put the champagne back in the fridge and sank into the rocking chair next to the window. I'd always been more of a stayer than Sarah.

I watched the cars cruising along below. I could just make out the lights of the city's major train station off to my left. Melbourne was bubbling with life here at night in the middle of the city, as opposed to the silent suburban streets of Perth. Engines revved and horns sounded as groups of young people called out to each other. A car stereo blasted Eminem's angry lyrics onto the street.

I was too wired to contemplate sleep so I heaved myself out of the chair, with some difficulty, and went in search of my new book, wondering how much of the plot I'd remember tomorrow.

A folded paper bag fell out onto my lap as I opened the front cover. The hurried writing was barely legible:

Mel

Just in case, here's my number.

Matt

I gasped for air as my stomach took a dive. I stared at his writing until my eyes crossed and the words blurred. Despite my best intentions, my longing for him had only grown through the night.

I debated with myself for an hour and a half, by which stage I was just about sober.

It was past one-thirty in the morning.

With trembling fingers, I reached for my phone and sent him a text.

Are you still up?

CITY LIGHTS

MATT

I caught one last glimpse of Mel out of the corner of my eye, before Lydia and I headed out to the airport car park. She was watching us. A trickle of acid burned the lining of my stomach.

I forced myself to listen to Lydia, who was breathlessly recounting how she'd asserted herself with the cake decorator yesterday. They had argued back and forth for half an hour, with the woman finally agreeing to knock a hundred dollars off the price of the four-tiered carrot cake. I smiled at Lydia's joy over something so trivial.

Choosing a carrot cake had been Lydia's one and only break with tradition for the wedding. I'd initially suggested it, my reason simply being we both loved carrot cake. After much heated debate between Lydia and her mother, carrot cake had won the day. By that stage I regretted suggesting it in the first place. The cake was now known as '*Matt's* carrot cake' and on the rare occasion I dared raise issue with Lydia's mother about her ridiculous plans for the wedding, I was pointedly reminded that I'd gotten my way with the cake.

'Anyway, I was just, like, bursting to tell you last night, but then I thought, no, I'll surprise him with it at the airport! I know how much this cake means to you, Matty, and now it's a bargain too!' Lydia beamed.

'You're a champ, Lyds. Well done, babe.' I hoped I sounded enthusiastic enough.

'Okay, now tell me everything, I'm absolutely dying to know what happened. Didn't you have phone coverage there or something? You didn't call,' she said lightly, still smiling.

'Yeah, nah, no coverage. Was out of range the whole time,' I mumbled, scratching hard at my stubble.

'So, are we going to be rich, Matty?' She looked at me with eager eyes.

Time to come clean. 'Maybe one day, babe, but not because of the mining boom in WA,' I said without taking a breath.

The smile vanished. She crossed her arms.

We stood in awkward silence facing each other from opposite sides of her tiny silver hatchback.

'Right then, I see.' There was no small amount of contempt in her voice. 'Why didn't you take the job, Matt? Why? You know how much I wanted you to accept it. It was, like, it was perfect for us.'

'It wasn't perfect for me.'

She pursed her lips and looked down at the ground. 'You didn't give it a chance. How do you know?'

I sighed, exasperated. 'Because I know myself. I know I would've been miserable.' I leaned my elbows on the roof of the car and told her about the woeful accommodation, the stinking hot weather, the red dust everywhere that you could taste when you swallowed, the thousands upon thousands of flies, the eerie quiet at night, and the fact that everyone was there purely for the money, nobody chose to live there for any other reason. 'And you already knew how I felt about the long hours and all the flying. Come on, Lyds, give me some credit for at least going there to check it out.'

She didn't answer, but climbed into the driver's seat and slammed the door.

I stood there for a minute and lifted my face up to the sun. The sky was cloudless and the air was warm. Any other time, this would've been a glorious Melbourne day.

I crammed myself into the passenger seat and rested my hand on her leg as she reversed out of the parking space. 'I'm sorry. Don't be upset with me. Please?' I said quietly.

Her face softened just a little. 'I just think it was worth a shot, that's all. Doing it tough for a year or two, it could've set us up for life. But I can't exactly make you take it, can I? And Mum and Dad would just, like, die if I went myself. So I guess that's that then.'

She drove in silence for a little longer, but then she started telling me about some of the strange patients she'd come across at the hospital that week and it seemed I was forgiven. I studied Lydia as she babbled happily now. She was energetic and engaging and she looked gorgeous. I definitely still fancied her, but something had shifted during the course of that flight. I was full of doubt. Did I actually love this woman? I didn't know. But what I did know with a cold certainty was that nobody should marry anybody unless they knew beyond a shadow of a doubt that they were desperately in love with them and couldn't bear to live without them. The wedding was four months away.

Shit.

I couldn't pull out, it would shatter her. She didn't deserve the humiliation of being jilted at the altar. And her dad would kill me. For real. I remembered what he said to me when Lydia and I became engaged – 'I know my daughter loves you, Matthew, and she'd be devastated if I didn't give my blessing to this union. But my gut tells me you'll hurt her. You're too broody for my liking and I don't trust broody people. And you're cocky. I don't like cocky. That girl is my angel, and if you ever hurt her I'll make you regret it. Do you understand me, boy?'

Up until now, I'd been offended by her dad's doubts about me. Yet I would have quite willingly cheated on her that morning with a stranger. He was right not to trust me.

I stroked her hair as she drove. She would never cheat on me. Lydia could never be unfaithful to anyone, she was just too decent and innocent. Her world was black and white, and she didn't break the rules.

This was the first time in our relationship I felt unworthy of her. She deserved to be with someone who'd appreciate her effort to stand up to her iron-fisted mother over a wedding cake. She deserved someone who was so blown away by her stunning looks and sweet happy personality, he'd take any job in any place just to please her. And most of all, she deserved someone who wouldn't try to seduce another woman on a plane.

I thought back to three years earlier, the day she'd turned up for her five-week placement at our clinic. Tom and I had high-fived each other at our luck to have landed a hot twenty-year-old student. Unfortunately for Tom, he had his girlfriend Emma, now his wife, to consider. I had nothing holding me back though.

As well as being pretty, Lydia was confident and friendly, which at the time ticked all the right boxes for me. I asked her out on her last day of work with us. My chest puffed when she said yes. She was far more attractive than any girl I'd gone out with before.

We had heaps of fun in our first year together, it was one big party as we bar hopped most weekends with her university crowd. I'd missed that since graduating five years earlier. I'd been too caught up in hospital work and then later had become bogged down with the responsibility of running a business.

Being with Lydia made me feel young and free again. She was always looking for the next good time and I happily followed her. She was an eternal optimist who'd never contemplated life not being perfect for her. Life wouldn't dare.

It was good for me to be with somebody like her. Over time, some of her sunshine penetrated my thick cynical walls and I started to think maybe the world wasn't all doom and despair after all.

She refused to hear any details about my work with Amnesty International, finding it too depressing. And she didn't stand for my moods when the volunteer work got me down.

'Get a grip, Matty,' she'd snap, rolling her eyes. 'This execution in Bangladesh is awful news and I know you feel bad about it. You did all you could to stop it but you can't win every time. Now stop wallowing, all right? It's not going to change anything. You're alive, you're healthy and you've got me. Life is good! Come on, mister, we're going out. Get up!'

A few months into our relationship, I told her I was the happiest I'd been since my brother died.

'I'm happy too.' She smiled. 'And I'm happy that you're happy. I remember thinking you looked so sad when I met you, Matty, but you don't look sad any more.'

She'd listened to me describe the night my parents had a knock on the door to announce that Rob was in intensive care. We threw coats over our pyjamas and somehow the policewoman who drove us to the hospital managed to go through countless red lights with all of us unscathed. Mum wailed at Rob's bedside, Dad cried silently beside her, and Holly and I stood back, dumbstruck, until the doctor turned off Rob's ventilator and his heart stopped.

Lydia sniffled as I spoke. 'Matty, that's the saddest story I've ever heard. How about I give you a nice massage to help you forget?'

The massage led to great sex, which certainly took my mind off Rob. So I never got to tell her how I'd sat and watched him, being dead, for over an hour, and how I was struck by how silent and still he was. No breath sounds, no chest rise and fall, no fidgeting. I never got to tell her about how I practised being still in bed that night while I listened to my parents fall to bits in the dining room. And about how being still became my secret thing to do when I first went to bed every night, at least until I moved out and had girlfriends sleep over and I had to act normal. And how every now and again, I still did it when I was on my own. But Lydia never found out about any of that. Instead we had great sex. And I never brought the topic of Rob up again until the flight with Mel, where she'd listened the way I wished Lydia had listened.

Lydia was well aware of her appeal, and she paid careful attention to her appearance. Her skin was always soft and smooth, her hair shiny and sleek, and her muscles toned to perfection. Sex with her was fantastic; she was adventurous and up for anything, so I was always looking for ways to get her into bed. And the fact that she wasn't in my bed every night drove me crazy.

She still lived at home with her mum and dad.

From the start, the biggest downer in our relationship was her parents. They'd migrated from England ten years earlier when her dad's accounting firm sent him to Melbourne to start up the

Australian arm of the business. Having no other relatives here seemed to have made them unnaturally reliant on each other. Her older brother was in the navy and always away, which made Lydia feel even more obligated to her parents.

I spent a few evenings a week at their house. Her parents were begrudgingly civil towards me, but only just, and they made it clear they didn't want me crashing in on their exclusive club of three. Early on Lydia protested that her parents adored me and that I'd misunderstood them. But later, as they made less and less of an effort, even she couldn't keep pretending.

Eighteen months into our relationship, Lydia's not so subtle hints became increasingly difficult to ignore. She was hungry for a proposal. She wasn't satisfied being just a girlfriend any more – she was ready to 'move forward' and 'take it to the next level' and 'keep the momentum going'. She cut pictures of diamond rings out of catalogues and glued them onto the cereal boxes in my pantry. I'd never been in love before and I figured that what I had with Lydia was close enough to it. I was also fully aware that I was punching well above my weight and that I'd be stupid to let her go.

Since moving out of home I didn't have all that much to do with my own parents. They still lived in rural Daylesford, about an hour and a half's drive away. But when I was tossing up whether to ask Lydia to marry me, I rang Dad for advice. Both my parents thought the world of Lydia, and Dad told me to go for it.

'She's brought some life into you, Matty. You're a new man thanks to her. She'll make a beaut wife for you, son. And she'll breed high quality kids too!'

Tom echoed Dad's words. He and Emma were also huge fans of Lydia. I could picture an easy, happy life with her so I took their advice. I proposed on bended knee following a Valentine's Day dinner at a fancy restaurant overlooking Albert Park Lake. Her delighted screams and hysterical phone call to her mum warmed my heart.

Alone in bed the following night, however, I couldn't get rid of the metallic taste in my mouth, no matter how much water I drank. I practised being still for a long time that night.

Almost immediately following the engagement, the wheels started to come off. It seemed that overnight the easy-going girl I'd fallen for had become an obsessive bride. Lydia lived and breathed the wedding, scaring the hell out of me as the plans got bigger and bigger. Our once fun weekends were now taken up with reception venue viewings, meetings with videographers and countless hours trekking around claustrophobic bridal fairs, comparing ugly ice sculptures and over-the-top floral centrepieces.

I complained. A lot. We had our first real fight when I asked if she could please scale back the two hundred and seventy-five guests. But Lydia was adamant her special day would be nothing less than the perfect fairy-tale she'd dreamed of since she was a little girl. And who was I to argue with that?

I went to Tom for sympathy but he just laughed. 'She's a classic Bridezilla,' he said as he slapped my back. 'Em was the same. They lose the plot, but once the wedding's done she'll be right. Just agree, agree, agree if you want to be happy, mate. Happy wife, happy life.'

As well as the massive expense of the wedding to worry about, I was kicking myself that we hadn't discussed money before I'd proposed. We had very different ideas about our future lifestyle – I had to work out a way to make more money, and I had no idea how I was going to do that.

The longer we were engaged, the more the feeling of foreboding grew but I stamped it out by focusing on all the good things about her. I hoped things would change once we were married and that I'd be happier then. But I'd never had the conscious thought that I might not be in love with her. Until now.

The few short hours I'd had with Mel on the flight had put a magnifying glass on everything that was missing in my relationship with Lydia. I'd seen the possibility of having more, of perhaps having it all. The connection I felt with Mel was the real thing. Of that I was certain. My gut couldn't lie.

Lydia smiled at me as she pulled to a stop at an intersection. I smiled back.

Yes, Mel might be my dream woman, but she was married and not a part of my life. Lydia was here, and I had to marry her, and that had to be okay. I had to talk myself out of thinking this was a mistake, it'd only create resentment and that would make things toxic. I really didn't want that.

My dad was right, she'd changed me for the better and made me happier. Once this stupid wedding was over with, and the flight with Mel was a distant memory, then things would be great again. I would eventually forget I'd ever had doubts. I'd grow to love her more in marriage, especially once she was the mother of my children. How could I not?

By the time we pulled up into my driveway, I'd convinced myself that everything was going to be good between us again. It came crashing down quickly.

She leaned across to kiss my cheek. 'Welcome back,' she chirped. 'I can't come in though, I've got heaps of stuff to catch up on at home.'

'Come on, babe. Come inside, just for a bit.' I slid my index finger along the line of her cleavage. I desperately wanted to have sex with her. It always helped to remind me why we were good together. 'I can't, Matty, I'm busy,' she said coyly. 'Plus I'm having a fat day. I feel all, like, yucky and wobbly.'

'Oh for Christ's sake, Lyds, not again,' I moaned. 'You're *tiny*. There's not a gram of fat on you, and it's been over a week. Please come in?'

She shook her head firmly. 'No, Matty, it's not happening today. I feel huge. I had *rice* yesterday!'

I rolled my eyes and looked out the window. Her obsession with the scales had soared to new heights as the wedding date grew closer. I'd forgotten how much that annoyed me, having had a few days break from hearing about it. Between her fat days, PMT days, tired days and headache days, there were none too many days left for having sex at all. And I was quietly stressing, all too aware of Tom's complaint that sex dried up once he'd been married for a while.

But sitting in the hot car in the driveway, I knew there was no use trying to argue my point any further.

'Okay then, I'll see you at dinner. Thanks for the lift.' I kissed the top of her head and got out of the car, feeling frustrated in more ways than one.

As I waved goodbye, the dissatisfaction and resentment churned in my stomach. How could I be this angry with her and at the same time feel like a total prick who didn't deserve her?

I sighed as I unlocked the front door to the shared entrance and made my way upstairs into my apartment. It smelled musty. I pushed hard on the creaky windows and let in some air. I looked through the mail I'd collected on my way in and hunted for food in the pantry. The best I could find was an open tube of Pringles.

I threw myself down on the faded blue sofa and crunched on the stale chips while I flicked through the TV channels. There was a one-day international cricket match live from Adelaide. I watched, disinterested. The small apartment I usually loved coming home to felt dull and empty. I reached for the phone and called Tom.

'Hey Matt, you home yet?'

I breathed out with relief at the sound of Tom's voice, 'Hey. Yeah, I'm back. You got any patients left?'

'Nah, I'm done, finished up a while ago. So, how was it?'

'Like I thought it would be. You free for a drink later this arvo?'

'No, I can't. But I'm just about to get a coffee up the road now.' He sounded tired. 'Why don't you come hang out for a while? We could go over last month's stats.'

I lunged for my keys. I could talk to Tom about the chaos in my head. He had a knack of putting things into perspective whenever I needed it.

Walking into the garage, I did a quick once over of my red hotted-up Commodore before getting into the driver's seat. I smiled as I heard its big engine come to life. That car could always cheer me up. I drove straight to the nearest fast food drive-thru and scoffed down a burger and a large Coke as I headed into the city.

The traffic slowed along Flinders Street. People were out in their hundreds. Tom always worked Saturdays while I worked late on Thursday and Friday nights, so I wasn't used to the city on a weekend early afternoon. The grey suits and blank faces were replaced with colour. I heard the sound of families and the sound of happiness. Then I saw the lunatic in the caftan who hung out on the corner of Swanston Street with his bagpipes and I closed the windows.

A few minutes later, I parked in the reserved space in the car park closest to the clinic and strolled over to the coffee shop a few buildings away. It was packed, and loud with conversations and the grinding of coffee beans. The queue was longer than usual, but the coffee here was worth it so I hopped into line. Tony, the always smiling barista, stretched his arm across the counter when I got to the front of the queue, and gave me a slightly too firm handshake.

'Heya, Matt! Haven't seen you for a few days, mate. How's that beautiful Lydia, your beautiful lady? You take her for romantic summer holiday, eh?'

'She's great thanks, mate,' I replied automatically. 'Just me who went away this time. It was a long few days without one of your espressos, Tony.'

'You leave her all alone and you go away by yourself?' He laughed as he started on my coffee. 'Mate, you stupid or something, eh?'

I smiled.

'I still can't believe she pick you, not me! Still, she got plenty a time to change her mind. You tell her Tony still waiting!'

I made myself laugh at the line I'd heard almost every day for the past three years.

Tony had made a major fuss of Lydia ever since the first time she walked into his crammed coffee shop. The middle-aged, short, stocky Sicilian, with a comb-over, was just another in a long list of men who probably fantasised about her in the shower.

*

Tom smiled broadly when he saw me walk into the clinic a couple of minutes later. 'Look at you, you messy bastard. You lose your razor?'

I grinned and gave him a one finger salute.

'What's the verdict?' he asked in a casual voice but with an anxious face. 'Do I still have a partner?'

I told him about what went down in WA and he looked as relieved as I felt when I said I definitely wasn't taking the job.

'How'd Lyds take it? Not good?'

'She'll get over it.' I shrugged. 'How's Shamu?'

It was unfair to compare Tom's wife to a killer whale but Emma was eight and a half months pregnant with their first child. She was snappy, grumpy and miserable the last time I'd seen her a fortnight ago. It didn't help that as well as having ankles the size of soccer balls she was also in terrible pain with sciatica. I didn't miss her company.

'She's bloody scary, that's how she is,' Tom groaned, looking very hard done by. 'Last night she's snoring for Australia, right, so I gently shake her awake, and ask her in a real nice way if she can cut it out so I can get some sleep. Whoa, *big* mistake. Mate, did she let me have it! I'm counting down the days till this baby comes out and I'm not shitting myself around her any more.'

I laughed. Emma had never been diplomatic at the best of times, I could just imagine how much she'd be breaking Tom's balls now.

'Things been okay here? How was the locum?' I asked.

Tom brought me up to date before we began the joyless task of reviewing the debtors' list, as well as the week by week revenue. At times like this, the money we saved by not having a bookkeeper didn't seem worth it.

An hour later, we leaned back in our chairs, relieved that we'd made a small profit last month. January was traditionally a slow time for us, when many of the surrounding businesses shut down over the summer school holidays, so the good figures were a surprise and extra sweet.

But I'd struggled to concentrate on the numbers while my mind raced. I took a deep breath. 'Tom, mate, um, I need you to remind me why marrying Lydia isn't a huge mistake.'

He looked up sharply from the papers he was filing away. After a short silence he ventured, 'Ahhh … because you love her?'

I stared blankly at him. He gave a low whistle and sat back down.

'All right then, how about because she's the best thing that ever happened to you?'

'Go on.'

'Well, she's smart, she's friendly, everyone loves her. She's great fun, she's caring.' He took my silence as encouragement to keep talking. 'She's a bloody stunner too, don't forget. And last, but in no way least, to quote you, "she's a firecracker between the sheets".'

I nodded.

He was on a roll now. 'Whereas you, mate, are a pale scrawny loser with a face that looks like a slapped arse and the personality of a wet mop.'

We both laughed.

'For reasons unknown to anyone bar God,' he continued, 'and going against all laws of nature, she actually loves you.'

The smirk quickly disappeared off Tom's face when he saw the look on mine.

'What's going on, Matt?'

'We've got nothing in common,' I explained. 'She acts like I bore her a lot of the time. And to be honest, sometimes she bores me too.'

'Since when?' Tom's voice was high-pitched now. 'You've got loads in common with her. You're in the same profession, you both love having a drink, catching a band, you play tennis together. What are you talking about, you dickhead? She's not boring. And by the way, you *are* boring.'

'Excuse me?'

'You are! You're shit boring! Look how much you crap on about all that Amnesty bleeding-heart bull, on and on in this monotone blah, blah, blah voice about politics for fucking hours. It'd send anyone to sleep.'

'Thanks, mate,' I said. 'You make me feel all warm and tingly.'

But I was far from offended. It was our normal way of speaking to each other. I knew if the situation ever presented itself he'd take a bullet for me, and I felt the same way about him.

'What's brought on the cold feet?' he asked.

'I met someone on the flight coming home.' My shoulders relaxed as I said out loud what had been eating at me for the last few hours.

He frowned. 'Are you taking the piss?'

'Do I look like I'm joking?'

He stared intently at me, before erupting into thunderous laughter. I glared at him as he slapped his leg and threw his head back.

'Oh God,' he gasped for air as he wiped the tears from his eyes. 'That's a classic, mate. You want to ditch your fucking perfect fiancée for some chick you met on a plane? Hang on, it is a chick, isn't it? Not a bloke, right?'

I pushed my chair back and stormed out of the office, heading for the front door. Tom jumped to his feet and followed me. 'Sorry, Matt. Come on, mate, I'm sorry.'

I stopped and he put a hand on my shoulder. 'I'm good now. Seriously. Tell me about it.'

As pissed off with him as I was, I still wanted to get it off my chest. So I sat down on the couch in the waiting room while Tom stood in front of me, leaning against the desk, trying desperately hard to look serious.

I told him everything. Starting with the surprise erection when I'd noticed Mel in the departure lounge, to the way I'd embarrassed myself when I'd first spoken to her on the plane. I told him how we'd clicked with each other so perfectly when we talked. Finally, I described what she looked like, how beautiful she was, how sexy she was. I even described the clothes she was wearing and the way they hugged her body.

Tom's eyes grew wide. 'That's the chick that came here,' he said, in a barely audible voice, nodding to himself.

'What?'

'She was here, just a few minutes before you got here.' He spoke clearly now as he counted off on his fingers. 'Black top, big tits, tight jeans, long brown hair, red lipstick.'

I gaped at him, my jaw hanging.

He grinned smugly. 'Yep, saw her. There was a blonde chick with her too.'

I made him give me a blow-by-blow recount of what happened. I kept pushing him for more details and pressuring him to try and remember everything.

'She knew my name,' said Tom. 'Did you tell her my name?'

I nodded, remembering.

'Yeah, for sure it was her, all right. Looks like you got yourself a stalker, Matt. Good effort.'

'Fuck,' I breathed.

'Exactly.' Tom nodded. 'She was a total psycho, mate.'

'She didn't say anything about me, did she?' My voice got stuck on the words. I coughed to clear my throat.

'Nah, nothing.'

I stood up and paced the room. My heart rate was going mental. I forced myself to take deep breaths.

She had been here!

Had she come looking for me? No, I told her I didn't work Saturdays. And if she wanted to contact me she would have taken a business card. Why did she come and then run away like that? My head hurt as I tried to process it all.

Tom broke into my frantic line of thought 'She's really not as hot as you said she was, you know. If anything, the friend's hotter, to be honest.'

I shot him a filthy look.

'And she looks way older than you, Matt.'

'She's only thirty-seven,' I snapped.

He raised both eyebrows and said nothing for a minute. Then he muttered, 'She's not a patch on Lyds, mate, not even close.'

'She's incredible.' I met his gaze.

His loyalty to Lydia wasn't unexpected. But I was frustrated and annoyed that he wasn't taking me seriously. He thought it was a joke. I suppose I'd laugh too if I heard someone else tell the same story. Still, I wanted to convince him that this wasn't as dumb as it sounded.

'It just fitted with her, Tom. Everything fitted. She seemed to understand me. She was interested in me.'

'It's not hard to act interested in someone for less than a four-hour flight, Matt,' Tom said logically. 'So you had a great conversation with a woman who gave you a hard-on. Don't blow it out of proportion. You've got Lyds and she loves you. Don't be an idiot.'

I nodded silently, looking at the floor.

'You haven't made plans to see her again, have you?' he asked in a suspicious tone.

I shook my head. It dawned on me just how close I'd come to crossing paths with her here and my chest tightened.

'Mmm, good.' Then he added, as if it was an afterthought, 'She single?'

I shook my head once again, avoiding his eyes.

'You're doing well to stay as far away as you can from that scenario then, mate. It's got disaster written all over it.' The warning was clear in his voice.

I exhaled heavily. He was right. Of course he was right. But knowing that didn't change the way I felt.

I didn't tell him about how I'd left my number in Mel's book, he'd only judge me more. In any case, she probably wouldn't even read her book over the weekend, so she wouldn't find the note until she was on the flight home or already back in Perth. Then it'd be too late.

Tom and I walked out to the car park and he told me to call him if I wanted to talk some more.

My brain was spinning on the drive home. Knowing Mel had come to the clinic was torture. She was interested enough to track down where I worked. I knew she was staying at a city hotel, but I didn't know which one. There was absolutely nothing I could do to reach her. I thought I might implode.

But there was a persistent voice in my head that repeated the same two words over and over. She'll ring.

While I was stopped at red traffic lights, I fantasised for what felt like the hundredth time about having sex with her on the seat in the plane. It was immediately followed with guilt about Lydia.

Back home I headed straight to my bedroom where I threw myself on top of the futon and stared vacantly at the flaking paint on the ceiling. Lydia was none too impressed at the idea of moving here in a few months' time to begin married life. But being only a half-hour drive to work, and with a small sandy beach in walking distance, Williamstown was ideal for me. I liked its mix of old and new architecture, and there were lots of great restaurants in a strip across from the bay.

My apartment was over a hundred years old and although it had been renovated several times in the past, it was in serious need of improvement again. I just hadn't been motivated enough to do anything about it yet. I looked past the chipped tiles and rusted gutters, to the green wooden shutters, the ceiling roses and the stained-glass doors. This place had so much character, but Lydia still thought it was a dump.

So we'd recently started house hunting in the upmarket suburb of Malvern, where her parents lived. It wasn't long before I knew we had no chance of ever being able to afford any one of the dozens of houses we inspected. It was hopeless.

But the housing nightmare was a problem for another day. I put that stress out of my head and rang my parents.

Mum answered just as I was about to leave a message on the answering machine. 'Hello?' she panted.

'Hi, Mum, it's me. You sound puffed.'

'Matty! Welcome home, love. I was just out the front picking flowers to take down to the cemetery for Robbie after Mass.'

There was the silence that always followed the mention of Rob, and then she called Dad to join us on the speaker phone. Bloody speaker phone. It echoed, and we always spoke over each other, but my parents still got a buzz out of the novelty of it, twenty years after it had been invented.

I spent fifteen minutes catching up with them and describing my time in WA. It comforted me to be a part of their predictable conversation. They both said how excited they were about seeing me in two Saturdays' time.

Once a month, Lydia and I, along with my sister, her husband and my nephew, made the trip to Daylesford to spend a day at Mum and Dad's. I always looked forward to this time with my family – I could let my guard down on their sprawling country property.

After I hung up, I went back to staring at the ceiling and was asleep in minutes. When I woke up much later, afternoon had become evening. I was expected at Lydia's in half an hour. I had a five-minute shower and considered shaving, but decided to make the most of the weekend and leave it until Monday morning.

My stomach rumbled. I made a promise to myself to stock up with a decent grocery shop tomorrow. In the meantime, I had Lydia's cooking to look forward to. Thank God it wasn't her mother's turn tonight. I couldn't face Chow Mein again.

Lydia's father, Kevin, stood aside to let me into the house when I arrived at six-thirty.

'Matthew!' he barked in a military voice. 'Hear you've decided to stay on in that crappy little clinic you only half own. A decent mining job not good enough for you, is it?'

'Evening, Kev,' I said cordially. 'Nice weather we're having.'

He growled under his breath.

'Hello, Matt, Lydia's just freshening up. Welcome back.' Lydia's mother, Beverley, planted a stiff kiss on my cheek as I walked ahead of Kevin into the kitchen. With neither of them going by their full names, Lydia's parents had the misfortune of being known as Kev and Bev.

We stood around awkwardly while we waited for Lydia to join us.

'How's all that "Save the Whale" carry-on going?' Kevin sneered.

'Oh, Kev,' Beverley giggled behind her manicured hand. 'We know Matt saves humans, not whales.'

I cringed. 'It's going very well, thank you, Kev. We're lobbying the Libyan government this month.'

'Why?' they asked in unison.

'Because there are four men there facing life imprisonment,' I said, reaching for a cracker and downing it in two bites.

'Why?' Again, in stereo from them both as they looked at me with matching expressionless faces.

'They were caught having sex with one another.'

Why did I do that? Why? I knew what was coming.

'HA!' Kevin bellowed. 'Let 'em rot, I say! Should've been drowned at birth, the lot of 'em.'

Just then, Lydia bounced into the kitchen and wrapped her arms around my neck. With my eye on Kevin, I kissed her mouth for just a few seconds longer than was appropriate in front of her father.

'What are you guys talking about?' She smiled.

'Your future husband here is telling us he's a gay pride activist now,' Kevin snarled, patting down his grey bushy moustache. I realised he looked just like the man on the tube of Pringles I'd had at home today.

'Daddy! Don't be mean to Matty just because he likes the gays. I think that's nice of him.'

'I'm not a gay activist, I'm a human rights activist. Gay men are human.' I clenched and unclenched my fists inside my pockets.

Lydia reached in and squeezed my hand. 'Matty, I've made lasagne for dinner, honey,' she said in a higher voice than usual.

'Thanks, babe.' I gave her a forced smile.

Kevin wasn't through with me. 'Why don't you join the Cancer Council or something worthwhile like that, Matthew, instead of wasting your time writing letters to defend dirty Arab fags?'

Beverley giggled nervously. Lydia froze.

I silently counted to ten. 'I'm pretty busy as it is, thanks, Kev. Between working in the crappy little clinic and standing up against homophobic bigots, it doesn't leave much time to join the Cancer Council. I agree with you though, it's a great cause. Maybe you'd consider joining yourself, seeing as though you're retired. I could make some enquiries for you if you like, mate.'

'Don't you give me lip, boy,' he hissed.

'Okay you two, that's enough talk about cancer and what not,' Lydia said in a sing-song way. 'Come and have some of my yummy lasagne. I made it from scratch.' She led me to the dining table.

Lydia had her work cut out for her, trying to keep the mood light. Luckily she wasn't interested in having more than a mouthful of the lasagne she'd slaved over, so she was able to talk solidly throughout dinner. I felt sorry for her, she was almost working up a sweat.

I normally tried to let Kevin and Beverley wash over me, but my tolerance for them was at an all time low. Barely over an hour later, I pleaded jet lag and made for the door.

Lydia followed me out. I leaned against the car with my arms around her waist.

'Honey, I'm sorry about my dad. He shouldn't talk to you like that.' She chewed at a fingernail.

I shrugged.

'He just doesn't understand what you do, that's all. He really doesn't mean what he says.'

I sighed. 'I know, Lyds, it's okay. I'm just really tired, babe.'

There was no point getting into it any further, Lydia worshipped her parents. The few times I'd tried to tell her how offensive I found them, she'd been devastated and defended them. I didn't want her to feel caught in the middle any more than she already did. Once we were married, then I'd make myself scarce whenever she wanted to spend time with them. I hadn't shared this plan with her yet, though.

I kissed her goodnight and drove home, where I sprawled out on the couch in boxer shorts and watched an old James Bond movie on television.

'At least he's getting sex,' I thought aloud as I watched a young Roger Moore in action.

It was eleven when the movie finished but I was nowhere near able to sleep thanks to the long afternoon nap. For a lack of anything else to do I went back to bed and obsessed about Mel.

I jumped when the phone sounded its text message alert at one-thirty in the morning.

Are you still up?

What? Oh my God! It was her. It had to be her. But what if it wasn't her? What if it was a message from some random person meant for another number? Should I text back or call? Call. Yeah, call, that way I'd know for sure it was her. I rang the number, my palms sweating.

She answered on the first ring. 'Hi,' she whispered. 'I think I'm drunk.'

I gulped. She sounded even sexier on the phone than she did in person. I was hard immediately. I had to go to her. Now.

'Where are you?' I asked, adrenaline coursing through me.

'I'm at the Old Colonial on Flinders Street. Do you know it?'

'Yeah.' I could barely breathe.

'Matt …' Her voice was shaky. 'I don't know what I'm doing. I shouldn't have called you. I just found your note and—'

I cut her off. 'I'm on my way. I'll ring when I get there. I'll be less than half an hour, okay?' I was already up and pulling on my jeans.

'Um, Matt …'

'I'm coming.' I hung up.

I was out of the house and in the car in less than two minutes, speeding towards the city. There was more traffic than I expected at this hour and I swore violently when I had to stop at a red traffic light for the second time.

My head was spinning. What should I say or do once I got to her? If she really was drunk like she'd said, then she might fall asleep before I reached her, so I pressed my foot down harder on the accelerator pedal. I flew over the West Gate Bridge, weaving in and out of lanes like a maniac, gesturing wildly at cars in my way. I pulled into a parking bay at the front of the hotel fourteen minutes after our phone call had ended. Surely that was some sort of land speed record between Williamstown and the city.

I rang her number and again she answered on the first ring.

'Matt, I'm sorry,' she whispered. 'This is crazy. I'm freaking out. I'm not coming down.'

I'd spent the last few hours thinking I'd never hear from her again. And now that I was this close, I couldn't just forget about it and go home.

'Please come down, Mel.'

'But I'm drunk.' She sounded scared. 'And I'm so confused.'

'Let's just go somewhere and talk? You messaged me, I came.' I tried to keep my voice low and even. 'Go on, Mel, come down. What's the worst thing that could happen?'

There was a long silence.

'Okay,' she whispered. 'I'll meet you in the lobby.'

I quickly picked up an old newspaper and a pair of thongs off the passenger seat and threw them over the back, and then brushed the seat clean with my hand. I got out of the car and made myself walk slowly into the hotel.

The lobby was empty, except for the desk manager who I ignored. I took a seat closest to the front entrance. I watched the lift and I waited.

Stay calm, I repeated silently.

I was beginning to worry she'd changed her mind again, when the bell sounded and the lift doors opened. She walked out.

My heart jumped at the sight of her. Her red dress clung to her irresistible curves and, with her hair held up, she looked as glamorous as a Hollywood movie star.

Her eyes scanned the lobby for me. I stood up and stuck my hands deep into my pockets. When she saw me, she smiled her mind-blowing smile and gave a small wave.

'Hi, Matt. It's nice to see you again,' she said softly once she reached me.

'Hi.' I said, more calmly than I felt. 'My car's outside.'

I led her out into the warm night, neither of us speaking. As I opened the car door for her, her hand momentarily brushed mine. It was the first time I'd actually touched her and my breath quickened. I could feel her eyes on me as I drove away from the hotel.

'Where are we going?' she asked finally, breaking the silence. I realised I was driving over the Yarra on autopilot.

'My house?' I looked straight ahead as I spoke.

She exhaled loudly. 'Would it be okay with you, Matt, if we go somewhere else instead? Um, you know, because …' She didn't finish.

I turned to look at her. 'Yeah, sure. Of course. I'll take you to one of my favourite spots then.'

While I drove, the radio played low. I imagined reaching over and taking her hand. My heart was racing. Every now and then she looked over at me and smiled. I felt very alive.

Twenty minutes later I pulled up into an empty car park at the foreshore in Williamstown. From where we were parked, we had a view across Port Phillip Bay. The city lights twinkled at us from the other side of the black water.

I unbuckled my seatbelt and turned to face her. She did the same.

'This is pretty.' She spoke so softly, I could barely hear her.

'You don't seem very drunk, Mel,' I said, thankful I was able to keep a level voice and pretend to be in control. I reached over to hold her hand, holding my breath until she squeezed her thumb over mine.

'No,' she said, staring intently at me.

I stroked the back of her neck with the tips of my fingers. She shut her eyes. Her perfume washed over me.

'You're so beautiful,' I said and leaned towards her.

But before I could live out all the fantasies that had been playing in my head since the airport in Perth, she turned away from me and clasped her hand over her mouth.

'Mel?'

'I can't do this! I just can't.'

I sank into my seat and rested my head back.

'Matt, I'm sorry. This is so wrong. I'm married. My God, I'm married!' she said, turning back to face me again. Her eyes were filled with tears. 'I don't know what I'm doing.' She hunted around in her handbag, finally pulling out a tissue and wiping her eyes. 'I can't do this to my husband, and I couldn't face my kids if … I couldn't live with myself. I can't ruin everything I have for this moment here with you. I love them. I can't.'

I flicked my hazard lights on and off while I watched her, and listened to her, and tried to slow down my breathing.

'I'm confused,' I said finally. 'You're not coming across as someone who's in love with her husband. You texted me in the middle of the night. What's going on?'

'I really do love him. I do,' she answered slowly. 'Just not in the way I should. I'm not sure I ever have. It's complicated.'

'I think I might hate him,' I mumbled.

'Don't hate him. He's a good man, Matt. He married me because I was pregnant and scared to go it alone.'

Whoa! What? 'You didn't marry him because you were in love with him? You married him because you were scared of being a single mum?'

She nodded.

'Well, that puts things in a different light, doesn't it?'

'It doesn't change the fact that we're married, Matt.'

'How did you get together with him in the first place?'

'You really want to know?' she asked.

I nodded.

'He was an anaesthetic registrar working at the hospital where I was on rotation in my final year. He was thirty-four then and he was a real charmer, way out of my league. The women on staff threw themselves at him. So I was surprised when he showed interest in me. And flattered. I guess I was dazzled by him.' She let out a wistful sigh. 'We'd been seeing each other for just over six weeks when I discovered I was pregnant. I was devastated, but I couldn't think about having an abortion. So I told him and he told me that he loved me and he asked me to marry him. I pictured the alternative – bringing up a baby all on my own – and so I accepted. We were married four months to the day after we first met.'

'Four months? That's fast.'

'You don't say! I wasn't sure at all about my feelings for him, but I hoped that marriage and children would bring us closer together.' She paused. 'And to a large extent they did.'

'So, what, you grew to love him?'

Mel nodded. 'In many ways, yes. I mean, we have a lot of fun with the kids, we support each other's careers, we have heaps of friends.' She bit on her lip. 'I have been happy, Matt, I'm not lying.'

We sat in silence for a minute before she continued. 'Living with a smart, caring man who makes me laugh isn't exactly a chore. I've never felt like Adam was my soul mate, that's for sure, but I can't sit here and tell you I've been miserable in my marriage, because I haven't been.'

'Obviously things aren't that wonderful or we wouldn't be here now, would we?' I persisted.

She nodded and took a deep breath. 'Six months ago, for the first time in my life, I didn't sleep all night. And then it happened again, and again. I'd lie there with this growing feeling that I was missing something. I felt empty inside, even though I was living this perfect dream life. I've just gradually been getting more restless and edgy and feeling more and more disconnected with Adam but not really knowing what I wanted. Then I met you and it all made sense to me.' She tucked her hair behind her ears. 'I know what I've been missing now, you see.'

I was speechless.

'But anyway, what about you?' she continued. 'You're engaged. Don't you feel guilty?'

'I don't want to be engaged any more,' I said, meaning it.

'But that's crazy, Matt! You're just about to be married.'

'I obviously shouldn't be getting married if this is where I want to be.' My voice cracked. 'I don't think I can go through with this wedding now.' My stomach churned and my throat felt dry and irritated. I started playing with the hazard lights again. Mel stared straight ahead.

'Do you feel like going for a walk? I need some air,' she said after a few more minutes of silence.

I cleared my throat. 'Sounds good.'

We walked along the grassy foreshore for a while. She took off her shoes and swung them in her hand. I led her to the edge of the path, where we sat, dangling our feet above the water. The street lights behind us cast just enough light over the bay so we could see the tiny waves lap against the rocks beneath us.

While we sat, I again found myself telling her things I'd never told anyone, just like I had on the flight. 'I often wonder where Rob is, where he went after he died. It does my head in, the not knowing. I wonder is he still the same Rob but in another space? Does he watch over us? Is the old Rob gone and he's reincarnated as someone or something totally different? Is he lonely? Is he hanging out with other dead people? Is he peaceful or is he miserable? Does he feel anything? Or is he just a dead body, just another rotting corpse at the cemetery and it's all over?' I rubbed the sudden sore spot on my chest.

'I don't know,' Mel said. 'I imagine my mum flying. It's weird but that's what I picture. Just her spirit flying above the clouds. Floating. Free. Flying over all the places around the world she never got to see when she was alive.' Her voice drifted off.

'I like that. I wish I thought that, it sounds nice. Do you picture your dad's spirit flying too?'

She frowned. 'Hmm. No, I don't.' She looked at me with a confused expression. 'I wonder why I'd never pictured my dad flying?'

I shrugged.

'That's really weird. I've never once wondered about my dad's spirit after he died. Whenever he crosses my mind, I just feel kind of sad that he's no longer around.' She took a deep breath. 'Wow.'

We sat in silence, and then she let out a small laugh. 'Today on *Dr Phil*,' she said in a deep American accent, 'Mel finds out the truth about why she can't picture her father flying.'

She smiled a broken smile and it melted me.

'I'm really good at denial,' she said quietly. 'Maybe I resent my dad more than I ever thought I did.' She looked up at me. 'Matt, it's so strange, I feel like I can say anything to you.'

'Same here,' I said. 'I feel like right now, here with you, is exactly where I'm supposed to be. Which means something's about to go wrong.'

'Why do you say that?'

'Whenever I feel happy, like really happy, or when things are going really well, I'm always waiting for something bad to happen. I feel as though things can't be good for long, they have to go wrong. That's how I feel now.'

'That sounds like you've got symptoms of post-traumatic stress, Matt.' She had her doctor's voice on, a kind and caring doctor's voice. 'Have you ever been to a counsellor? Since you lost your brother?'

'No, never.'

'I think you're holding in a lot of pain. Counselling might really help you. That fear of things always going wrong, that's not something you should have to live with.' She patted my leg and an electric shock ricocheted up my thigh.

'But I'm way too cool and together for counselling,' I said.

She laughed and a lock of her hair fell over her eyes. I drew it back off her face and stroked her cheek with my finger. She locked her eyes on mine.

'Your laugh is the biggest turn on,' I murmured.

'Really?' She smiled. 'I never feel sexy. As in never, ever. I feel sexy around you though. I feel young again.' She drew slow patterns on my leg with her fingers. 'Being here with you, just sitting here and talking, and looking at the city lights and the water … it's just this perfect moment in time. This is a memory I'll treasure forever. Thank you.'

And there it was. I'd just admitted to being happy and something had to ruin it. She was already putting me in the past and calling me a memory.

I shifted my leg and her hand slid off it. She sighed and lay back on the grass, her legs still dangling over the edge. I did the same. The moon was out and the sky was light over the city.

'Do you believe in fate?' she asked.

'Yeah, definitely,' I said.

'I don't.'

'Really?' I was surprised. 'You don't think *this* is fate? Yesterday we didn't even know each other.'

She didn't answer.

'Shooting star!' She pointed out a few seconds later.

I saw it dart across the sky. I made a quick wish. It didn't come true.

'Matt, I'm getting cold,' she said suddenly and shivered.

I stood and helped her to her feet.

Once we were back in the car, I asked her what she'd like to do next. She hesitated in answering and I was worried she'd ask me to drive her back to the hotel.

'There's a cute cafe nearby,' I suggested.

'At four in the morning?' she asked, wide-eyed. 'Wouldn't it be closed?'

'You're in Melbourne.' I chuckled. 'Nothing closes here.'

'I'm happy just to stay here for a little longer. It's nice. But is there anything else you want to do?'

I grinned and raised my eyebrows.

She blushed. 'Except for that.'

'Honestly, I'm happy staying here and talking if you are.'

She took a deep breath. 'You know, as much as I don't want to ask, I kind of want to know. What's … your relationship like?'

It didn't slide past me that she'd avoided using Lydia's name.

I sighed. 'It's not great. I'm really confused about how I feel about her which makes me want to call off the wedding, but I don't want to hurt her. It's pretty fucked up. I'm not sure if I love her.'

'Why are you engaged to her then?'

'Because I'm an idiot who proposed to a woman because she wanted to be engaged. It didn't seem like the worst idea in the world, but as time's gone on I've realised I don't actually enjoy spending time with her like I used to. And now, well, now I feel painted into a corner and I don't know what to do next.'

'I envy her, you know. She's the one who gets to have you,' she said softly. 'And she's so pretty and so *young*. I saw her at the airport, she's like a supermodel.'

I laughed. 'I saw you watching us. I wanted to grab you and make a run for it.'

'Really?' She smiled, clearly surprised. 'But you looked so happy with her.'

I shook my head. 'Lydia didn't stand a chance after I met you.'

'So what *are* you going to do next?'

'I don't know,' I said honestly. 'What I do know is that I want to be with you. That's what I want.'

'Really?' she said again, and then she surprised me by asking, 'What's sex like with her?'

I paused. 'Good.' I couldn't lie.

'Oh.' She bit her lip.

'But I know it'd be better with you,' I said, leaning in close to her. 'It would be really, really good with you.' I put my hand on her thigh and traced circles on her bare skin.

'What are you doing?' she whispered. But she didn't push me away.

It was all the encouragement I needed.

I leaned in closer and kissed the exposed skin on her collarbone. She inhaled sharply and turned her head towards me. I kissed her mouth hard. She reached for my hair and laced her fingers through it while her tongue found mine. There was nothing awkward about what we were doing. It had been years since I'd experienced a spark like this, the thrill of a first kiss, and this one held more promise than any first kiss I'd had before. I poured everything I was feeling into it, poured my soul into it and as she responded, I knew she was doing the same. I couldn't imagine ever feeling more connected to someone or being more aroused than this.

I slid my fingers along her thigh, inside her dress and, even through the fabric of her underwear, I found my mark. I pressed down. My hand trembled.

'Come home with me,' I breathed into her ear, adding slow circular pressure with my middle finger.

'Oh God,' she said in a low voice as her pelvis rocked slightly under my touch.

'I know you want to,' I murmured in between small licks around her ear.

She moaned softly. She was rocking harder now and breathing rapidly. I worked faster, watching her respond to me. She turned her head towards me and our lips touched again as she reached for my jeans. When she felt my erection her sigh escaped into my mouth. We kissed deep and slow.

Then she pulled her head away with a jerk. 'No. Stop!' she said, flicking my hand away.

I drew back quickly and my elbow banged against the dashboard. She jumped in her seat.

'Sorry! I knocked my elbow.' I touched her arm and lowered my voice. 'I didn't mean to startle you.' It hurt where I was straining against my jeans, and my elbow was throbbing.

'I want to go back to the hotel now,' she said, avoiding my eyes. 'I have to go back, I'll regret it if I don't.'

'So that's it?' I asked hoarsely. 'You want me to drive you back and just forget about you?'

'Yes, that's it. If I stay with you any longer, Matt, things are going to happen that I'll never be able to undo. I don't trust myself. I'm calling time on this. Now.' She straightened herself, fixed her dress, and gave me a quick nod. Her eyes were cold.

I knew I'd lost. I dropped my head into my hands.

'Matt, I'm going home today,' she said as if she was talking to a child. 'I'm married and you're engaged. There's no future in this. And I can't just have a one-night stand with you, that's not who I am.'

'I don't even *want* a one-night stand. I want *you*. I'll follow you back to Perth if you let me. You don't have to tell him, he doesn't even need to know about me until we get to know each other better. This can't end now.' I knew it was hopeless and I sounded desperate, but I was grasping at anything.

She was silent for a minute. 'Take me back to the hotel, Matt, please.'

I turned the key in the ignition and drove away from Williamstown without a word. It was 5 am when I stopped the car outside the hotel. I was thirsty.

'Do you want to go get a drink?' My voice came out stiff and formal.

'No, thanks,' she replied in the same tone.

We were silent again. The air burned my lungs as I breathed. I became hypnotised by the flashing green neon sign at the car park next door.

'You do realise we're missing out on something incredible here, don't you?' I said, squeezing the steering wheel hard.

She swallowed audibly. 'Yes.'

'This isn't just some random thing between us, you know.' I turned to look at her. 'It's fate.'

'I know.'

'I've fallen hard here, Mel.'

She looked at me mournfully. 'I want you so much, I've never wanted anyone more. You don't know what you've done to me.'

'So how can you ignore it?'

Her eyes filled with fresh tears. 'Because I'm married, I don't have a choice.' She opened the car door. 'I have to go.' She reached for my face. 'I'm so sorry.'

I said nothing.

'Bye, Matt.' She touched my closed mouth with her lips and ran her fingers once through my hair. She got out, gently closing the door behind her. Still, the sound it made when it shut hurt my ears.

I watched her walk towards the hotel and disappear through the doors.

It was only when the sun rose that I drove home. I had to freshen up. Lydia had arranged a nine o'clock meeting for us with yet another wedding photographer.

VACANT

MEL

I barely made it across the length of the lobby to the lift before I came apart. My ribs hurt from crying. I fumbled around for the key card and unlocked the door to the suite with shaking hands. Still heaving, I tiptoed inside. Sarah hadn't moved. She snored rhythmically, her face completely concealed by her hair.

I walked over to the window and looked down at the street, my tears dripping onto the sill. Matt's car was still there. Leaning my forehead against the cold glass, I whispered I was sorry, again and again.

My heart urged me to run back down to him before it was too late. My brain told me to draw the curtains and go to bed.

I took the phone out of my handbag and turned it off. Leaving the curtains open, I slipped off my shoes and crawled into bed. I tugged hard at the sheet, pulling it up to my chin and curling my knees up.

So this was what being in love felt like. I was lucky to have been spared it for thirty-seven years.

*

Sarah sat up just after 9 am, grumbling obscenities and holding her forehead. She looked over to where I lay facing her, my eyes swollen.

She snapped to attention and was at my side in a flash. 'Honey, what happened?'

I was too far gone to lie to her. 'Sare, I think I've fallen for someone.' I hid my face in her lap and sobbed.

Our planned morning of brunch and the markets in St Kilda was forgotten.

'Mel, tell me what happened.'

I shook my head violently. 'No, I can't tell you. I don't want to tell you. I'm too ashamed.'

'You know I won't judge you. This is me, honey, I'm here to listen. Just tell me, let it all out. You'll feel so much better for it, I promise.'

But I shook my head again. 'No, not yet. In a bit, okay?' I blew my nose.

'Okay,' she said, 'we'll talk when you're ready.'

I lifted the sheets up to let her in and she slid into bed beside me, wrapping her arms around me. We stayed that way until I eventually ran out of tears and began to settle down. Sarah ordered us breakfast from room service. I remained in bed.

While we waited for it to arrive, she found the note from Matt on her bedside table. I'd jotted a message to her underneath his: '*Sare – I'm with him. Call me if you wake up and I'm not back.*'

Sarah studied the note for a few seconds and then slowly walked over to the bin, tore it in half, and dropped it inside without a word.

'Let's get you changed.' She used a motherly tone as she pulled fresh clothes out of my case. 'Can I run you a bath? Would you like that?'

'No, thanks.' I stared out the window. It was grey outside.

'All right, honey, but you have to get dressed at least.'

I obediently got out of bed and changed clothes.

'Go and wash your face, sweetheart. It'll make you feel better.'

I splashed cold water on my face and brushed my teeth. Who was this stranger staring back at me in the bathroom mirror? Could I have aged this much overnight? My face was red raw. It was no wonder Sarah looked as alarmed as she did.

We ate a silent breakfast, side by side on Sarah's bed. I chewed and swallowed a slice of toast mechanically. It tasted of warm cardboard. After a few mouthfuls, I put the plate back onto the tray.

'Are you ready to talk now?' Sarah asked as she smoothed a strand of hair off my face. She hadn't eaten much either.

I nodded and the tears resurfaced. She listened to the whole story without interruption. When I was done she hugged me tightly.

'Oh, Mel, what a mess. Look, it was one night, okay? A lapse, nothing more than a lapse. Now you're going home to the other side of the country, back to your family. And he's got his life here. Don't beat yourself up too much about it.'

'But I think I'm in love with him,' I said through the tears.

'Sweetheart, you're an intelligent woman. You and I both know that's not true. You're still caught up in last night. You just need to get on that plane home and you'll be able to put it all in perspective tomorrow, you'll see.' She gave my hand a tight squeeze.

Her soothing voice was so calm and she was so assured of what she was saying. I had never loved her more.

'Please don't tell Ryan,' I begged.

'I promise I won't. I'd never betray you in that way, you know that.'

'Thank you.' I gave her a grateful smile.

'Do you want to come back to Sydney for a few days? We could do a proper debrief, hey?' she suggested. 'You could tell Adam you wanted some more time with me. You could say I nagged you into it. You don't have to face him today if you're not ready.'

'No, thanks, Sare.' I was sorely tempted by her offer. 'I need to go home and be with him and the kids, get back to normal. I have to put this behind me somehow.'

My flight home was leaving in two hours, and Sarah's soon afterwards. We needed to think about getting to the airport. We crammed our shopping haul into our suitcases. Sarah even managed to make me smile as she made a big performance out of jumping up and down on her overfull case.

The desk manager farewelled us as if we were his dearest relatives.

Sarah and I sat close by each other in the back of the taxi on the way to the airport. She played air guitar, mimicking the pained facial expressions of the musician at the Indian restaurant the night before. Then she used the calculator on her phone to add up how much money she'd spent on clothes yesterday, choosing to stop when she saw how quickly she hit four figures. She successfully got me through the taxi ride without tears.

Although it had always been awful for us to say goodbye, this time the pain was more acute than ever before, and we cried shamelessly at the airport before heading off to our respective gates.

I looked around the departure lounge. Matt knew what time my flight home was scheduled. Maybe he'd come to the airport.

Maybe he'd be waiting for me, and he'd ask me again to be with him, to go home with him. Maybe I'd say yes this time.

But he wasn't there.

I sat down and stared at the departures screen until it was time to board. I couldn't turn on my phone and risk myself calling him.

I remembered very little about the flight home. The time passed quickly as I stared vacantly out the window. I may have even nodded off at one stage and, by the grace of God, the elderly lady sitting next to me didn't once look my way.

Walking across the domestic terminal back in Perth, I remembered the excitement I'd felt being here less than forty-eight hours ago. Yesterday I was carefree, excited. I was normal then. Now Matt had changed everything. How could I go back to normal again?

I applied my makeup carefully in the airport bathroom. I looked less ravaged now, after a few hours free of tears and two layers of under-eye concealer. I'd be able to pull off being nothing more than a little hungover.

I drove home at a snail's pace, the lead weight in my chest slowing me down. Technically, I hadn't consummated anything with Matt, but I wasn't fooling myself that I hadn't been unfaithful to Adam. I'd shared my heart with another man. It was a complete betrayal, nothing less. Wonderful, kind, generous Adam, the father of my children. Why didn't I feel more guilty? Why was I wishing I'd slept with Matt? Who had I become?

As I pulled into the garage, I heard the sound of laughter coming from the back garden.

'She's home, guys!' Adam shouted jubilantly. 'Mum's home, everyone!'

The three of them rushed into the garage. Their happy faces broke me a little more.

Adam kissed my cheek and grabbed my suitcase from the boot of the car. 'Shit, Mel!' he said with a laugh. 'This is heavy. Am I going to need to remortgage the house?'

I smiled and followed him inside with my arms around our children and my mind on Matt.

Once safely inside the sanctity of the ensuite, I turned on my phone. There was a single text message from him, sent at ten past seven.

I'm leaving now. I've been sitting here hoping you'd come back down. I wish you weren't married. I don't regret what happened. I hope you don't either. Bye.

My fingers traced over the words on the screen.

I'd promised myself on the flight home that I'd never contact him again. But I couldn't let him think I'd ignored his message. Just one text message, I would at least give him that.

Lily knocked loudly on the bathroom door. '*Muuum*, hurry up! How long are you going to stay in there for? I want to see what new stuff you got me.'

'I'll just be a minute, Lil,' I said in a light voice.

Matt, I hope you understand why I had to leave. I could never regret you, but my life is with Adam. Please understand. More than anything, I hope you find happiness xx

'Mum, who are you texting from in there? And why are you texting in the toilet anyway? Yuck!'

Lily was still standing outside the bathroom. I thought she'd left.

'Oh, I'm, um, I'm texting Sarah, love. I'm just making sure she got home safely.'

My phone beeped. It was another text message from Matt. All it said was '**Bye**'.

'Can you please come out now, Mum? Did you get me those skinny jeans I asked for?'

I turned my phone off again, pulled the wife and mother mask firmly over my face, and stepped out of the bathroom to resume my life.

'Yes, baby, I found your size in black and denim so I bought you two pairs,' I said, kissing the top of Lily's head. 'Come and I'll show you.'

We all passed a quiet afternoon at home, which was rare for us. Adam and I sat in the living room with steaming cups of tea. The children stood in front of us, playing Mario Brothers on the Wii together.

Looking at my perfect, fair-haired, lanky children teasing each other good-naturedly while they jet skied by remote control, and then at my perfect husband, reading a magazine and humming to himself, I realised that the only thing wrong in this scene of family bliss was me. I didn't feel like I belonged. None of them were living a lie like I was. The enormous room was suddenly suffocatingly small.

Rather than leaving me feeling refreshed and ready to take on life again, which was the whole idea, the weekend away had left me resenting that I had to come back at all. Was this how my father felt when he was having an affair? Did he sit in our family home wishing he was elsewhere, until he couldn't take it any more and left for good? Well, I would not destroy this family like he had destroyed ours. Nothing could make me tear apart our home. This was it for me now.

But I felt like I was caged. I could almost feel the barbed wire tearing at my skin.

Later in the afternoon, Adam followed me into the bedroom while I unpacked. I held up the clothes I'd bought and he complimented them as he looked up from over the top of a golf magazine. I slipped two new sets of lingerie into a drawer while he was reading.

When I was halfway through unpacking I had a flash of guilt, and took a seat next to Adam on our bed. 'Thanks for looking after the kids this weekend, love. I really appreciate it.'

'You're very welcome, doctor,' he smiled, still reading. 'But you owe me.' He looked up with a glint in his eye.

I couldn't swallow.

He rubbed his hands together. 'Let me think about this. Weekend on my own, dealing with hideous teenagers, wife spending all our money … Mmm, an hour of you on top should cover it. I'll drive the kids to youth group and when I come back, you can pay up.'

'Is that right, Dr Harding?' I fixed a smile on my face. 'A whole hour, hey?'

'I'm setting a timer.' He grinned and resumed reading.

The telephone rang. Neither of us made an attempt to answer it. Nobody called the landline except telemarketers.

Lily came into our bedroom a minute later. 'Mum, that was Sarah. She rang to see if you got home safely because she said she couldn't get through on your mobile. Is she deranged or something? Weren't you guys just texting each other? I asked her but she went all quiet and then she goes, "Oh, well, just say hi again from me then," in this real strange voice. Weird, huh?'

'Hey? What's this about?' Adam asked.

Act normal. Quick, think of something!

'Oh, geez,' I said with a shrill voice. 'She's funny!'

'But Mum,' Lily persisted, 'you were texting her from the ensuite and she texted back. I heard your phone beep. Why is she ringing to check whether you got home safely? Is she losing it?'

Shut up, Lily!

'That's not a nice way to speak about Sare, Lil,' I said, my voice trembling. 'She's really sleep-deprived. We were up very late in Melbourne. People do silly things sometimes when they're over tired, okay?'

Adam put down his magazine and looked at me for what felt like an eternity. He had a curious look on his face. I looked away and busied myself hanging up more clothes. I was sure he'd notice me shaking as my heart crashed violently about and my body twitched.

After a prolonged period of awkward silence, he stood up. 'Come on, Lil. It's time for youth group. Go round up your brother.' He guided Lily out with his hand on her shoulder, pausing in the doorway. 'You're paying up when I get home, Mel,' he added with a smile.

As soon as they were gone I raced to my handbag and hurriedly deleted the messages Matt and I had sent each other. That was a close call, and exactly what I needed to end communication with him. With a pang, I deleted his number as well. It was clear from his last text that he wasn't planning to contact me any more either. I told myself that was a good thing.

I took a quick shower and changed into one of my new sets of lingerie, applied vanilla moisturiser all over my body and re-did my makeup. I lit a white scented candle that had sat on our chest of drawers collecting dust for months, and drew the curtains closed.

Adam and I had sex at this time every week. It was a recurring alert in the calendar on his phone. He said it always made his day to receive the notification that read 'Getting some today!' When he'd shown it to me, I'd laughed to hide my horror.

He also made suggestive jokes every Sunday morning and afternoon, and then in bed that night he'd comment on how great it had been. I always responded that it was indeed great. We did have sex after special occasion dates too, and on the very odd Friday or Saturday night, if we'd both had a few too many drinks.

As I checked my reflection in the mirror in the flattering light of the candle, I decided things had to change. We needed to make an effort to break this monotonous cycle we'd fallen into. I couldn't be with Matt, so I had to make it better with Adam. I wanted a proper sex life. I needed a proper sex life.

It seemed bizarre to me though, that when I heard Adam drop his keys onto the bench downstairs and call out gleefully that he was on his way up, I felt as if I was about to cheat on Matt.

Adam stopped in the doorway of our bedroom. He looked at the candle and then at me, standing with one knee bent and my back against the wardrobe in the red satin bra and knickers.

'Whoa, Mel! Did you just buy those?'

I smiled and nodded.

'Well, well,' he said in a husky voice, 'I love them. Take them off.' He started to undress as he walked towards me.

'Adam,' I purred, 'do I look beautiful?'

'Uh-huh,' he said distractedly as he concentrated on undoing his shirt buttons.

'Honey, look at me. Do I look beautiful?'

He glanced up for a quick second. 'I said yes. Hey, why are you still in those? Let's get naked.'

I felt the cold seep down from my neck and along the length of my spine. I spoke slowly. 'I'm still dressed because I want you to look at me. I want you to tell me I'm beautiful.'

'But I just did, twice. And who wants to waste time looking? You've got your hour on top, doctor. Now where's that timer gone?' He chuckled. His shirt was off. He walked over to where I stood and reached around to undo my bra.

I shrank away from his touch, taking a step back. 'Do you really think I'm beautiful? You don't act like you do.' I looked deeply into his eyes to see if I could find the truth there for myself.

'For the third time, yes. And if you take a look at my pants, I think you'll find the proof there,' he said quietly. He crossed his arms over his chest and stood facing me. 'Are we actually going to have sex today, Mel?'

I sighed. 'Adam, I want to feel like the most beautiful woman in the world to you. I want you to have to hold yourself back whenever I'm around. I want to feel like I blow you away when I'm dressed like this,' I finished limply.

He threw his arms in the air. 'Well, of course I think you're pretty, but come on, mate, we've been married forever. How could I function if I had to hold myself back every time I saw you? It wouldn't be feasible.' He reached for my hand and gave it a squeeze. 'I'm used to seeing you in your underwear. But I noticed these, didn't I? I told you I loved them. I'm half naked trying to shag you, for God's sake! How blown away do I have to get? Come on, Mel, come to bed.'

I withdrew my hand from his, slid open the wardrobe door and pulled out a dressing gown. 'Pretty and beautiful aren't the same thing,' I snapped as I put on the gown and walked briskly out of the room, blowing out the candle as I left.

I heard Adam swearing under his breath as I closed the door behind me.

I walked down to the kitchen in a huff and made myself a cup of coffee. I sat there fuming, picturing how Matt would have reacted to seeing me in tiny red satin knickers.

And then I stopped. Jesus! What was I doing? Adam didn't deserve this. He was just being himself. And it wasn't as though he'd said anything awful. He'd complimented me and wanted to be intimate with me. He just hadn't been completely over the top about my appearance. And after fourteen years of marriage, how could I even expect that of him?

I realised that it was ridiculous to expect a scorching hot romance with Adam after all this time together, especially considering we'd never been scorching hot to begin with. He couldn't suddenly change and satisfy me in the way I wanted him to. It wasn't fair to compare him to Matt, he could never give me that sort of illicit and dangerous excitement. And as my husband, he shouldn't have to. What he did every day to show his love for me should be enough. This wasn't a Mills and Boon novel or a romantic movie, this was life. I had a really great man here. I had to forget Matt.

I let the dressing gown drop to the floor and made my way back upstairs. I found Adam sitting on the edge of our bed, getting changed into his volleyball uniform.

He turned and looked at me when I walked in. 'You are beautiful, Mel. You're very beautiful. I'm sorry,' he said in a more serious tone than I'd heard him use for months.

I took a deep breath and went to him. He really was a wonderful man. But I felt nothing when he touched me. Not a thing.

*

During that first week I was back home, my phone felt like an explosive in my handbag. Every time it rang or the text message alert sounded my heart skipped a beat. But it was never Matt. I was both relieved and crushed.

I failed miserably trying to forget Matt and focus my energies on Adam. Matt saturated my brain and there was room for little else. I obsessively recalled every moment we'd had together. The side of me that knew I'd done the right thing by cutting contact with him paled in comparison to the side that raged with regret that I didn't have sex with him and that I hadn't begged him to follow me back to Perth.

When we weren't making scheduled love once a week, the only affection Adam gave me was a peck on the cheek in greeting and farewell every day, with his arm briefly touching my waist. Aside from that, and his jokey way of lightly smacking my bottom, he never touched me.

The conversations I'd had with Matt meant more than all of Adam's one-liners, which seemed to be the only thing he was capable of.

To be touched and to be listened to. To have had it for one night and then have it taken away was too unfair.

As my resentment towards Adam overtook the guilt of cheating on him, the daydreaming about Matt became more and more frequent. I didn't try to reel it in at all. I allowed myself to unravel as I pined for another life that I couldn't have. I allowed myself to completely slip away. It was a voluntary, deliberate decision. And I was stupid enough to think that going down this delusional road wouldn't end in a mess for me and my husband, and for our children.

When I finished work at lunchtime each day, rather than grocery shop or catch up with friends for a coffee or head home to get chores done, I wasted hours sitting on the beach staring at the horizon, before reluctantly picking up the children from school. At night I rarely slept, while thoughts of Matt consumed me. I had just enough sleep to keep me functioning on the most basic of levels.

I googled his clinic and was dismayed to find a notice that the site was being upgraded and temporarily unavailable. I couldn't Facebook stalk him – I didn't even know his surname. And I didn't trust myself to ring the clinic to find out in case he answered.

Each day I went through the motions of preparing school lunches, going to work, coming home to help with homework, doing the laundry, taking Nick to football training and Lily to dance practice, preparing the evening meal, washing dishes, and finally collapsing on a sofa beside Adam to watch drivel on television, and I felt myself sink further and further into the fantasy of escape. My life was so incredibly dull. How had I not noticed this before?

Nick and Lily showed no interest in me unless there was something I could do for them. Adam continued to treat me as the buddy he also happened to sleep with. I'd built my life around this family and had lost myself in the process. The sexy interesting passionate woman Matt had met on the plane didn't exist here in this house with these people.

I wanted to rediscover the woman I was beneath the wife, the mother and the doctor. So even though Matt wasn't here, I lived as though he was. I imagined he was with me, that he couldn't get enough of me, and I lived solely according to this fantasy.

I was surprised by how responsive Adam was to me as night after night I nudged him awake in the early hours of the morning so I could squeeze my eyes shut and pretend he was Matt. It was all I could do not to call out Matt's name when I climaxed.

'I love how much sex we're having,' Adam murmured one night. 'Hot sex too. It's bloody excellent.' He grinned at me. 'You're trying some new moves there. Where did you learn those? Should I be worried?'

'I'm reading a bit of erotica at the moment.' I kept my voice casual. 'Makes me horny, I guess.'

'Well then, we need to keep you well stocked on the horny books, mate.' He chuckled.

He was enjoying more regular and more active sex with me? Who knew! I wondered why, if he enjoyed it so much, he never instigated it when it wasn't our allotted time. And anyway, whether he was happy with our sex life or not, it was too late. My body was his to have, but my heart and mind were elsewhere.

'Give me the name of that author and I'll hunt down more of her books. I love what this erotic reading is doing to you,' he said before dozing off.

Of course he hadn't noticed I never actually spent any time reading.

I started wearing nicely tailored skirt suits to work instead of the pants and boring blouses I always used to wear. I got out of bed earlier every morning to fit in a session at the gym before taking the children to school. It was something I hadn't done for over a year even though I was still paying the membership fees. I obsessively watched what I ate and it showed on the scales. The transformation gave me a secret confidence. It kept me going.

'Wow, you look hot, Mum!' Lily remarked one morning as I walked out of the bedroom in a fitted peplum top over a pencil skirt and new heels. 'You know, you look different since you came back from Melbourne.'

I laughed. 'You think so honey? Well, I'm trying to be more like the yummy mummies I saw in Melbourne. I'm still in my thirties, aren't I? I can still be hot, right?'

'For sure. Go, Mum!' She gave me a high-five and I floated down the stairs, thrilled with myself.

Later in the week, a friend joked while we stood waiting near our cars to pick up our daughters from school, 'Who are you having an affair with, eh, Mel? Nobody wears skirts that tight for their husband.'

I turned bright red and laughed. 'I'm just sick of myself, so I'm making more of an effort, that's all.'

'I'll bet Adam's finding ways to knock off early every day to get home to you.'

'If only!' I scoffed.

I pretended I could see Lily coming out of school and walked away.

Adam hadn't said a word about my changed appearance. I was sure he hadn't even noticed that there was anything different about me at all.

At least Sarah knew what was going on inside me. It was an enormous relief to be honest with her, and to vent, and to have one person I could speak to about Matt. We spoke of little else. Not that she told me what I wanted to hear. Our phone calls were the same every day, me pretending to listen while she talked about her children and her work and then her trying to talk sense into me while I pined for Matt.

'Mel, all this talking and sharing, this intimacy you say you had with Matt, why not go there with Adam?' Sarah suggested, not for the first time, during one such call.

I sighed. 'I've tried, believe me. He's not interested.'

'But when? When was the last time you really tried? It sounds like you gave up on him years ago. Maybe he's wanting more now too. Why not give it another shot?' she insisted.

'All right, I'll try again,' I said with no enthusiasm. 'It's just not the same as with Matt.'

'Mel.' Sarah's voice took on a harder tone. 'Of course it's not the same. You've got that "just met, can't keep your hands off him" rush with this guy. Of course it's more exciting than the man you've been living with half your life. For goodness sake, listen to yourself. All these things you've been saying you love about Matt, you have right under your nose already.'

'You just don't understand, that's the problem.'

'I do understand, it's that I don't agree with you, not that I don't understand that's the problem. Mel, like I told you yesterday, and the day before, and the day before that, you only had one night with Matt. You don't actually know him at all. He turned it on for one night, any guy can do that. For all you know you're wasting your time dreaming about a wanker.'

'He's not a wanker! He's the best guy I've ever met,' I snapped.

'*Adam's* the best guy.' She sighed. '*You've already got the best guy.* You're having some sort of early midlife crisis, and it's not about Adam, it's about you.'

I rolled my eyes as she kept talking. 'Mel, you have to stop obsessing. I mean a couple of days after you got home, fair enough, but now it's getting ridiculous. It's completely self-destructive. You need to let it go. You had your fun and now it's over.'

I'd heard it all before from her. Sarah refused to accept that I wasn't, and had never been, madly in love with my husband. In her eyes I was simply having a temporary brain freeze that I could snap out of.

But she was a good listener, and that was all I wanted from her. She didn't have to understand as long as she listened. It didn't bother me that I was frustrating her, I just wanted to talk about Matt. But she'd clearly had enough for today so I changed the subject.

'How's Paris going with the little cow who's been bullying her?' I asked.

'Oh, look, she's doing better …'

After the phone call ended, I thought about what Sarah had said and I decided to follow her advice even though I was sure she was wrong. I had nothing to lose by making more of an effort to become closer to Adam so I may as well try.

The following Sunday morning, after dropping Nick off at his first football practice match for the season and Lily at a friend's house for the day, Adam and I sat out on the back veranda, him with a green tea and me with a strong cup of coffee. It was a perfect Perth summer's day.

We'd had a late night the night before, celebrating the fiftieth birthday of one of Adam's colleagues. Adam had held court at the party for hours, with his collection of funny anecdotes that I knew by heart. Then he'd danced with his friends' wives, twirling them around with gusto and galloping them all over the dance floor.

I'd watched the other women's smitten expressions, and wished he had the same effect on me. But I'd woken up this morning with a new resolve that Adam and I would sit together and have a conversation spanning longer than five minutes.

'You up for a skinny dip in the pool?' He rubbed his hands together.

'What? No! Adam, I want us to sit here and talk. We only ever talk to organise things. We never talk about ourselves.'

He screwed up his face. 'Talk's overrated, mate. It's for girls.'

I shook my head. 'Now, Dr Harding,' I began with a smile, 'your wife would like to know what's on your mind these days. How are things at the hospital?'

As if on cue, Adam's phone buzzed. He excused himself and got up to call the hospital from inside the house.

I sipped my coffee and waited.

He emerged a few minutes later, in shirt and tie, jingling his car keys. 'Sorry, honey.' He bent down and kissed my forehead on his way past. 'Gotta go.'

'Adam! You *promised* you'd stop doing weekends this year. You've got a locum, remember? What was the point in hiring him if you never actually use him?' I glared at him.

'Can't this time, love,' he said unapologetically, and left.

Four hours later Adam walked back into the house, whistling to himself. By that time I'd brought Nick home from football. He was hungrily making his way through his second meat pie while he watched cricket on the television.

Nick had seemed more embarrassed than pleased when I'd turned up early to watch him play once Adam had left for the hospital. I was hurt by his refusal to acknowledge me when I happily waved to him from the boundary line. I asked him about it on the drive home.

'Mum, I'd look like such a loser waving to my mum in the middle of a practice match. The coach would cream me. It's serious at this level, you know.' He was clearly frustrated at how little I understood him.

'I'm sorry, love,' I gulped. 'Would you prefer me to wait in the car next time?'

'Yeah, I would,' he said, ripping at the Velcro strap of his sports bag with aggression. 'And I don't know why you came in that tight dress and high heels to pick me up either. It's not like you were going anywhere fancy. One of the trainers said something about you I didn't like. Dad would've decked him if he heard him.'

'Sorry, Nick,' I said, my voice hoarse.

'Actually, maybe just Dad can drop me off and pick me up from now on. No offence.' And then he'd taken his iPod out of his bag, plugged his ears with headphones, and hadn't spoken to me again.

It was difficult not to cry while I drove the rest of the way home.

Adam smiled widely at me now as he went to join Nick on the couch and they proceeded to speak in serious tones about the cricket score.

'Honey, do you want to go up to the marina for a late lunch?' he called out to me from the living room. 'Maybe we can pay your son to take a bloody shower while we're out.'

'I already ate,' I lied. 'Why don't I make you something here instead?'

'Any pies left?' he asked.

I went and stood between him and the television. I had to see for myself if he was joking. 'What? You mean to tell me that you, Adam Harding, are asking me to warm you up a processed frozen meat pie that you will actually put in your mouth and eat?'

Nick was also staring at him with his jaw open. Never in his life had he seen his dad eat frozen food. In fact, I sometimes sneaked through fast food drive-thrus on nights when Adam worked late and the three of us would hide the evidence before he came home. The kids hated it if he ever packed their school lunches. Adam was the eat-fresh Nazi.

'Yes! Get me a pie, woman!' He laughed. 'I need comfort food, I had to go out and work on a Sunday. It was rough out there, mate, and Nick's pie smells so good.'

'Wish Lily was home to see this.' I smiled at Nick as I walked back into the kitchen to get the last two pies out of the freezer. 'Dad eating a meat pie.'

Adam stood up and followed me. 'Do you want to go for a hit of golf after lunch then, Mel? Beautiful day for it.' He took a swing with an imaginary golf club.

'No, thanks. I don't feel like golf. Why don't we just stay home and talk?'

'Ah, shit. Still with the talk! I feel like I'm in trouble. *Adam, we need to talk.*' He imitated my voice. 'Come on, honey, let's do something fun. It's the weekend. Stuff the talking!'

'Adam.' My tone changed. 'Please. I just want to sit and talk with my husband. How was work today? Why did they call you in? What was the emergency? I'd like to hear about it.'

His face clouded over. 'It was nothing,' he muttered. 'Don't want to talk about it. It's boring.' Then his eyes brightened. 'What's not boring, however, is golf! Come play a quick nine, Mel. Go on, mate.'

'No! I'm *not* playing golf, okay? I want to know about your morning. I should be allowed one decent conversation with you. It's not too much to ask. How. Was. Your. Morning?' I asked through clenched teeth.

Adam's expression suddenly changed. He walked a few feet away from me and then turned back around. There was a hard look in his eyes I didn't recognise. My breath caught.

'All right then, I'll tell you about my day, since you're obviously so desperate to know.' His voice was low. 'I got called in to give an epidural to a woman in labour with a child she knew was dead inside her. Kind of thought I shouldn't handball that one to the locum his first year out, what do you reckon?' he said in a sarcastic tone.

I flinched.

'So I got in there and I had to time the needle between her screaming and writhing with each contraction while she cried out her baby's name over and over. How I managed to put it in the right place with the way my fucking hand was shaking, I don't know.'

He paused to look at the ground, and then lifted his eyes to meet mine again. 'I had to stand around while she delivered her dead baby. And I watched her husband hold that cold blue little boy and tell him how much he loved him. Then the midwife wrapped the baby in a blanket and his mum nursed him and sang him a lullaby. And all I could think of was Nick when he was born, and how we got to take him home, and how this couple would have to bury their son instead.'

Adam's eyes brimmed with tears as his voice broke. 'That was today, Mel. Do you want to know what happened at work on Friday?'

I didn't reply. I stood unmoving, my hand still on the frozen meat pie.

'Friday,' he said in a mock cheery tone, 'I gave a general to a young guy who'd come in to the ED with stomach cramps a couple of days before. None of the idiots there could figure out what was wrong with him and he was getting sicker and sicker. So they called in the surgeon who decided to open him up and have a look. I stood next to the guy's wife in pre-op and gave her my standard lines, you know, "Nothing to worry about blah, blah …"

She didn't buy it, she was white with panic. She had these two little kids hanging off her. "You take care of him," she said.'

Adam was crying now. It was the first time I'd seen him cry since Lily's birth. I gulped back my own tears watching him.

'So we go into theatre and the surgeon gets in there. Do you know what he found?'

I shook my head.

'He found four litres of pus in this guy's abdomen. Those dickheads in Emergency missed a burst appendix for two whole days. He died ten minutes in. I went with the surgeon to tell the wife. She was waiting with the kids back in the ward. You can imagine it.'

Adam sighed as he sat down on one of the bar stools. He wiped away the last of his tears with the back of his hand.

'I'm so sorry, love. I'm sorry you've been through that.' I held out a tissue but he shook his head.

'That's what it's like at work, Mel,' he said, deflated. 'Are you happy now? Have we talked enough? I can keep going if you want.'

'But, Adam, I'm a doctor too. We should help each other through things like that. We should talk it out together. It's wrong that I have no idea that this is what's been happening in your life over the past two days. I'm your wife, talk to me, tell me! Why do you have to hold it all in?'

He looked at me and slowly shook his head. 'You still don't get it, do you? Even after all this time together, *I don't want to talk*!' he shouted. '*I want to forget*! When I come home to you, you're my sanctuary. I'm not holding it in, I'm letting it go. I want our life to be happy and fun to make up for all the shit I have to deal with at work. I don't want to come home and rehash it all. I want to play golf!'

'I'll come and play golf with you, Dad.'

We both turned to see Nick standing in the doorway. He was carrying his own golf clubs in a bag over his shoulder and he had Adam's golf bag in his other arm. He looked at me with obvious resentment that I'd upset the man he worshipped.

I put Adam's pies in the oven and slammed the door shut. 'Go play golf, Adam. Go have fun. Forget about trying to have an adult relationship. Let's just keep pretending everything's perfect and never talk about anything that bothers us. You know, last time I checked we were married. I thought being married meant you had someone to talk to. Obviously I was wrong. I'm going upstairs,' I hissed as I pushed past him and then Nick.

It was the first time we'd argued that aggressively, especially in front of either of our children, and before I reached the bedroom the guilt kicked in. I'd provoked him and upset him, and upset Nick.

But maybe, I reasoned, it would be worthwhile. Maybe my words would get through to him and we could try to have a real relationship at last. Maybe then I would get over this relentless obsession with Matt.

But less than five minutes later I heard Adam's booming laugh coming from downstairs, followed by Nick's laughter. They both roared obscenities at the cricket on the television, and then they went off to play golf. Neither of them said goodbye before they left. I could just imagine Adam doing a quick scan around the carpet before he left to make sure every last remnant of our fight was swept well enough under it.

I picked Lily up from her friend's house later in the afternoon and we spent a couple of hours beading pearls and gluing sequins on a purple leotard. Her first ballet competition for the year was still a couple of months away but this was one of three complicated outfits we had to make for it, so we were starting early.

It was so easy to be with Lily. She talked happily the entire time – about Charlotte and Hattie, who were still fighting about Charlotte tagging everyone except Hattie in her post about having the best friends ever; about Miss Drew, who was so mean and strict and horrible, and never turned on the air conditioning at ballet even when it was really, really hot; about how she wished her breasts were big enough to need a proper bra, not just a crop top; about how Ruby was Team Gale and how could anyone be Team Gale and not Team Peeta, when Gale was the one who made the bombs that killed Prim, whereas Peeta risked his life over and over to save Katniss; and about how it was only six days until the school disco and all the stupid boys said they weren't going, which was just as well because they were so dumb anyway. And there was no pressure for me to respond to any of it with more than nods and the occasional, 'Oh really?'

Adam and Nick came home in buoyant spirits.

Adam smiled sheepishly at me. 'Dr Harding, good to see you. Missed you at golf. Nick isn't as cute in his golf pants as you are in yours.' He winked. 'By the way, I chucked out the meat pies. Couldn't do it when it came to the crunch, mate.'

'It's good to see you too.' I smiled, instantly softening towards him.

However, despite both of us being friendly to each other, the tension hung around for the remainder of the day. It was the first Sunday night for as long as I could remember that we didn't have sex while Nick and Lily were at youth group. Nothing was said, but when Adam came home from dropping the children off, instead of coming to find me he settled himself in front of the television. I joined him in the living room and sat on the other end of the couch, pretending to read.

He stood up after half an hour. 'I'd better go get ready for volleyball, Mel.'

I hated this uneasiness between us. I would never pressure him to have a real discussion with me again. It wasn't worth it. It didn't change anything anyway.

'Adam, are you okay?'

'I'm as good as gold, honey,' he replied, walking away.

When he returned from his volleyball match the children were back, and they all watched television until it was late, then he came upstairs. I was already in bed, waiting.

I cuddled up to him. He put his arm around me, pulled me in closer and stroked my hair. It was an uncharacteristically intimate gesture from him. It felt strange, but in a good way.

'I'm sorry I shouted at you today,' he said. 'I never want to shout at you. It makes me feel like a pig.'

'I'm sorry too,' I said. 'I'm sorry I pushed you into talking about work when you didn't want to. I'm sorry I didn't play golf with you.'

He was silent for a while. Then he said, 'I'll try and talk more about stuff if you want me to. I just want to make you happy, Mel.'

I had to stop trying to turn him into someone he wasn't.

'You do make me happy,' I said, my arms wrapped tightly around him. 'You just be yourself, love. If you don't want to talk, then don't talk. I want you to be happy too.'

I slowly slid my fingers down his rippled stomach. 'I missed our Sunday session, Adam,' I murmured. 'I'm not very tired. Are you?'

He swallowed audibly. 'Sorry, Mel. All the shit that went down today has kind of killed my sex drive. I'm not up for it tonight, honey.' He pulled his arm out from under me and yawned.

I lay awake next to him for what seemed like a never-ending night. It was the first time in over fourteen years he'd knocked me back. I finally fell asleep with a heavy heart, and dreamed only of Matt for the two short hours I slept.

The insomnia became a real problem at work. Whereas before I'd always been alert and motivated, I found myself growing lethargic and apathetic. I could only blame part of it on the constant fatigue. The argument with Adam had only served to confuse me further. Instead of waking up to myself, I was even more fixated on Matt.

I was much slower than usual with my patients, who quite often had to repeat their symptoms to me several times before I registered them. This led to frustration for those left in the waiting room, which in turn led to a tense environment for Cheryl, the receptionist.

Cheryl was no slouch, and she hadn't taken long to detect the changes in me. She said nothing at first, but I noticed her sidelong glances at my daring new wardrobe, and her exaggerated sighs as I came out late yet again to call in patients who'd been waiting for too long.

We were both in the tiny kitchenette making coffee on the day she confronted me.

'Mel, what's wrong with you? You've been like a zombie since you came back from Melbourne.' She stood facing me. 'Tell me what's up.'

I sighed a long sigh. 'I'm not sleeping.'

It wasn't a lie.

'Well then take something to help you sleep. I'm worried about you. You're doing a crap job with your patients, well, worse than normal anyway.' Despite her sarcasm, she seemed genuinely concerned. 'Why aren't you sleeping? Want to talk about it? I've got three minutes.'

'No, no, I'll be fine, thanks, Cheryl. Nothing to worry about, really. Sorry about the patients. I know I'm too slow. I'll work on it, promise. I'll be back to my usual level of crappiness soon, okay?' I smiled brightly at her and took my coffee back to the consulting room.

But I couldn't drink it. I'd poured milk in it. I always had my coffee black.

That evening, while she helped me prepare dinner, Lily excitedly relayed a conversation she'd overheard between two other students in the school toilets. 'So they're actually going to go through with it, Mum! Can you believe it?' Her green eyes shone with glee.

'That's fantastic, sweetie,' I said, chopping the carrots.

'Mum,' Lily's voice dropped. 'You weren't listening, were you?'

'Of course I was, honey,' I lied in my most convincing tone.

She rolled her eyes. 'No. You weren't. You think it's fantastic that Maddie's going to sneak Vodka Cruisers into Hannah's party?' She waited for my reaction.

I opened my mouth, but couldn't come up with anything.

'You've gone all weird, Mum,' she said, with a look of distaste on her face. 'It's like you're not even here half the time. You're just obsessed with how you look and you just stand there and veg out and you don't even hear me or Nick when we ask you things because you don't care. I'm sick of it!' She threw the peeler she'd been using onto the floor and stormed out of the kitchen, her footsteps echoing all the way upstairs. I heard her bedroom door slam.

I muttered a curse at myself. What sort of mother had X-rated daydreams while having a conversation with her daughter? How bad had I become for her to think I didn't care about her?

Nick walked into the kitchen soon after Lily had walked out. 'Mum, did you remember the batteries?'

Oh no. It was the third day in a row I'd promised I would buy them for his calculator. I bit my lip. 'Oh, honey, I'm so …'

Nick didn't wait to hear my excuse. 'I knew you'd forget again,' he said. 'I got in trouble with Mr Byrne for not having a calculator again. I'll ask Dad to get them for me tomorrow. *He'll* remember.'

I was alienating my children for the sake of a fantasy. But I couldn't let the fantasy go. No matter what. I sickened myself. It was another night with no sleep.

The following day, a pharmacist from a nearby store rang me at work to check up on a prescription. I'd prescribed an adult dose of an antibiotic for a baby. It was the first serious mistake of my career.

The baby's mother stormed into the clinic later in the morning, demanding to see me. My hands trembled as I tried to usher her into the consulting room but she pushed me away. She pressed the heel of her hand hard against my collarbone and I took two quick backward steps to prevent myself from falling. With her baby daughter on her hip, she hurled abuse at me in full view of everyone in the waiting room, before one of the male doctors heard the commotion and escorted her outside.

'My baby could've died because of you, you hopeless bitch!' she called out over her shoulder as she was being shown to the door.

Cheryl found me crying in the consulting room. The walls were adorned with photos of Adam and me beaming on our wedding day and on many holidays thereafter, as well as the children's school portraits. My medical degree and practising certificate were also proudly displayed.

I was losing grip on all I held dear.

That was the first night I took sleeping tablets.

The tablets worked beautifully and left me feeling much better rested and at less risk of being sued for malpractice, but they didn't bring back my spirit.

I felt like a fraud with Adam and the children as I hid behind the veneer of my smile. I became a better actress, and Nick and Lily, who, like all children, wanted to see only the goodness in their parents, seemed to believe I was back on board. Adam went on the same way so my insincere attempts to be more present appeared to make no difference to him at all.

At work I was back to being efficient, but I had a new cynicism towards my patients. Being a doctor had always been my vocation, my passion. Now it was just a job. I simply couldn't be bothered. Even when I attended births at the hospital, which were usually emotionally charged for me, I was zoned out.

I was sitting at my desk on a Friday morning, writing out a sick leave certificate for a woman who was as healthy as a horse, when my text message alert sounded. I finished the appointment with the fake sick patient, the third one to think she'd fooled me that week. Once she'd let herself out of the room, coughing twice for effect as she did so, I hunted around for my phone in my handbag.

My heart caught in my chest when I read the message.

What's Mel short for?

It had been one month and five days since I'd seen him.

He hadn't forgotten me!

I replied immediately.

What's Matt short for?

I suddenly felt so alive.

The phone beeped within seconds.

Yeah, that's funny. Now tell me your name.

My heart raced. This was dangerous. What I did now would determine which way this would go. I could have him. I could definitely have him. Oh God, the very idea.

But I couldn't have him. I chewed a nail. Adam. I had Adam. And I had Nick. And I had Lily.

Stop.

His response took a little while longer to come this time, but when it did it sent my head into a spin.

You stop. Stop pretending you don't want me. We've got unfinished business to attend to you and me. I'm coming to find you.

I wanted to stand on the chair and scream, 'Of course I want you! I want nothing but you. I'm obsessed with you. I think about you all day and dream of you every night. Come! Come take me away with you. We can talk and touch and I won't say no and we can touch some more. Please come!'

Instead the married mother texted back.

Enough now.

His reply came quickly.

And when I find you, I'm going to fuck you until you cry.

THE HUNT

MATT

I drove to Lydia's house with a lead weight in my stomach. I was breaking up with her and I wasn't going to back out this time. I couldn't let the wedding get closer by even one more day. It was only three months away now. I had planned to break up with her over a month ago, after I'd first met Mel. But things hadn't gone according to plan then.

Lydia had turned up at my house the morning after I stayed up all night with Mel at the car park in Williamstown, announcing herself with five musical toots of her car's cloying horn. She let herself in as I dragged myself up to go meet her at the front door.

'Well, hello there, Matthew.' Lydia smiled her prettiest smile, placed both of her arms around my neck and kissed me deeply.

I immediately forgot about how I was going to break up with her and instead tried hard to swallow the golf ball–sized lump in my throat. She was such a sweet gorgeous girl. She had no idea what I'd been up to with Mel and I felt like a scumbag.

'Good morning,' I mumbled between kisses, instantly aroused.

She was dressed in a tiny pair of cut-off denim shorts and a fitted singlet that didn't quite cover her belly button. It was easy to think I didn't want her when she wasn't in my arms dressed like that.

She let go of me and took a step backwards, her eyes shining. 'Back in a sec.'

She turned around, skipped out the front door and bounded down the stairs while I watched from the landing. She reappeared a minute later, struggling under the weight of four green recyclable bags overflowing with groceries.

I rushed downstairs to take the load off her.

'I woke up extra, extra early to buy your groceries,' she said. 'I knew you wouldn't want to shop today. Hey, you wouldn't believe how, like, quiet it is at the shops this early on a Sunday, Matty,' she said brightly. 'And I've brought stuff to make your favourite chocchip pancakes for breakfast!' She handed me the two heaviest bags.

'But I thought we had to go meet that wedding photographer this morning?' I said, confused. 'We haven't got time for pancakes.'

'Uh-uh, not going.' She shook her head. 'Emma rang last night. She told me how you talked to Tom yesterday and how you were, like, so shitty about me and the wedding.'

I froze.

'She gave me a tongue lashing and a half! She said you'd had it up to your ears with the wedding plans and the house hunting. You should've told me, Matty, instead of moaning to Tom about it.' She had a hurt look on her face.

'I tried to.' My voice was scratchy. I put the grocery bags down on the bottom step and leaned against the railing.

'I guess you did, but I thought you were just having a whinge, like a typical man. And of course I want to move into a better house, but it doesn't have to be right now.' She sighed. 'But Em said I'm putting too much pressure on you and that I need to pull my head in or else,' she said with a grimace.

I stared at her, dumbstruck.

'So anyway,' she continued, 'I'm really sorry, honey. I don't want you to be, like, all stressed. I'm sorry, I've been feral about the wedding.' She smiled, seeming embarrassed. 'I postponed the photographer until this arvo, Matty. From now on, I'm going to do all that extra wedding stuff with Mum. Em said you'd be happy with that. And I promise, promise, no more house hunting till we both agree we can afford to buy. But,' she added with a laugh, 'that doesn't mean I want to, like, live in this mouldy shoebox forever, okay?'

'Okay.' I could barely get the word out. I was still gaping at her.

This was the last thing I expected. My well-planned strategy to call off the wedding had turned on its head. By some miracle, Lydia was back to being the sweet thoughtful person I'd fallen for.

'So, we've got all morning to chill out together.' She stepped in closer and then she gave my neck a quick sexy lick, lowering her voice to the seductive tone she knew turned me on. 'But before I cook you an obscene amount of pancakes, I think you need to, like, work up an appetite. Don't you think?' She raised an eyebrow and slid her hand up and down the front of my shorts.

So we didn't break up after all.

In fact, forty minutes later I was reading the sports section of the paper Lydia had bought, while she sang to herself in the kitchen making pancakes. The smell of maple syrup and melted chocolate filled the house. I was surprised by how happy I felt. Lydia's sunshine had worked its magic again.

Later in the morning, she suggested we go for a walk along the foreshore together. I told her I was too tired. The idea of going back there, just hours after I'd been there with Mel, felt wrong.

'Oh rubbish, Matty, you're so not tired, you're just lazy.' She laughed. 'You had an early night. You would've been home from my place by, like, eight-thirty, and I'll bet you were asleep not long after. Come on, let's go. The markets are on today. You can buy me something nice!'

On the foreshore, we walked past the spot where Mel and I had sat together, baring our souls to each other.

I pulled Lydia in closer to me and she beamed. 'Everything's better now with you and me, isn't it, Matty? You're not miserable any more like Tom said?'

'Yeah, babe. It's all good now.'

The Sunday market was in full swing at the park at the end of the foreshore. I bought Lydia a gemstone bracelet that was a huge rip-off in an effort to shake off some of my guilt. She was rapt and put the bracelet straight on. We passed a quiet hour strolling around the market, then we sat huddled together on the grass listening to the hypnotic voice of a folk singer, playing her guitar on the small stage in the middle of the park. Finally we started to head home, and I only relaxed when we were back at my apartment.

We sat out on the balcony and had a coffee while we laughed together at the idea of Tom and Emma's impending parenthood.

'Can't you just picture Em, Matty, mouthing off at Tom for, like, putting a nappy on the wrong way or making noise when the baby's asleep?' Lydia giggled.

'That poor bastard's got no idea what's coming.'

She looked at her watch. 'I have to go, honey. I'm swinging past home to pick Mum up for the photographer. She's so excited, bless her.'

I could just imagine.

Lydia sat herself on my lap. 'Now you're sure you don't mind me doing wedding stuff without you? Is that really what you want?'

'Absolutely, babe, you're the expert,' I said wholeheartedly. 'I've got no idea, and you'll have fun doing it with your mum.'

'Well, if you're sure. All right, I really have to go now or I'll be late. See you Tuesday night?'

'Who's cooking?' I asked with narrowed eyes.

'Mum.'

I groaned, 'Bloody Chow Mein. Awesome.'

'Matty!' She laughed despite herself. 'Don't be mean, it's her specialty.'

'It's her only fucking dish, of course it's her specialty.'

She smacked my leg and hopped up to her feet. I walked her down to the driveway, and we kissed for a few minutes standing against her car. I tried to coax her into coming back upstairs with me but she refused. Wedding plans were calling.

My phone beeped in my pocket as I walked back up into the house. I stared incredulously at the display. It was a text from Mel. The timing of it, less than thirty seconds after I'd seen Lydia off, was uncanny.

Matt, I hope you understand why I had to leave ...

I read the rest of the message, in which she practically admitted she was in love with me, but was going to stay with her husband. So I sent a text straight back.

Bye.

It was over. She had her husband, I had Lydia.

Why was it then, that after spending a near perfect morning with my lovely smart sexy fiancée that for the rest of that day and night and for the entire drive to work the following morning I thought only of Mel?

Knowing Mel had gone home to another man made me irrational with jealousy. They'd been married fourteen years and had two children. It wasn't outrageous that after only a few hours with me she wasn't prepared to throw all that away. I couldn't blame her. It was just that when I remembered the taste of her tongue in my mouth and how the heat of her breath had mixed with mine, I physically ached for her and all reason was put aside.

But then, when I'd been with Lydia, I'd enjoyed every minute. It was as if I'd rediscovered her all over again. When I was lying in bed next to her I couldn't believe I'd planned to break off our engagement over a married woman I'd never lay eyes on again. I had told myself as I lay there with Lydia that I had to wake up to myself and see this thing with Mel for what it was, an impossible fantasy brought on by a bad case of cold feet.

Those thoughts turned to dust as soon as Lydia left and Mel's text arrived. It was just fucked. The whole thing.

As I pulled up into the car park near work on Monday morning, I forced myself to focus on all the positives I had with Lydia.

The previous morning with Lydia had shown me that I could be happy with her again and we could still have a good life together. I just had to find a way to control my overactive imagination that kept conjuring up images of Mel and me together and then everything would be okay.

The clinic was unlocked, the lights were on, and the radio was playing softly when I walked in. The smell of toast and freshly brewed coffee came from the back office.

I sat at the front desk and glanced at the computer monitor displaying the list of the day's patients. Having time off always resulted in a crazy week crammed with patients upon my return, and today was no exception. I had twenty-one patients booked in with only half an hour off for lunch, finishing at seven o'clock.

I yawned and went to say good morning to Tom.

He was sitting with both feet up on the desk and his arms crossed behind his head. 'Still thinking about the chick from the plane or did Lyds shag you back to reality?' he asked, failing to hide his smirk.

'You're an interfering arsehole.'

He roared with laughter.

After twenty-one assessments and treatments, along with answering a slew of phone calls, processing payments and scheduling in further appointments, my legs ached, my head hurt and my thumbs burned from overuse. Tom had long gone home to Emma, and I was finally ready to call it a day.

I took my time tidying up the clinic and preparing for the next day, I was in no hurry to return to an empty apartment. Lydia played netball on Monday nights, and I knew where my thoughts would go the second I was home alone.

It wasn't as though I'd made it through the day without thinking of Mel. She slipped into every tiny gap between dealing with patients. It didn't help matters when I was caught in traffic on Flinders Street on the way home, which left me sitting stationary in the car for ten long minutes, directly outside the hotel where she'd stayed.

'It'll get better. You'll get over her,' I told myself firmly.

I was determined to make it work with Lydia. I kept reminding myself that Mel had chosen her husband, and that Lydia actually *wanted* to spend her life with me. I tried not to think of Mel when I had sex with Lydia, and to see Lydia's bubbly personality as endearing rather than irritating. I pretended not to notice when Lydia quickly changed the computer screen to hide a real estate website when I walked in on her one evening. At least she wasn't putting direct pressure on me any more.

Lydia stayed true to her word and shielded me from the wedding plans, simply keeping me informed on a need-to-know basis. I took her on romantic dates – to fancy restaurants where she played with her food, and to an outdoor cinema, which was a more successful date – but when I surprised her with concert tickets for one of her favourite bands, I really hit the jackpot. She loved that.

I spent more time with her parents, and was always on my best behaviour around them, just to please her. Lydia and I were getting along better than we had for the past twelve months.

But still, the memory of Mel's eyes, her hair, her taste, haunted my dreams no matter how much I tried to forget her.

Early on a Saturday morning I picked up Lydia for our monthly visit to my parents' house. She climbed into the passenger seat with a massive smile.

I leaned across to kiss her. 'Hi, gorgeous. You look sensational.'

She did look great, but then again, when didn't she look great? Today she was wearing a white shirt tied into a knot above her flat belly, and a long loose red skirt. With her figure she could pull off any look, so she liked to shop for clothes virtually every week. I dreaded the day she'd have to cull it all to fit into the tiny closet she'd be sharing with me in Williamstown.

'Guess what?' Lydia squealed. 'You'll never, never ever in a million years guess!'

'So why bother?' I laughed. 'Just tell me.'

'The resort in Port Douglas double-booked us with another couple,' she said, feverish with excitement.

'And that's good?'

'Yes, Matty, it's very, very good. The manager rang to say she was, like, terribly sorry about the mix-up, but because we'd booked the room first, and because we'll be honeymooners, she's giving us the presidential lagoon suite for the same price. *The Presidential Lagoon Suite*! Remember, Matty? The room I was totally dying for but you said we couldn't afford it. Remember?'

I kissed her again. I had no recollection whatsoever of the suite she was talking about, but if it made her this happy, then I felt happy for her. We drove off for Daylesford in high spirits, singing along with the radio, in between catching up on the last couple of days. But as we approached the turn-off to my parents' house, Lydia went quiet. It was the same every time.

I rubbed her leg. 'Babe, relax. You'll be fine.'

'She hates me. She's just going to stare at me again and roll her eyes at everything I say.'

'Holly doesn't hate you, I promise. She's just a rude cow generally, to everyone. Mum and Dad love you to pieces, Lachy worships you. Don't let her get to you so much, it only gives her power.'

'I love your parents too, and Lachy, of course. I just want Holly to like me. She thinks I'm not good enough for you, I can tell. She thinks I'm, like, a bimbo, just because I'm not obsessed with human rights like she is,' Lydia said bitterly.

She was completely justified too. Holly was openly horrified when I introduced her to Lydia for the first time, and she'd rung me in a rage after Mum told her the news we were engaged.

'Are you out of your fucking mind?' Holly had roared. 'You don't even love her, you dick! She's so wrong for you. What the hell are you going to talk about for the next fifty years, pedicures and spray tans?'

'I do love her!' I'd shouted back. 'What would you know?'

'I know you, Matt,' Holly said in a calmer voice. 'I know what makes you tick. She's not for you. One day you'll meet someone else and realise you're only with Lydia because she's hot and she liked you back.'

'Well, Mum and Dad are rapt. They know me and they think she's perfect for me. So do Tom and Em.'

'Matt, nobody knows you like I do. They see you temporarily cheered up because you're with a nice girl and they're grateful you're not the moody shit you were before. But that doesn't mean she's the one for you. Things might be okay now, while you're still shagging every night, but later on you'll want someone who's on your wavelength. Just think about it, okay? It's not too late to back out.'

'Piss off, Holly.' I'd hung up the telephone and immediately blocked out everything she'd said.

Now, as I pulled into the gravel driveway of my parents' place, Holly's words came into my head again, sending a chill down my spine.

Lydia's smile was back as she rushed out of the car and threw her arms around my mum. I watched them hug. I couldn't help but compare my soft and cuddly mum to Lydia's glamorous ice queen mother whose facial expression remained the same no matter what her mood was, thanks to the wonders of Botox. Lydia loved them both. But then again, Lydia loved everybody.

My dad walked out of the house, a huge grin on his weathered face, carrying Lachlan up high on his shoulders. Lachy had brought a lot of healing to our family. We all doted on him. Even tough-as-nails Holly turned to jelly around her only child.

'Uncle Matty!' Lachy shouted, waving one arm as he held on to his grandfather's head with the other. 'Look how high I am! I'm even higher than you!'

I jogged over to them, feeling the tension leave my body as it always did when I was near my dad.

After a long morning tea around the large oak table on the front patio, Holly's husband Brandon, and Lydia, Lachlan and I played an extremely competitive game of backyard cricket, which went on until lunchtime. The others heckled us from the comfort of their banana lounges.

Brandon, an engineer who'd met Holly at university, came alive during the cricket match, but as soon as it was over he withdrew into his shell and hid behind a newspaper for the remainder of the day, with the exception of lunch where he sat mute. I'd known Brandon for ten years but still couldn't manage a proper conversation with him; it was like talking to a sulky teenager. But according to Holly, who adored him, he was the world's greatest husband and father, so I was happy enough to have him in our family, even though he was the dullest man on the face of the earth.

After a barbeque lunch, Lydia was helping my mother clear away the dishes when Holly approached me with a determined look holding a manila folder. Her messy brown curls flew around her face and her eyes sparkled, the way they always did when she was about to be annoying.

'Go away with that,' I said. 'It's the weekend, Holly, my down time. I don't give a shit about whatever's in that file.'

She ignored me and sat down next to me, tucking her gangly legs under the table and slapping my thigh as she opened the file. 'I need you to proofread this letter I've drafted for the Governor of Texas.'

What was she, deaf?

I tried to stand up, but she grabbed my sleeve and pulled me back down. She slid across a photo of an unsmiling skinny bald man who looked to be in his fifties. 'This is Howard Clyde. It's an urgent action one. Final appeal against his execution failed yesterday. It's happening in two weeks. Here, check this and tell me if it's missing anything so I can get the emails going.'

I wasn't getting out of it. I read the letter twice. The crime was sickening.

'It's good, I can't think of anything I'd add to that,' I said with a queasy feeling in my gut at the details I'd just read.

By then, Lydia had finished helping in the kitchen and she came up behind me, leaning in with her arms around my neck. She saw the file laid out on the table.

'Ooh, he looks nasty, doesn't he?' She giggled and then she stepped back. 'Electric chair, oh no! What did he do to deserve that?'

'Nobody deserves the death penalty,' Holly and I automatically replied together, which made Lydia laugh.

'No way, you guys, depends what the crime was. Some people totally deserve to die. So … what was the crime?'

I sighed. 'Lyds, the crime makes no difference. We're opposed to the death penalty in all cases. No exceptions. The right to life is a fundamental human right.' I felt my heart rate rising.

Lydia rolled her eyes as she took the papers from my hand. 'Yeah, yeah, Matt,' she said, and started quoting me back to myself. 'The death penalty appeals to our lowest instincts as humans. It's despicable and it isn't even an effective deterrent … I know, you've said it all before. But let's see what this creep actually did.'

The colour drained from her face as she read. 'If I had a gun I'd pull the trigger on him myself,' she said when she was done. 'I can't believe you're trying to save his life. What a waste of your time, Matt.' She didn't look at Holly, she saved her look of distaste for me. I was about to answer when she said, 'I'll leave you guys to deal with that alone, I think. Hey Lachy, bet you can't catch me!'

And she ran off, with Lachlan running after her around the garden.

Holly looked long and hard at me. 'Yep, there goes your soul mate, Matt. Peas in a pod, you two.'

Two weeks later, Lydia and I were in her lounge room watching television while her mother prepared another mouth-watering Chow Mein. Lydia's mobile phone rang and we both jumped.

Tom had left work early that morning when Emma had called to say her waters had broken and labour had started. Lydia and I had been obsessively checking our phones all evening.

'It's Em,' Lydia gasped before answering the call. She listened for a minute and then she started squealing, bringing both of her parents rushing into the room. 'It's a boy!' she screamed in my ear. 'She had a little boy, Matty!'

I swallowed the lump in my throat and nodded. I couldn't get to the hospital quickly enough.

Emma's room was overflowing with visitors when we walked in. Lydia and I stood shoulder to shoulder with the others. Emma looked exhausted. Her hair was matted to the sides of her head, she had dark blue circles under her glazed eyes and deep cracks in her white lips. But she was somehow so beautiful to me as she sat up in bed, her white nightgown straps falling off her shoulders.

Standing beside her, Tom looked completely stunned. He was almost incoherent when I asked him how Emma's labour had been.

Little Mitchell Thomas Stone – swaddled in a blanket and being passed around from person to person like a football – stayed fast asleep, unaware of the fuss surrounding his safe arrival.

I watched Tom stroke Emma's cheek, and she looked up at him with a warmth that made me want what they had. Having a baby together had clearly created a whole new level of intimacy between them. I thought of Mel having gone through this with her husband, twice, and my jaw clenched involuntarily.

'Don't open your eyes now, Mitchell, whatever you do. There's a seriously ugly dude in your face,' Tom cooed at his baby when it was my turn to hold him.

I ran my finger along the tiny creases on Mitchell's knuckles, and then I stroked the top of his warm pink head. 'Why did your nice mummy name you after that good-for-nothing daddy of yours, hey Mitch? Poor little bugger.'

I laughed along with the others, relieved I'd managed to hold in the tears. Tom would never have let me live it down if I'd cried in that room. I was amazed at how much I already loved this baby, and how overcome I felt holding him. It was hard to believe the pimply, girl-crazy eighteen-year-old doofus I'd met at a pub crawl on uni orientation day was now a father.

We stayed with Tom and Emma for an hour and then, along with most of the other visitors, left them to enjoy their son in peace.

I hugged Lydia tightly when we got out of the car back at her parents' house. 'I want to make one of those with you, babe,' I said huskily.

'How cute was he, Matty? See his squished-up little nose? Ooh, and his fuzzy red hair!'

'Mmm, hmm.' I nuzzled into her neck. She smelled sexy. 'Let's make one.'

She giggled.

'I'm serious, let's make one. Come back to my house now and make a baby with me.' I started to nibble at her ear.

She pushed me off, laughing. 'Get away, you crazy person.'

'Why not?' I smiled. 'Don't you want one?'

'I most certainly do not want one, thank you very much,' she said, still laughing. 'Talk to me in, like, ten years or something.'

'Ten years?' I exclaimed 'Are you for real?'

'Yep, if you're lucky. Maybe twelve years actually.' She kissed my nose.

'But doesn't it make you want one after seeing Mitchell?'

'No way!' Lydia squealed. 'Are you kidding me? What about my career? What about the beautiful house we want? How long do you think it would take to pay off a mortgage once we have a kid? I'm in my early twenties, Matt. God, don't write me off yet! I don't want to be like Emma – that's it for her, game over. Mitchell's gorgeous but, eww, I wouldn't trade places with her for anything.'

I took a step back from her. 'Is that really how you feel about kids, "eww"? I thought you loved kids. What about Lachlan?'

She nodded. 'I do love kids, especially little Lachy, he's a star. But I don't want them for myself, not for years and years. I'm so not ready to lose my body yet, no way am I wearing incontinence pads when I go running like the mothers I treat. This body's all yours for a long time yet, mister. Hey, maybe later we could, like, adopt a child from one of your sad countries then I won't end up stitched up and sore and swollen like Em,' she added with a grin.

I stared at her as if I was seeing her for the first time.

She was oblivious to the sudden death of our relationship. 'I'd better go in, Matty. I can see Dad peering at us through the curtains and he doesn't look impressed.' She giggled. 'He's hilarious, isn't he?'

I drove home in a daze. What was I doing marrying this woman who was still a stranger to me after three years together?

I knew since her talk with Emma that Lydia had tried her best to make me happy, but she couldn't change who she was. The things that were important to her, like the big house, weren't at all important to me. There was a massive difference in our world view when it came to human rights and now she wasn't keen on having kids either. It was all too much.

I'd given it my best shot. It hadn't worked. There was no way I could marry her. The next morning as I drove into work, I found myself once again stuck in peak hour traffic outside the hotel where Mel had stayed. I remembered the way she'd looked at me when she walked out of the lift that night, and I admitted the truth to myself for the first time.

It wasn't just lust. It wasn't just a meeting of the minds. It was love. I was in love with her.

I had to put a stop to the wedding and then go find Mel. We belonged together. If I went to Perth and told her I loved her, and that I wanted to make a life with her, maybe now after having had a month to think about things, she just might consider it. She'd admitted she wasn't satisfied in her marriage. I was certain she was in love with me and not him. Well, almost certain. I couldn't die wondering.

But first, I had to break up with Lydia. She had a busy few days coming up so I wasn't going to see her until the following Thursday night. And I was flat out too. With Tom away and a locum covering for him, I had less time to stress out about Lydia anyway.

Tom came into work on Thursday after the clinic was closed to go over the monthly business figures and get organised for his return to work the next day. He wasn't scheduled to come back until the following Monday, but Emma's parents and sister from Ireland were staying so he was desperate to escape the house.

He walked into our office to find me sitting with my head in my hands.

'You okay, mate?' he asked, putting his hand on my shoulder.

I'd kept my feelings to myself since my initial confession to him a month ago. But I couldn't keep this from him any more. He deserved to know. 'I can't marry Lydia,' I said, my voice heavy. 'I'm not in love with her. I've tried. We want different things from life. We're just too different, Tom. We'd never be happy.'

Tom sat down opposite me with a blank expression on his face. I silently willed him to speak. I wanted a reaction from him. He picked at fluff on his trousers.

After a while he looked up. 'It's that chick from the flight, isn't it?'

I nodded.

'Have you been cheating on Lyds?' he asked matter-of-factly as he took off his glasses and cleaned them on his sleeve.

'Almost. Yeah. Once.' I scratched my head and swallowed hard. 'I'm going to Perth to find her. I'm calling it off with Lyds tonight.'

He sighed loudly, 'Oh shit.'

'Sorry,' I muttered.

We sat in silence for a few minutes longer, with Tom drumming his fingers on the desk. 'This is huge. You sure you know what you're doing? I think you're making a big mistake.' He frowned.

'I'm sure.' Now I'd said it out loud, it seemed ridiculous I'd taken this long to decide when it had been so obvious all along.

'What about us?' asked Tom. 'What about this place? I need you here, especially now, mate, with the baby and all that. You can't move to Perth permanently, Matt.' He looked intently at me.

'I don't even know if she's going to want anything to do with me. I'm only going for a week to find out.' I took a deep breath. I felt bad for what I was about to do to my friend. 'I won't leave you in the lurch,' I was quick to assure him. 'If I end up leaving, I'll help you find another partner and I'll stay on till they've settled in and it's all running smoothly. Don't worry.' I knew it wasn't that simple.

'Oh, Jesus,' he moaned. 'This place is ours, Matt. Mine and yours, not mine and some physio I've never met. I thought we were in this for the long haul, mate.' He pulled at his shoelaces.

I gulped down the guilt. 'I know, I'm sorry. But she might boot me back here, you never know. I've already lined up the locum to stay on next week to cover for me.'

Tom rolled his eyes, then sighed and nodded.

I imagined myself in his position. 'I'm being a crap friend. I'm really sorry, mate, I am. I know the timing's terrible with the baby and everything. But if I don't follow this through I'll just be a huge mess and not able to focus on anything here anyway. I have to try, Tom. I think it's the real thing with her.'

We left the clinic together, both in a morbid mood, not having touched the pile of paperwork. I asked about Emma and the baby, but Tom brushed me off.

He put his hand on my shoulder when we reached our cars. 'Good luck,' he said sadly. 'I hope you get what you want, mate.'

'Thanks. I'm really sorry.'

He dismissed that with a shrug. 'Ring me if you want later on,' he said. 'You know, after you tell Lyds.'

So this was it. This time I was going to break up with Lydia and I wasn't going to chicken out.

I drove straight to Lydia's parents' house, rehearsing what I was going to say to her. I'd never before felt so sick with anxiety. It was only when I heard the gravel on the driveway crunch under the car's tyres that I realised I'd arrived. I couldn't remember any of the drive. I was expected for dinner, so the porch light had been turned on for my benefit. This was the last time I'd ever be welcome here. I took my time walking to the front door.

My heart sank when Lydia greeted me with her warm smile. No backing down this time. I hesitated when she stood back to let me in.

'What is it, Matty?'

I didn't know how to start. 'Can we go for a walk?'

'Right now? But dinner's just about ready.'

'Yes, now. Please.'

A worried look came over her face when she saw my expression. 'Mum, Dad, I'm going out for a walk with Matty,' she called out over her shoulder.

'Take a jacket!' Beverley squawked.

'It's bloody well dinnertime!' Kevin bellowed.

'We won't be long, Daddy.'

'You better not be, I'm hungry!' he roared over the noise of the television.

Lydia smiled nervously. 'Come on, Matty, let's get out of here before Mum brings out a coat and gloves.'

I took her hand and we walked slowly along the street past a few houses. I knew I was being a massive coward, but it was easier to do this in the dark without having to make eye contact.

My mouth was dry. I licked my lips and took a deep breath. 'Lyds, I don't know how to say this, babe,' I began shakily, looking down at the footpath, 'but I, I just, I don't want to … I don't want to get married.'

She stopped abruptly and turned to look at me. 'Matt, if this is your idea of a joke, it's really not funny,' she said, her voice quavering.

'I'm not joking.' I felt the tears stinging my eyes and blinked them away.

'Why?' She barely let the word escape, her own eyes instantly full of tears.

My shoulders slumped. 'I don't think I'm in love with you.' I couldn't look at her as I imagined the effect my words were having.

'What?' she exhaled in a whisper.

'I'm sorry, babe, but I'm just not convinced of my feelings ... and you deserve better. I can't do this to you. I can't go through with the wedding when I've got this much doubt.'

'You can't do this to *me*?' she asked through her tears.

We stood there in silence under a streetlight, neither of us looking at each other. I reached for her hand and she took a step back, shaking me off. She leaned against a neighbour's front fence and picked at the leaves of a hibiscus bush.

'I'm sorry,' I offered pitifully.

'It doesn't make sense.' She started to pace. 'Is there someone else? Is that it?'

'Of course not,' I murmured, my heart pounding. 'No.'

'Well, I don't believe you don't love me.' She looked around frantically, as though she would find answers in the air around her. 'It might just be, like, cold feet. That happens to heaps of guys, doesn't it?' she said, her eyes pleading. 'Do you think that's all it is, maybe? Just cold feet?'

I shook my head. 'I don't think so. I haven't been feeling right for a while. I'm going back to Perth. I need to get away for a bit.'

'What? Why?' she asked, taken aback.

'I just need to get away.'

'For how long?' she demanded loudly, hysteria creeping into her voice.

'A week, maybe.'

Lydia took a step towards me. 'Matty, I know you love me, I know it. I think you're just scared.' She fiddled with the buttons of my shirt.

I couldn't speak. The tears fell freely down my face now.

'Please, Matty, don't ruin us,' she said thinly.

I held my arms out and she collapsed against me as we both cried.

'Go then, and come back in a week,' she said. 'You do love me, Matty. Maybe you just need, like, a little space to get some perspective.'

'Okay, babe.' I wiped hot tears away from her cheeks, hating myself as I spoke the words that I knew weren't true. 'I'll go and think about it for a week.'

'Okay then.' She breathed deeply. 'Okay then.'

I walked her the short distance back to the house, gave her a long hug goodbye and left quickly. There was no way I was going inside. I was finished with Kevin and Beverley forever, thank God.

I drove home slowly, imagining Lydia in her pink bedroom, curled up on her fluffy pink bed, crying to her mother. I was surprised by how calm she was when I left. I'd pictured her completely losing the plot. She was probably in shock. It'd come later on, when the reality of what I'd said really hit her.

It hit her sooner than I'd banked on.

I'd been home for about five minutes when a text message arrived.

I hate you! Don't bother coming back. I won't be here waiting. Go to hell.

I went straight to bed in my work clothes, pulling the sheet up over my head.

The next morning I slept in till late, feeling strangely hungover. I rang the locum and asked him to work in my place. My head hurt and my stomach was cramping. I rang Tom and told him I wouldn't be in. He asked about Lydia and I filled him in briefly on what had happened the night before.

'Sounds to me like there's still hope for you guys, the way you left things,' he said.

'No, mate, there isn't.' I was adamant.

'Em thinks you're a huge wanker, by the way. She said she doesn't want to see you when you get back.'

'She'll come round.' I tried to sound casual, but I adored Emma and I couldn't deny that it hurt. 'She'd love Mel,' I said defensively. 'You both would.'

'So her name's Mel, huh? Mel what?'

There was a pause while I silently swore at myself. 'I don't know.'

Tom guffawed loudly. 'You really are a tosser, mate, you know that? You don't even know her bloody name! Listen, dickhead, hang up, then ring Lyds and tell her you were drug-fucked last night and you didn't know what you were talking about, and beg her to take you back.'

'See you next week,' I snapped and hung up.

The skin on the back of my neck prickled. I wondered what I would think of him if he cheated on Emma with a woman he'd just met. I'd want to kill him. But the difference was that he and Emma actually did belong together.

Stuff him.

I had a shower and fried myself some sausages. I was surprised at how much better I felt once I'd washed and eaten. I managed to push Lydia and Tom right out of my mind. My thoughts were only on Mel. I had a new focus now and there was nothing and nobody to stop me. I was going to find her.

Problem was, I didn't know her name, and I had no idea where in Perth she lived or where she worked. I felt as though I understood her so well, but I didn't know the most basic details about her.

My fingers shook as I grabbed my phone and sent her a text. It was something I'd stopped myself doing every day leading up to this one.

What's Mel short for?

After the longest five minutes of my life, I received her reply.

What's Matt short for?

I laughed out loud as our texts pinged back and forth. With my groins tingling, I sent her a final text.

And when I find you, I'm going to fuck you until you cry.

She didn't reply. She didn't say no, or don't. I took it as an invitation to find her.

I spent the next couple of hours online, until I located and listed the phone number for every medical centre in Perth. There were hundreds. Now I had to narrow it down.

I phoned them all and gave every receptionist the same prepared speech: 'Hi, I'm looking for a female doctor who's been recommended to me. I think it was Mel something? Melinda maybe? Melissa? Melanie?'

In the end I had a shortlist of clinics. I was exhausted but euphoric.

I booked a flight to Perth for two days' time, on Sunday. Starting the following Monday, I'd lined up three consecutive days of appointments with all the possible Dr Mels. I would complain of an upset stomach to every one until I found the right Mel.

I slept soundly that night.

When I woke up late the next morning, the guilt about Lydia had settled in again. I hadn't contacted her all day yesterday. I should have at least done that. I still didn't have the nerve to ring and check on her. So I did what many gutless wonders had done before me. I sent a text.

Lyds, I hope you're okay. I'm so sorry about everything. I'll call you next week. I'll pay for everything as far as wedding costs. I'm going to Perth tomorrow. Take care. Matt.

She didn't reply.

I stared at the photo of her that was the wallpaper on my phone, taken on holiday in Tasmania seven months ago. It was of her holding a snowball and grinning in anticipation of the pain she was about to inflict on my face. I imagined my life without her in it any more as I deleted the photo.

There was no way we could continue as friends. She'd find out sooner or later that I'd left her for someone else, and that would make things ugly. So Lydia would disappear completely from my life. I'd never hear her laugh, or snuggle up with her watching a movie, or taste her pancakes, or talk to her on the drive to Daylesford, or have her in my bed ever again. My heart tightened.

I rang Mum and asked if I could spend the day with them. I told her I was feeling down, and that I'd explain everything when I got there. The concern in her voice and her excitement at the idea of seeing me unexpectedly made me wish I made the effort to spend more time with her.

I drove along the wide, empty roads that led to Daylesford, thinking how even though I was nearly thirty years old, in times of stress I needed my parents as much as ever.

When I reached home, Mum had just finished baking a bread and butter pudding and it was cooling on the kitchen bench. She hugged me hard. She smelled of talcum powder, my favourite smell ever since I was a kid.

As I reclined on a banana lounge on the back porch, overlooking the rolling green hills, I emptied out my heart about Lydia to my parents. I left out the part about Mel. They both said everything I needed to hear to comfort me, as I knew they would. My mum and dad were as solid as they'd been my whole life in their unconditional, unwavering love for me.

I stayed all day. After our talk, Dad and I played a long and intense game of chess, and then I set the table and stood around in the kitchen while Mum added the last minute touches to a roast chicken dinner. She was a brilliant cook, my mum, and it was comfort eating at its best.

I left their house late in the evening with mixed emotions. If things worked out with Mel and I moved to Perth, what would my parents and I do without each other?

It was with a strange sense of deja vu the next day that I packed a bag and made my way to Tullamarine airport. I checked in quickly and headed to security.

As I passed through the screen, it beeped repeatedly until I found myself with no watch, no belt, no shoes, and being treated with great suspicion by the two customs officers on duty.

'Any metal implants?' one of them asked flatly.

'Just my balls of steel, mate.'

He didn't appreciate the joke. 'I could fine you for that comment,' he snarled.

So naturally, I was summoned over for the 'random' bag check. Every bloody time.

Once I was a free man I went to the departure area and boarded immediately. I'd chosen a window seat again, towards the back of the plane, and I watched with intrigue to see who would be sitting next to me this time. The smile was wiped off my face when a seriously overweight woman with lime green highlights through her hair, threw herself down heavily in the seat beside mine.

She wore a tight tank top emblazoned with the words 'Zero to Bitch in Sixty Seconds', that left far too much of her belly uncovered. She was hauling a grubby toddler.

She smiled at me with chipped teeth. 'Awesome, spare seat between us. There ya go, Jayden, now I don't have to have ya on me lap for the whole fucking flight.'

It was a long flight.

I was mauled by the little boy, who climbed on and off his seat incessantly and clambered onto my lap to press his nose against the window, and I found myself nodding inanely at his mum, who didn't stop talking to me for the entire flight while chewing a big hunk of purple gum. When the plane did finally land, she burped and then asked me for my phone number.

I got off that plane faster than I knew I could ever move.

After picking up a hire car, I drove back to the same hotel at Scarborough Beach. I checked in just after 2 pm and wasted no time changing into board shorts. I raced down into the surf, where the waves smacked my body, leaving big red welts. I body-surfed without much skill, but loved being out there anyway.

The beach was crowded with surfers, swimmers, and children who ran in and out of the shallows with delighted screams. I stood on the sandbar twenty metres off shore and took in Scarborough. The enormous clock tower monument stood in the centre of the roundabout, and on either side people strolled along the cafe and hotel strip. The foreshore buzzed. There was a real holiday vibe to the place.

I lay on the sand after a swim and the sun's rays seemed to point straight at me. I felt as though I was being welcomed home. I shut my eyes and soaked it in.

I was on a high for the whole afternoon, knowing that within the next three days I would hopefully be with Mel again. Every now and then, an annoying voice in my head warned she might not share in the excitement of seeing me, that she might have sorted stuff out with her husband … but I drowned the doubts out with positive thoughts of us together.

Monday morning, after a big buffet breakfast overlooking the ocean in the hotel restaurant, I set off early to meet the first prospective Mel.

Dr Melody Withers worked at a clinic ten minutes north of Scarborough. I stifled a laugh as the round, grey-haired doctor, dressed in yellow baggy pants and masseur sandals, ushered me into her room.

As the day wore on, I started to lose my sense of humour. Driving from clinic to clinic in an unfamiliar city wasn't easy. I grew more and more irritable the longer I sat in sterile waiting rooms, and then in stuffy consulting rooms listening to the same advice for my supposedly upset stomach, from each doctor that wasn't her.

After having seen seven doctors in a day, I returned to the hotel at five o'clock, tired and grumpy. I stayed in the suite and watched a horror movie on TV, with a hamburger and a beer.

When the movie finished, I sat on the balcony listening to the crash of the waves and hoping to God that tomorrow wouldn't be another wasted day.

I walked into yet another busy waiting room at five minutes to twelve on Tuesday morning. Its red, black and white Ikea-style furniture made it feel eerily like my own waiting room.

I reported to the receptionist on my arrival, a tough-looking fortyish woman with a rectangular jaw, her hair pulled back so tightly it made her eyes squint. There was the usual crowd in the waiting room – old people, and mums with their toddlers. This was the fourth clinic of the day and I was already fed up. Soft elevator music came from the stereo and the television was muted and tuned to an American daytime soap opera.

I took a seat and waited.

Then I saw her walk out holding a file. Her hair was up in a high ponytail, and it was as though she was gift-wrapped in a tight navy skirt and a white blouse that hugged her breasts. She glanced down at the file, called out my name and looked into the room.

I forgot to breathe.

THE PATIENT

MEL

It was nearing the end of my shift just before noon on Tuesday. I'd been booked out solidly with twelve patients so far, and I only had two more to see before finishing up.

I hadn't had a chance to look at Matt's text messages since starting work that morning, so I pulled my phone out of my handbag and had a quick flick through them, smiling as I felt the familiar surge shoot up through my insides. Since they'd arrived four days ago I'd re-read them dozens of times.

I guarded my phone closely, keeping it on silent and never out of my sight whenever Adam was around, just in case Matt sent any more. Even though it was risky leaving the messages in the phone, I figured it was only a small risk. Adam was not a snoop, which was just as well, because I couldn't bring myself to delete them yet. Matt's ability to turn me on with a handful of typed words was thrilling.

I knew of course that nothing could come of it. He'd never find me. He didn't even know my full name, let alone where I lived or worked, but the rush of knowing he wanted to find me was enough excitement on its own.

The same day the messages had come from Matt, I went out with some mothers from Nick's old primary school class. I sat through dinner, smiling and nodding, twirling fettuccine around and around on my fork, while I lived in my parallel universe. I didn't join in any of the several conversations going on around me, I wasn't even listening. I just drank and daydreamed.

One friend complimented the dress I was wearing, telling me I looked lovely. It was the same red cocktail dress I'd worn in Melbourne.

'Thanks, Cath, you look lovely too,' I'd replied demurely, while thinking, *There's a sexy twenty-eight-year-old man out there who also thinks I'm lovely. Very lovely.*

I arrived home late, almost rolling out of the cab. I tossed my handbag and keys onto the tiled floor near the front door, and followed the series of dimly lit down-lights that illuminated a pathway up the stairs to our bedroom. Adam was spreadeagled on his back on top of the covers, breathing deeply. He was naked but for his Calvin Klein boxers, which left little to the imagination. I needed an orgasm. There was too much pent-up energy down there, I had to release it. I kicked off my shoes and climbed on top of him.

He stirred. 'Did you have a good time?' he murmured while I kissed and sucked on his neck.

'Yes. I'm about to have a better time now.' I licked under his ear.

'You're a tad drunk there, mate. Come home horny, did you?' He pulled my strap down and kissed my shoulder.

'Shh,' I whispered. 'Talk's overrated, remember?' I didn't want his voice to ruin this.

He chuckled softly and I felt him becoming aroused. I grinded against him. I was so ready for this. His breathing got faster as he began to move under me.

'Fuck me. I need you to fuck me,' I breathed in his ear.

He stopped immediately and pulled his head back sharply. 'What did you just say?' He held me away from him, his hands pushing against my shoulders.

Oh no, I didn't want him to stop now. I tried to push myself back down onto him. 'Nothing. I didn't say anything,' I whispered.

He was wide awake now. 'Mel, why did you say that? It's vile.'

I rolled over onto my back, my mood well and truly dampened. 'Relax, Adam, it's just a word. You say it all the time.' I stood up and began to undress, frustrated beyond words at the missed opportunity.

His face was thunderous. 'I say it when I'm angry, as a swear word. I don't – *we* don't – say it in that context. It makes you sound cheap. I don't like it.'

'Okay! All right! I'm sorry, I won't say it again.' I slipped into satin pyjama shorts and a loose ribbed singlet.

Adam turned his back to me.

I rolled my eyes. 'Adam, for God's sake, I'm sorry! I didn't think you'd be offended. Don't be so buttoned up.'

'It's not who you are, Mel. When you talk like that, it's as if you're pretending to be someone else,' he said in a sulky voice, still facing the other way.

I switched off the bedside lamp and climbed into bed, lying as far away from him as was possible without falling off the edge.

I'm not pretending to be anyone. This is me. If you knew me better, you'd know I find talking dirty extremely erotic. If you knew me better, you'd know I want you to be waiting up for me when I come home from a night out, that I want us to sit up with a bottle of wine and talk about you and me and our family and our future and our dreams. You'd know I want you to take me in your arms late at night and hold me for hours while you tell me all your secrets. You'd know I want you to kiss me, I mean really kiss me, out of the blue and for no reason except that you saw me and wanted to. You'd know I want you to tell me I'm beautiful, every single day, and to look at me in a way that actually *would* make my belly flip. And you'd know that, more than anything, I want to be absolutely, no-holds-barred, mind-blowingly fucked, as hard as any woman can possibly hope to be fucked, every once in a while!

That's what I thought. What I said was, 'Goodnight, Adam.'

Adam was up and out of bed well before me the following morning. It was the same every weekend. By the time I walked downstairs, he'd already been for a run and a surf, had showered, breakfasted, and was ready for the day. There were no lazy mornings in bed together.

He was standing at the stove when I came into the kitchen, and he smiled his big broad smile at me. 'Morning, sleepy head.'

'Good morning, Adam,' I said softly. 'Good morning, you guys.'

Nick and Lily were seated at the breakfast bar, making their way through their omelettes. Neither of them acknowledged me with a reply, though Lily looked up and one side of her mouth lifted slightly.

'I'll get your coffee in a sec and your omelette's just about done, honey,' Adam said as he tilted the frypan this way and that, making the perfect omelette as always.

'I can get my own coffee. Thanks for the omelette though, smells great.'

'Here you go, all ready.' He smiled warmly again. 'But you better eat it nice and quick, hey? I've booked you in for a deluxe pedicure followed by a one-hour relaxation massage at Divine.

Your appointment's at ten-thirty. I'm taking these two horror heads ten-pin bowling while you're there. Thought it'd be nice after a late night. Sound good, doctor?'

I smiled with what I hoped looked like a genuine show of gratitude. 'Sounds fabulous. Thanks, darling. Love you.'

'Love you too, mate,' he winked.

And that was Adam all over. Wife drama, done with. Sufficient amount of spoiling and sucking up, sorted. Let's get on with the day.

Pity I hated everything about Divine and its shellacked, Botoxed beauticians. Pity I'd never told Adam this.

Two hours later I found myself lying face down, my toenails now a startling shade of coral, while a stranger's doughy hands kneaded my flesh and a recording of synthesised whale noises played in the background. I was feeling slightly asthmatic from the sandalwood incense that found its way to my nose through the hole in the padded table.

Why, oh why, had I said the F-word to Adam? I could've been curled up at home with a coffee, reading the paper instead.

When I returned home from the morning of pampering, we performed the weekend ritual of ferrying the children to and from training and then friends' places, before I started on the housework. For years I'd refused Adam's offers of hired help; another woman cleaning my home seemed unnatural to me. I knew I'd be the sort of person to clean before the cleaner came anyway.

Adam laughed when he walked in on me singing along to the dirty lyrics of Rihanna on the radio as I scrubbed the spa bath in the ensuite. He stuck his head around the corner with a quizzical grin on his face. 'What's gotten into you, hey? I never hear you sing. Thought there was someone being flayed in here.'

I sprayed him with disinfectant as he mimicked my singing voice.

'Raunchy lyrics there, doctor? Tomorrow night when the kids are at youth group, I would happily do what you were just singing about if you like.'

The explicit thoughts about Matt and me that I'd just been having were replaced with shame and guilt. I wasn't guilty enough though because the thoughts returned minutes later.

And that was how it continued all weekend. The switch in my overworked brain flicked continuously from Matt, to guilt over Adam, Matt, guilt. It flicked on and off through a raucous dinner out with the children and two other families on Saturday night; through church on Sunday morning; through lunch in Fremantle with some more of Adam's loud friends, and even through our Sunday evening lovemaking, which was significantly more intense than normal as I arched and slid and moaned and sucked in ways I wished I could with Matt. Adam delivered nicely on the orgasm, but still I found myself feeling hollow afterwards. And Adam's over-enthusiastic vocal afterglow irritated me no end.

I was relieved when the weekend was finally over and I was away from Adam again. I had the distinct feeling he'd suffered through the weekend as much as I had. He'd been extra funny and chivalrous and complimentary – he must've been exhausted from the effort of it all. It was probably why he'd arranged for me to be shipped off to Divine for a couple of hours on Saturday, but I couldn't be sure.

As well as giving me a much needed reprieve from Adam, it had been relatively quiet at work yesterday. But today had been far too busy for my liking. I'd confirmed a pregnancy to a couple who'd been struggling for years with infertility; I'd vaccinated two screaming toddlers and pacified their distressed mothers; I'd argued with a patient over his excessive use of suppositories, and I'd poked many a stick in a mouth with the instruction to say 'Aah'. And I cared about none of it.

Re-reading the text messages just now had me wishing I could go home and touch those parts of me that I very much wanted to touch. I couldn't picture any words turning me on more than the ones on my phone.

I sighed as I stood up, straightened my skirt, headed out to the hallway and picked up the next patient's file from the pigeonhole. Only two patients to go, then straight home where I could relax and do lovely things to myself while I thought about Matt.

I looked at the name on the file and cleared my throat. 'Matthew Butler?' I announced loudly as I looked into the crowded waiting room.

He stood up. 'Dr Melissa Harding? I'm Matthew Butler,' he said in his gravelly voice.

My jaw dropped and I felt myself redden as the blood rushed to my cheeks. The next few seconds played out in slow motion, as I stood gaping at him and squeezing my thighs together in an attempt to stop what was going on between them.

He seemed self-conscious, standing a little hunched, hands in his pockets and his head cocked to one side. His hair had grown and was messier than before. It suited his three-day growth. He wore a loose white singlet, faded board shorts and rubber thongs. He looked even younger than I remembered. And Jesus Christ, those eyes!

I was vaguely aware of Cheryl looking from me to him and then back to me again. Perhaps everyone else in the reception area had also turned to look at us as we stood unmoving, staring at each other from opposite ends of the waiting room, but I didn't notice.

'Come through,' my voice cracked. I could hardly get the words out.

I walked into the consulting room with shaky legs. I could hear his footsteps behind me. He followed me in and closed the door.

I turned to face him. 'You found me,' I only just managed to say before he pushed me hard against the door and slammed his knee between my legs.

His mouth was on mine and he kissed me so fiercely that the back of my head hurt against the door. He wrapped one arm tightly around my waist, pressing me into him, while he undid the zip of my skirt and yanked it to the floor. He let out a moan when he saw the lace G-string I was wearing. He dropped to his knees and within seconds his wet tongue was inside me, darting in and out.

I moaned loudly and he stood up and held a finger to my lips. 'Shh, Mel,' he stage whispered. 'There are patients out there. Easy, baby.'

He threw off his singlet and let his shorts drop after pulling out a wrapped condom from the pocket. His arms and legs were lean and beautifully defined. A huge tattoo in some kind of Aramaic script was spread across the taut muscles of his flat stomach. And his erection, my God, wow. I watched mesmerised as he deftly slipped on protection.

I couldn't have been any more turned on.

I unbuttoned my shirt, unclasped my bra and pushed my breasts against him.

'Keep your shoes on,' he whispered.

He lifted me up higher against the door, and with my legs wrapped around his waist, he pushed himself so forcefully inside me, I had to bite my bottom lip not to yell out.

Our foreheads touched and we stared into each other while he rocked me up and down, slowly and rhythmically. My stomach dived as he sucked on one nipple and then the other, moaning softly as he did so. I licked the delicious hairs on his toned chest and the salty skin of his neck and shoulders.

He looked at me with a devilish grin.

'What?' I smiled.

He raised his eyebrows and with my legs still around him, he carried me across to the desk chair and sat down with a thud, pulling me on top of him. It felt even deeper when he moved inside me now. So wonderfully deep.

I cupped the back of his head and plunged my tongue inside his mouth. We kissed with crazy desperation. He tasted of coffee and sex.

He pulled his face away and held mine in both of his hands. 'This is what I wanted to do to you on the plane. Just like this.' His breath was hot and rapid.

'I wish you had,' I replied breathlessly. 'I wanted it so badly in your car.'

'I know you did,' he panted, 'but it's okay because I'm fucking you now.' He whispered those last four words over and over in my ear as we picked up the pace.

His hands slid up and down my back, sending shivers racing along my spine. He pulled my legs further apart so his fingers could play lightly between my buttocks, while his tongue left wet tracks all over my neck and breasts. It was the best thing I'd experienced in my lifetime.

I didn't have long to go. I didn't want to finish just yet. I wanted to cling on longer to this amazing feeling. But I could feel the build up coming from way, way down, and the promise of what was to come was too enticing for me to try and stop it. I shut my eyes and felt that build up rising in me, more and more. He placed his hands firmly around my waist now and lifted me up and down on top of him, harder and harder, until I opened my eyes and his face blurred in front of me. I mouthed a wide O and completely lost myself. The pulses were hot and heavy and almost painful. My toes curled and my teeth buzzed. It was ecstasy. And it went on and on and on until I was almost willing it to finish.

He waited until I stopped arching my back and then he pounded so fiercely inside me that I gasped each time. It hurt so beautifully.

His body gave a sudden shake and he muffled a loud groan in my neck. I relaxed, and we rested our heads on each other's shoulders while we heaved and sweated.

A few moments later, he lifted my head up so we were face to face, and he looked at me with tenderness and a deep satisfaction. 'Melissa, that was the bloody best doctor's consultation I've had in my life. I want another appointment in half an hour.' He laughed silently, shaking his head.

'I think I've fallen in love with you, Matt.' I could feel the tears welling up, burning my eyes.

'I think I've fallen in love with you too. Hey, hey, it's okay, don't cry. I love you,' he murmured as he rested my head back down on his shoulder. 'I love you, Mel.'

He stroked my hair while I wept openly with joy, relief and indescribable heartache.

AFTER

MATT

Mel stripped the sheet off the examination table and draped it around us. I sat with my back against the door and she leaned in against me, seated between my legs, my arms wrapped tightly around her.

She listened as I told her about how much I'd struggled with my feelings over the past month, about the break up with Lydia, and how I'd managed to track her down to this clinic.

She lifted her head and looked at me with unmasked emotion. 'I can't believe you came all the way here and went through all of that just for me. It doesn't seem real,' she said, shaking her head.

'I would've done anything to find you. I'm obsessed with you.' I kissed her bare shoulder.

'You couldn't be as obsessed as I am with you. I'm almost insane.'

'Good,' I murmured.

The skin of her inner thigh was soft and warm against my hand. I nuzzled into her hair that I'd pulled out of its ponytail.

'How long can you stay?' she asked.

'I have to catch a flight home on Sunday night.'

She counted on her fingers. 'That means we have five days together after today. That's hardly any time.' She sounded anxious.

'Mel, I'm not letting you go again. Don't worry. I'll only go home for a bit to sort out work and the house. Then I'll come back.'

'For longer?'

'Forever.' I smiled as I said the word.

'You mean *forever* forever?' she whispered.

'Forever and ever,' I promised and kissed her neck.

'Oh, Matt,' she sighed. 'Let's get out of here. Let's go back to your hotel. My kids both have stuff on after school today so we've got till five until I need to be home.'

I scoffed. 'Five? Are you serious? You're spending the night with me, I've travelled across Australia for this.'

She was silent for a few minutes, biting her lip and staring into space frowning, and I began to worry that I really would be spending the night alone.

Then her frown changed into a smile. 'Okay, I think I know how I can manage it. Yes, I think I have a way.' She looked at me. 'A whole night with you – this is the best day of my life.' She kissed my mouth hard. 'I need to go home and pick up a few things first, and then I'll come meet you at the hotel.' She stood up, trying to take the sheet with her but I held onto it, wolf-whistling as she bent over to pick up her clothes. She blushed and ordered me to turn around so I couldn't watch her getting dressed.

But I kept my eyes fixed on the body that I'd now made mine. 'If only you knew how many dirty dreams I had of you in those tight jeans you wore on that flight, Mel.'

She laughed. 'Do you know how hard it was finding skinny jeans high-waisted enough to hide this jelly belly?' She patted her stomach.

'Do you know how hard it made me to see those skinny jeans on you?' I grinned.

Once she was dressed, she went to her desk and sat on the same chair we'd just had sex on. She picked up the telephone and spoke via the intercom to the receptionist. 'Cheryl, I've run quite late with this new patient. Can you please move the next patient across to one of the others and give her my apologies? I've got an important appointment at Nick's school I have to get to.'

There was a long pause before a voice came through the speaker. 'Is that right? Fine then, I'll sort it out.'

Mel grimaced as she thanked Cheryl and hung up.

I looked around the consulting room and felt my chest tighten when I stared at the framed photographs on the walls of Mel in her husband's arms. He was undisputedly better looking than I am. He would have been perfect on a dentist's poster with his straight white teeth and his smug 'all men want to be me, all women want to do me' smile. My gaze drifted to the portraits of her children. They both had their father's colouring, but Mel's eyes and her smile. The kids whose family I was here to ruin. I quickly looked away. Why did she have to be married?

'Shall we head off?' Mel interrupted my unpleasant train of thought. 'If you go out first and then I'll join you at the hotel as soon as I can.'

I gave her the details of the hotel and then we kissed until we were both breathless, standing there in the middle of the consulting room.

When I left, I marched straight past reception. The receptionist followed me with her eyes and I pretended not to notice. She made no attempt to stop me from pushing open the glass door and walking out without paying.

INSTINCT

MEL

We kissed each other goodbye standing in the consultation room, and then he walked out. I missed him as soon as he left. I couldn't get enough of him. I wanted to feel him moving inside me again.

I played his promise over in my head as I drove home. Forever. He said forever.

Because he loved me. He loved me!

I quite literally wanted to jump with joy.

But Sarah's voice kept ringing in my ears throughout the drive home, ruining my happiness. I'd called her from the clinic as soon as Matt left, delirious with the news that he was here in Perth. What was I thinking calling her? Of course she'd throw a wet blanket over my happiness.

'Don't do it, Mel, don't spend the night with him. Once you get home, text him – don't call him – and tell him you made a terrible mistake. Tell him to go back where he came from.'

'What? No! I can't do that. You don't understand …'

'Please, Mel,' she interrupted. 'Taking this next step is going to ruin your life. It's just a fixation, it's not real. Your life with Adam is real. Think of the consequences, think of what would happen if Adam found out where you were tonight. It'd all be over, everything, gone. Think of your kids. Mel, think of Nick and Lily. Don't risk your children over this.'

I tried to block out her voice. Adam wouldn't find out, I would make sure of that. And what Adam didn't know couldn't hurt him. So in fact I wasn't risking the children at all. Everything was going to be fine because Matt and I loved each other and that was the most important thing. We'd find a way to make this work.

But then my own voice joined in with Sarah's. 'You're going to pay for this, Melissa.'

I changed my focus to remembering how Matt had sucked my fingers one at a time. My belly double-flipped and I told the negative voices to leave me alone.

They didn't. Instead the voices grew louder when I stepped into the house. I stood in the back doorway and looked around. Adam's golf clubs were leaning against the pool table; the children's plates and half-drunk glasses of juice sat on the breakfast bar. A note I'd written to them this morning saying *Don't forget sports bags, both of you!* had fallen onto the floor. I stayed glued to the spot. I swallowed hard as my eye caught the photo from last year that we'd had enlarged to a poster-sized canvas print – all four of us, our arms flung up above our heads and our mouths wide open in smiling terror on a rollercoaster at Movie World.

'What are you doing?' I whispered to the empty house. 'Why isn't any of this enough for you? What are you doing to this family?'

'It's not too late to pull out,' the voices, mine and Sarah's, chimed in together. 'There's nothing that says you have to go through with this.'

I had a sudden feeling of deflation. Tiny butterflies of doubt spread their miniature wings and flickered around inside me.

Just then, my phone beeped in my handbag.

I'm waiting. I'm so hard it hurts. I want you in those tight jeans.
No knickers. And when you get here ask me to fuck you some more.
Hurry.

I was wet the second I finished reading the message. Just one
night. I absolutely had to be with him for just one night. Tomorrow
I'd reassess things with more clarity. Because after reading that
message, no amount of doubt could beat the compulsion I had to
spend the night with him.

I raced upstairs to our bedroom, humming loudly to drown out
the voices while I manically changed clothes and threw anything
that came to mind into a large bag. I tried to avert my eyes from
Adam's clothes in the walk-in robe we shared, and when I found
that impossible, I gave up packing altogether and left the room. I
managed to make it back downstairs without looking into either
of the children's bedrooms, in fact I made it out of the house
without noticing one more thing that could in any way tempt me
to change my mind. I drove two blocks before pulling over into
a side street to text Adam. No way could I call him and hear his
voice.

Hi love, a patient called and she's in labour. It's a home birth –
my first! Heading off there now and will stay until it's over. It might
take a while. I ducked home and grabbed an overnight bag, just in
case. Kids making their own way home around five. Can you make
sure you're home soon after, please? There's leftover spaghetti in
the fridge. Will have phone turned off during the labour. Love you x

It took three times longer than usual to type the message. My
fingers fumbled and shook and made it almost impossible to hit
the right keys. I was overcome with dizziness and sweat by the
time I pressed *Send* and I realised I'd been holding my breath. I
opened all four car windows and swallowed big gulps of fresh air.

The dizziness settled down and I wiped my drenched forehead, cheeks and neck with cool baby wipes that I had in the glove box.

Once I was breathing normally again, I reapplied my makeup, and drove along the road towards Scarborough. Towards Matt, towards the night it felt I had waited for my whole life. The voices nagged me to turn the car around and go home before it was too late, but I didn't listen.

SLEEPOVER

MATT

Once back at the hotel, I cheerfully cancelled the remaining doctors' appointments I'd lined up. Then I sat on the balcony with a coffee and watched the activity of Scarborough below. The sun beat down on the bare skin of my arms and legs, and the strong sea breeze blew my hair into my eyes. I loved this place.

As I sipped my coffee, I could smell her on my fingers. I felt pure happiness and relief. My thoughts drifted briefly to Lydia but I shut her out of my mind again. Guilt wasn't going to ruin this moment.

I had mentally rehearsed a speech for Mel dozens of times as I'd sat in each doctor's clinic. I was prepared for a long debate to try to convince her that we belonged together. But when she'd walked out into the waiting room and I saw the look on her face, I realised that everything I'd planned to say was no longer necessary. It was all expressed in the minute we stood across the room from each other, without saying a word.

I thought about what she said later. About how she'd been desperate from missing me this past month. The icy doubt that had been swirling around in my head melted away and I relaxed. She loved me back and she loved me hard.

Two hours after I'd left the clinic, she arrived at the hotel. She'd changed into the jeans I adored, and wore a white fitted tank top with no bra, her nipples clearly visible.

'I missed you, Matthew. I was so lonely all by myself,' she said, as her hands made their way up my chest. 'Can you please, please, fuck me some more?'

I pulled her jeans down to her knees and carried her over to the bed. I undid the Velcro at the front of my board shorts, slipped on a condom and slid inside her while we were both still dressed. It was over in minutes but just as good as the first time.

I peeled off her tank top and began licking the warm skin just below her breasts while I waited for my erection to return. I was nowhere near finished with her yet.

Later I checked my watch and was stunned to see it was past six o'clock. We were both starving, so I hunted for snacks in the mini bar while Mel investigated what we could order from room service.

I tore open a packet of M&Ms and laughed, 'Hey Mel, these were made for us, for the Matts and Mels!'

She reached into the packet and took one out, suggestively putting it in her mouth. She rolled her eyes with exaggerated pleasure and moaned as she sucked on it. It had been so intense with her so far, but now I could just enjoy her. Tonight, and for the rest of my life.

We sat out on the balcony, sharing beers, a satay chicken pizza, and a bowl of scorching hot wedges. Even on a Tuesday evening, it was still buzzing below on The Esplanade, with people out for dinner or having gelati or fish and chips on the foreshore, and others making their way back up from a day at the beach, bodyboards tucked under their arms and wetsuits half off.

The air was fresh enough now for Mel to rug herself up in my denim jacket over her jeans. Her hair was flying everywhere in the breeze and it was wildly curly. Who knew? I never wanted her to straighten it again. The golden light of the sunset catching the side of her face gave her a goddess-like glow, and as she ate and laughed and played with her hair, I sat mesmerised.

'Do you know I can pinpoint the exact second I fell in love with you?' she said dreamily.

'What, you mean I didn't have you at "hello"?'

'Um, Matt, considering your "hello" looked like this –' she turned to face me with her tongue hanging out and her eyes bulging '– surprisingly, no, you didn't have me at "hello".'

I pretended to be offended. 'It was romantic! Love at first sight. Chicks love that shit.'

'Oh, come on, give me a break.' She laughed. 'That wasn't love and you know it.'

'Okay then, I actually do know the exact second you fell for my irresistible charms.'

'You do not,' she said.

'It was when I ranted about Amnesty and politics, wasn't it?' I raised my eyebrows.

'How did you know that?'

I let my tongue hang out and my eyes bulge. 'Wasn't hard to guess,' I said smugly.

She reached across the table and lightly punched my arm.

'If it makes you feel any better, Mel, you had me way before "hello".'

'What do you mean?'

'I saw you in the departure lounge in Perth. You were leaning up against a pillar, and I was sitting squashed between two old ladies, and, hmm, how do I put this? It wasn't just my eyes that noticed you. Other parts of my body kind of stood to attention.'

'Really? With two old ladies sitting next to you?' She laughed. 'Oh, Matt, how embarrassing!'

'Tell me about it. Then you came and sat next to me on the plane in that low-cut top and with that sexy perfume on. What hope did I have?'

She shook her head and laughed. 'You perv!'

'Mmm, yep.' I smiled, 'I was hooked from the second I saw you. It was like you'd done some sort of black magic on me.'

'I get that a lot.' She nodded. 'It's a burden to be so bewitching.'

I guffawed. 'So you've got loads of other guys flying across the country in search of you, do you?'

'Yes, but you're the only one who I let have his way with me. Lucky you.' She grinned. 'And while we're on the subject, once you did decide to turn into a crazed stalker and ring hundreds of medical centres, why didn't you just describe me? If you'd said, "I'm after a doctor called Mel, she's got long brown hair and she looks as though she'd be in her late thirties," you would've narrowed it down to maybe one or two clinics.'

'Ah, crap!' I groaned, realising how stupid I'd been not to do that. 'Do you know how expensive and boring it was going to all those bloody clinics? I couldn't use my Medicare card more than once a day, and some of those doctors ran over an hour late.'

Mel was just about crying with laughter. I decided now was the perfect time for revenge.

'Yeah, well at least I waited until after we'd kissed before *I* stalked *you*.'

'What do you mean?' She looked confused.

'Don't you remember doing reconnaissance work at my clinic with your friend, pretty much straight after the flight that Saturday?' I popped a potato wedge into my mouth. 'Hmm?'

The mortified look on her face was priceless. 'Oh God! How did you find out about that?'

I laughed, almost choking on the wedge. 'It's not often that women run away from Tom.'

'I'm so embarrassed, I could die. Argh,' Mel groaned. 'Tom must think I'm a nut job.'

I nodded. 'Um, yep, he does actually. So you and me, we're even with the stalking thing now, don't you think?'

'I guess,' she replied, still blushing. She gave a little shiver. 'It's getting cold out here.'

'Let's get back inside.' I stacked the dishes onto the tray, looking out at the ocean. It had a more dangerous feel now that the sun had set.

'I want you,' she purred once we were back in the room. She took off the jacket and wrapped her arms around my waist.

'What? Again? Already?' I'd never had to perform five times in such a short space of time before and I was already more than a little tender in that area. 'You're kidding me, aren't you? Please tell me you're not serious. It'll fall off, Mel, have mercy on me.'

'Do I look like I'm joking?' she said in a sexed-up voice as she turned her back to me and climbed out of her jeans. She looked over her shoulder invitingly. 'You snooze, you lose, Matthew.'

Afterwards we lay on top of the covers, cooling our overheated bodies. Mel rested her head in the crook of my arm and traced the three linear symbols of my tattoo with her index finger.

'What does it say?' She lifted her head up slightly to get a better look at it.

'It's Hebrew, it means "Be willing",' I said quietly. 'Saw it in a documentary and it resonated with me.'

She shut her eyes and breathed deeply. 'That's the sexiest thing,' she whispered. 'When did you get it done?'

'I was eighteen.'

'Did it hurt?'

'Like you wouldn't believe,' I said, meaning it.

'Poor Matt,' she cooed and slid herself down so she was between my legs. She laid a trail of feathery kisses all over the tattoo. 'Better?' she asked, with a smile, looking up at me when she was done.

'Better.'

Once she was lying beside me again, I traced a small 'M' on her right hip, a few times over with the pad of my calloused thumb. 'Right here,' I murmured. 'Get one.'

She smiled. 'But it hurts. You said.'

'It's worth the pain.'

She turned to face me and stared long into my half-closed eyes. 'Worth the pain,' she whispered. And we lay there in silence, our fingers clasped tight and our eyes locked, until it was very dark.

'I have to pee,' she announced when I was three parts asleep. 'Talk among yourselves.'

A thought occurred to me when she disappeared into the bathroom. 'What did you tell your family you were doing tonight?' I asked her when she came back.

Mel stopped in her tracks and the colour drained from her face. She took a moment to answer. 'I told Adam I was at a delivery – a home birth.'

'Oh.' That was clever of her. 'Did he mind? Is it normal for you to be out overnight at a delivery?'

'Um, no. I have stayed out late at the hospital before, but I always come home at some stage through the night.' She remained fixed in that one spot.

'So, how did he react to you saying you'd be staying out all night?'

'I don't know, Matt. I sent him a text message and then I turned the phone off.' She was getting more visibly distressed by the second, wringing her hands and chewing on her lip, so I dropped it.

It pleased me that she could do that, turn off her phone without waiting for his reply. And even better was that she had quite obviously given him very little thought since she had been here with me for all this time. He couldn't be that important to her. But then I thought, if she was able to disregard her husband in this way, what did that mean for me? A little alarm bell went off in my brain but I was quick to silence it. She loved me, she didn't love him. That was the difference. She would never treat me that way. Would she?

'If you need to ring home tonight, don't let me stop you,' I said stiffly.

She shook her head. 'No, no, it's too weird. And anyway, this is *our* time. I just want tonight to be about us. Can we please not talk about Adam any more? Please?'

'We're going to have to talk about him at some stage, Mel. We need to figure out what we're going to do.' I said this even though I wished I never had to give him another thought.

'I know, but please let's leave that conversation for another time,' she said, finally coming back to bed to sit cross-legged at my feet. 'All I want for now is to live in this very moment, here with you.'

'Okay, I won't ask about him any more.' I patted the mattress next to me and she moved up and sat closer. 'There's so much I want to know about you though. Tell me everything.'

She told me more about her childhood and her parents, and about her best friend, Sarah. She told me about the first time she had sex. 'I'd just started university, he was studying law. We met at a ball and I was pretty drunk. It was a one-night thing. It was in his bedroom, with his parents asleep down the hallway. I couldn't believe how much it hurt, Matt. I hated every minute of it. I didn't sleep with anyone else for months afterwards.'

I felt ridiculous at how jealous I was of the man who had her first.

'When was the first time you fell in love?' I asked.

She didn't answer for a while. 'I don't remember ever thinking I was falling in love with someone. Lust, excitement, maybe. Love, no.' She ran a hand through her hair. 'I mean obviously I loved Adam, I just don't recall *falling* in love with him. Just you, Matt, I've definitely fallen in love with you.'

I kissed her forehead. 'Same here, you're my first too.'

She moved onto talking about her children. 'It's like a life sentence of worry, you know. From the moment I discovered I was pregnant I worried about them. And it doesn't get better as they get older, it gets worse. I'm more worried now than ever before. And there's huge pressure to stay alive for them!'

I wondered what they'd think of me. I was daunted by the idea of having to build a relationship with the children whose home I broke up. For the second time that day, I shut them out to save myself the guilt.

By midnight, we were too sleepy to stay up and talk any longer.

'Hey, Matthew, do you want to have a sleepover together?' she murmured.

'Mmm-hmm,' I nodded, taking her into my arms.

Neither of us stirred all night, so she remained nestled in close beside me until the sun came in through the window and threw light over our bed, warming my back and shoulders and waking me up. I was careful to move slowly as I propped myself up on my elbow to watch her sleeping.

If there was any way I could have stopped time and frozen my life right there in those seconds before she woke up, I would have done it. I had everything I wanted in that moment.

Her soft noises were child-like and her expression peaceful as she slept with her back to me. Her smooth olive skin showed no signs of her age. Her long lashes were matted together with yesterday's mascara, and then there was that gorgeous long honey brown hair with streaks of blonde that were caught by the sun. The mound of her breasts was visible underneath the sheet and one arm was draped across her stomach. She was wearing her wedding and engagement rings. The whiteness of the square-cut diamond taunted me. I was suddenly afraid and wanted her awake, so I gently blew along the length of her arm.

She opened her eyes wide and stiffened. There was no mistaking what she whispered in that instant.

'Oh fuck.'

My heart muscles contracted hard.

'Sorry I woke you,' I said in a strangled voice.

She turned to look at me and immediately smiled a warm sleepy smile.

'Good morning, Matt. I love you.' She stroked my naked chest, and somehow I convinced myself that everything was going to be all right.

TIGHTROPE

MEL

The phone rang and rang before Cheryl picked up.

'Hey, Cheryl, it's me,' I said in a weak voice. 'I'm not feeling too great today. I think I'm going to stay home in bed. I feel pretty fluey.' I got the words out quickly and held my breath.

'What's going on, Mel?' Cheryl asked after a solid thirty seconds of stony silence. 'What the hell is going on here?'

'I'm sick. I need to rest,' I snapped. How dare she question me?

'Whatever,' Cheryl replied with a sigh and hung up.

I was outraged. I was her boss! She needed to be reminded of that next time I saw her.

Matt walked into the room brushing his teeth. 'How'd it go?' His words were muffled with toothpaste.

'My receptionist just hung up on me,' I said in angry disbelief. 'She doesn't believe that I'm sick.'

He laughed. 'Why are you so angry? You're not sick, she's right.'

'Argh!' I growled at him and he disappeared back into the bathroom, still laughing.

'Matt, I'll be about an hour,' I called out, still fuming about Cheryl as I packed my things. I wished I'd had the presence of mind to pack properly. In my flustered state yesterday I hadn't even managed to pack one complete change of clothes or any clean underwear. I'd just had to share Matt's deodorant.

He re-emerged and enveloped me in his arms. The fury fizzled. I took in his fresh morning smell. He kissed me, gently at first and then a little deeper. I so loved the way he moved his tongue inside my mouth. It was like a sexy dance. I dropped my hand down to the zipper of his cargo pants.

'Go home,' he said against my lips. 'Come back for that later.'

We'd already had sex that morning. I'd initiated it to take away the sick feeling deep in my gut at waking up in a bed that wasn't mine and Adam's. Now, only an hour later, I was hungry for it again. Something had switched on inside me and I simply could not get enough sex with this man.

'Just a little one,' I begged, pushing my pelvis against his.

He shook his head and pulled away. 'I have to pace myself, I'm at risk of permanent injury.'

I could feel his erection against my hip. 'You'll survive,' I reassured him as I slid my hand inside his pants.

Later, as I drove along the highway in the direction of Mosman Park, the sick feeling in my gut returned. I thought I'd feel satisfied after having spent the night with Matt, and be in a clearer frame of mind to know what to do next. But instead I was more mixed up than ever.

When I thought about Adam, my stomach churned. I imagined him finding out about Matt and I couldn't bear it. But I would not give up Matt, I was resolute about that. For five days he would be my focus. So that meant for five days I was going to have to try to avoid Adam. The children were so busy with school and after-school activities and their friends, that as long as there was food on the table they wouldn't even notice if I was around a little less for a few days. But it was going to be trickier with Adam.

The sick feeling intensified as I pulled into the driveway at home. Adam's car was in the garage. He wasn't at work.

It wasn't until this morning when I turned on my phone that I saw the message from Adam, wishing me luck with the home-birth delivery and telling me not to worry about a thing at home. There was no mention of him not being in surgery today.

Oh God, had he found out somehow? I thought I was going to be sick. If he accused me, what would I say? My brain was completely blank. I wished I could drive away right now and avoid seeing him, but I had already opened the garage roller door, which was noisy enough to be heard from anywhere in the house. And having been out overnight at a supposed home-birth, I'd be expected to come home at some stage this morning. There was no way out of this. I got out of the car and slowly walked into the house.

I let out a huge breath when I heard him call out from the lounge room. 'Is that you, Dr Baby Whisperer? Hello there!'

'Hi love,' I sang out, almost crying with relief. 'What are you doing home?'

He bounded into the kitchen, wearing nothing but boxer shorts. 'Day off!' He held a massive palm up and I accepted his invitation to high-five. 'Surgeon's sick. Gastro. All surgeries called off today.'

'Great!' I squeaked.

He bent over to kiss my cheek, then stepped back and looked me up and down. 'Is that what you wore to the delivery?' he frowned.

I blurted out my first thought. 'It was a home birth, why would I get dressed up for that? I wanted to keep it casual.'

He raised his eyebrows and tilted his head down so he was looking at me over his glasses. I hated it when he did that, I felt like I was back at primary school.

He spoke slowly. 'As in – 'no bra' casual?'

Shit! Why now was he noticing what I wore? He *never* noticed my clothes.

'Do you know I can clearly see your nipples through that singlet?' he said accusingly.

'As if I would go bra-less, Adam,' I scoffed. 'Don't you remember how messy births are? I had to get changed and this was all I had. I didn't think to pack a spare bra.'

That seemed to appease him. His expression relaxed.

'You must be wrecked, you look like you've been going hard at it all night. I hope you cancelled your patients this morning so you can rest up,' he said.

'No,' I replied with a sad shake of my head. 'I have to go in. I just came home to change.'

I'd have to dress in work clothes now, and pack other clothes to change into once I was back at the hotel. 'I was going to organise another dance mum to take Lil to ballet this afternoon because I'll still be at work, but now that you're home, Adam, could you do it please?'

'Sure, I can take her. What about dinner? Shall I barbeque some steaks and throw a salad together for when you get home?'

'I'm off to the movies with Steph tonight, love, remember?' I was quick with the lie.

'Completely forgot,' he grinned. 'So, steaks for me and the kids then. We'll miss you. That's two nights straight you're not home for dinner with us.'

The pit of my stomach couldn't have felt heavier. It was so easy to lie to Adam. His forgetfulness meant that he was not the least bit suspicious.

I wanted badly to get away from him so I could stop lying. And to stop being reminded that he was such a decent person while I was just the opposite.

'I'd better shower and run, Adam.' I escaped the kitchen that felt as if it was closing in on me, and locked the bedroom door to make sure I would be alone in the shower to feel my shame privately.

DEEPER

MATT

I held Mel's hand in mine, as we crossed the promenade and walked down onto the beach. She was skipping a little to keep up with me so I slowed down. I wasn't used to having a girlfriend who wasn't tall enough to match my stride.

'You sure you don't mind being out in public with me?' I asked her as I pulled my sunglasses down over my eyes.

'Nobody in Scarborough would know me, trust me. And even if they did, they wouldn't be expecting to see me with you so they wouldn't notice me anyway.'

I hadn't expected that she'd be happy to be out and about with me before first coming clean with her husband. But I liked that we were out in the sunshine at the beach together and not holed up out of sight all day.

The tide was out and we left a trail of footprints in the white sand. It was like caster sugar, not yellow and heavy like the sand in Melbourne.

At Mel's urging, I filled her in on my picture perfect childhood before Rob died. She stopped me at the mention of his name.

'Tell me what happened with Rob.'

'He wrapped Dad's station wagon around a streetlight three weeks after getting his licence.'

'Jesus Christ.'

I nodded.

'That's enough to destroy a family,' she said.

'Well, yeah, it did. My main memories of the years after that are turning the music up in my room to drown out Mum's crying, and the screaming matches between her and Holly.'

'What was Rob like?' Mel asked.

'He was a cocky smartarse,' I smiled. 'But he was my best mate. I used to tag along when he went to the footy with his mates, and we spent hours kicking a soccer ball around the backyard. He always made time for me. We were really close.'

'Did you and Rob look alike?'

I stopped and reached into my pocket for my wallet. I slipped out the family portrait I carried everywhere. Mel took it and covered her mouth with her hand, her eyes disbelieving.

'I know.' I nodded.

'I would never have believed that wasn't you,' she gasped. 'You're identical.'

'Yeah.' The heaviness in my chest returned, uninvited as always.

Mel stroked my face 'Oh, Matt, I'm so heartbroken for you.'

I sighed. I could only imagine how hard it must've been for my parents to watch me grow up and become a man who was the mirror image of their first son.

She gave me back the bent and faded photograph. 'Tell me about Holly.'

I laughed. 'Shit, where do I begin with Holly? She's a nightmare, my sister.'

'Is she? Why?'

'She just is. She fell to bits after Rob died. She tried to commit suicide at fifteen, poor Mum was the one to find her. She's still got the scars that remind me of that day every single time I see her.'

'Oh, no. That's awful.'

My heart tightened at the memory of it. 'Anyway, after that she was medicated and she's been on meds ever since. But she goes up and down, you know? She's done pretty well for herself though, considering everything she went through. She's happily married, great career, she's a good mum.'

'Good for her.' Mel smiled. 'What's her husband like?'

I took a deep breath. 'Brandon? Mmm, to put it nicely, he's a drip.'

She laughed. 'What did she see in him, then?'

'That he's a drip!' I laughed too. 'I think that's what she was looking for. Someone intelligent but with no free will of his own. He goes along with everything she wants and she's the type of person who has to have every single thing go her way so they're a perfect match. And he's really understanding about her illness, he's got a lot to deal with.'

'What do you mean?'

'She's high maintenance, Mel. When my nephew, Lachy, was born, she had this episode of post-natal psychosis and it was so intense that she rang Brandon at work and said, "You'd better come home quick because I'm about to kill the baby."'

'Oh my God!' Mel exclaimed. 'I hope she got help for that.'

'She did, she was in hospital for three whole months. Brandon took extended leave and he was buggered going between her in hospital and the baby at home. Even through that, he still thought the world of her. He bloody worships her. She's pretty lucky, really. It's just me who's stuck with the world's dullest brother-in-law.'

Mel stopped every now and then to collect shells, which she tucked into the front pocket of her shorts. As she picked up another shell, I bent too and spotted one that was half buried in the wet sand. I washed it off in the water before opening her hand and placing it in her palm.

She gave me a confused look. 'It's all chipped and grey. Thanks a lot.'

'Yeah it's one messed-up shell, that one. It's not like the perfect ones you're used to. Will you keep it? Even though it's damaged?'

She looked at me and then at the shell and her eyes filled with tears. 'It's my favourite. I love it.' She didn't put that shell in her pocket, but held it tight in her hand.

'How's your work with Amnesty International going?' she asked a few minutes later. 'You must feel so proud doing what you're doing.'

'At the moment, there's not that much to be proud of.'

'Oh? Why's that?'

'I got an email last week from the office of the Libyan ambassador here. For a couple of months we've been campaigning to have life sentences overturned for four men over there whose only crime was being gay. Anyway, the email said that he'd been in touch with government officials back in Libya, and they were standing by the sentence. No appeal. So all that work and we achieved bugger all.'

'Do things like that make you feel like you're fighting a losing battle sometimes?' Mel asked.

'Yeah, at times like that it totally feels like pushing shit uphill. But then, when you're just about ready to chuck it all in, you get a win and it keeps you going. Like late last year, Holly was heavily involved in a massive campaign to release a thirteen-year-old Somalian girl who was sentenced to death by stoning for adultery when she'd been raped—'

'I think I heard about that,' Mel interrupted.

I nodded. 'Yeah you may well have, it was all over the news. Because of all the media attention Amnesty managed to get, it mobilised people and they pressured their own governments to speak. Amazingly lots of governments did, and even more amazingly, it had an impact on the government in Somalia. The girl was pardoned and allowed to go home.'

Mel's eyes were wide. 'Holly sounds like a force to be reckoned with.'

'She is. She's like a dog with a bone about her work. I think she's trying to fix as many injustices as she possibly can. Like it's some way of coping with the injustice of losing her brother, which she can't do anything about. Maybe I'm doing the same, I don't know.' I scratched at my neck.

Mel stepped in front of me so we were facing each other. She looked as if she was about to cry again. 'Oh Matt, I'm so in love with you.'

She kissed my mouth. When she drew back I smiled, embarrassed and happy. I checked the time. 'Are you hungry? Should we have lunch?'

'I wish I'd met you fourteen years ago,' Mel sighed as we sat under a tree on the foreshore, having finished the kebabs and cans of Coke we'd just bought from a beachfront takeaway cafe.

'Yeah, me too,' I laughed. 'I would've been fourteen years old and totally up for it!'

'Oh God, I keep forgetting how young you are.' She slapped her forehead. 'How can this age difference not bother you?'

'It just doesn't.' I smiled. 'Besides, I feel older than you anyway.'

She nodded. 'I feel that too. It's just, I don't know, I'm worried you'll trade me in for a newer model as soon as the novelty wears off. I mean, I'll be forty in three years.'

I shook my head. 'Mel, as you get older I get older. And how can you be worried about something as stupid as that? This is me here, I already traded a newer model in for you.'

'I still can't believe you did,' she said with a rueful smile. 'Here comes Matthew Butler, folks, forget your daughters, lock up your mothers!'

'I'll show you lock up your mothers, woman!'

She squealed as I stood, scooped her up into my arms, and marched back across the road. My arms ached but I kept carrying her all the way up in the lift, only putting her down in the bedroom.

Sex with her was beyond anything I'd ever imagined possible. It was in turns fierce and frantic, and then mesmerisingly slow. She turned my brain into a fuzzy mess with the slightest of her movements, and I held nothing back. I gave in to her like I'd never done before.

We took a shower together, a long shower, and there was no better sight than Mel on her knees before me, the water dripping from her hair. She wasn't shy about bringing me to my knees either, and then we finished with fast and hard wet sex against the slippery shower wall.

After another room service dinner that evening, I walked back in from the balcony, to find her on the bed, one knee bent up, in a skimpy white lacy bra and a tiny pair of matching knickers. She twirled her hair around her finger.

'I have to go home, Matt. I'm sad. Come over here and make me better.'

I stood in the doorway and watched her in wonder. 'Melissa, you're the most beautiful woman I've ever laid eyes on. I just want to look at you like that forever.'

She shook her head slowly. 'You always know the perfect thing to say.'

I pulled my phone out of my back pocket. I took photo after photo of her while she posed for me on the bed, and then I asked her to take her knickers off and I filmed her while she touched herself, at my request, her eyes wide open looking straight at me until she climaxed.

I climbed on top of her when she was done. 'I've never watched a woman do that before,' I whispered in her ear. 'That was the hottest thing I've ever seen.' I breathed, more aroused than I ever thought was possible. 'Can I film you again tomorrow? Please, can I?'

'Anything you want, I'll give you. Anything.' She dug her nails into my shoulders and whispered, 'Come inside me, I want you close.'

'Closer than this?' I asked as I pushed myself inside her and moved slowly.

'Yeah, closer. It's not close enough,' she panted. 'I want all of you inside me. I want you to live in there. Be inside me always.'

I traced her neck with the tip of my nose. 'It's okay, baby, I'm here. We're close. Always.'

'Don't you ever leave me, Matt, I'd die.' She sounded on the verge of tears.

I shook my head as I reached down and held her hips still. 'Never, I'll never leave you. I promise.'

I pinned her down so she couldn't move and continued to thrust inside her, not so slowly now.

She dug her nails in deeper and shut her eyes. 'Oh, Matt,' she breathed as I felt her squeeze tight around me.

She was more mine every time.

I sat alone in the dark after she'd gone home and thought about how for the first time in my life, I was starting to believe in the idea of soul mates. Before I'd thought it was pathetic. Not now that I'd found my own soul mate.

It was a comfort and a relief to have finally found someone who wasn't put off by my intensity. I didn't have to reel in my feelings around her, and it didn't frighten her away when I shot off at the mouth, which was a first for me. Everyone had always told me to shut the hell up. But Mel always wanted to hear more.

Both of us were hopeless daydreamers, admitting to spending long hours staring into space, trying to figure out the meaning of our lives, or thinking of nothing at all.

'I could've daydreamed professionally this past month!' she laughed. 'But it's been awful in a way too, I haven't felt like a good mum, ignoring the kids. And at work, my heart just hasn't been in it. I've made bad mistakes this month, I can't go on like that.'

'I know what you mean,' I agreed. 'I've been totally tuned out at work too. I feel bad about it. I hope my work ethic comes back when I start over again here.'

'So, can you truthfully see yourself working here in Perth?'

'Absolutely. I love it here, I can't wait to move over. I want to explore more of WA too, you can show it off to me, hey?'

'I'd love that.'

She told me about the places in WA that held special meaning for her, the most special being the coast a few hours south of Perth.

'The Aboriginal name for it is "the place of love",' she said about the southwest town of Yallingup. 'There are these enormous rocks in Yallingup, called Canal Rocks, where the tide comes crashing in between them. It's so beautiful, the noise and the foam everywhere. I'm definitely taking you there. And we absolutely have to go exploring the Ngilgi Cave together. The stalagmites in there are stunning. And then there's Busselton Jetty, it goes out almost two kilometres – we have to go there, oh and Dunsborough coastline is so beautiful, plus there's all the little cafes there, we have to go there too.' Her eyes danced.

'It all sounds perfect.'

I looked forward to the day when we could take holidays together, and have no time limits, unlike now. Mel had gone home with another man, and I was here on my own again. And then she'd insisted she had to go to work tomorrow as well.

'What? You can't be serious, Mel.' I'd protested. 'Can't you just call in sick again?'

'No, Matt, I can't. I'd feel too guilty. And you know what? I also can't go for a third night in a row without being home for dinner with my family. So I'll come and see you tomorrow after dinner okay?'

No, that wasn't okay at all. 'Surely, you could at least pop in to see me after work and tell your family you've had to work late or something and then go home, have dinner and come back.'

'Sorry, I can't do that, Matt. I have to go straight home.'

'So you're telling me that out of the few days I'm here in Perth, I'm not going to see you for a whole twenty-four hours?' I looked at her in confusion.

'I'm sorry, I don't see any way around it.' She played with the strap of her watch, avoiding my eyes.

'I've just told you a way around it.'

Her face clouded over, and the silence that followed gave me an uneasy feeling. I preferred the happy Mel, the Mel that I got when I pretended to ignore the fact that she was married, compared to the cold, distant Melissa she became if I challenged her about it.

So I had no choice but to wait for the couple of hours I would get with her at the end of the day tomorrow, before she went home again.

I checked my watch. One am. I'd kept myself awake in the hope of a goodnight text from her but my phone had stayed silent. So I gave up and went to bed, trying unsuccessfully to block out the image of her in bed with her husband.

The next evening, Mel let herself into the hotel room a little after nine. I was sprawled on the bed watching a gardening show, bored witless.

'You were very naughty today,' she scolded.

Soon after waking up, I'd decided that I couldn't go through the whole day without seeing her. So I faced the glare of her receptionist and showed up at the clinic. It had been well worth it to be with her for those twenty minutes in her office where we gave the treatment couch a workout.

'Very naughty indeed, Matthew Butler.'

'Yeah, but you loved it.'

'Not as much as you're going to love this,' she said as she pulled off my shorts, bending her head down.

She was very quiet after we had sex. It was a type of quiet that scared me. Her thoughts were clearly not here in this moment. I asked how her day had been but she simply shrugged. I suggested we take a walk down onto the beach.

'Okay, whatever you like.' She was far, far away.

'Mel, you're really quiet. Are you all right?' I asked, once we'd walked in silence all the way down to the shore and sat on the sand, listening to the waves crash in the dark.

'I'm scared of this, Matt. And of what it's doing to me,' she said as she made finger patterns in the sand. She turned to face me. 'It's so different, this love between you and me, this obsessive, manic, "die without you" love. I've never really got it before now, how people do crazy things for love, how powerful it can be and what it can do to you. How it can turn you into someone you don't even recognise. It scares the hell out of me. I'm scared for you, for my kids, for Adam, for everyone.' She had an intense, desperate look on her face.

I didn't know what to say. 'I'm scared too.' I kissed her, knowing I was far more scared than she ever could be. I was witnessing her doubt, whereas I had none. At least she was safe in my love; I was certainly not feeling safe in hers at the moment. What would another day back with her family do to her tomorrow? She wasn't anywhere near as present tonight as she had been last night.

'Why do you love me, Matt?' she asked as she settled back against my chest.

'Because you complete me,' I said jokingly, to cover up the panic that was creeping in.

She giggled at that. At least I'd broken her negative thoughts. 'You complete me? Think of your own lines, boofhead! I really want to know, Matt, why do you love me? Am I worth all of this? It's so complicated.'

'What's complicated? It's completely straightforward. I love you beyond all reason. I love your sensitivity, your intelligence, your—'

'Oh look, the poor little thing,' she interrupted, pointing to an injured seagull hopping along the shore, its bent spindly leg tucked up underneath its belly.

I heard the sea-eagle first, the flap of its wings was audible even over the sound of the wind and water. Mel smiled up at it but I felt my stomach lurch. This was bad.

It hovered above us for a minute, its white belly and wing span stretching well over a metre wide, and then it lunged down with incredible precision and snatched the unsuspecting seagull in its claws.

Mel screamed and I threw myself over her as the eagle dived towards us. It soared back up, high into the sky, with the screeching seagull in its grip. And then it was over. The noise and the birds disappeared into the night sky.

Mel was shaking when I let go of her. Neither of us spoke for a while. I found it hard not to be sick and kept swallowing it down.

She rocked herself as she spoke in a flat voice. 'I'm a bad person. I'm a bad person doing bad things to others. I don't deserve to be happy. I deserve bad things to happen to me. That was a sign, I can feel it. Bad things are coming, Matt.' She covered her face with her hands.

'It's just a bird, Mel, just nature,' I tried to reassure her, but she wouldn't hear it. 'Come on, baby.' I helped her up. She was still trembling. 'Let's go back up inside and I'll tell you all those millions of reasons why I love you.'

'I want to go home,' she said as we neared the hotel entrance.

My heart sank to the lowest depths. 'Please don't go home now, come up for a little while. I'll make you a coffee, and we'll talk, and you'll settle down.'

She nodded and came upstairs. Instead of a coffee, we lay on top of the covers on the bed. I put my arms around her and she started to cry.

I whispered, 'Hey, Mel, do you know what I do when I'm upset?'

'What?'

'I see how still I can lie.'

'Why?' she whispered.

'Because it reminds me of how peaceful Rob looked when he was dead. It's weird but it works. Want to try?'

'Okay.'

We practised being still together.

Half an hour later, she finally spoke. 'I need to go home now, Matt. I'll call you in the morning.'

'I feel like I'm about to lose you, Mel.' I reached for her hand in the dark.

'I love you,' she replied, squeezing my hand, which did nothing to help me feel any more secure.

I walked her down to the car park and kissed lips that didn't kiss me back. I closed the car door for her, watched her drive away, and then walked back in through the hotel sliding doors with a great sense of foreboding.

DIVIDED

MEL

I was exhausted. And irritable. And confused. And I hated myself.

'What is it, mate?' Adam rolled onto his side to face me in the dark. 'What's bugging you?'

'I can't sleep,' I sighed.

'You haven't been yourself lately. I think you're doing too much, you've hardly been home for days. You need to slow down, Mel.'

He hadn't cracked a joke or dismissed me. I was so grateful for that, I started to cry. I'd cried lying next to Matt, and now here I was only a few hours later, crying next to Adam.

'Hey, hey,' Adam said tenderly, reaching for my face and wiping my cheek with his fingers. 'What's wrong? Why the tears?'

I tried to remember why I'd been so full of resentment for him this past month, why he annoyed me so much that I went off and found salvation in Matt. Nothing came to mind. Nothing that warranted this kind of betrayal anyway. It wasn't Adam. It had never been Adam. It was all me. When I fell in love with Matt I needed a scapegoat, otherwise I would've had to own up to my treachery. Blaming Adam for not meeting my needs suited me better than facing my truth.

My initial euphoria at Matt's arrival in Perth was short-lived. I only managed to exist in that blissful bubble of denial for two days, which was while I avoided my family altogether. I barely saw or spoke to Adam or the children, and instead indulged myself in my love for Matt, uninterrupted by thoughts of them.

But as soon as I was back in the family fold, reality burst that happy bubble. I'd somehow convinced myself this past month that my children didn't need me, that they didn't care about me, when the fact was I had stopped needing or caring for them, and they'd simply reacted to that. I'd started to believe that my sex life with Adam was cold vanilla ice-cream, whereas the truth of the matter was that as soon as I showed an interest in sex Adam had jumped on board and we'd had really great hot chocolate-type sex. The issue was me – I didn't want to acknowledge the great sex with Adam because that took away my excuse to cheat on him.

What I wanted from Adam, when I was honest with myself, was that he become Matt. I wanted him to be as deep and troubled as Matt. And I wanted him to be obsessed to the point of insanity about me, just like Matt was. For a month I'd done nothing but fantasise about a life of profound conversation and intense passion with Matt, and I thought it was all I could ever want. But then I got a taste of that life. With Matt I had the most exhilarating sex and the strongest emotional connection of my life, and it still wasn't enough. Because I still needed Adam and Nick and Lily and our life together.

When I came home it was as if I was seeing them for the first time in a long time, without the self-pity that had made me blind to them. And I fell in love with them all over again.

And then when I left them after dinner to go and meet Matt, I tried to recreate the magic of the past two days, because I desperately wanted to keep that fantasy going. But I couldn't do it. The fantasy was sullied now that I'd opened my heart to my family again.

I'd walked into the hotel, and straight into hot and heavy sex with Matt to try and numb my guilt, but now that the blinkers were off, even the most breathtaking sex couldn't make me happy. Matt was unhappy too, and I knew he'd remain unhappy forever if I continued to have him in my life. But I couldn't bring myself to send him away. He was a part of me now.

So although I couldn't give Adam and our family up, I refused to give Matt up either. And I had no idea what to do so that life would ever be okay again.

And that was why I couldn't sleep.

Adam broke the silence. 'I love you, Mel, I don't want to see you cry. Please tell me why you're crying.'

It hit me hard in that moment how much I loved him. He wasn't Matt, he could never be, but he didn't have to be. He had been the most important person in my life for the past fourteen years. I cried harder at the hopelessness of it all.

'Adam, I'm just so tired, so overtired,' I wept. 'I feel messed up. I'll be better tomorrow. I'm sorry.'

He stroked my hair. 'I love your hair curly,' he whispered. 'You should never straighten it.'

I cried even harder at that. Big wracking sobs.

'I know what will make you sleep peacefully.' He reached between my legs and started stroking me.

'No,' I whispered, clamming up. 'I'm too tired to be any good to you.' Sex was the very last thing I wanted.

'Who said you had to do anything? Let me,' he said in a husky voice as he slid down the bed, before peeling off my underwear and finding the spot where his kisses felt better than ever, ever before.

Maybe I was extra sensitive to the perfect wetness of his tongue and his lips, or maybe guilt and emotion heightened my sensitivity. Or maybe I'd simply never noticed how very good Adam was at this. Whatever the reason, I never wanted him to stop. I cried the whole time, my tears a mix of pleasure and grief. Despite myself, Adam gave me one of the most intense, powerful and memorable orgasms of my whole life.

And then I slept.

THE LAST NIGHT

MATT

She had a delivery to go to. That was the line. It was the same line she'd used on him. She swore on her life that she wasn't lying this time. I still didn't know whether I believed her. It was my second last night in Perth and she was going to spend it at a hospital, helping deliver a baby. Helping. Which meant she was dispensable, and yet she still chose to be there over being here with me. Or worse, there was no delivery and she still chose not to be with me. But by the firmness of her words and the tone of her voice, I knew I had no chance of making her change her mind.

I'd spent the whole day waiting for her like a cat on a hot tin roof. At five-thirty, two hours before she was expected, she called to cancel. She sounded sincere. She explained she had been the main carer for this woman throughout her pregnancy and that she'd be letting her down if she didn't attend the birth. She was very convincing. But then again, I'm sure she sounded sincere and convincing when she fed her husband lies too.

I thought back to a few days before. I was so sure of her then, of our future. Now I had no idea what was going on in her head. She was a different woman last night from the one who had left here the night before. Something changed in her over the course of the day between, and I was lost as to what that was.

'If I'm not going to see you at all today, then I want us to spend all day tomorrow together, and the next day, right up until I leave. For the rest of the time I'm here I want to be with you.' I held my breath and hoped she'd agree.

'Matt, how on earth am I going to do that?' she pleaded.

'Can't you think of something? I'm leaving, Mel, and I want to be with you before I go. I don't know how soon I'll be able to come back again. It might be a couple of months away. Don't you want to be with me before I go?' I choked. 'Do you still even love me?'

'Of course I do!' she said with feeling. 'I love you so much, it's killing me.'

I was relieved that at least she'd said that. I was standing out on the balcony, and I leaned forward against the railing. Neither of us said anything.

In the silence, I noticed a couple going for it on the sand below. It had been cooler today, and this late in the afternoon the beach was almost deserted apart from these two, and a few others out in the surf. The woman was topless and wore a black sarong around her slender hips. Then I noticed the person underneath her was also a woman. And topless too. Oh. Oh wow.

'I'm desperate to see you, Matt,' Mel said softly after a while. 'I will find a way to spend the whole weekend with you. I'll think of something, okay?'

'Okay,' I said, getting turned on very quickly by the scene down on the sand. The woman in the sarong moved further on top of the other one. Their pelvises were grinding against each other. I could come just watching that.

'I want to have sex with you so badly right now, Mel,' I said, a bit short of breath. 'I can see these two topless girls getting into it on the beach and it's making me so hard. I wish you could see this with me. It's really hot. They're rubbing against each other, Mel. They're kissing like crazy.'

She was silent.

'Mel, are you still there?'

'I'm still here,' she said softly.

'Mel?'

'Yes?'

'I wish I could watch you with another woman. Just sit back and watch you do things to each other, just like these girls are doing now.'

She breathed haltingly down the phone. 'Oh, Jesus.'

'Do you wish you were here watching with me?' I asked in a low voice.

She was silent again and then, 'Yes.'

'You love the idea of these two girls sliding all over each other. You want a girl sliding all over you, don't you?' I ventured.

'Yes,' she breathed.

'A really pretty girl, with beautiful long hair and a gorgeous body. Nice and naked. On top of you. Underneath you. Between you.'

She gave one of her sexy high-pitched sighs that I loved so much.

'You'd love that wouldn't you?'

'Yes.'

'You've fantasised about that before, haven't you?'

'Yes'

'You're desperate to try it, aren't you?'

'Yes.'

I almost couldn't hear her. 'Where are you?' I asked.

'In the bathroom. On the ward.'

'Is anyone else in there?'

'No.' She sounded breathless.

I looked at the girls, lying side by side now, leaning on their forearms and smoking cigarettes. I walked inside and lay down on the bed. I desperately needed to connect with Mel again, any way I could, and I was excited at what was just about to happen between us.

'Put your hand inside your knickers,' I told her.

'What?'

'You heard me. Suck on your fingers first. Make them soaking wet.'

'Okay,' she said. 'Okay.'

There was a short silence followed by another one of her sexy sighs and I knew she was doing what I'd asked.

'Shut your eyes, Mel. It's the pretty girl on the beach. Can you feel what she's doing to you?'

She didn't answer, she was panting.

'What colour is her hair, Mel?'

'Blonde,' she almost cried.

The sound of Mel's beautiful moans over the phone during her breathless orgasm saw me through the rest of that night.

Early the next morning, she was back in my bed again. I didn't ask what excuses she'd used to be free to spend the weekend with me. All that mattered was that she was back in my arms.

'I hope you understand that you're not leaving this bed all day,' I said, contented.

And we did literally spend the day in bed. We talked for hours in bed. We ate lunch in bed. We watched a movie in bed. We split the paper and read different parts of it in bed.

She'd forgotten her phone at the hospital. She fretted about it, but I talked her into not going to pick it up. I wasn't prepared to risk her having a change of heart while she was gone and not coming back.

As the sun was setting, we moved out to the balcony and took in a final sunset. Then we went back to bed for our last night together.

'Can we talk about the future now, please?' I asked before switching off the light.

'Tomorrow,' she said.

Tomorrow came.

'Now?' I asked.

'No, let's talk about the heavy stuff in the afternoon,' she said.

Later, I absently traced a freckle on the inside of her impossibly soft forearm as we sat out on the balcony having coffee.

'Mel, we have to talk about the future, no more putting it off. I'm about to catch a flight to Melbourne and I want to go back there with a solid plan.'

After our renewed closeness, I was more in love with her than ever. I was tempted to propose to her, but there wasn't much romance in proposing to a woman who was still married.

'Okay, all right, let's talk about the future,' she said, her face clouding over.

I told her the dream I'd been concocting over the last few days of investing in a shared clinic where we could work together, and of buying one of the new townhouses being built right on the beach here, on the opposite side of the promenade. We could live happily ever after, waking up to a Scarborough sunrise every day for the rest of our lives.

'Oh, I'd love that,' she sighed. 'If only I wasn't married, Matt. Why don't you go ahead and do it, though? You'd love living in Scarborough, and I'd visit you as much as I could.'

And just like that, it was over.

I shook my head violently. 'What? No way! What do you mean "if only" you weren't married? You're not *staying* married!' I said adamantly. 'If I move to Perth, you're getting divorced.'

Her eyes widened. 'Matt, you know I can't do that. I thought you said in Melbourne that you'd move here even if I didn't leave Adam. I can't leave him.'

'I meant short term, while you worked out what your feelings were!' I was shocked beyond belief to hear her say that. 'Do you seriously think I'd be happy for you to go back to him again now? It would do my head in. I'm not sharing you with him, not for one more day. You're going back there to tell him it's over and that you've fallen in love with me. No more lying, it's time for you to come clean.'

'But Matt, my kids,' she implored.

'What about your kids? Your kids will cope. You can't go on living a lie.' I stood up, too wired to sit any longer. 'You won't be the first person to ever end a marriage, you know,' I said harshly.

'I won't break up our home. I'm sorry, but I just won't do it.' She looked resolute.

I felt the panic inside me rise to the surface. 'Stop being such a pathetic martyr, Mel. You've said it yourself – you love me, you want *me*. It doesn't mean turning your back on your kids.' I squatted down next to where she sat and searched her eyes frantically. 'You still get to be their mum – I'm not asking you to leave them, I'm asking you to leave him.'

'But Matt, Adam needs—'

'That fucking anaesthetist you married has had you sedated for fourteen years. I've woken you up. Stay the fuck awake!' I was shouting now and I couldn't stop. I rose back up to full height. 'This whole time you've been thinking you're going back to him? What the fuck? I can't even wrap my head around that. Hasn't this meant anything to you? This is my life too. You expect me to be holed up somewhere waiting by the phone for you forever? You're fucking dreaming!'

She started to cry. 'I told you in Melbourne I'd never leave him but you came anyway. Why are you so shocked now? How was I supposed to know you'd changed your mind? You didn't say,' she shouted tearfully.

My eyelids burned and the front of my head pounded with pressure as I held in my tears. I hollered, '*I shouldn't have to say*! I'd only known you a few hours then. All I meant by that was for you to have time to see if it could work with us before you left him. How can you think it's still okay to stay married now? How can you even want to? You can't love me and do that to me, it's all bullshit. I'm just your plaything, your bit on the side, is that it?' I swallowed what tasted like poison and lost my battle with the tears.

'That's what you think?' she sobbed quietly now. 'That you're my plaything? I'm so in love with you I want to die right now. But I have a family. You can't ask me to do this.' She came and stood near me, turning my face so I was looking at her. 'I love you, but I love them too. I can't choose. The only way this can work for me is if I keep seeing you whenever I can get away. I'm sorry, Matt, that's all I can give you.'

I was mute with grief as she continued. 'I know what it's like to be shipped from house to house between parents, lying in bed at night wishing they still loved each other and that we could all be a family again. I won't do it to my kids.' She sighed tearfully. 'And Adam's done nothing wrong. He doesn't deserve to have his home torn apart and his children ripped away from him. I married him knowing exactly who he was and he hasn't changed. He's a wonderful man and a wonderful husband to me. I'm the one who's changed since I fell in love with you. How can you expect me to punish my family for my mistake?'

'So I'm a mistake now, am I?' I spat and stormed inside. I swore a string of expletives to myself, pacing up and down.

'Of course you're not a mistake. I didn't mean that.'

I brushed past her, opened the door to the suite and bolted down the hallway. I pressed for the lift but when the doors didn't open straightaway, I headed for the fire escape and ran down the stairs.

'Matt, come back!' Mel ran down after me but she couldn't keep up. I flew down all sixteen flights, ran out through the lobby, across the road and onto the sand.

I was breathless.

And I was broken.

I could feel the pieces of my heart shattering in my ribcage.

I saw with absolute clarity that I would never be to her what she was to me. It devastated me that she didn't love me enough to be with me, and only me. I found it hard to believe that we had so thoroughly misunderstood each other's intentions, and for the first time I judged her. What sort of person could string two men along the way she planned to do? She was prepared to live a lifetime of dishonesty. I'd thought she was better than that.

I walked a long way south along the shore, furiously kicking the sand until my legs hurt. I sat alone for a while on an isolated stretch of beach a couple of kilometres away. Then, feeling exhausted and miserable, I returned to the hotel to find her wrapped in a blanket, sitting on the bed, waiting.

I started throwing my clothes into my suitcase. 'I have to get to the airport.'

'This can't be it, Matt,' she sobbed.

'It is it if you go back to him. I'm not chasing you any more. I'm finished with that. It's all or nothing now. Either you love me enough to want to be with me or you don't. And if you don't, I'm out of here.'

'Go then,' she said looking straight ahead, her knuckles white from her grip on the blanket. 'Go home and marry Lydia.'

'How can you say that?' I shouted at her again. 'I'm not marrying—'

'She'll help you get over us,' she continued in a dead voice right over the top of me. 'You told me that she used to make you happy, maybe she will again. You can at least have a family with her. But I'm not leaving Adam. You've wasted enough time on me.'

I shook my head with disgust. I had to get out of here now. I'd come back for my case after she was gone.

'I'm going.' I was struggling to keep myself together. 'I'm not fucking marrying Lydia, all right?' I opened the door and looked at her one last time. My heart broke a little more. 'I love you, Mel. I'll always love you. Please change your mind. Tell me you'll leave him. Please.'

'You said you'd never leave me. You said it,' she sobbed into her hands.

I gulped. 'And you said you'd die without me.'

'I love you so much.' She lunged off the bed and clutched at my T-shirt. I unclasped her fingers and walked out of the room, without looking back.

RECKONING

MEL

There is always a day of reckoning.

Driving away from the hotel, I was swamped with tears. I turned onto the highway without giving way, narrowly avoiding a four-wheel drive, and a few seconds later I slammed the brakes hard enough to make the car screech and skid as I realised I was just about to go straight through a red light.

I made it past three more sets of traffic lights before abruptly cutting lanes to pull into a service station. Not having my mobile, I thumbed through a tattered phone book and then slotted coins into a payphone in the corner of the shop. I didn't bother hiding behind sunglasses, I was anonymous here so who cared what any of these strangers thought of me? And so the tears continued to pour.

I was put through to his hotel room and it rang for a while before he answered. 'Mel? Is that you?'

'I need to see you again. Can you please come to the clinic?'

'Have you changed your mind?' The husky tone of his voice was so much more pronounced over the telephone.

'No. Please come anyway? Just for half an hour, you have time before your flight leaves. Please let me be with you just one last time.'

He was silent. I waited.

'Please, Matt,' I begged.

'Do you honestly think I could say no to you?' he said finally.

I drove to the clinic in a frenzied state. When I arrived I ran out of the car and up the path, grazing my elbow on a tree branch as I passed. He was waiting outside the front entrance, his eyes red and swollen. I hurriedly unlocked the glass door and it swung wide open. Once inside the waiting room I flung myself into his arms. We had frantic sex on the floor right next to the front door, both of us professing our love over and over again.

I lay facing him in silence afterwards, stroking the body that was now so familiar to me. He played lightly up and down my spine with his fingertips, the way he knew I liked it.

'I've got a flight to catch, Mel,' he announced quietly at six o'clock.

'Just stay,' I whispered. 'Stay.'

'I can't.'

I sat up on one arm and looked into his eyes. 'Thank you for coming to find me. I'm so glad you did.' My voice broke. 'I don't even want to think about tomorrow with you not here.'

'Maybe tomorrow's the day you realise you need to leave him,' he murmured as he tucked a strand of hair behind my ear.

'I don't know how I'll live with myself either way,' I said mournfully.

He nodded. 'We'll wait and see what tomorrow brings, hey?' He kissed my forehead.

'Can I call you in the morning?' I asked. 'Just to know that you arrived safely?'

'Sure.' He smiled weakly. 'We'll talk in the morning.'

A morning phone call to cling to made it easier to say goodbye.

I got dressed, struggling to do up the button on my jeans. My fingers were inexplicably numb. We had one final lingering kiss, standing in the doorway, before we walked to our cars and took off in opposite directions, Matt to his home and me to mine.

I sobbed violently as I drove home. The road was barely visible through my tears. I tried to console myself with the thought that perhaps I would end up getting my way. I'd figured out exactly what I wanted two nights ago, after working late at the hospital. I decided that I wanted it all – Matt *and* my family with Adam – and I worked out how to stop feeling guilty and torn up about having it all. When I was with Matt, I would focus only on him and not let even a fleeting thought of Adam, Nick and Lily come between us. And then when I was with my family again, I would ignore any thoughts of Matt and focus completely on our home life. That way, I reasoned, I could give everyone my undivided attention when I was with them, and not tear myself to pieces any more.

I gave absolutely no thought as to how anybody else would be affected by this plan.

This was why I was so shocked by Matt's rejection of it. Perhaps, given some time to think it over, he'd see it my way. But somewhere deep inside me, I knew I'd never see Matt again. I couldn't bear the thought.

I stared through glassy eyes at a colourful bug making its sideways trek across the windscreen, and told myself to focus on my future with Adam. He'd sounded surprised, but not suspicious, when I'd announced on Friday night that Sarah had called me in great distress after a huge row with Ryan. I said she begged me to spend the weekend in Perth with her because she was desperate to get away and think things through clearly.

Adam said he never expected that kind of drama from those two, but of course I should spend the weekend with her.

As I set off supposedly to meet Sarah at the airport on Saturday morning, Adam told me how lucky she was to have a devoted friend like me. He and the children hugged me goodbye, among promises that next week I would spend loads and loads of time with them all to make up for my long absences this week.

'I'll Snapchat you lots this weekend, Mum,' Lily said, and it was at that moment I realised I'd left my phone at the hospital the night before.

'Shit!' I said loudly.

'What?' Adam asked.

'I forgot my phone. It's still sitting in my pigeonhole on the ward.'

'That's just as well your mum hasn't got her phone,' Adam said, ruffling Lily's hair. 'She can have peace and quiet with Sarah doing their secret women's business, without selfies from you interrupting them every five minutes.'

I drove straight to Matt's hotel after that conversation, relieved that there was now no pressure to call home while I was with him.

When I'd initially received the call on Friday from the hospital about my patient being well into her labour, I had actually been relieved to have an excuse not to see Matt that night. After the night before that, in bed reconnecting with Adam, I was more tortured than ever, feeling torn between the two of them.

But then I called Matt from the hospital to cancel our rendezvous, and the erotic experience I had with him on the phone, as well as the way my heart soared just hearing his rough-edged voice, compelled me to go back to him.

As soon as I was back with Matt, to the exclusion of my family, I told myself that this was it. This was the way I could have it all. So for the final weekend before he left, I gave myself to Matt completely – heart, mind, body and soul. I successfully managed to shut out all thoughts of my family when I was with him and I saw that as proof that my plan to hang onto him and my marriage could work. But now he was gone. And he was gone for good.

And it wasn't until now, driving towards home that I took a deep breath and stopped the hysterics and in a moment of absolute clarity all the pieces fell into place and I saw myself for what I was. A selfish monster.

It hit me hard. I thought about what I'd done to Adam and how I would have felt if he'd done this to me. I thought about what I'd done to my children by being so absent lately, and by putting their father last. By risking their home. I thought about the web of lies I'd built and the delusional state I had let myself fall into. I thought about the way I'd wilfully betrayed the trust Adam had in me. And I wanted to die.

I thought about how hard I'd been on Adam, especially recently, because he didn't live up to what I wanted. It all seemed laughably petty now, considering I'd just had an affair right under his nose. I had to make it up to Adam. I had to find a way to redeem myself.

He deserved so much more from me – Adam, who'd given me the passionate sex I'd yearned for the second I was open to it. I had to find a way to hang onto that passion without using it only as a vehicle to fantasise about Matt. I'd try hard from now on to be present and in the moment. I'd do whatever it was going to take to make him happy and satisfied from this day forward, and I'd never, ever look at another man again. I'd stop being a monster and start being a wife.

I found myself speeding towards home, to Adam. I wanted to hold him and love him and tell him I was sorry for all the things I could never confess to.

I wasn't driving home to a loveless sham of a marriage, which was the impression I'd given Matt. I was returning to a man who I couldn't imagine my life without.

There was so much about Adam I loved all at once that I couldn't process it fast enough. I loved his huge warm smile and his mischievous eyes. I loved how he always had a short black ready for me when I woke up on weekends. I loved the way he patiently explained movies to me when I found them difficult to follow. I loved watching him in his quiet moments with our children. I loved him in a way that was so different from my passion for Matt.

Adam and I were a team. We had history. Together we'd created a beautiful family and, before I'd decided to erupt a volcano in our lives six weeks ago, we'd had a peaceful and happy home. I wasn't a selfless martyr, sacrificing her own happiness to fulfil her family duties, the way I'd been feeling ever since the trip to Melbourne. I needed to be part of my family again, to make amends.

Now that the blinkers were off and I was seeing things clearly, I was astounded that I'd been naive enough to think Matt would accept the type of arrangement where he played second fiddle forever. How could I ever have thought that would satisfy him? Matt deserved a wife and family of his own. And realistically, how long could I have kept sneaking around to be with him? Surely, *surely* I would have grown a conscience at some stage.

I had to let Matt go. It was the only way I could live with myself and be a decent wife. I would never see him or have any contact with him again, whatsoever. It had to be a clean break. For his sake and for Adam's and for mine. It was the only way I could live with any integrity after this mess. I would not call him tomorrow. I would never hear his voice again. And I had never been in this much pain. Rationalising my decision to choose Adam didn't take away from the heartache. The idea of ever getting over Matt was a joke. I'd just have to learn to live with the pain, it was there to stay. That was how I was going to pay the price for being unfaithful. I was going to live with the burden of secret heartache and guilt forever.

As I turned the car into our street, I was thankful for the small mercy that at least it was Sunday night and the children would be at youth group. There was no volleyball tonight, Adam's team had a bye, so he'd be home alone and the timing could not have been better. Tomorrow was a new day. I could start again. I could wake up to the children with a new attitude. They would have their mum back. But tonight I'd begin being a wife again.

My heart raced when I spotted Adam's black BMW in the garage. I parked my car beside his and walked quickly through to the backyard to find him.

Then I stopped dead in my tracks.

He was sitting at the table on the back patio, nursing a beer. At least a dozen crushed beer cans littered the table around him. He was unshaven and his hair was dishevelled, his shirt creased and stained. His red-rimmed, unblinking eyes bored through me.

He knew.

I didn't know how, but he definitely knew. I couldn't swallow, my mouth was dry and I felt the hairs on my arms rise. The silence was interminable.

'Are you leaving me?' he asked finally, speaking in a monotone.

'No,' I whispered. 'It's finished.' I couldn't insult him by denying it.

I became acutely aware of my wet knickers, Matt's DNA. Matt's DNA in my knickers. I dropped my head.

He cleared his throat. 'It started in Melbourne, didn't it? That weekend with Sarah.'

'Yes,' I croaked, looking up again.

He nodded slowly. 'I've known you nearly fifteen years. What do you take me for?' He was chillingly calm.

'I'm so sorry, Adam.' I gulped. I desperately tried to stop the flow of tears. He deserved to have this conversation without me dissolving into hysterics.

'Am I an idiot in believing that this is the first time you've cheated on me?' He frowned, watching my eyes carefully for my response.

I shook my head vigorously. 'No, you're not an idiot, I promise you this was the first and the last time. I swear. Never before, never again.'

I walked a few feet closer to him and sat on the step. My legs trembled wildly as I bent my knees to sit.

His undisguised anguish made him look much older than his forty-eight years.

'I love you, Adam. I do.' My voice was heavy.

'I thought we were okay, you know. Good, even. I thought you were happy enough,' he murmured, not losing eye contact.

'*I was happy*,' I said adamantly. 'I lost my mind over this guy. I don't know what the hell happened. But it's over.'

His expression didn't change and his voice remained lifeless. 'I didn't kid myself into thinking it was perfect between you and me, but I thought it was all right. But obviously it was only all right for me, not for you. I knew the day you came back from that weekend, I knew something was wrong. You were different. But I just buried my head in the sand. I tried to ignore what you flaunted in my face, with your slutty clothes and your slutty mouth and all your disappearances.' He said the last sentence with venom. 'You're either completely delusional or you think I'm fucking blind not to notice.'

Despite myself, I cried harder. 'I'm so sorry. I'll spend the rest of my life making it up to you, if you let me. I know I don't deserve you but I do love you. I really, really do.' I wiped my face with a shaking hand and looked at him to see if he believed me.

'Huh,' he said under his breath. He shook his head and laughed quietly to himself. 'Ryan called me yesterday afternoon.'

I felt the ice gather around my heart.

'He said he'd tried your phone through the morning but it rang out. He wanted your opinion on a bracelet he was buying Sarah for her birthday. You can imagine how that conversation went.'

'Oh my God,' I whispered.

'So I went to the hospital to get your phone, to see if I could get some answers from it.' He let those words hang.

It was then that I noticed the bright pink phone case right there among the beer cans on the table.

I gasped. Oh Jesus! All of our explicit messages to each other – and there were many – were still on the phone. I'd taken naked photos of Matt in the shower. I had footage of Matt giving me oral sex from start to finish. It couldn't get any worse.

Adam watched me as I furiously tried to catalogue what other horrors were on the phone.

'So, was he right, in those texts he sent you before he found you and shoved his face between your legs?' Adam asked, his voice strained. 'Was he right? Did you do what he said you'd do?'

'Did I do what?' I croaked.

He was silent for a minute, before he spoke in a rasp. 'Did you cry when he fucked you?'

I shut my eyes.

He picked up a can, tilted his head back and chugged another few mouthfuls of beer.

'Please don't leave me,' I said in a small voice.

He sighed loudly. His fingers tightened around the can in his hand and he crushed it, while he looked at me with cold eyes. He pushed his chair back, the steel legs scraping against the wooden decking beneath it. With a sweep of his arm he sent cans flying off the table and clattering onto the floor. He stood up and walked past me to the garage, taking his keys out of his pocket.

'Adam, you can't drive like this. Please don't get in the car,' I begged him.

He turned and walked slowly back, stopping less than a foot away. He squatted down until we were face to face, his narrowed eyes full of disgust. I could smell the beer on his breath. My blood was pumping rapidly.

He rested his hands on his knees. 'Fuck you,' he said in a low voice.

He stood up again and walked away. He got into his car, slammed the door and revved the engine. The tyres screeched as he sped away.

I didn't move. I sat there and cursed myself to the fiery depths of hell for what I'd done to him. Adam had given me a life that turned my friends green with envy, and this was how I'd thanked him.

I sat in silence on the step outside, my stomach in knots, until I heard the children's voices coming from the front garden. They were shouting their goodbyes to the friends who had driven them home.

I stood up. The echo of my shoes on the stone tiles as I walked through the empty house was deafening.

I forced a smile on my face as I opened the front door.

My beautiful kids. I had an outburst of love at the sight of them. If nothing else, I still had my kids.

Lily's eyes lit up when she saw me. 'Mum! Hi!' She threw her arms around my neck and launched into a spiel about her day. 'Guess what, Mum? Kate Young got her tongue pierced behind her parents' back!' she squealed and waited for my reaction. Then she took in my appearance. 'You look *really* crap, Mum. Are you sick or something?'

'I'm all right. Think I might be coming down with a cold. I missed you guys.' I put an arm around Lily and smiled at Nick. He'd been standing patiently beside his sister as she spoke.

'Hi, sweetheart. Come and give your mum a hug.' I held out my free arm to him.

He came over reluctantly. Over the last six months he'd become increasingly uncomfortable with any form of physical contact from any of us. It worried me, but Adam had laughed it off.

'All his affection's going to his penis, Mel,' he'd said. 'There's nothing left for us, mate.'

'How's my boy?' I smiled at Nick now, as he slipped out of my hug.

'Yeah, good. Where's Dad?' He looked over my shoulder.

'He's gone down to the rec centre, love. They asked him to fill in for another team that was short,' I lied smoothly.

'Hey, Mum, you should see Dad, he's a total mess!' Lily said dramatically. 'Apparently some guy he worked with died yesterday and now Dad's gone all depressed. Someone called Phillip. We didn't even know he existed and now all of a sudden he was one of Dad's best mates.' She gave me a knowing look. 'Do you know what, but? We don't even think he's telling the truth. Nick and I think Dad's losing it. He looks all gross and he sat outside, like, literally all night drinking. He was smashed. Today he just sat there for the whole entire day, just sat there! It was really creepy, Mum. I reckon it's that midlife crisis thingy.' Lily stood tall, clearly proud of her observations.

I turned to Nick. 'Has he really been that bad, Nick?'

'Yep,' he replied matter-of-factly.

Lily continued, 'Yeah, we tried to ring and tell you but you forgot your phone at work, remember? Anyway it was kind of cool, wasn't it, Nick? Dad let us stay on our laptops for ages last night and he didn't check our homework so Nick didn't do any, did you, Nick? Tell Mum, don't lie. And we even had pizzas delivered for dinner, with Coke and everything!' Her eyes sparkled at the scandal of it all. 'I can't believe he went to volleyball,' she continued. 'He probably cheered up because you were home again, Mum.'

I was raw with pain.

I fried Nick and Lily some eggs for dinner, which they ate in front of the television. The idea of having anything to eat myself made me want to vomit. I played up the excuse of a cold coming on and headed upstairs, after retrieving the phone from outside.

I checked the text message screen and it was empty. The camera roll was empty. Adam had deleted everything.

Sitting on the edge of the bed, I sent Matt a text message.

I'm so sorry, Matt, but I won't be calling you tomorrow, or any day after that. I have a family. Don't know what I was thinking. Adam knows about us now. I'm so desperately sorry. For all of it.

His two-word reply came moments later.

Okay then.

I was shocked by the physicality of my pain as I read it.

Later in the evening, the children came upstairs to their bedrooms. Nick closed his door and the light went out immediately. Lily plugged her iPod into speakers and listened to her current favourite song on repeat for almost an hour.

By ten o'clock the house was silent, but for the noise of the cicadas outside.

I wondered where Adam was and fretted about his safety. I thought of Matt, and my chest tightened. I had lost them both on the same day. It was the least I deserved.

I ticked off the hours on the digital clock as I sat in the dark waiting.

Adam came back in the early hours of the morning. I heard the rolling sound of the garage door and a freezing shower of dread poured down on me. I sat up taller in bed, my senses on high alert, and waited.

He didn't appear.

I heard him crack open another can downstairs.

There is always a day of reckoning.

THE WEDDING

MATT

I married Lydia.

THE COST

MEL

I walked into work on Monday morning with my palms sweating at the idea of facing Cheryl. I imagined the icy stare and the pinched mouth. But when she looked up from the computer, her expression was one of concern. I burst into tears.

She followed me into the consulting room and sat in the chair opposite mine. She didn't say anything, she didn't attempt to comfort me. She didn't even look at me. She just sat there, waiting, staring into space.

'It's over, but Adam found out,' I wailed.

'Adam's leaving you?' she asked, more as a statement than a question.

'I don't know,' I said through tears. 'He slept on the couch last night and he left this morning without a word. I don't even know where he is. He's not at work. The receptionist said he's taken the day off sick. His phone's going to voicemail.'

Cheryl straightened some papers on the desk and nodded. 'He'll settle down. He loves you to pieces. Give him time.'

'I hate myself,' I howled. 'I hate what I've done to him, and what I've done to Matt. I just want to crawl into a hole.'

'It will pass, Mel. Everything passes.' She reached for the tissue box and handed me one.

I blew my nose noisily and calmed down a little. 'Why are you being nice to me?' I looked at her suspiciously.

'Because I care about you,' she replied.

'Thanks,' I sniffed. 'You didn't tell the others, did you?'

She gave me a filthy look.

I wiped at my tears. 'Well? Aren't you going to ask for all the gory details?'

She laughed under her breath. 'Mel, it was enough to have to tidy this room up after he'd been here on two separate occasions. The smell of sex nearly bowled me over. I don't need any more detail than that, thanks.'

'Sorry.' I was nowhere near as embarrassed as I should have been. I was already too exposed.

'If you want somebody to talk to, I'm around.' She stood up. 'Your eye-liner's smeared. Unless you want to be Dr Raccoon today, you better go to the bathroom and fix yourself up. You're booked out this morning. And you better run on time and do a good job, Mel. I've had it up to my ears with patients getting aggro out there because of you. You said it's over, so your time in la-la land's finished now. Got it?'

I nodded and smiled gratefully at her before she walked out. I knew she'd never bring any of it up again. She wasn't half bad, Cheryl.

I threw myself into work that morning. I wished I could have worked longer hours to avoid going back home.

Those first few days after Adam found out about Matt were the stuff of nightmares. Adam's resentment knew no bounds. He didn't once look in my direction or utter a single word to me. I found out from Nick that he'd passed his scheduled theatre list to a locum and that he'd cancelled the week's appointments at his suites.

The only time Adam spent at home was in the wee hours of the morning, when he slept on the couch downstairs. Once awake, he would shower and change before disappearing again, without explanation, to God knows where.

I alone had created this change in him. My happy-go-lucky, life of the party, impossibly handsome husband was gone. In his place stood a white-whiskered, bleary-eyed sombre man. I'd sucked the life out of him. And I had no idea how I could make it better.

I missed Adam. I missed having him to talk to. Now that it was gone, I realised how much his conversation meant to me. I didn't care if it was brief, or casual, or even what I'd regarded before as meaningless chatter, I just missed talking to my husband. If the children said or did something sweet or funny or annoying, if the computer crashed, if I found a bargain price on shoes, if I sliced my finger while cooking, he was always the one I could tell, the only person in the world who was interested. But not now. I discovered that the 'meaningless' chatter actually mattered a lot.

On top of that, I desperately missed Matt. Going from being with him so intensely to having no contact with him at all left me with a severe case of withdrawal. I ached to feel his stubble under my palm, to listen to his throaty low-pitched laugh, to have him read out loud to me. I didn't eat or sleep, and I felt as if I had the flu. My entire body hurt, down to my bones.

I knew Matt well enough to know how much he'd be missing me too, and how unhappy he'd be back home in Melbourne. I'd sucked the life out of him as well.

I looked in the mirror and saw a woman who had taken her amazing husband for granted and made a mockery of her marriage.

The same woman who then chewed up and spat out a beautiful man who was prepared to throw away everything important in his life just to be with her.

What Adam thought of me couldn't have been any harsher than what I thought of myself. I was profoundly miserable.

And for the first time in nineteen years, I didn't have Sarah to make me feel better. After screening her calls for the first two days, I plucked up the courage to dial her number. I'd delayed ringing because I knew I had a lot of explaining to do, and I wanted to avoid that conversation. But I was in no way prepared for the extent of her anger, or for the reception I received when I finally made the call on Tuesday evening.

'Hi,' she said coldly.

I gulped. 'I'm sorry, Sare. Sorry you got caught up in it. I shouldn't have done that to you.'

'No, you shouldn't. But you did anyway,' she snapped.

'Sare, please,' I said, 'please don't be mad. I need you, I'm so devastated.'

'For fuck's sake, Mel! Stop thinking about yourself for a minute.'

It was the first time she had ever shouted at me. I felt the wind get knocked out of me as she continued. 'It's not all about you. Do you know how much shit I'm in? Ryan hasn't talked to me for four days. He says he can't trust me any more. "What sort of fucking weekends do you two have together? Trawling weekends?" he accused me. He reckons we went out on the pull together in Melbourne. He thinks I might have screwed someone too.'

'What?' I asked incredulously. 'That's ridiculous.'

'No, it's not ridiculous,' Sarah said in a high-pitched voice. 'I'll tell you what's ridiculous. You thinking you could get away with it, that's what's ridiculous. I mean, what the fuck? Who does that? Who spends a whole weekend with another man when she's married? Poor Adam, is all I can say. That man loves you so much. You're so, so lucky. And just because he's not completely perfect in every little way, that in no way excuses what you did to him. And the kids. And all you can think about is how sad *you* are? Do you know what? I'm going to hang up now. I can't do this with you at the moment. You exhaust me. You've been exhausting me since you laid eyes on that dickhead and I'm over it. See you later.'

I heard the dial tone in my ear and the misery engulfed me.

By Wednesday, the children were alarmed enough by Adam's behaviour not to be consoled by my lies that he was simply dealing with the loss of his fictitious friend from work. It didn't explain his refusal to acknowledge me, or his obvious neglect of them. They were old enough to realise that something was seriously wrong with their father.

'Mum, I'm freaking out that Dad's going to kill himself or something,' Lily cried in the car on the way home from school, on what she knew was usually Adam's day to pick them both up. He hadn't even bothered to check with me that I could do it instead.

'He used to be so normal and nice before, but now he doesn't even talk, and he looks scary. It's like he's stopped loving us,' she wailed, gasping for breath.

'Don't be such a drama queen, Lil,' Nick snapped. 'He's just having a rough time of it this week. He'll be right, won't he, Mum?'

I detected the slight note of panic in his voice. 'Of course he will, darling,' I said in my most reassuring tone. 'You know Dad, guys. He loves us like crazy, he's probably just lying low to protect us from seeing how upset he is. Obviously Phillip meant a lot to him and he's grieving privately. He'll be back to his normal self really soon, I'm sure. He's not going to do anything stupid, Lil, don't worry, darling. He's a very sensible man, your dad. Hey, who wants to sneak a Macca's thickshake?'

As ridiculous an overreaction as Adam committing suicide seemed, Lily's words scared me, and I stewed over them while my temporarily pacified children slurped noisily on their thickshakes. The thought that he might do something bad had crossed my mind more than once in the past three days. He was unreachable on any level. I had no idea what was going on in his head and that terrified me.

I confronted him that night. I was waiting up for him in the dimly lit lounge room when he staggered in at two o'clock in the morning, reeking of bourbon. He tried to brush past me, but I held onto his arms with all my strength and ordered him to look at me. His arms felt as hard as he looked. His eyes met mine for a split second and then he looked away in disgust.

The ominous whir of the ceiling fan directly above us was the only sound in the room.

'Adam, I know you hate me,' I began, 'but this can't go on. You're a father and a doctor, and you're losing the plot. Your children are genuinely worried you're going to try to kill yourself because of the way you've been acting. You have to stop this.'

He scoffed and rolled his eyes. 'As if I'd top myself,' he said bitterly, looking off to the side.

'Adam, look at me. How long are you going to pretend I don't exist?' I demanded.

He glared at me with contempt. 'How long have you pretended that I don't exist?'

I winced. '*I'm sorry*! I'm very, very sorry. It's over with him, I promise you, and I'm prepared to do whatever it takes to make things better between you and me. But I can't do anything while you refuse to talk to me, and when you're never even home.'

He shrugged me off and sat down heavily on the couch, letting his head drop into his hands. 'Give me time,' he said quietly. 'I can't talk to you yet, I can barely stand to look at you. Do you know the things I saw on your phone? You've destroyed fourteen years of marriage and trust. Give me more than three days to get over it, okay?'

'You're right. I'm sorry,' I agreed. 'But please, please stop going out drinking all day and night. Just be here for the kids. You're scaring them. Forget me, but please stop punishing them. Nick and Lily need you.'

'Yeah, well they needed you last week and where were you?' Then he sighed. 'All right, I'll stop going out. As long as you understand I'm only here for them.'

I nodded, relieved. At least I wouldn't be worried about his safety if he was home.

My words had the desired effect and by eight o'clock that morning Adam had cleaned up his act. He was sober, clean-shaven, and he'd made breakfast for the children. I overheard him apologising to them, blaming his behaviour on his grief for the friend he'd made up. Nick and Lily were in high spirits when I dropped them off at school. They had their father back.

But Adam continued to completely ignore me. He responded to my attempts at conversation with one-word answers or often with nothing at all, and he avoided eye contact with me.

'Dad, why aren't you talking to Mum?' Lily asked him warily, in front of me. She'd just witnessed my greeting to him go unacknowledged when I'd arrived home from the grocery store. 'Are you getting divorced or something?'

'No,' Adam said sharply before leaving the room.

'Did you do something really bad, Mum?' She turned to me. 'I haven't seen Dad say one word to you, even though he's being all nice to me and Nick again.'

Nick was playing on his DS nearby, and he froze.

'Yes,' I said steadily, looking Lily in the eye. 'I did do something very bad, but it's private between me and your dad. He's really, really angry with me at the moment, and that's okay, he's allowed to be. But we love each other very much and we'll sort it out soon, I promise.'

Nick exhaled loudly and stood up to walk out. Before he reached the doorway, he turned to look at me with narrowed eyes. 'There's only one thing you could've done to make him this upset,' he said knowingly.

I felt my face burn with shame.

Lily's eyes widened. 'What does he mean, Mum?'

'Lily, I told you, it's between me and Dad.'

'Well, I'm going to go ask Nick then,' she said with attitude. When she was halfway across the room, she spun around on her heels and gaped at me. 'Oh my God,' she breathed, her face showing that she got it. 'Did you have sex with someone else, like adultery?'

'Lily, it's *private*!' I yelled at her, slamming my hand down hard on the bench. My palm stung.

'Oh my God,' she said again, with a horrified expression, and quickly followed her brother upstairs.

Adam and I never confirmed or denied my infidelity to Nick and Lily, but the balance of power in my relationship with both of my children was reversed permanently, starting from that afternoon.

Adam returned to work the next week, much to my relief. With the exception of his continued disregard for me, he seemed to be getting back to his old self again. His laughter once more echoed through the house as he fooled around with the children.

As much as I missed his attention, in a way I was relieved I wasn't required to interact with him yet. Once I'd realised how much Adam and our marriage meant to me, I'd expected to be able to bounce from Matt and launch headfirst into blissful married life with Adam. I hadn't accounted for needing time to grieve for Matt.

I fell apart whenever I drove anywhere by myself, when I was in the shower, and any other time I was away from prying eyes, even in between patients at work.

I had no photos to linger over, no letters from him, absolutely nothing but the seashell, all chipped and grey, that I kept in my wallet so it was with me wherever I went. I held it to my heart obsessively, again, when no one was watching.

'Focus on Adam,' I kept telling myself, as I craved Matt. I knew I couldn't move forward with Adam if I continued to pine for Matt, so it was just as well that Adam had no desire to move forward with me yet either.

Losing Matt affected me in ways I hadn't expected. Shopping for groceries had never been painful before, but now almost every aisle had some reminder of him – a packet of M&Ms here, his favourite crisps there. I was looking for deodorant for Lily when I noticed the brand Matt used on a nearby shelf. I sprayed it on my arm and inhaled his familiar scent until I was lightheaded. It was a blessing I didn't shop near where I worked so I didn't risk any of my patients seeing their doctor collapsed in the deodorant aisle, sniffing her forearm and sobbing. I compensated for my guilt by walking back through the shop and buying all of Adam's favourite foods, as well as an excessive amount of sugary snacks for the kids' school lunches.

The following week I was going through Nick's school bag looking for his lunch box, when I came across an envelope addressed to Adam and me. It was torn open. The letter inside was dated the day before.

> *Dear Mr and Mrs Harding,*
> *Nicholas has failed to hand in this term's major assignment in Society and Environment. The due date was last Monday. Nicholas's given reason was that there are problems at home diverting his attention away from his studies.*
>
> *I would like to arrange a time to meet with one or preferably both of you to discuss this.*
>
> *I am prepared to grant Nicholas a week's extension to complete the assignment.*
>
> *Please ring the school to organise a meeting with me at your earliest convenience.*
> *Yours sincerely*
> *Clifford Hill*

I put the letter down on the table in disbelief. Nick had never been a keen student. Adam and I often had to nag him to finish his homework before he was allowed to go outside to kick his football around. But this was the first time he hadn't turned in an assignment, to my knowledge.

I couldn't work out what it was that I was most upset about: that he'd used our problems as an excuse to slack off at school, that he'd opened a letter addressed to us, or that he'd kept the letter a secret.

I stormed up to his bedroom with the letter flapping in my

hand. I found him sitting at his desk, with the sports lift-out from the paper spread out in front of him.

'Nicholas, would you care to explain this to me?' I asked in a near hysterical tone.

He stood up, ashen-faced, when he saw the letter being waved about manically in front of him.

'Not really,' he mumbled, crossing his arms and taking a step back.

'How dare you!' I screamed. 'How dare you hide this from us? Why didn't you do this assignment?'

'Didn't feel like it.' His tone was suddenly defiant. He straightened to his full height so that he was looking down at me.

'*What*? You didn't *feel* like it?' I barely recognised my own voice, which was an octave higher than normal. 'I don't care whether you feel like it or not, this is your school work, it's your future. You have a responsibility and a commitment to do it.'

He scoffed and rolled his eyes. For the first time in my life I had to stop myself from slapping his face.

'Who are you to talk about commitment? You can't even commit to your own husband,' he sneered.

His words took my breath away. I had no response. Luckily for me, Adam walked in, obviously having heard the ruckus. He brushed past me and stood only a few centimetres away from Nick.

'What did you just say to your mother?' he growled, his voice menacing.

'Nothing, I, I …' Nick stammered.

'*Sit down*!' Adam roared as he kicked the desk chair and pointed to it.

Nick sat down, his eyes wide with terror, a line of sweat forming across his hairline.

I left the room.

From inside my bedroom with the door closed, I couldn't make out Adam's words but his shouting was constant for several minutes.

Nick knocked on my door ten minutes later and walked in with his shoulders slumped and his head hanging low. 'Sorry, Mum,' he muttered, struggling to maintain his composure. 'I won't ever disrespect you like that again.'

'Thank you, Nick,' I gulped.

I looked for Adam and found him out in the garage, ferociously scrubbing the rims on the wheels of his car.

I lightly touched his shoulder. 'Thank you. I don't deserve you to defend me.'

'You're still his mother. No son of mine talks to his mother like that,' he said without looking up.

Adam spent three straight hours the next afternoon hovering around Nick in the dining room while he made him complete the assignment. We never did make that appointment to see his teacher.

The next day I rang Sarah.

'Hey, Meliboots,' she said when she heard my weak hello, and I immediately dissolved into tears. She listened for a long time and soothed and comforted me the way she'd always done before.

'I was angry last time we talked,' she said later in the conversation, when I'd settled down and begged her to forgive me. 'I said what I had to say. Doesn't mean I don't love you, Mel. You're still my favourite person.'

I asked how things were with Ryan.

'Don't worry about that,' she said dismissively. 'It's all good. He believes me now. And he knows people make mistakes, so he hasn't got a problem with you. Adam will come around too, don't worry. Promise him it will never happen again, and really mean it, and he'll come around, you'll see. I know him, he'll forgive you.'

She was right, he did. Eventually.

The turning point between Adam and me came the following Saturday night, thirteen days after my return home from the weekend with Matt. Not forgiveness yet, just the turning point. Adam was the keynote speaker at a hospital fundraising ball, so we had no choice but to attend together.

He didn't speak to me during the half-hour drive there, which was the longest amount of time we'd spent alone since I came home. He grunted when I complimented him on how handsome he looked in his tuxedo, and he made no comment about my appearance, even though I was dressed to the nines.

Once we arrived at the ball he was in his element, entertaining an entourage of fans. I stayed politely on the sidelines as always, smiling and joining in the conversation only when required. Neither of us danced.

After dinner, one of his colleague's wives asked me where I'd bought my beaded necklace.

'I made it.' I smiled, instinctively reaching my hand up to play with the Murano glass beads.

'Wow, it's beautiful, Mel. I didn't know you made your own jewellery. Aren't you clever?'

'Yes, there are lots of things about Melissa you don't know, Sue,' Adam said acerbically. 'She's very clever at hiding things, aren't you, Mel? In fact I'm still discovering some *very* interesting things about her myself that I had no idea about.'

'Adam!' I snapped, and shot him a warning look he pretended not to see.

Sue smiled uncomfortably and found an excuse to leave us. Adam then moved on to the next person and started a long and detailed analysis of the performance of the Australian cricket team in the latest one-day match, his back turned to me the whole time.

I found the bathroom and locked myself in a toilet stall. Kicking off the painful twelve-centimetre Louboutins, I flipped the toilet lid down and sat on it with my evening dress around my hips and my feet up against the door, until I heard things winding up in the ballroom. Then I fixed myself up and went to find the husband who hated me.

Adam had had too much to drink and seemed somewhat more relaxed as I drove us home, just after midnight.

I decided to take advantage of it. 'Please can we talk, Adam?'

He was silent.

'Please? I need to know what you're thinking.'

'You need to ask? Can't you guess what I'm thinking?'

And the deluge began.

I drove us to a car park facing the Swan River. I stared at the procession of headlights on the freeway that crossed over the river while I faced my husband's wrath.

He pummelled me with questions about the affair, most of which I refused to answer, to his fury. I admitted to meeting Matt on the flight to Melbourne, seeing him again that night, and sneaking off to the hotel when he later found me in Perth. I confessed to sleeping with him and using Sarah's make-believe problems as an alibi. But no matter how hard Adam pushed me, I didn't divulge the intimate details of our relationship that he demanded from me. I lied about it at every turn.

'Did he get any footage of you naked?'

'No.'

'Did you blow him?'

'No.'

'Was he bigger than me? Better than me?'

'No. *No!*'

'Well what was so good about him then?' he roared.

'Nothing. Nothing at all,' I cried. 'I told you, I went crazy, I lost my mind. It was just sex.'

'If you don't give a shit about him, then let me talk to him. I was going to call him when I found the filth on your phone but stopped myself when I realised you'd be there with him,' he growled. 'I have the right to tell this arsehole what he needs to hear.'

'I'm begging you, Adam, please don't ever call him. It'd kill me if you did,' I said desperately.

He gave me a sideways glance. 'Do you know what? I think you actually love this prick you're protecting,' he said through gritted teeth.

'No, I don't,' I lied, avoiding his eyes.

He snorted. 'So if you don't love him, but you took that huge risk of getting caught, then he must've been a fucking good screw.'

'Don't,' I winced.

'Tell me,' he said with a sarcastic laugh, 'what did he do that's so good you ruined your marriage for it? In what way did he *fuck you* that made it worth abandoning your children to run away with him for the weekend? Tell me the kind of *fucking* you want that I haven't give you. Because I saw the video of him going down on you and quite frankly, I give you better than that.' His nostrils flared.

'Adam, please, please *stop!*'

He had been relentlessly grilling me for over an hour and he was becoming more and more upset, as was I, at the humiliation of it all.

I began calmly, 'Adam, I know there's nothing worse I could have done to you. I know that. I can't tell you how much I hate myself for it. You deserve better than me. I've always known that you're too good for me,' I said with emphasis. 'And then I went and proved it right. But I promise you it's finished. I'm never going to see him again. I wish I could show you my heart so that you could see how sorry I am that I hurt you. I know it's going to take a long time to move through this, if we ever can. If you even want to. I know it's selfish of me but I desperately want you to forgive me. Because I can't imagine my life without you in it.'

He was quietly listening, not moving a muscle as I spoke.

'But, Adam, you have to stop these questions. I know you want answers, but I'm not going to give you any more to imagine than what you've already seen for yourself. You deserve to know everything, of course you do, but I'm scared that the more I tell you, and the more you can picture me with him, it will destroy us irrevocably. Do you think there's any hope that you can forgive me, even without knowing all the details? I'm so sorry.'

He was silent for a long while, and then he let his mask fall.

'I don't know if I can ever trust you again,' he said, his tone much less aggressive, his eyes locked on mine. 'And that kills me. Everything I believed about you is gone now. Everything I believed about us, it's gone. There's no safety in this marriage for me any more. I've seen what you're capable of, and I'm shocked. I think of you with him and it makes me sick. I can't stop replaying it in my head, I really can't. It's driving me crazy. I feel like a failure, a loser. I couldn't keep my wife from looking elsewhere for sex. I don't know where to go from here. I don't know if things will ever get better between us.'

His eyes were tortured. I could see how real and how deep

his pain was. He'd been concealing it from me by avoiding me up until now.

I touched his arm. 'You're not a failure, Adam, I'm the one who failed you. And I didn't go looking for sex, I promise. I know it sounds clichéd but it really was something that just happened. I didn't plan it. I was bored with myself, with life. I was looking for an adrenaline rush, and I had an instant attraction to him. It was bad timing for me to meet him when I did. But I swear to you, Adam, I love you very, very much. I want to make you believe in us again. Please let me try to gain your trust back.'

It was as though he hadn't heard me. He took a deep breath. 'I've always known you didn't love me the way I loved you. I just pretended to ignore it. I've spent our whole marriage convincing myself I made you happy, that you didn't marry me only because you were pregnant. I wanted so much more from you, I wanted us to be closer, but you always held back from me.'

'No I didn't,' I said, instantly becoming defensive. I withdrew my hand from his arm. *Me* holding back? What about him?

'Yes, you did, Mel. You held back. From the very start you held back,' he said adamantly, giving me a sharp look. 'For about the first five or so years, every time we had sex I felt like you were just going through the motions. We can tell when women do that. And I know you very well, better than you realise So, I stopped trying. I didn't make demands on you any more. I thought if we did it just once a week, it'd be enough.' He ran his hands through his hair. 'And then all of a sudden you were right into it. And I loved that. Then I figured out pretty quickly that it wasn't me you were into. But still I thought if I satisfied you and gave you great sex, maybe you'd see what you could have with me, and it'd bring you closer and make you stop thinking of whoever else you were thinking about. So I tried my best to turn you on, but clearly that didn't happen. I'm just a sucker.'

'Oh, Adam.' I was reeling. 'I don't know what to say. You *have* given me great sex.'

He sighed. 'No, we've never actually had great sex, because it takes two people to do that. You can't have great sex with a woman who's a million miles away, thinking of someone else.' He stopped for a second and looked out his window. 'Obviously I didn't satisfy you. I couldn't feel like less of a man than I do now. And that makes me *so* angry because I wanted our sex life to be fantastic. If you'd wanted it. But you never wanted it with me.' He let out another big sigh.

'Adam, I honestly never got that vibe from you, that you wanted to be passionate with me.' I was so confused. 'I always felt like I wasn't pretty enough or sexy enough for you, like I had to ask you to notice me. You've never been all over me. You just sort of mucked around, like sex was a big game to you, not like you seriously wanted me.'

He looked at me as if I was thick-headed. 'What? I've never made you feel pretty? Why do you think I asked you out in the first place? Because I thought you were ugly? You think I married you only because I knocked you up? I'm not a friggin' saint, you know. I think you're incredibly sexy and gorgeous, I always have. But it turns me off when you want me to say it all the time. You should just know I feel that way without needing to be constantly told. You're just so bloody needy. "Adam, look at me. Adam, am I beautiful?" Give me a break! You were always beautiful to me, even before you met that fucking bastard and turned into a Barbie doll overnight. And like I just told you, how could I be all over you when I knew you weren't interested in me? I mucked around because I was insecure about it. I'm the one who's never been good enough for you.' He swallowed. 'Not the other way around.'

'Adam, I never, ever thought I was too good for you,' I said fiercely. 'I've just felt for our whole marriage that you've never opened up to me, never been passionate about me, about us. How could we get closer without talking about our feelings and our fears and our dreams? I've always wanted more from you too. But I didn't get it, so how could I bond with you sexually? Don't you see that it's all connected?'

He took a while to answer. He loosened his tie and rolled his head around. Only two weeks after being with Matt and professing my undying love for him, I now found myself desperate to have sex with Adam right there in the car. And I had no idea why. I was angry and hurt, and wishing he'd been this open and honest with me years earlier, so maybe we would have had a decent marriage. But still, here I was, burning with the need to have sex with him.

He broke into my thoughts. 'You can't expect me to open up to you when from the very start it's been clear I'm not the type of man you wanted,' he sighed again. 'I'm not the sort of person to sit and spend hours analysing my feelings. To me we could still be close without having to do that. Why not just go through life loving each other and standing by each other, raising a family together and having a laugh, and having great sex? Why do we have to sit and stare at each other, talking deep and meaningful crap, to feel close?'

I unwound the window and took big breaths of cold air.

'You're the only person in my life who makes me feel shallow,' he went on. 'And you, of all people, should know better. I'm not shallow, I just don't dwell on things like you do. Life's too short. Why waste a second not being happy and trying to forget insignificant problems instead of analysing them to death? And, I probably would have been happy to talk to you more and open up to you if I didn't feel so judged by you, it didn't exactly inspire me to expose more of myself. I've had my defences up around you for our entire marriage; it's a bloody exhausting way to live. But you know what? I tried to make the best of it and I honoured our wedding vows. And I don't know if I'll ever forgive you for not standing by your vows too.' He rested his head back against the seat and shut his eyes.

I was stunned into silence. I didn't have the words to tell him how sorry I was. I'd spent our whole marriage frustrated at how little he understood me, when all along I'd never made the effort to try and understand or accept him. I was sickened by how selfish I'd been. And on top of all that, I'd betrayed him in the most hurtful way imaginable.

I reached for his hand and silently thanked God when he didn't pull it away. I stroked each of his fingers with the pad of my thumb.

'Honey, from the bottom of my heart, I'm so sorry,' I said, after a while, stroking his arm and then his face. He kept his eyes shut and I kept talking. 'There's a lot we never had in common. You weren't into the deep and meaningful stuff and you're right, I did judge you and I did hold back from you because of that. And then I didn't even realise that I was holding back from you, so I became angry when you weren't all over me the way I wanted you to be. Everything has fallen into place for me now, I understand you for the first time, I think. I really hope we do get through this and that one day you will find it in you to forgive me, because I think we've finally got a shot at making our marriage really, really good. Now that I know what an idiot I've been, and what I've cost us all these years. I love you. I really love you. Don't give up on me, Adam. Please don't give up on us.'

He shrugged. He looked spent from all the talking, his face was drawn. He'd held so much in for so long, I could only imagine how fragile he must have felt now that he'd laid it all out there. But I was very grateful he had. Now we had a future. If he could forgive me.

'Please just keep talking to me,' I begged him. 'I miss you. I need you. Please don't shut me out any more.'

He nodded. 'I'm tired. Let's go home.'

'Will you come back to our bed tonight?' I asked with baited breath. 'Please come back.'

He nodded again, but he looked miserable. I knew it was up to me to repair this relationship. After all, I'd single-handedly created all the damage.

When we arrived home, I approached Adam in the bedroom as he undressed. I worked hard to push Matt out of my head as I helped him undo his shirt buttons. He was reticent at first, but it took no more than a few of my kisses on his chest for him to respond.

He pulled my dress off and pushed me down onto the bed. Panting heavily, he climbed on top and we were having sex within seconds. It was unlike anything we'd had together before. It was gritty and it was raw and it was incredible. In reclaiming his wife for himself, he didn't hold back and, being desperate to prove my love for him, neither did I. We ravaged each other. It was vastly different from the sex I'd had with Matt. There was less of a soulful connection, but I had no guilt, and that was a beautiful thing.

When it was over, we lay still and silent, holding hands, until Adam fell asleep. I stayed awake all night. Why had I made such a mess of this life with Adam? Why hadn't I seen him in this light fourteen years ago? I thought of all the time wasted and of all we had missed.

THE HONEYMOON

MATT

'Are you absolutely sure you won't come with me, Matty?' Lydia asked one last time while I rubbed sunscreen on her spray-tanned back.

'Positive, thanks, babe. I really want to finish this book, it's getting to the good bit.'

'Why don't I just tell you what happens and then you can come with me?' She laughed.

'You better not! Look, there's your man turning up now. Go have fun. See you in a couple of hours, hey?' I wiped my hands on a towel and gave her a quick pat on the bottom.

'Okay. Bye, honey.' She kissed my cheek and ran towards the tour guide who was dragging an ocean kayak into the water.

It was the fifth day of our honeymoon.

The guide stood in the shallow water, looking around and checking his watch. His face broke into an enormous grin when he saw Lydia jogging towards him in her tiny black bikini, the breeze blowing her cropped blonde hair.

I sat up on my elbows and watched them from where I lay on the sand. He helped her onto the kayak. From the tinkling sound of her laughter, he was obviously a comedian as well as a tour guide. He was bronzed, blond and buffed. He was flirting with her already, smiling sleazily and wrapping his arms around her as he demonstrated the correct rowing technique.

Lydia lifted her sunglasses off her eyes and rested them on her head. Then she tilted her head back so she was eye to eye with him, and I saw her smile the smile she knew worked every time.

I should've been fuming. I should've walked over there and kissed my wife or put a protective arm around her to make my presence felt before he took off with her for two hours.

But I remained where I was. I wasn't in the least bit jealous. And I knew why.

Before she paddled off, she looked over her shoulder and smiled as she waved at me. I waved back, thinking about how I knew with absolute certainty I didn't love her, and never would.

What the hell had I done?

Lydia and her admirer soon disappeared from sight out on the warm aqua waters of Port Douglas. I sank back down onto the sand and let my mind wander back to the last night with Mel, before I returned to Melbourne with my tail between my legs, begging Lydia to forgive me. After some token hysterics, she happily continued to plan the wedding. I'd blamed the break-up and my subsequent walkabout interstate on an outlandish case of pre-wedding jitters.

On that last night in Perth, when I was waiting to board the plane back to Melbourne, I received a text message from Mel.

I'm so sorry, Matt, but I won't be calling you tomorrow, or any day after that. I have a family. Don't know what I was thinking. Adam knows about us now. I'm so desperately sorry. For all of it.

I was suddenly lonely. So I rang Tom's home number. Emma answered the phone.

'Hi, Em.'

'Do you know what bloody time it is here?' she whispered angrily.

I slapped my forehead. 'Oh crap, Em, sorry! I forgot about the time difference. I'm just at the airport and wanted to talk to Tom. Did I wake the baby?'

'No, you didn't.' Her tone was clipped. 'He's always awake. So am I. I've forgotten what sleep feels like. Tom's asleep, and I'm not waking him up.'

'S'okay, I'll see him at work tomorrow anyway. Sorry, Em. Hope you get some sleep,' I croaked. 'See you later then.'

'Matt, wait,' she said as I was about to hang up. 'Are you okay?' she asked, reverting back to the warm voice I was used to hearing from her.

'Not really,' I murmured. 'She's not leaving her husband.'

Emma sighed. 'They never do, Matt.'

I nodded to myself.

'Lyds has been a wreck all week,' she said. 'She'd take you back in a heartbeat, you know.'

I gave a loud sigh.

'Come home and sort yourself out, Matt. Come home and marry her.'

So I went home and married her.

And now as I lay on the sand, all I wanted to do was to turn back the clock and be in the hotel room once more, with Mel's fingernails running up and down my bare chest.

But instead I came back to Melbourne and made the biggest mistake of my life. I was angry as I sat there alone on my honeymoon while my gorgeous new wife was turning on someone else.

And I directed that anger not at Lydia, but at Mel. She'd sent me a text about the chipped shell I'd given her on the beach in

Scarborough. She'd lost it, the message said. That was it. That's all she wanted to tell me. When I replied that I'd lost her she didn't respond. I'd had my heart ripped apart by her and she was more worried about losing a stupid shell than losing me. I wanted her to know I wasn't waiting for her any more. I wanted her to feel what it was like to be stood down in favour of someone else.

I took my phone out of the beach bag and sent her a text.

I'm on my honeymoon. I married her, just like you wanted. Happy now?

I wasn't expecting her to reply as quickly as she did.

You fucking arsehole.

I read her venomous message in disbelief. I loved this woman. She loved me. What were we doing apart? How could things have gone this wrong?

I wrote her another text.

I love you Mel.

But I never sent that one. Instead, I found and deleted every photo and video that I'd taken of her. I was a married man after all.

RESET

MEL

It took the best part of a year to rebuild our marriage. The initial talk in the car park opened the floodgates, and after many more tearful conversations that spanned over months and months, Adam slowly started to forgive me.

We had some very dark days when I was sure he'd leave me, and I was tempted to leave a handful of times myself.

He'd sometimes walk into the house after work and stare at me in a way that made my stomach twist because I knew immediately what he'd been thinking about. Or out of the blue he'd bark a random question about the affair, and then slam doors or leave the house for hours when I refused to answer.

One day I came back inside from hanging out the washing to find him sitting on the couch, bent over my phone.

'What the hell are you doing?' I became hysterical. 'Let it go, Adam! It's over! It's been over for more than two months. When are you going to learn to trust me? *I'm not in touch with him!*'

'I'm a long, long way off trusting you yet. Doing stuff like checking this,' he said unapologetically, waving my phone in the air, 'is helping me trust you. It reassures me.'

'It has a delete setting that I know how to use, you know,' I snapped, roughly wiping the tears from my cheeks. I snatched the phone out of his hand.

Sometimes it felt as if the marriage wasn't even worth the effort of saving, that it was all just too hard. But the morning after that first ground-breaking talk, Lily jumped onto our bed and shook me awake.

'Mum, Mum, guess what? Dad's making you breakfast! See Mum, he loves you again. It's going to be okay now.' Her eyes shone.

I took my daughter into my arms and felt real hope for our family. I hung onto moments like those to get me through that awful first year.

As the weeks and months crawled past, the children watched our slow progress with keen eyes. As they saw their father begin to forgive me, they relaxed once more. Nick, who'd hardly acknowledged me since discovering the affair, slowly let me into his life again.

'Hey, Mum, what's for dinner?' he asked, throwing his bag on the floor after football training one evening.

'Home-made pizza,' I said without looking up from slicing onions.

'Awesome!' He walked into the kitchen and planted a kiss on my cheek. 'You're the best, Mum,' he said as he picked at some shredded mozzarella.

My heart soared. Nick's rejection of me had been one of the worst repercussions of my infidelity. He never did quite completely forgive me though, I never fully got him back.

And in those first difficult months, as I chipped away at rebuilding my marriage, I still ached for Matt every day. I longed to know what he was doing, where he was going, how he was feeling. I continued to carry the guilt that came with knowing Adam loved me more than I deserved and that he still didn't have sole ownership of my heart.

I wondered if Matt missed me as intensely as I missed him. It surprised me that he never called. Even though he'd been adamant that if I returned to Adam then he was done with me, part of me still thought he'd continue to try to make contact. He had obviously not been bluffing. If he had called I would never have answered, but still it bruised my heart and my ego. Was it possible he'd already met someone else? Or could he have reunited with Lydia? I didn't know which was worse, but both thoughts were equally selfish of me. Would I ever learn how to change this awful flaw in myself?

On a day where things seemed particularly hopeless with Adam, I went as far as keying Matt's number into the phone, but I never pressed *Call*. I knew it would only lead to more pain for all of us if I did. And I was under no illusion that Adam hadn't found a way to check my phone records, even though I had all the passwords. Adam would have found a way around that for sure. The consequences of ringing Matt would be catastrophic, and just knowing that was enough to stop me from doing it.

Each day I didn't cry over Matt, I congratulated myself on surviving another 'clean' day. It was like a drug addiction. At certain times I craved a hit of Matt so badly it made it impossible to take a deep breath, sit still, or have a single other thought.

And then there was the day when I fell off the wagon and sent him a text. I couldn't help it. I was too shattered.

It was the night of Lily's ballet competition. The venue was on the other side of the river, and crossing the city in peak hour traffic was something I'd neglected to factor in. Lily became increasingly panicky, checking her watch obsessively as we remained stationary in the car, a sea of red brake lights ahead of us.

We made it to the hall five minutes late and in my rush to get her inside, I unwittingly left the car unlocked and my handbag in the backseat. Unaware the car was being broken into, I sat in a musty corridor, on a wobbly chair surrounded by other stage mums. I took my phone out of my pocket and read celebrity gossip online to distract myself from worrying about Lily's performance.

She emerged forty-five minutes later, relieved and elated, not knowing the results of her individual dance yet, but confident she'd done her best. We put our arms around each other and walked out to the car, only to discover the stereo gone and my handbag missing.

I was too caught up cancelling credit cards over the phone to realise what was gone. But later that night, as I went in search of the shell before taking a shower, I remembered my wallet had been stolen. I realised then I had nothing left of Matt. Really nothing.

That's when I sent the text.

I lost the shell.

He didn't reply. It was past midnight in Melbourne, after all.

I imagined another woman in his bed and felt unhinged with jealousy. In Scarborough, whenever I lay there panting and sweating after sex, he'd leaned on his elbows, pursed his lips, and gently blown cold air all over my hot skin, top to toe. He'd laughed at my delight and told me it was the 'Matthew Butler signature move'. Was he doing the same thing to some other girl tonight? Was she prettier than me? Did she turn him on more than I had? Was he obsessed with her now? Overnight, I chewed my fingernails so far down my skin bled. At six am my phone vibrated.

The shell is replaceable. I lost you.

The message reminded me of the hold he had over me and I wasn't equipped to deal with it. My only thought for the entire day was to pack a bag and get on the next flight to Melbourne. But God help me, I loved my husband and my children too much to go through with it. I was tortured to the point of insanity.

'Focus on Adam,' I begged of myself.

In my moments of weakness that was my mantra: 'Focus on Adam.' I would run through the mental list of all the things I had to be grateful for, and when that failed, I'd ring Sarah. She'd listen to me weep for Matt and then gently remind me of the reasons I'd broken up with him. More than once she read me the riot act and told me to pull my head in.

'Get counselling,' she told me, many times over. 'You need professional help, you're clinically depressed. Don't you recognise the symptoms in yourself? There's no life in your voice, Meliboots, you should hear how dead you sound. That fuckwit Matt's killed something in you. I hate that guy.'

But I simply couldn't talk about it to a stranger, even though I knew Sarah was right and I was in dire need of therapy. Because I felt too ashamed to tell anyone else what I'd done.

I didn't dare tell Sarah I'd been hanging on to Matt's shell for months, so I had nobody to commiserate with over my loss. I couldn't even comfort eat, the way I'd always done in the past. I had no appetite from the day Matt and I left each other.

And somehow, after everything, Matt still managed to break what was left of my heart, even after he'd left. Out of the blue I received a text message from him.

I'm on my honeymoon. I married her, just like you wanted. Happy now?

It was cruel and his intention to hurt me was devastating. How could he not have warned me he was getting married? His anger towards me was palpable. Well, I was angry now too. He'd said he could never marry her. He'd acted insulted when I suggested he go back to her, as if he'd rather die than do that. And now he'd done it, he'd actually gone and married her. My tongue felt thick as I swallowed the rage.

I immediately broke my vow to not contact him and replied quickly and viciously. Then I cried myself stupid for hours.

When Adam brought the children home from a church youth conference later in the evening, I was sound asleep. They didn't wake me and I stayed asleep until the alarm went off the next morning. I immediately wanted to take another sleeping pill when I opened my eyes to a new day where Matt was married.

I never heard from him again. That final interaction had cheapened and demeaned all we'd had together, but it went a long way in helping me to finally focus on Adam instead of Matt. And from that day on, if he ever popped into my head during sex, I immediately shut those thoughts out and made myself open my eyes to see that it was Adam I was with. That had to be a good thing.

'Bluff it till you become it,' Sarah had told me earlier when I'd confessed to her that I sometimes felt like a fraud when I was with Adam. 'You'll get there, I believe in your love for each other. I think you don't give it enough credit.'

She was spot on. Adam and I grew closer the more I made myself spend time alone with him, have fun with him, listen to him, attend to him. It worked. Bit by bit, I went from bluffing being someone who was in a happy marriage to genuinely becoming it.

The fundamental differences between us didn't change but we both made more of an effort to be upfront. Our once glossy relationship was far more volatile as a result, but it was real for the first time.

His lack of trust in me, and my ongoing burden of guilt, were obstacles that proved harder to overcome. It was a matter of making the most of our life together, despite the invisible chains around each of us, pulling us in different directions. Happiness took work. Sometimes the tug of those invisible chains around my neck chafed me till I bled invisible blood.

But I preferred this life, pain included, to the one of pretence we had led before. We were no longer strangers to each other. I'd come tumbling down off the pedestal Adam had put me on and I liked having my feet on the ground. I think Adam also liked that I'd been brought down a peg or two and humbled by this spectacular fall from grace. And I liked that he was openly vulnerable for the first time since I'd known him. I loved that. We were different and that was okay. We weren't born soul mates and that was okay too.

And our sex life improved beyond my wildest expectations. We were intimate frequently and spontaneously. I told him what I enjoyed and what I didn't, and he did the same. We were both quick learners. And I discovered that once his defences were down, and he was confident that I was 'into it', he was a sensational lover. As we lay in each other's arms, out of breath with exhaustion, we regretted that this wasn't the way it had always been.

Towards the end of that year I could honestly say I was genuinely happy with Adam. Not ecstatically, over the moon, shout-it-from-the-rooftops happy – my self-loathing made that impossible. But I was much happier than I had ever envisaged being with Adam. And he was happy too.

Matt was never far from my mind, but he wasn't taking up as much space in it. I tried harder to forget him. My chemical addiction to him was still there, but the longer I went without a hit, the easier it was to get through another 'clean' day. After months and months of staying clean, it got to the point where I couldn't remember the last day I had cried over him.

A little more than two years after the dreadful night of my return from the weekend at the hotel, Adam and I went to Fiji to celebrate his fiftieth birthday. Nick was sixteen by then, Lily was fifteen and we were happy to leave them in the care of friends' parents. They were outraged that we would leave them behind, but we both wanted time out just for us, so we told them to get over themselves and waved goodbye.

DONE

MATT

I couldn't do this any more, I was finished. Lydia was finished too. She barely raised an eyebrow when I told her I wanted out. As long as she got Otto, she said. He was hers not ours, she said. I'd given him to her for her birthday in a desperate attempt to provide some of the love I couldn't give her myself.

So she'd taken the dog in the padded Chanel dog carrier and clip-clopped in teetering heels out of our house and back to her parents'. Nearly two years of marriage down the drain and neither of us could care less.

I snatched the envelope holding the divorce papers off the desk. As soon as they were signed and witnessed, I'd have a second chance at life. I almost skipped to the car.

FIJI

MEL

I fell in love with Adam in Fiji. The kind of love that makes your palms sweaty, and your heart race so fast it makes you dizzy. And I fell for him hard.

We'd been married sixteen years and never had more than the odd night without kids around us. We'd never had a honeymoon. This was it. We made the most of every minute and the more minutes that went by, the more I discovered just how great we could be, him and me.

It started with happy hour cocktails standing around the main cabana, surrounded mostly by young honeymooners. It was a disco theme night. Adam's blond chest hair stuck out from the mostly unbuttoned pink satin shirt he'd tucked into astoundingly high-waisted blue flares, and my short silver-sequined dress resembled a disco ball. We both enjoyed more than a few cocktails and I actually had fun dancing with him, which surprised me because I'd always dreaded it before. I think it was because there was nobody else he was trying to impress that night. He didn't ask anybody else to dance, which was a first, it was just about him and me.

Towards the end of the night, the limbo stick was brought out to a round of cheers. I'd always been unnaturally flexible, so I figured I had a good shot, despite being much older than most of the other women taking part. I figured right.

As the DJ pumped out 'Knock on Wood', I kicked off my platform shoes and arched backwards, clearing the low pole easily. In the end it came down to me and one other woman, playing off for a free cocktail. I turned to look for Adam to give him a thumbs up. He was leaning back in a wicker chair, staring at me in a way that made his thoughts abundantly clear. He'd never looked sexier to me.

And right there in the sweltering disco hut on the beach, with bright spinning lights and music blaring around us, with just a look, my husband made my belly flip for the first time in our marriage.

'I love you,' I mouthed, pointing at him, and he smiled. I think it was the first time he ever truly believed me.

We snorkelled together through warm lagoons along fluorescent-coloured reefs with tiny fish nibbling at our elbows, and we had sunset picnics on our own private beach, delivered to us by the cheerful staff. We relaxed for hours on the balcony of our luxurious hut, soaking in the magnificent views of the surrounding Pacific Ocean while we sipped Pina Coladas.

It was a honeymoon that was worth waiting sixteen years for. I'd fallen in love with my husband and I couldn't wipe the smile off my face. Every single day that week I'd experienced the best, best sex I'd ever had, and I knew there was lots more of that to look forward to when we got home again.

Were we always on the same page in Fiji? No. Did Adam roll his eyes when I asked him to list his greatest hopes from one to five, and his greatest fears too? Yes. Did he tell me to stop ruining the moment when we were relaxed sunbathing with stupid pointless shit like that? Yes. But did he make me laugh until I literally wet my pants, did he massage my feet while we reminisced about when our children were small and the funny things they used to do and say, did we use every excuse to hop into bed and have hot humid sex that left me completely sated, and was my heart content every morning when I woke up and found myself wrapped in his arms? Absolutely.

We left Fiji a solid, unbreakable team.

We were settled, happy, and living the good life. It had been two and a half years since the affair and it never came up any more. Adam and I had moved on from that. So of course Matt chose that time to shake us up again.

Adam had been unusually quiet through dinner with the kids. He stared at his plate without blinking, and Lily's daily blow-by-blow recount of what happened at school went without his usual funny interjections.

Once dinner was over and the kids were upstairs, I asked him if he was okay, looking at him with concern as I scraped leftover food into the kitchen bin.

He nodded thoughtfully.

'You don't seem it. You sure? What's on your mind?' I put down the plates and walked over to where he was still sitting at the table.

'I met Matt today,' he said, looking away.

What did he just say?

'He's different from what I expected.' His voice was heavy.

I thought I was going to be sick. I tried to breathe and control the upheaval of chicken schnitzel rising in my throat.

'Oh my God.' I pulled out a chair and sat down. 'What happened?'

He turned to look at me with the saddest eyes. 'I can't talk about it. It was quick. Only a couple of minutes. He was at the clinic.'

'Oh, Adam. I'm sorry. I'm so sorry.'

He gulped and nodded.

'Dad!' Nick called from upstairs. '*Daaad*! Come watch this, it's awesome!'

He stood and walked slowly upstairs.

I didn't have another chance to be alone with him for the rest of the evening until he joined me in bed. I hadn't touched the mountain of ironing I'd promised myself I would do that night. I'd just sat on the bed staring into space instead.

What the hell had happened today? Why was Matt even here in Perth? Why would he go to Adam's clinic? What did he say to Adam? I imagined ten different ways that conversation would have gone down and every version was ugly. I imagined how it must feel to come face to face with the man who'd slept with your wife. I agonised about it all evening.

Adam sighed wearily as he took off his clothes and climbed into bed. He reached across and switched off the bedside lamp. I felt around in the darkness for his hand under the sheet and intertwined my shaking fingers through his. He gave them a squeeze.

'Please tell me what happened, Adam.'

'I can't.'

'Honey, I don't know what to say. I haven't heard from him. I didn't even know he was in town. Promise. There's nothing going on between us, I swear.'

'I believe you.' His breath was unsteady.

'Adam, are you crying?'

He still didn't answer. I rolled onto my side to face him and touched his cheek with my palm. It was wet. It broke my heart.

'Oh my darling, I'm so sorry you're hurting. I love you.'

He stopped pretending he wasn't crying. 'He was smug. About you. He was so smug.'

'What did he do, Adam? What did he say?'

'I really don't want to go into it, Mel, please.'

My mind raced into overdrive that night as I lay wide awake listening to Adam's peaceful snores once he'd fallen asleep. Matt was here! He was right here. And he'd found Adam. He obviously wanted me to know he was here. Why? What for? Had he come back to claim me? Oh, please God, no. Please don't let him show up at my clinic next, it would kill me. Not for any reason other than I couldn't bear to cause Adam any more pain.

It was when I had that conscious realisation that the man lying next to me was actually the love of my life, that I fell asleep too.

THE CONSULTING ROOM

MATT

'Excuse me, where's the bathroom?' I asked the girl behind the front desk at the specialist suites. My consultation with the orthopaedic surgeon was finished and the date was set for surgery on my left shoulder. He estimated full recovery would take no longer than six to eight weeks, which seemed optimistic, but I guess we'd have to wait and see.

I started down the hall for the bathroom, when the sun reflecting off a metal name plate on an open door caught my eye. And I stopped.

Mr A Harding – Anaesthetist

I glanced into the room. It was empty. I hesitantly took a step inside and looked around. The room was as sterile as a consulting room could get. White on white. The biggest desk I'd ever seen was at one end, with a massive leather swivel chair behind it. The brag wall on the opposite side of the room was intimidating. There were a dozen certificates up there at the very least. There were a couple of smaller frames on the desk. Photos? I walked over, picked one up and turned it around.

It had been two and a half years since everything had ended. But when I saw her smiling face and her smiling eyes, it all rushed back. All at once.

The door swung open and hit the wall. I jumped.

'Hey buddy, can I help you there?' he bellowed.

Buddy. Instant friendship.

He came into the room and made for the desk. As he walked past me, he gave my back a big unnecessary slap and I got a strong whiff of his aftershave. It was the same as mine. I wondered was it sheer coincidence, or was it Mel's doing that we smelled the same?

He was huge, built like a tank. Slicked blond hair, piercing blue eyes. Biceps bulging inside his designer shirt. Silk black tie, pointy leather shoes, Rolex on his wrist. He was a jock. A big smug rich jock.

'No, I'm good, thanks. Wrong room, I think.'

'Who you looking for, mate?'

His voice. Jesus, why so loud?

'I just the need toilet actually. This clearly isn't it though.'

And then came the laugh. It rattled my eardrums. It was the loudest, most irritating laugh I had heard. Ever.

This was who she wouldn't/couldn't leave? This?

'I know your wife.' It was out before I could stop myself.

The laughing died down but the grin stayed there. 'Do you? You know Melissa?'

'Mel. Yeah, I do.' I stared into his eyes.

A few seconds went by.

'Really?' No trace of a smile now. 'That so?'

'We know each other well. Really well.'

'Get out.' His voice was suddenly an octave deeper and barely more than a whisper.

'I enjoyed fucking your wife senseless,' I said, looking at the framed photograph of Mel in my hands before putting it back down on the desk. 'She was desperate for it.' I smiled a tiny smile when I saw the effect that had on him.

He inhaled deeply and blew the air out hard. The muscles at the front of his neck twitched. 'Get the fuck out of this room, you piece of shit, before I do something to get myself thrown in jail,' he hissed, his white lips curling. Rows of frown lines cracked the perfection of his tanned forehead.

Although my hands were shaking and my legs felt weak, an evil pleasure worked its way up my chest and warmed my ears as I approached the door.

'Tell her I said hi,' I said with my back to him. I gently closed the door behind me.

As soon as the door was shut, the warmth drained from my body and the regret smashed into me like a wall of cold water.

I hurried out of the building and took in big gulps of fresh air. The ground was spinning. I walked to my car and kicked the back tyre as hard as I could, three, four, five times. I leaned against the car, panting, and threw my head back.

'Fuck! *Argh*! You arsehole! Why? Why?' I shouted at myself as I pounded at my forehead with closed fists.

All this time I thought I hated him, but I didn't. I hated myself.

BIRTHDAY

MEL

Five months later, on a scorching January day, I turned forty. My birthday was heralded by a massive party thrown by Adam aboard his brand-new, astronomically priced yacht named *Sweet Lily*. It was the second largest privately owned yacht in Perth.

When I first heard of his plans, I argued with Adam that I didn't want a huge party, that it just wasn't my cup of tea. But he insisted that I deserved spoiling so a big party it was.

Of the hundred and twenty people he'd invited on the night, about fifteen of them were my friends. I took extra care applying my makeup and wore an elegant black silk cocktail dress, befitting of Dr Harding's wife.

Sarah came into my bedroom looking like a screen goddess in a cream sheath. She'd flown into Perth with Ryan and their children the previous day.

She came over to zip up my dress. 'Jesus, Mel, look at your body! When did you get so toned? This is the best body you've ever had.'

'You think? Thanks, Sare. I've been running with Adam in the mornings.'

'Are you kidding? You're running? You never run!'

'I do now.' I laughed.

'Well it's showing on you, honey, you look sensational.' Sarah looked me up and down admiringly.

I blushed. 'I'm surprised by how much I enjoy doing it actually. I'm fit enough to be able to talk with him while we run now. A few months ago I was only able to grunt a word or two. That's why I'm enjoying it now, I think, it's nice to have that time together at the start of the day.'

'I can't tell you how happy it makes me to see you two happy again, Meliboots.' She smiled and tilted her head. 'Do you still think about him though? You know … Matt?'

My breath caught at the sound of his name. 'Of course I do.' My happy mood dived. 'But I'd never do anything about it so you don't need to worry.'

'Did he ever try to contact you after he went to Adam's clinic that time?'

I shook my head.

'I thought he might have and you wouldn't want to tell me.'

'No,' I promised. 'I haven't heard from him since he told me he was on his honeymoon.' It still hurt that he sent me that message, even now after three years had passed.

'I wonder if he lives here?' she mused. 'He was at specialist suites. That's not exactly a touristy thing to do.'

'I don't know and I don't plan to find out,' I replied firmly. This wasn't a conversation I wanted to be having, especially not before my birthday party. 'Let's go back out to the boys, I haven't shown Adam this dress yet. Do you think he'll like it?'

'How could he not?' She gave me a hug. 'I'm proud of you, Mel.'

When she left, I looked at myself in the mirror. My body had indeed changed. The curves Matt had so loved were gone.

I could hear Adam and Ryan laughing together downstairs. It was the first time they had seen each other since Ryan had inadvertently exposed my affair to Adam. To my eternal gratitude, both of them pretended that that ugly chapter in our friendship had never taken place. But I couldn't help noticing the exaggerated camaraderie and laughter between them. It was as though the more noise they made, the more they hoped they could drown out the identical thoughts they were having.

My party was loud and busy. Adam had draped thousands of fairy lights all over the boat, and it sparkled as we sailed around the Swan River. Perth had turned on a magnificent balmy evening and the sky was littered with stars. There was a disc jockey on board and the tiny rented dance floor was well occupied all night. Everyone raved about the delicate finger food that had been supplied by a swanky inner-city restaurant. I didn't touch it.

I mingled to the best of my ability and then stuck close by Sarah.

At eleven o'clock I blew the candles out on a four-tiered chocolate mud cake from an award-winning French patisserie. Adam gave an irreverent speech that had all the guests rocking with laughter and then, in front of everyone, he presented me with a pair of Tiffany platinum and pink diamond earrings.

I kissed Adam long and hard as our audience wolf whistled. But I shut them out and kept kissing him, pulling him in closer towards me. I wanted to convey in that kiss how much he meant to me, how grateful I was that he had forgiven me and how hopeful I was that the old cliché was true and that life did begin at forty.

THE ARTICLE

MATT

Leaning against the letterbox in the sunshine I whistled as I unrolled the newspaper. The front page headline caught me mid-breath. I thought of him immediately. But when I went on to read the story and realised it actually was him, my vision blurred and I felt dizzy. I gripped the letterbox to steady myself and read the name again to make sure I wasn't mistaken. It was him.

My first instinct was to find Mel, to comfort her. But I knew I couldn't. I folded the newspaper and tucked it under my arm. I unlatched the rusty lock on the gate and walked along the narrow path, somehow not feeling the scorching asphalt burn the soles of my bare feet as I rounded the corner and headed to the beach.

As much as I thought I'd succeeded in closing my heart to her, I now found she was preserved in it. My heart was in fact a shrine to her. Every feeling and thought of her was unchanged. I remembered the shape of her calves as she stood on her toes and stretched wearing nothing but my old T-shirt. I remembered the condensation marks left on the wall in the shape of her palms and breasts. I remembered how she ate toast going around in a perfect square until all the crusts were gone first. I remembered the sound of her laughter and the taste of her skin.

I found an unoccupied spot of shade under a Norfolk Island pine and spread the paper out on the grass. I read the entire article again.

I wished I could go to her.

But of course I couldn't.

THE BIRD

MEL

Adam died the morning after my fortieth birthday party.

He was out surfing at Cottesloe Beach when he had a brain haemorrhage, the result of a previously undiagnosed aneurysm, and he drowned.

A seven-year-old boy playing on the shore was the first to see his washed-up body at nine o'clock in the morning. By that stage Adam had been dead for over two hours.

I was still in bed, nursing a hangover, when two policemen knocked on the front door. Sarah came up to the bedroom, her stricken face white and her hands twitching.

'Mel ... honey ... get up, darling. You have to come quickly, love. Something's happened.'

I ran down the stairs, two at a time.

'Liar!' I hissed at the solemn young policeman who broke the news to me, before slumping onto the floor at his feet.

Leaving Ryan at the house with the children still sleeping, Sarah drove me to the morgue where I identified Adam's bloated and blue body. He smelled of the ocean. They couldn't shut his eyes. Thank goodness the children would never have this image of him in their memories. Thank goodness I was here to see him and hold him one last time.

I stroked my husband's lifeless arm and kissed his cold cheek. We'd been asleep with our arms around each other only a few hours earlier.

Sarah and I didn't speak on the drive home except for when I asked her to turn on the heater. She looked at me quizzically, but then saw my shaking thighs and set the control to full on that blistering hot day.

Back home I watched Nick and Lily's innocence evaporate before my eyes when I told them their father was gone. The loss was immediately and irreversibly drawn on their young faces. Their grief compounded my own tenfold. They were inconsolable.

The following days were a cloudy haze of survival. I stared blankly at the television as Adam's death was reported in the nightly news bulletin, as though it was happening to someone else. I didn't know when I was crying and when I wasn't. My existence seemed surreal as I chose music and Bible readings for his funeral.

Lily slept in our bed on Adam's side, and Nick slept on a blow-up mattress by the side of the bed at my request. I had to have them near me. I fretted about them the minute they were in another room. I needed them close to me to catch their tears and hug them through their sobs.

Nick, Lily and I met with the local pastor to discuss Adam's eulogy. The pastor was a close friend of Adam's and we trusted him to speak on our behalf as none of us felt up to doing it ourselves.

'Make sure you say he was the best dad there ever, ever was,' Lily said emphatically.

'And the best husband,' Nick added quietly.

The tributes to Adam poured in and the huge church overflowed with mourners. Knowing the state I was in, Sarah insisted I take a sedative before the funeral. As a result, the service was awash in a thick white fog and I never really remembered much of what was said. I just sat there, flanked by my children, in disbelief that my husband would never escape that polished dark wooden box with the shiny brass handles.

Nick stood up at the end of the service and walked slowly to the coffin. He grabbed a handle along with Ryan and four other friends. His whole body trembled as he carried his dad and best friend out of the church. My six-foot-two, broad-shouldered son crumbled under the weight of his grief and he nearly dropped his end of the coffin twice.

As I shook hands and accepted the condolences of hundreds of people, I agreed with them that this was no ordinary man who had died. The world was now a duller place without him.

It was thirty-nine degrees as we stood around Adam's empty grave while the pastor blessed the coffin, one final time before it was to be lowered into the ground. I ignored the beads of sweat that mingled with my tears as I tried to stop my legs from buckling under me. Lily's howling pierced the still air.

I heard the distinct sound of flapping above me and looked up, as did everyone. An eagle peered down into the grave and then circled low over the congregation. There was no question in my mind it was the same bird from Scarborough and that it had come to find me.

You were right. Its message was clear. *You did deserve bad things to happen.*

'Go away!' I screamed at it. 'Go away!'

Nick held me firmly as I frantically swiped my black straw hat at the sky.

'It's all right, Mum, settle down. Look, there it goes. It's gone now. See? All gone. All better now.' He spoke as he would to a baby.

People murmured among themselves as I wailed at Adam's coffin. 'I'm sorry Adam. I'm so, so sorry!'

When we arrived home for the wake, to the smell of coffee and sausage rolls, and to the funny stories about Adam that were being passed to and fro, everyone behaved as though my outburst hadn't happened.

Sarah stayed on with us for another two weeks while Ryan went back home with their children. She cooked, cleaned, washed, organised, hugged, consoled, listened and talked us through those initial black days. But then her own commitments led her back to Sydney, and I was forced to get a grip and attempt to start running my own life again.

I didn't want to stay home any more once she'd gone, it was too horrible in the house without her there, and so I went back to work. It was time to start picking up the pieces and join the real world again. Nick and Lily went back to sleeping in their own beds each night and I learned to sleep alone.

The children both had summer jobs that I encouraged them to return to, purely for the distraction. Nick had recently graduated high school and Lily was just about to start Year Twelve.

Our enormous house was eerily quiet without Adam's larger than life presence to fill it. The light and life of our family had been snatched from us and we struggled to keep our heads above water without him.

I dug deep to try to be resilient for the sake of the children, but in my private moments I disintegrated with anger and disbelief. My first thought each morning was that I'd dreamed the whole thing, but then I'd turn over and Adam wasn't there in the bed beside me. I rang his phone more than once out of habit, only to get the disconnected message, and I called out to him at some stage nearly every day to a reply of silence. I could have sworn I heard his voice and his laughter in the house at least twice after he died.

I'd gone through this process before when my father, and then my mother, had died. But that grief was nothing compared to this grief. The injustice of Adam's death, in the prime of his life, made it too hard to bear. He would never walk his daughter down the aisle, he would never see his son become a father, he would never enjoy the fruits of his hard work in retirement.

The children were just as outraged as I was.

Lily was looking for a snack late one afternoon, when a packet of Adam's organic popcorn fell out of the pantry and onto her foot. I walked into the kitchen to find her furiously throwing all of his health food onto the floor. Her face was red and blotchy and she looked so very, very young.

'It's just, well, there was no point to it, Mum,' she sobbed in a child's voice. 'Eating this stuff didn't keep him alive, did it? What was the point?'

'I know, sweetheart.' I started to cry too, it never took much to get me going these days. 'He just loved being healthy, Lil, it made him feel good about himself. He should have just pigged out on chips like we do, hey?' I said, stroking her wet face.

She smiled and wiped at her eyes.

'Here, let me help you.' I grabbed a large bin-liner from the cupboard. 'Let's turf it all. God knows we won't want to eat any of it.'

Nick came into the kitchen and he reached the high shelves for us. The three of us didn't take long to clear out all the wheat-free, lactose-free, gluten-free, sugar-free, artificial colour-free, flavour-free, preservative-free food that Adam had insisted upon in his quest to be a fit and healthy old man, who'd still be swimming in the ocean on the morning of his hundredth birthday.

We ordered two thick base supreme pizzas, and ate them on the floor in the lounge room, toasting Adam as we downed a two-litre bottle of soft drink between us. Looking back, I think we all started our healing journey that day.

But I was haunted by the bird. No matter how much I tried to forget the eagle, it swooped in whenever there was an empty recess in my mind and taunted me. I had been dissatisfied with Adam for so many years, and then finally when I woke up to myself and loved him for who he was, he died. Karma. Sweet and simple.

Six weeks after his father's death, Nick left home with two friends to begin a gap year in London that he'd booked months before. I'm sure he was thankful for a new adventure to distract him. Lily and I outdid each other with tears as we made our way home from the airport. Our men were gone. It was just us girls now.

She supported my decision to sell the house, and we moved into a modest three-bedroom townhouse, two blocks back from the shore at City Beach. If we stood on tip-toes in the bathroom we could see a sliver of ocean.

Adam's life insurance policy had left us well looked after, so with the exception of our personal effects and a few sentimental things, I donated the entire contents of our home – down to the sheets on the beds and the food in the pantry – to charity. I numbly stood back as the St Vincent's and Red Cross vans came and cleared away the remnants of my married life.

Filling our new home occupied Lily and me for many weekends, the retail therapy a welcome distraction for us both. After three months the new house was a home, a real home, compared to the show home we'd lived in before. It didn't echo. But I wished that getting the house I finally felt comfortable in hadn't come at the cost of losing Adam.

I surprised myself with how little I missed of our old lifestyle together. I only missed Adam. Not our family friends, not our social club, not our golf club, not our lifesaving club, nor any of the church groups. I found that I actually wanted very little from life apart from my children and a few girlfriends, my career, some good books and the beach.

Fortunately Lily was still around. I needed her perhaps more than she needed me. She gave me purpose. She was my reason for being that first year without Adam. I was there to cook meals for her, to do her washing and to give her a shoulder to lean on through her most important year of school.

She shared my grief in a way that comforted me. If I suddenly remembered some special or funny thing about Adam, I knew Lily would listen to me relive it. Like the way he hated the commercials for discounted rugs with such passion that he would swear loudly at the television, 'They're always ninety per cent off, you dickwad.' Or his habit of spraying the air dramatically with air-freshener whenever any of Nick's footy friends left our house, while he performed the sign of the cross and mumbled exorcist-type prayers.

We snuggled in bed on many nights and cried as we watched home movies of our family, comically narrated by Adam. One was of Lily's first day of surf lifesaving training. She was seven years old and she looked adorable splashing about in the shallows in her little yellow swimming cap, with her top front teeth missing.

At one point, Adam turned the camera around onto me as I sat on the sand nearby, with Nick wrapped in a towel between my legs. He zoomed in close until the whole screen was taken up by my face, hair flying everywhere, as I cheered enthusiastically for Lily.

'Would you look at her, hey?' he said under his breath, but it was caught on the microphone. As with many of our home movies, we filmed them but never got around to sitting down to watch them. It was the first time I'd seen this.

Lily, curled up next to me under the covers, turned to smile at me. 'He loved you so much, Mum.'

I nodded, unable to speak and knowing more than ever that I had never deserved him. Somewhere in my mind, the eagle screeched at me.

As though she could read my thoughts, Lily said, 'Don't cry, Mum. You loved him too. When you had to choose, you chose him.' She found my hand and gave it a squeeze. Lily acknowledged and forgave me my affair with that one sentence.

I hated to imagine how I would have survived that first year without her. But I was anxious about Nick being so far away from us and dealing with it all on his own. Every weekend when he rang home though, he insisted he was much happier being over there. He assured me that the friends who'd travelled with him were a great support, and that his work as a barman in a busy London pub was the perfect tonic for him.

But sometimes when we finished speaking and Lily took the phone, I could hear her consoling him, and it was obvious that he was crying on the other end. Once when she was close by, I was able to hear every word and I was exposed to the true extent of his pain.

'I wish it was her, Lil,' he said, his voice breaking. 'I hate myself for thinking it, but I really wish it was her, not him. I wish I still had Dad.'

It felt as if a rock had been hurled at my chest. My child wished me dead.

'No, you don't. You know you don't, Nick,' Lily soothed. 'You would've been just as bad if it was that way around.' She spoke in code, not realising I could hear his side of the conversation.

'Maybe,' he said, in between muffled sobs. 'It's not that I don't love Mum, you know? I don't really know what it is. Just seems unfair it was Dad, not her.'

'Yeah, I know,' Lily replied. 'Same.'

I knew exactly what it was that made them both think it was unfair that I lived while Adam had died, and that tortured me.

My grief gave way to an ever increasing guilt. I convinced myself that Adam's death was for no other reason than karmic retribution for my affair, and I let this thought consume me. I began sinking fast.

Cheryl stormed into the consulting room one morning while I sat writing notes between patients.

'All right, Mel, out with it, what's up? You've got that psycho obsessive look from the old days on your face again lately. Is Mr Tall Dark Facial Hair back on the scene?'

I turned my head sharply and snapped, 'No, he's not. In case you've forgotten, my husband died nine months ago. Maybe *that's* why I'm not myself.'

'Bullshit, Mel, I know you.' She took a seat. 'What's up?'

'How dare you!' I raised my voice. 'Accusing me like that. You don't know anything.'

'Mel, I know you,' Cheryl reached over to grip my hand. 'I'm accusing you of nothing. But I'm worried about you. What's up? Talk to me.'

I sighed and slumped my shoulders as I told her about my belief that I'd caused Adam's death by cheating on him. I told her about the eagle that pecked away at my conscience night and day.

She was silent for a while and then she shook her head. 'You know what?' she said. 'You're even more self-obsessed and melodramatic than I thought you were.'

I swallowed to stop the tears. 'Thanks, Cheryl. I feel heaps better now.'

'Your husband died because an artery burst in his brain.' She articulated every word slowly and clearly as if she was talking to a deaf foreigner. She leaned forward in her chair. 'You're the one who showed me the autopsy report, remember? It's a miracle he lived with that aneurysm as long as he did. You know, it's not always about you, Mel. People don't die because three years earlier their spouse slept with someone else.'

'What about the sea-eagle?' I challenged.

She raised her voice. 'For Christ's sake, Mel, listen to yourself. It's a *bird*, a common Western Australian bird. It's not the same bird from the beach, your personal messenger of doom! Those birds are everywhere. But I tell you what, at least this finally explains your performance at the cemetery. I thought you had sun stroke, flapping your hat around like that and screaming like a banshee.'

Despite myself, I laughed. Then I sighed. 'I can't stop thinking about it. I hear the flapping in my head all the time. And it talks to me in my nightmares.'

She grinned. 'Then get one of the other dickheads around here to prescribe you some strong anti-psychotic drugs.'

I gave her my most withering look.

'Listen, Mel,' she said sincerely. 'Whenever that bird comes into your mind say to it, "You have no meaning. I made you up. Now leave." And see if that works. Try to talk yourself out of this craziness.'

I nodded and she stood to walk out. When she reached the doorway she stopped and said, 'I really need a new job.'

'Why?'

She turned to look at me and smiled. 'Because I've just had to tell my boss what to say to the imaginary eagle in her dreams. You're taking me down with you, girl.'

I took Cheryl's advice and practised her mantra whenever the eagle spread its wings across my brain. And amazingly, the more I said it, the more it worked.

And for the first time in my life, after having recommended it to countless others, I finally gave in to Sarah's incessant pleas and I saw a wonderful psychologist, Jayne, who worked out of her own home, and whose simple, down to earth nature appealed to me. I met with her every week, and sat on her couch and drank coffee while she guided me through sorting out the muddle in my head.

Jayne was able to make sense of the confusion, shame, self-hate and guilt that were my constant companions since I first laid eyes on Matt. She had to repeat the same message many times over many sessions, until I started to believe her.

'The verb love is what counts, not the feeling of love. When you *feel* love, it's selfish, it's just for you and it affects nobody but you. But when you *act* love, you're committing the act of loving somebody. Do you understand this concept?'

I nodded.

'Good. So let's apply it you, Mel. During your affair, you didn't love Adam. You may have felt a selfish *feeling* of love for him, but you *acted* in a way that didn't love him. You need to own that betrayal of him. But here's the thing you really need to concentrate on, so listen carefully. When you stopped that affair, when you made the choice to *act* love only for Adam, then you loved him again. That you continued to have lingering *feelings* of love for Matt is irrelevant. You acted love only for Adam. You loved him wholly and honestly and exclusively, and that's what counts. What you need to do now is to grant forgiveness to yourself for the dishonest act of the affair – but only for the affair, nothing that you felt afterwards needs forgiving. There's no need to regret feeling love for Matt once you let him go. The only thing you need to forgive yourself for is that you acted in an unloving way towards Adam during the time of the affair. That's it. And he forgave you for that affair well and truly, a long time ago. Now you must do the same. At some point you have to let go of this guilt. It's useless to you. Free yourself, Mel, and allow yourself to feel that love you experienced for Matt without shame. Matt was a very important part of your life. Acknowledge it.'

For the first time, instead of berating myself for starting the affair, I acknowledged the fact that I let it end even when I was falling in love with Matt and that this had been a sign of the strength of my real love for Adam. I realised that I had as much control over my heart to make it forget Matt as I had power to make rain. Eventually, the more I accepted that, the more I freed myself from the eagle's sharp claws and slowly began to shed the guilt I'd held onto for so long.

The guilt at not regretting my affair with Matt had held me back from living freely. Because, despite the carnage it caused to all of our lives, I could never regret falling in love with him. Accepting that freed me.

And living without guilt gave me new life. Lily noticed the change in me. I began eating proper meals, started shopping for trendy clothes and shoes again, and started leaving the house to meet friends for dinner or a movie. Lily saw that I was going to be okay and she started concentrating on her own life.

To her credit and my utter amazement, she not only graduated from high school but performed extraordinarily well. She was accepted into the Faculty of Medicine to pursue her goal of becoming an anaesthetist, just like her dad.

In her first year at university, she fell insanely in love with an earnest young architecture student named Ben. Seeing her happy again warmed my heart, and I grew very fond of Ben, a blond, well-built young man who could've passed for a younger Adam, and who wore his love for Lily on his sleeve. As I expected would happen, she spent increasingly less time at home.

After his year away, Nick returned home from London. He didn't move back in with me, instead choosing to live with friends in a rented flat near the university in Fremantle, where he studied for his Bachelor of Education. He seemed to have aged several years in the time he was gone. He'd let his wavy blond hair grow long and his face was covered in stubble. He was bigger and broader than his father had ever been, and he received just as much attention, if not more, from the young women around him.

His time overseas had helped him recover from Adam's death, but he still displayed his grief more openly than Lily did. It was imprinted in his eyes, no matter what his expression. I worried terribly about him. He was too serious for a young man – he rarely smiled and his laugh was hollow. He didn't visit me very often at all, and when we did spend time together he was distant and polite. I don't think he ever really got over my betrayal of his hero. I couldn't blame him. But I took comfort in the fact he at least remained close to his sister.

I was grateful when football season began again. It gave me an excuse to see him every week as I sat in the stands with Lily and cheered him on. He waved when he saw us as he ran on and off the field.

I gradually settled into this new phase in my life, and time dulled my pain. I found my greatest comfort through work. Now that the children were independent, I finally had the time and the motivation to do some more study. I applied for a Post Graduate Diploma in Obstetrics. And when I attended a home water birth for the first time, I cried with joy at how beautiful the process could be, and I knew that this was where my new career dream lay. I wanted to deliver babies in their own homes.

After I graduated, I split my time between working at the clinic and delivering more and more beautiful babies, as word spread that there was a GP with a Diploma in Obstetrics who specialised in home water births.

This replaced my brokenness with hope. And on top of that, being a GP meant that I got to hold the babies and watch them grow when they were brought into the clinic for regular check-ups and vaccinations. The relationships I built with these mothers and their children filled the void in my heart.

I still ached for Adam every single day, but the pain was easier to live with. I felt guilty about this so I revisited Jayne's couch, and she again urged me just to accept my feelings. So I didn't force myself into grieving for Adam as much as I thought I still should.

And I kept a private corner of my heart just for Matt, but the years faded some of my memories of him. I still prayed for him every night to a god I didn't know if I believed existed, and I still wondered what he was up to and if he was happy.

In a weak moment once, when I was feeling extra lonely, I searched for him on Facebook. He wasn't there. I took that as a sign and didn't pursue tracking him down any further.

On a drizzly, winter Saturday morning, I found myself driving past a tattooist shop on my way to a work conference. I did a quick U-turn and pulled up outside. The sign on the window simply read 'Tattoo' in black Gothic letters. I grabbed my purse and ran in out of the rain.

Inside it looked as I expected – dark and dingy, with old brown vinyl furniture. The stench of stale cigarette smoke combined with marijuana was overpowering. The three men gathered around the front counter wouldn't have been out of place in a bikie gang. They looked amused at the sight of me as I ignored the voice in my head telling me to get the hell out of there and took a step forward. A one-eyed pit-bull terrier on a studded leash sitting near the counter growled a warning in my direction.

I explained what I wanted done, trying hard not to appear intimidated.

'No probs, babe. Come through the back room, eh?' The oldest of the men, aged perhaps forty, led me into a curtained-off section.

I quashed down thoughts of Adam's face if he could see where I was right now and instead I flicked through an album filled with horrific images of snakes with daggers through their heads and evil looking Japanese masks. The tattooist drew the design I asked for in a small room next door. He reappeared five minutes later, stroking his goatee. 'First one, eh?'

I nodded.

'No probs.' He sat down next to me. 'Gonna need ya to take off yer jeans but, eh?'

I did a quick mental recall of the underwear I had on and agreed. He turned around while I stripped off and lay down on the leather table. I'll never forget the menacing buzz of the tool or the exquisitely sharp pain when it first pierced my skin. I'd never thought anything could be more painful than giving birth. I was wrong. I bit hard on the knuckle of my bent index finger.

'Stop wriggling, babe,' he said firmly as he worked and whistled.

Less than fifteen minutes later it was over. I inspected it in the foggy full-length mirror and smiled.

Driving home rather than to the conference, my hip throbbing, I felt calm and I felt happy. I had Matt's 'M' on me at last. Except it wasn't just M for Matt, it was M for Marriage, and for Making it through, and for Moving on, and most importantly it was M for Mel. M for Me. I didn't do it to remember Matt, I did it to remember that I was strong enough to get through anything. Maybe I'd pay the price for the feelings I'd had for Matt if I had to stand before a god one day, but for now I was at peace with it and at peace with myself.

I carried on.

SERENDIPITY

MATT

I stroked her cheek with the back of my fingers, marvelling at the delicate softness of her skin. The touch of her and the smell of her hypnotised me. The worries of the day melted away and my breathing slowed down until it was in sync with hers. She was curled up tight, lying on her right side with her hand tucked under her cheek, purring contentedly in her sleep as I lay facing her. Her brown hair stuck out a little behind her pink ear and I moved my hand to stroke it. She stirred, mumbled something indecipherable, sighed and resettled herself back into her dream.

My God, I loved her. I loved her fiercely. So fiercely, it made me mad with it. My heart leaped and soared high into the heavens whenever she smiled, and I knew it was just for me. I spent countless hours staring at her, absorbing her while she slept. Every day brought with it a miraculous new discovery about her that made her even more wondrous to me.

Kelly walked in, her arms full of folded nappies. 'You still lying there?' she whispered, smiling indulgently at us.

'Come and feel this bit,' I whispered back, and she put down the nappies on the change table and gently crept up beside me onto the doona. She stroked the nape of Ava's neck where my fingers had just been.

'Oh,' she mouthed, 'so soft.'

'Mmm-hmm,' I went back to stroking Ava with one hand and slipped the other around Kelly's waist, bringing her down alongside me on the bed.

'This is nice,' she said quietly, intertwining her legs through mine. 'I hope she sleeps tonight. She's already slept for an hour and a half. It might be fun and games later on.'

'I'll stay up with her. Why don't you try and get a little nap in now too?'

'Mmm, maybe,' Kelly sighed and shut her eyes. I kissed the top of her head that was resting on my chest.

With an arm around my wife and an arm around my baby, it was a perfect moment. These moments were rare, life was busy. But I let myself enjoy it as I took in the sweet clean smell and warm feel of mother and daughter.

I reflected back on the events of the day, from the mundane – vacuuming the guest rooms and trimming the front lawn edges, to the more interesting – a conversation at breakfast with a wealthy retired Canadian couple, both in their seventies, who were taking a break by the seaside after two months trekking in Nepal.

And then I let my thoughts drift further and further back, as they sometimes did. Back to Lydia. I'd heard from Tom and Emma a few months ago, that she was shacked up with a divorced investment banker twice her age. I didn't ask for any details because I honestly didn't care. What a terrible and foolish decision getting married was, for both of us. We entered the marriage surrounded by deep oceans of doubt, and once the wedding was over we quickly drowned.

The divorce was fast and easy. Lydia wanted out as much as I did by then, and neither of us entertained the idea of fighting over our shared property. We were too desperate to sniff fresh air.

There was no point in hanging around Melbourne for much longer. The regret gnawed away at me while I lived with memories of Lydia everywhere I turned. It was time for a new beginning. And after thirty years of smog and cold, I was ready for a move west.

Leaving my parents was messier than the divorce. Mum was desolate. No sons left around her, she had sobbed. But this was my life, and I would not stay somewhere I didn't want to be just to appease Mum. She didn't get over the move until her third or fourth visit to Perth, when I think it finally dawned on her that it was a done thing and that I wouldn't be coming home in a hurry.

Dad was emotionally remote for a while, but was more empathetic towards me much sooner than Mum. And he loved the Bed and Breakfast. I waited on them hand and foot every time they came. I set them up in the most luxurious room, with Mum's favourite Sauvignon and fresh figs for Dad. And I didn't let Mum lift a finger, despite her protests, while I served them hot breakfasts and grilled seafood platters for lunch out on the veranda. She grew to really enjoy that side of things. I did allow them to potter in the cottage garden and we proudly displayed the burgundy roses Mum picked in bud vases at dinnertime on the centre of the table.

Starting the Bed and Breakfast from scratch was not an easy thing, by any stretch. There was the break-up of the partnership of the clinic with Tom, who was sure I was having another of my mental crises. It wasn't a breezy decision to give up on the profession that had provided so well for me, and to abandon a business partnership with my best friend. Thankfully, the friendship remained intact and Tom's family were almost annual guests at the Bed and Breakfast. One summer I had both his and Holly's families staying at once, a real Melbourne reunion.

The decision to leave the business, and indeed Melbourne, was brought on because I had not forgotten Mel's passion for her work and for where she lived, and I was always envious of that. I craved that kind of passion and I knew where I would find it.

So I put everything I owned on a truck that was headed across the Nullarbor and had it all delivered to my new address in Scarborough. With the money Tom paid me for my share of the business I was able to put down a sizeable deposit, but I still found myself with a massive and terrifying mortgage on a beaten-down weatherboard house on a big plot of land, one block away from Scarborough Beach. The beach I wanted to see every day for the rest of my life.

For a year I continued to work full-time in somebody else's physiotherapy clinic, and every single afternoon and all through the weekends, I worked on the house. Most nights I saw midnight with either a paint roller or a screwdriver in my hand.

It was a good thing my dad had insisted on me helping him renovate the Daylesford property when I was a teenager. Having that experience under my belt saved me thousands in labour costs. My back ached and my knees creaked, and I overused my shoulder so much it needed surgery. I had no social life to speak of, but slowly my vision for the house came to fruition.

Surprisingly, once I opened the doors to the public I barely had to advertise. It appeared that the Bed and Breakfast market in Scarborough was largely untapped and ready to be cracked open. With only a cheap, do-it-yourself website I was up and running, and within three months I was already booked out for the three months after that.

Perth is a big city, so I knew the odds of ever running into Mel were slim. There were two million people buffering us, but still I wondered if I would ever run into her. What would we do? Hug awkwardly? Shake hands? Would she pretend she didn't recognise me? Or would she give me a death stare and storm off? After all, our last communication years before had hardly been friendly. Maybe she'd hung on to that anger all that time. In any case, I never did run into her or hear from her again. For the best, I thought.

I had held on to the anger myself for a long, long time. I was angry married, I was angry divorced, I was even angry when I moved to Perth. But the solitude, the house that grew more beautiful every day under my care, and the roar of the waves at night on Scarborough Beach as I slept appeased my angry soul. I softened, and then I forgave, and then slowly I started to forget.

They say you never forget your first love, but I did forget her in a way. Certainly there were parts of her, some of the things she said and some of the things we did together, that would be forever burned in my mind. Occasionally now I still thought about her and very, very occasionally I fantasised about her, suffering the guilt afterwards as I looked over at Kelly sleeping unaware next to me. But for the most part, I forgot her.

It was a gradual kind of forgetting. One day I realised I couldn't quite picture the shape of her face as well as I used to. I forgot the tone of her voice. I couldn't recall her mannerisms when I daydreamed of her, which became less and less frequent.

The strong feelings for her surfaced momentarily, years ago when her husband died. I resisted the urge to call her then, although I'd been very tempted at the time. He wasn't in the way any more, and maybe I could have won her over again if I'd tried. But my head ruled my heart. It could never be clean with us. And I didn't want that. I wanted more than that. I wanted to know she was with me not because he was gone, but because she had chosen me over him. So I let her go for good. It was a kind of relief when her husband died. That was when I knew for sure I'd never take her back.

When I did happen to think of her after he died, I always thought of her fondly. Mel had unlocked my heart. She was the first person who gave me hope that I could be understood, and that even with all of my hang-ups, I could be accepted and loved. I was forever in her debt for that. If it wasn't for her, I'd probably still be living a two-dimensional life, forcing down Bev's Chow Mein every Thursday evening. Mel opened my eyes to the possibility of a real connection. But she was never really mine. It took years to get over the anger, but I did get over it.

And then I met Kelly.

Ironically it was her resemblance to Mel that grabbed my attention in the first place. She sat cross-legged on a seat opposite mine during a local Amnesty International meeting, revealing a sexy calf that peeped out from her loose skirt, and a tantalisingly manicured foot that dangled a sparkly silver thong. She swung her foot to and fro, and I was unable to concentrate on a word being said as I followed its gentle rhythmical motion. Her red painted lips, long brown hair and curvy body were achingly familiar. She stirred up intense sexual desires that had laid dormant inside me for what had felt like forever.

But her resemblance to Mel stopped there. She was nothing like Mel in any other way. Kelly was excitable and loud and irreverent.

She snorted when she laughed, and when she laughed too hard she snorted and cried all at once. She was a vocal advocate for marginalised people, and a passionate human rights defender who felt personally wounded at social injustice. She was also a keen netballer who had no qualms about a bit of 'argy-bargy' on the court if it meant a goal for her team. And she was a newly qualified teacher, whose brain worked at the speed of light, coming up with new, art-inspired learning ideas that were so exciting to her she felt the need to wake me in the middle of the night to describe them to me with great detail and grand arm gestures.

Kelly was strong and tender, opinionated and open-hearted, loud and vulnerable all at once. And she was unattached and willing to be loved wholly and only by me. I adored her. We fell in love in a minute and were married a few minutes after that, or so it seemed.

Our love affair started like a bushfire, I couldn't keep my hands off her. And then over the years the fire eased to a steady smoulder. And now, with Kelly nearing the end of her maternity leave and Ava almost a year old, and with both of them safe in my arms, I wished it was possible to freeze this moment in my life.

Between the busy Bed and Breakfast business, our continued human rights activism, and of course the day and night job that was Ava, we rarely stopped. But here we were, all three of us, resting peacefully.

I looked out the window and saw the clouds reddening. It was nearly twilight. The next day would be our first family Christmas. I closed my eyes and slept soundly.

CHRISTMAS EVE

MEL

I was bursting with excitement as I showed a patient into my consulting room. It was on days like this I couldn't imagine not having chosen this as my vocation.

The young woman took a seat next to me with her eleven-month-old son asleep in her arms and her two-year-old boy, who was one of the very first babies I had delivered in a home-birth, standing at her side. Her face was racked with anxiety and she eyed me frantically.

At the start of her third trimester of her second pregnancy, she'd come to see me for a routine exam, and commented off-handedly about a constant ache in her left hip that wouldn't ease no matter what she tried. She suspected it had something to do with the pressure on her back from the baby's position. But she didn't understand why she had a massive bruise on the hip, because she was sure she hadn't knocked it against anything.

I examined her as I struggled to hide my emotions. That sort of bruising and unexplained constant pain usually meant only one thing.

Two days later, after I'd sent her off for hurriedly arranged blood tests, a scan and a biopsy, I gave her the earth-shattering news. She had malignant bone cancer.

Her reaction at the time was indicative of her incredible will. 'So get rid of it then,' she'd said calmly.

I assisted at the emergency premature delivery of her baby so she could undergo radical surgery a week after his birth. She was devastated at her inability to breastfeed her son because of the danger posed to him from the chemotherapy treatment. This upset her far more than the terrible pain and scarring that the removal of some of her pelvis had caused her, or the hideous side effects she suffered from the chemotherapy. Over the months I watched her with helplessness, offering pitifully inadequate remedies for her mouth ulcers, stomach cramps, rotting nails and intense nausea.

Even as the chemotherapy ravaged her body, she took her toddler to playgrounds and Wiggles concerts and baked him cookies. She also gave her new baby a ten-minute massage every day after his bath, including the days she vomited up to ten times.

She never walked into my consulting room without a smile, except for the week before, when she'd come in complaining about a sudden and severe onset of leg pain on her opposite side.

From her research on the internet, she knew all about the dire implications associated with secondary tumours. I sent her for an emergency scan at a radiology centre in town and the results had just been emailed through before I led her into the consulting room today.

'Nadine, the tests are clear,' I said placing my hand over hers as soon as she sat down. 'There's nothing but a normal cancer-free leg there, sweetheart. It's all clear.' I felt the tears pricking my eyes.

She stared at me while my words registered. 'Okay,' she whispered as a trembling smile formed on her lips. She started to cry.

I stood up and put my arms around her, enclosing the baby between us. 'You're okay now, Nadine,' I soothed. 'Everything's okay now.'

She nodded mutely.

'You've got a disc protrusion between the fourth and fifth lumbar vertebrae in your spine. All you need is a good physio!' I laughed and wiped away my tears as well as hers.

I'd discovered a wonderful local physio who I used all the time, since Matt had opened my eyes to the long-term benefits of physiotherapy.

'Take this referral, go see the physio. She'll help you get rid of that pain, and then go home and raise your kids,' I ordered her.

'Sounds like a plan to me, Dr Harding,' she said softly.

Her toddler jumped into my arms to kiss me goodbye when I gave him a candy cane on their way out. Now what other job in the world gave a buzz like that?

Later that afternoon, I took it upon myself to do the unthinkable and tidy the desk in my consulting room. It was Christmas Eve and there were two glorious weeks off stretching before me. The motivation to clean up came from knowing how terrific it would feel coming back to a fresh clean room in the New Year.

'Oh dear,' I muttered when I opened the top drawer and for the first time in several years saw the mess for what it really was. How did I let it get so bad? Crumpled sick leave certificates were strewn among referral sheets, loose staples, pen lids, pencil sharpenings, bent paperclips and clumps of Blu Tack.

I buzzed Cheryl.

'What now?' Cheryl didn't like being buzzed.

'Have we got any big black garbage bags? Really big ones?'

'Why? Did you kill someone?'

I laughed. 'No, but there is a chance of finding a small animal carcass or two in here. I'm cleaning out my desk.'

'Jesus, Mary and Joseph – it's a Christmas miracle! I'll bring some in to you.'

An hour later I was on to the third, final, and most neglected drawer. I flipped open a navy blue clipboard with a chewed corner and when I saw what was inside, I smiled, and cried, and then cried some more.

On a white sheet of copy paper, in black ink scrawled in his illegible crooked writing was a note I'd never seen before.

You are one messy woman! This desk is a pig sty.

   So I've just given you a really good seeing to (again). You pretended you were all busy and annoyed that I showed up when I was supposed to be waiting for you at the hotel like a good boy. I think we can both agree I am many things, but a good boy I most certainly am not. Well, you're not annoyed any more! You just smirked your way out of here to go to the bathroom to wash up. You were particularly sexy this afternoon, I must say. Those tiny red knickers, oh my God!

   So when you find this letter (which may be never, judging by the state of this desk), I want you to get turned on remembering that time with the sexy red knickers and the stethoscope. And then I want you to come straight home to me. I reckon home will be a nice townhouse right on the beach at Scarborough, or maybe we'll have moved down South like you've always wanted to, who knows? Point being, you are to read this letter and then come home and give me some lovin'. M

After all these years, I had something that came from him. One beautiful piece of paper to remind me of a time when my heart had been ripped open and an unexpected love affair changed my life entirely. I had reminders of Adam everywhere I looked, and now, finally, I had something from Matt. No matter how brief it had been, it had still happened. We had completely fallen for each other. I remembered how it felt to be so giddy that I'd let myself be carried away in an impossible dream. And I remembered how that one week with him freed me from my previous life of lies and opened up a new life of truth. Matt led me to Adam and he led me to myself, I had so much to be thankful to him for. I pressed the note against my heart, grabbed my handbag and left for the day. The clinic was empty. I locked up and walked out into the brilliant sunshine with a new spring in my step.

I arrived home from work and immediately kicked off my shoes and shed my skirt suit, which now lay in a tangled heap on the bedroom floor. I slipped into a loose satin nightgown, its cool feel refreshing against my skin. I pulled the Marian Keyes book I'd had on the flight with him out of the bookshelf and tucked the note in the front cover.

I flopped down now onto the soft leather recliner in the lounge room, armed with a packet of chocolate biscuits and a steaming cup of wickedly strong coffee. I was still smiling. I could revel in the feeling of finding a long lost love letter because I had literally nothing to achieve for fifteen whole days.

I planned on doing as little as humanly possible with the exception of eating lots of fruit mince pies, reading the latest Marian Keyes novel, and slouching around watching reality television. I still had this week's deliciously voyeuristic episode of *The Real Housewives of Beverly Hills* waiting for me.

Both the children were away this Christmas. Nick was surfing with friends in Bali. He'd phoned yesterday sounding very excited about the quality of both the surf and the nightlife there. There seemed to have been a shift in him over the last few months, a positive shift. The sexy giggles of a girl, who was clearly very close by, made me smile.

Lily was spending a few days with Ben's extended family at an old homestead in the heart of Margaret River. For her birthday he'd given her a small ruby ring that never left her hand. Things seemed to be getting quite serious between those two.

When she called a few weeks ago to tell me she'd been invited to Christmas with Ben's family, I convinced her that I relished the idea of sleeping in with absolutely no pressure to prepare a fancy Christmas dinner. She was hesitant about leaving me alone, but I insisted she go with my blessing. I didn't cry until she'd hung up. Thank God for Sarah or I would have been all alone. And that would have been unbearable. I loved my tranquil life, but on Christmas Day, who wants tranquil?

Sarah, Ryan and their brood were due to arrive in Perth later tonight for a few days on the beach before driving North to Monkey Mia. At first I'd been looking forward to the indulgent Christmas lunch we'd booked at a flashy new bistro overlooking the ocean in Sorrento. But then Sarah had let slip that their friend, Harold, who'd recently relocated from Sydney to Fremantle, was joining us at lunch.

For the last three months I'd heard about nothing but Harold in every phone call with Sarah. Divorced Harold was lovely. Single Harold was great looking and had bucketloads of money. Available Harold knew nobody in Perth, and wouldn't it be sweet of me to call him and make him feel welcome? Sarah had the bit between her teeth and now she'd taken things one step further and invited him to Christmas lunch. Up until today I'd been holding a grudge about the set-up, but now I was on holidays and in a great mood, and I'd found a love note to keep forever.

Maybe Harold would turn out to be not so bad after all. He was a GP, so we already had that in common, as Sarah had pointed out dozens of times. I had to admit that it'd be kind of great to have a man in my life again. Matt's note reminded me of what I was missing. Could I kiss a Harold? Hmm, quite possibly not. I'd find out tomorrow.

I wondered what the future held for me while I sipped my coffee. The children had moved on with their lives, so was it time for me to turn a new leaf? I was a free agent for the first time since my early twenties. As much as I loved my job, I didn't have to keep working at the same clinic, or anywhere, if I didn't want to. I certainly had enough to retire on, but I'd miss the work. I'd miss the babies and their mums. Maybe a sabbatical would be a better idea. I could take a Pacific Ocean cruise. I could go spend a year in Tuscany and learn Italian. I could go to Mexico and fall in love with a chef who'd cook me chilli burritos.

My middle-aged bladder interrupted these exciting thoughts by signalling a need for a visit to the bathroom. As I looked at my reflection in the mirror while I washed my hands, I was reminded of Matt's humanitarianism. *That's what I should do. I should do something for others. Something to make the world better.* Maybe that was why I'd found the note. Perhaps it was to inspire me to do more with my life now that I had the opportunity. It definitely felt like the right time to take a leap of faith and throw myself into a good cause. But what? What would I find rewarding? What would I be good at?

'Give me a sign, God,' I said out loud, looking upwards. 'What should Melissa do with the rest of her life? Should she marry a

Harold, or should she fall in love with a Mexican, or should she save the planet? If you really are there, oh Heavenly Father, and I didn't waste a thousand Sundays going to church all those years, then please give me a sign. Thank you. Amen.'

My first authentic prayer in forty-two years and it was done standing next to the toilet. No sooner were the words out than the chimes sounded from the front doorbell.

I looked up at the ducted vent in the ceiling. 'Impressive speed there, God, with the sign giving!'

I threw on a dressing gown and walked quickly to the front door.

'Merry Christmas, ma'am.' A tall and strapping young African man smiled warmly at me. He was wearing an ID badge.

'My name is Joseph. I am here on behalf of *Médecins Sans Frontières*. In case you have not heard of us, may I show you this?' He held up a brochure with a photo of a doctor holding a child on his lap while administering an injection, surrounded by other African toddlers and babies and women.

'We are looking for good people like yourself to be a part of our regular giving scheme in supporting the volunteer medical staff to reach less fortunate people in third-world and war-ravaged countries. Is this something you would consider this Christmas, ma'am?'

I took a deep breath and my amazing new life began. 'Are you looking for more doctors too?'

ACKNOWLEDGEMENTS

Settle in folks, a seven-year journey means I have a lot of people to thank!

I was lucky enough to be given not one but four wonderful editors to work with. So first up, a huge thank you to my team of editors at HarperCollins. To Anna Valdinger, thank you for taking a punt on this unknown first-timer, for believing in my story and for holding my hand when I was new and lost. And to Mary Rennie, who took over when Anna became a mumma to an adorable baby boy, thank you for leading the charge in taking this book where no HarperCollins eBook had gone before and putting in the hard yards to secure the print deal. Thank you for all the care you've shown me along the way as well. To the lovely Madeleine James, thank you to you too for all your hard work in bringing the final story together. And an extra massive thank you to the best structural editor on the planet, Dianne Blacklock. Your keen eye and wise words made a world of difference. Thank you for making me laugh so hard during the editorial process that isn't supposed to be a funny business.

To the rest of the HarperCollins team, you guys rock! The loveliest publishing director ever Shona Martyn, my tireless publicist Alice Wood, otherwise known as Double A (Amazing Alice), my wonderful marketing and promotions manager Sarah Barrett, the genius Matt Stanton and the cover design team who made me cry when I first saw this stunning cover, my main man Brendan Mays and the social media team, and the brilliant Karen-Maree Griffiths and the go-get-'em sales team, especially my gorgeous Western Australian manager, Theresa Anns – I'm beyond blessed to have you all in my corner!

To Jacinta di Mase, how do I thank you in just a few words? I somehow landed the best literary agent in Australia, if the not the world. I will forever be grateful for the great leap of faith you took in putting your name behind me and for your fierce tenacity in finding me a publisher. Your vision for how the story should unfold made it what it is. Thank you for sticking by me through all the ups and downs. You continue to be my backbone, even now.

To the brilliant Meredith Whitford, thank you for taking the original manuscript and transforming it from a first draft piece of drivel into a ridgey-didge novel. Your insight, advice and ideas changed the course of my life.

To Nikki Williamson, thank you for pushing me out of my comfort zone to bring out the guts in this story. I apologise for all the things I said behind your back every time you made me re-write. I owe the *oomph* in the book to you.

To the authors who I'm lucky enough to have as my very own team of mentors – Jenn J McLeod, Alissa Callen, Monica McInerney, Jennie Jones, Alli Sinclair, Renee Hammond, Stephanie Pegler, Rachael Johns and most of all, the amazing Natasha Lester. Thank you for the time you've taken to show me the ropes, for being great sounding boards, for cheering me on and especially for throwing your weight behind me to get me on the map. You've all become such dear friends to me and I love you to bits.

To my soul-sisters in crime – Deborah Disney (forever my swami), Engy Albasel Neville, Jennifer Ammoscato and KJ Farnham. I hit forty and thought I had already met all my best friends, and then I met you lot! Thank you for all the love, support, wisdom and laughter you bring me, I love you four so very much and I'm glad we're walking this crazy journey together.

Lots of love also to the gorgeous authors I've met through HarperCollins and through the Romance Writers of Australia – a girl can't go wrong with this much support around her.

To the book reviewers who brought *Love at First Flight* to the masses by supporting me so passionately on social media and on their blogs and who gave me street cred – Renee Conoulty, Marcia Bezuidenhout, Melinda Hence, Laura Tait, Samantha Janning, Jade St Clair, Monique Mulligan, J'aimee Brooker, Rowena Holloway, Arielle Deltoro, Melissa Amster, Melissa Sargent, Margret Best, Leanne Albers, Karan Eleni and Sharon Taylor Xuereb – I owe you the world lovely ladies!

To John Kurtze and Len Klumpp – two more unlikely supporters would be harder to imagine but you both increased my readership numbers immensely and on top of that you are both such lovely gentlemen, thank you.

To my beautiful non-author-world friends who made the best chapter-by-chapter critics as the story was created, Sarah McWilliams, Daniella Hassett, Donelle Marcar and Nina Casella. Thank you for the hours of editing and for guiding me in the right direction countless times – love you all.

To Heidi Lauri, how lucky am I that my beautiful friend comes over to snap a few shots in the backyard and it's good enough to be my official author photo? Thank you, Heids, for bringing out the best in me – love you.

To Kathryn Wilshire and Catherine Kolomyjec and the SHC family – your kindness and encouragement blew me away. Thank you, our family is so lucky to belong to a school community that we cherish so much.

To my first readers, my extraordinary girlfriends, your enthusiasm, encouragement and ongoing support has touched my heart – love you all. And thank you gorgeous Emma Cockman for the title!

To my mum and my dad and my big loving family, especially my cousins who are spread all over the world and yet we still manage to remain so close, thank you for your belief in me and for flogging the book far and wide – best family ever. I love you all so very, very much. Mum, thank you especially for being the loudest and best cheerleader of all time.

To my beautiful kids, Tommy and Lara, thank you for putting up with a crazy writing mummy with so much love and encouragement. I love you, love you, love you. You are my two most favourite people in the whole wide world.

To my husband and soul mate, Paul, they say you write what you know and I have known great, great love. Thank you for your unwavering strength and kindness. Thank you for being the one who picked me up every time I fell over. You carried me from an idea in my head to the book this ended up being. I love you with my whole heart.

Maeve Binchy, Marian Keyes, Stephenie Meyer, Adriana Trigiani and Rosamunde Pilcher – your words rocked my world, thank you for writing them.

And finally to you my readers, I could never put into words how much you've enriched my life with your kind words and support. I never dreamed that my story would connect me to so many beautiful people the world over. Thank you for being the reason I write.

BEAUTIFUL MESSY LOVE

TESS WOODS

Available August 2017

When football star Nick Harding hobbles into the Black Salt Café the morning after the night before, he is served by Anna, a waitress with haunted-looking eyes and no interest in footballers famous or otherwise. Nick is instantly drawn to this exotic, intelligent girl. But a relationship between them risks shame for her conservative refugee family and backlash for Nick that could ruin his career.

Meanwhile, Nick's sister, Lily, is struggling to finish her medical degree. When she meets Toby, it seems that for the first time she is following her heart, not the expectations of others. Yet what starts out as a passionate affair with a man who has just buried his wife slips quickly into dangerous dependency.

Scarred by tragedy in their own way, each of these characters must face prejudice and heartbreak to learn just how much beautiful messy love can mean.

SUNDAY

NICK

I draped a heavy arm over my grainy eyes as the sunshine broke through a gap in the blinds right onto my face. Why did sunrise have to be so damned early? It was just rude. It was Sunday, for Christ's sake. People needed to sleep.

I smacked my lips together, tasting last night's Jack, and turned to face the other side of the bed. It was empty, the sheet was pulled halfway down in a neat diagonal and the indentation from her head was still on the pillow. I listened for any sounds of Bridget in the house. She might have been the type to settle in with a coffee watching Netflix while she waited for me to wake up or, worse, be in the kitchen making breakfast. But all I heard was the distant hum of a lawnmower, my dog Bluey and the Alsatian a few doors down barking in a duet, and the sound of traffic off the main road.

At least I didn't have to take her out for breakfast, my tried and tested way of getting girls out of my house without hurting their feelings. Taking them out for breakfast was usually enough for them not to run to the papers. I hated those breakfasts, with their awkward daylight small talk and the exchanging of phone numbers and the fake promises to meet up for dinner during the week. But they were a necessary evil.

Thankfully Bridget seemed to have accepted our night together for what it was and left without expecting a romance to spring from it. Hang on, it was Bridget, wasn't it? Bridie? Could've been Bridie. Hopefully she didn't steal anything.

Shit, did she take any photos of me before she left? Would I be all over social media again today? Would I have Craig ranting at me, about how I was letting the whole team down *again* and how I was failing in my duty as a role model? My head pounded into the back of my eyeballs.

I reached for my phone and squinted at the bright screen while my heart raced at the thought of what I might find. Nothing. Thank God. I'd dodged another bullet.

I dropped my head back down on the sweat-soaked pillow and stared at the lock screen image on the phone. It was of Dad and me, standing back to back on the sand, holding our surfboards out in front of us. I was about sixteen when Mum took that shot of us on the Gold Coast. I stared at the screen until it blacked out.

'No more, Dad, I promise.'

I had half woken up just after 2 a.m. feeling dead inside as I watched the girl sleeping, her long legs entwined in mine. I'd wished in that sleepy moment in bed that we meant something to each other. I wanted to wake her up and apologise for what had happened between us. But I didn't. And now she was gone.

I'd met her for the first time a few hours before when she slid up behind me on the dance floor and wrapped her arms around my waist by way of introduction, before dropping one hand down and stroking my penis through my jeans in time with the music.

She'd never know that I watched her sleeping and wondered what it was that possessed her to come home with a complete stranger, and what made me do the same thing?

It had never felt good afterwards. But it felt particularly shit today. I didn't want to be that guy any more. I hated that guy.

I swung my legs out of bed, scrounging around for boxer shorts. I was through with this shit. Sunday was technically the first day of the week. New week, new attitude. No drinking, not even one drop, until the end of the season, or maybe ever. My team mates didn't touch alcohol for the entire season. They all took the responsibility of being in peak physical condition seriously. It was time for me to do the same.

I swallowed against the scratchy dryness of my throat and something inside me knew with full conviction that last night would never happen again. I'd finally had enough.

I'd had enough of having to watch my back for cameras whenever I was up to no good, enough of feeling seedy, of trying to piece together the movements of the night before, of possessive drunk boyfriends imagining something where there was nothing and looking for a fight; enough of feeling like an arsehole. I'd had enough of the whole deal. But most of all I'd had enough of not having any respect for myself or for those girls I ended up with.

Dad was the most respectful person I ever knew. He treated Mum like a queen. And look at what I did – I was worried that a girl whose name I didn't know had robbed me. How the hell had I turned out like this?

I found my boxer shorts turned inside out in a ball on top of my jeans, which were also inside out from my hurry to get out of them and into the girl last night. I slid my legs into the shorts and stood up.

Uh-oh. There was a sharp twinge in my left foot. I took another step, hoping I'd imagined it. I hadn't. The searing pain shot up my fifth toe towards the ankle. I put my head in my hands.

Not again. Please, God, not again.

I gulped down the dread along with two Nurofen, and kept the bulk of my body weight on my right foot while I hobbled through the house to the back door. I fiddled with the stiff lock and let Bluey in. He galloped past me, just about bowling me over, and raced mad laps all over the living room. Only once he'd sniffed out every corner was he satisfied that all was as he had left it the night before and he came to greet me. He bent his head down and licked the top of my bare left foot.

'How can you tell it's sore, mate?' I ruffled the top of his head. 'Clever boy you are, hey? You hungry, Blue? Come on, food time.'

Hearing the f-word, Bluey stopped his inspection of my injured foot and bounced around on his front paws. I left him scoffing dry biscuits on the back deck and made my way back to the bathroom to wash Bridget/Bridie and the remnants of last night off me. My foot throbbed under the hot water and I felt my career slipping away.

Don't panic – you don't know it's that.

But I did know, deep down I knew. I'd felt it for the first time with five minutes to go in the last quarter. It had started as a niggle but as I ran from one end of the ground to the other, it worsened until I was limping by the end of the match. Not so anyone would notice. Anyone except Lily that was. Nothing escaped Lily. I ignored her calls and texts yesterday because I couldn't face the barrage of questions I knew she'd throw at me.

I didn't tell anyone in the club rooms about it after the game. I didn't want to dampen the atmosphere of our first win of the season or the collective relief in the team that I'd seen out the whole game. Anyway, I reasoned, it could have been nothing more than lack of match practice.

It got worse in the evening, so I went into denial by getting blind drunk in full view of the entire coaching and management staff. Thanks to the alcohol, I didn't feel a thing last night. But this morning I knew.

When I was dried and dressed, had sunk a Red Bull, and felt strong enough to handle the sound of my own voice down the phone – as well as hers – I rang Mum's mobile.

Ross answered. I stiffened, even though it was him that I was really after. I told him about the foot and he said they'd come straight over. As far as orthopaedic surgeons went, there weren't many around more experienced than Ross. I trusted his judgement.

I limped back outside and patted Bluey's back. 'Sorry, mate, can't walk you. My foot's buggered. We'll see if Mum will take you for a walk, hey?'

Bluey bounded over to where I kept his lead and looked expectantly over his shoulder at me. Instead, I found his sodden tennis ball half buried in the grass. I pulled up a bar stool from the veranda and spent the next fifteen minutes throwing the ball around the small garden while Bluey sprinted to fetch it until he was panting.

With Bluey forgetting he'd missed his walk and happily snoring on the couch, I hopped around and did a quick tidy up of the house before Mum and Ross arrived. Not that it did much good, the place was a disgrace. I really did have to get a new cleaning lady. Sharon mysteriously disappeared late last year, along with a stack of hundred dollar notes I had in the top desk drawer. So it had been roughly five months since the floors were mopped or the shower had been scrubbed. It didn't bother me but it would bother Mum and she'd bother me.

The doorbell rang just over an hour after I spoke to Ross. It still unsettled me to see Mum with him. I wished it didn't. Ross was a genuinely good guy, he adored Mum and he was always friendly with Lily and me, never overstepping the mark. But he wasn't Dad, and every time I saw him, no matter how nice he was, it reminded me that it should be Dad by Mum's side.

After Mum's predictable 'Nick, your house is revolting. Have you no shame?' speech, I showed them the offending foot. Mum sat close by, watching, as Ross did the assessment while I lay back on bent elbows. He was silent as he prodded and twisted my foot with his large cold hands. I gasped sharply and cursed when he hit the spot.

He stroked his chin when he was done. 'Nick, I'm really not sure. Given your lack of pain through the pre-season and the fact those last lot of bone scans were clear, it could just be that you overdid it yesterday and it's only a bit of inflammation that will settle down. But it might be that the stress fractures have come back, mate. I wouldn't rule it out without an MRI.' He avoided my eyes when he said that.

I groaned loudly.

Ross turned to Mum. 'Mel, let's order an MRI, to be safe.'

Mum reached into her handbag and pulled out a referral pad that she handed to Ross.

They didn't stay long after that. We'd already said our goodbyes after dinner on Friday night before the match. They'd been living up north for a year now. They met in Kenya, Mum and Ross, when they were both volunteer doctors there, and then Mum followed him home to the outback. I wouldn't see them again until the finals. If we made it that far into the season. If I made it that far.

I shook Ross's hand at the front door.

'Catch you for finals, Nick.' He patted my back. 'I've got a good feeling about the Rangers holding up that cup this year with you leading the charge, mate. I can picture it clearly.'

I mustered up a smile. He tried hard, Ross.

It was only when they'd left that I realised I'd forgotten to ask Mum if she'd walk Bluey.

I sat on the couch with my leg up and called Craig.

'Nick, what's up? Tell me you didn't get into trouble when I left last night,' he groaned. 'We're going to need another serious chat about drinking during the season after what I saw of you yesterday.'

He sounded fed up. It was little wonder. He'd spent much of last year in damage control while I wreaked havoc all over Perth. It was only his second year coaching me but already he was exhausted.

'I know, I'm sorry. I promise no more drinking. Honestly. But, Craig, I'm ringing because my foot's bad,' I said heavily. 'It hurts to walk. A lot.'

He sighed. 'Shit.'

'Ross White, my mum's partner who's an orthopaedic surgeon, came over and checked it out this morning. He's written me up an MRI referral.'

'And? What does he think?' I could hear the tension in his voice.

'He said it's hard to say — it might just be inflammation. He's not ruling out stress fractures though.'

There was a long silence.

'All right, Nick, I'll call Aaron and get him to line up that scan for first thing in the morning. Stay off it all day, all right?'

Five minutes later, Aaron, the team's head doctor, called to say I had an appointment at nine tomorrow morning. MRIs normally had a three-day wait list.

As the pain became more and more intense, a knot formed in the pit of my gut. I couldn't afford to have stress fractures again this early in my career. It spelled disaster. And now I'd run out of painkillers too.

I drove to a local pharmacy where I was tempted to park the Range Rover in the disabled spot directly outside, but then I imagined the impact on the club if a photo of that appeared in tomorrow's paper. And today was the day I stopped being an arsehole, so parking in a disabled bay wasn't the way to go. I drove around the corner and parked in a regular spot.

'Oh, cool, Nick Harding! Look, Dad, Nick Harding!'

'Is too! Well spotted, Joshy! Onya Harding!'

I smiled, gave them a double thumbs up and limped into the pharmacy.

I walked in self-consciously, the way I did everywhere, knowing my every move was more than likely being watched. Luckily, it seemed empty, except for the voices in the dispensary.

As I passed by the birth control section on my way through, I had a quick flashback. Pretty sure that was the last condom in the box I'd frantically grabbed last night. I reached out for a pack but stopped myself. No condoms in the house meant no more Bridgets. And no more Bridgets meant no more hating myself after Bridget-type nights when I ignored Bridget-type text messages.

I left the condoms where they were, bought some over-the-counter anti-inflammatories and went into the coffee place next door for the first time since it had changed hands and been renamed Black Salt.

It was packed in there. Shit. This place used to always be empty. I was super careful to hide the limp.

People were sprawled out on black oversized beanbags and lounging around on red vinyl sofas. Two preschool-aged boys were attempting to climb a giant Buddha water feature in the corner. Couples swung on indoor garden swings and on hammocks tied to wooden beams. A group of teenage girls were writing their names on the blackboard-painted walls with coloured chalk dangling from twine. There wasn't a single table to be seen, just wine barrels painted with motivational phrases dotted around the place between the sofas.

Great, just what Fremantle needed – another overpriced hipster café.

'Yeah! Haaaarding,' a guy around my age drawled from a beanbag. 'Yer a bloody legend, mate!'

'Good to have you back, Harding,' his mate chimed in. 'We missed you, mate.'

I smiled, gave them the regulation double thumbs up and walked extra, extra carefully to the queue at the counter, biting down on my lip as I put my full weight through the foot. Lots of sets of eyes were on me. I wished the windows to this place weren't tinted – if I'd known how busy it was I never would have come in.

When it was my turn to order, I leaned on the counter and forced a smile at the girl who hurried back from pinning the last order to the kitchen alcove.

'Hello and a warm Sunday session welcome, sir, to Black Salt Café. You're in luck because our amazing Best of Brunch food mood boards have landed. Our all day brunch is now served up straight on the chopping boards and it's fresher than ever!' Her huge caramel-coloured eyes peeked at me from a long fringe that fell over her face. The rest of her dark hair was super short and in punk style spikes. Even though she was tall and broad-shouldered, there was something in her eager-to-please expression that made her appear vulnerable, fragile almost. She was beautiful. Really beautiful. 'Have you a preference, sir, for which Best of Brunch food mood board you would like to sample? I can very highly recommend the Feeling Frisky Best of Brunch food mood board, because the glazed chorizo and the chilli lime squid on the Feeling Frisky Best of Brunch food mood board is a very good brunch combination, hokay?'

Did she just call me sir?

'Uh, actually I just wanted a take-away coffee, thanks.'

'Oh yes, of course, sir. I should have asked you that first, yes? Please let me explain to you the Craving a Coffee menu, hokay?' She took a deep breath and launched into another spiel. 'There is the Banging Brazilian Blend—'

'I'd just like a large flat white with one, if that's okay.'

'Of course, yes, sir. Gianni our barista will fix that for you personally, sir, hokay?' She smiled again.

'Excellent.' I smiled back at her. 'I'm just going to sit on the swing in the corner there while I wait, if that's all right.' I desperately needed to get off my foot.

'Oh, you will not be sitting with your friends in the "Chillax Zone"?' She pointed to the football fans who had called out to me when I walked in.

'Oh, no, um, no we're not friends.' I paused. 'I don't actually know those people.'

She frowned. 'Hokay. Very well, sir.'

I sat and swayed on the zebra-striped swing, not taking my eyes off her while she served the next few customers. She jutted her bottom lip out and blew air up her face making her fringe fly. She wiped sweat off her brow but the whole time her smile stayed genuine and warm with each person in line.

She wasn't my type, not by a long shot. My type was very much the Bridget type – the flirty, wouldn't say no to anything, wouldn't be out of place on the cover of *Maxim*, the longer the (preferably blonde) hair and the tighter the clothes, the better. Long painted nails, extra high high-heels – that type.

She looked over to where I was. I smiled at her. She stopped talking for a second and smiled back at me. Our eyes stayed locked. Whoa. I gulped and she blushed a deep red. She looked back at the customer she was serving, tucking rogue strands of fringe behind her ear and she started talking to them again, shifting her weight from one foot to the other. Could she sense me watching her?

A couple of minutes later, another girl walked up behind her and tickled her on the waist. She turned and laughed and untied her apron, pulling it up over her head and hiding it behind the counter.

At the same time, my ticket number was called out by Gianni, who looked more Australian than Vegemite. I was about to heave myself out of the swing when I saw her motion at me to stay sitting and she walked up to the coffee bar to grab the cardboard cup.

She walked towards me, looking at the ground. She had a loose black T-shirt on that hung halfway down her thighs with the words 'It's LeviOsa not LeviosAR' emblazoned across the chest. Her green zig-zag striped leggings were tucked into bright purple Doc Martin boots. I hadn't noticed it when she was serving me, but she had a good twenty leather bracelets stacked up high on both forearms.

Attitude hair, attitude clothes. Hmm, interesting.

'Your coffee, sir.' She said self-consciously, handing over the cup.

'Hey, thanks.' I took it from her hands and our fingers touched for a quick second. Whoa – again. Seriously, what was with that? I swallowed and said, 'That was really kind of you to bring over my coffee. You didn't have to do that.'

'But you have a sore leg, so of course.'

'How can you tell? I thought I was doing a good job hiding that.'

'No, not such a good job, sir.' She smiled, tugging at the bottom of her T-shirt. 'Is it very bad, the pain when you walk?'

'Nah, it's all right.'

She gave a little laugh. 'Australians always say, "It is all right" when it is not all right.'

I laughed too. 'Yeah, we do, don't we? So where are you from?'

'I am from Alexandria, in Egypt.'

I liked the sound of her husky voice. A very sexy voice.

'Oh? You're the first real-life Egyptian I've ever met. Have you been in Australia long?'

'A little more than a year since I came here, sir.' Her eyes had a distant look about them. They looked almost haunted.

'You don't need to call me sir, I'm just Nick.' I reached out my hand and she gave it a weak shake. Wishing I didn't have to, I let her soft hand go after a few seconds. 'So, what's your name?'

'My name is Anna, sir.' she nodded.

I laughed again. 'Not sir, just Nick. Okay? You really don't have to call me sir. My name's Nick Harding. Well, it's Nicholas Harding, but I prefer Nick.'

I waited but there was not a hint of recognition from her. Oh, that was great. Beyond great.

'It is a pleasure to meet you, Nick. Nice weather we are having, yes?' She smiled with her whole face and nodded at me quickly a few times.

My heart skipped a beat.

'It *is* a nice day.' I let my eyes rest on hers and she looked at her boots.

Gianni was watching us from behind the bar. He looked kind of pissed off.

'Hey, is it okay that you're here talking to me? Will you get in trouble with him?' I indicated with my chin in Gianni's direction.

'No, no,' she said dismissively.

'He keeps looking over, though. Is he your boyfriend? I don't want any trouble.'

She broke into a low husky laugh and looked over her shoulder at him, giving him a shoo-away sign with her hand.

'Gianni, my boyfriend? Not if he was the last man left on the Earth!'

'Is he really that bad? You'd rather let humankind die out as a species than repopulate with him?'

'Definitely. But he is a very nice boss, even though he is a terrible boyfriend to poor Renee.'

'Why does he look annoyed with us, though? Is it because you're talking to me rather than working?' I threw Gianni a warning look but it didn't stop him staring.

She shooed him away with her hand again, in a more pronounced way this time, and he finally looked away. 'My shift is finished. Ashlee has taken over for the afternoon.' She pointed at the girl behind the counter who was also staring at us. 'Gianni is not annoyed at us, rather he is annoyed that we are too far away for him to hear what we are saying. He is the kind of person who has to know everything.'

So she'd come over to chat instead of running for the door, like anyone else would have, after finishing a shift in a busy café on a Sunday morning.

'If you've finished your shift, do you want a seat then?' I patted the swing.

'It is hokay, I am happy to stand. So what is wrong with your leg?'

'Hurt it running. I'm having a scan to find out what's wrong with it tomorrow.' That was the truth after all. 'What does that writing on your T-shirt mean? What's a Leviosar?' I asked, dragging out the 'o' sound.

Her jaw dropped. 'Nick, this is one of the most famous quotes from *Harry Potter and the Philosopher's Stone*. You do not recognise this quote?'

I shook my head. 'I haven't read any Harry Potter books, haven't seen any Harry Potter movies either.'

'But, the story of Harry Potter is the most wonderful story ever told so I am afraid you are missing out greatly by not reading it, sir, not sir, Nick.' She looked genuinely worried about me not having read it.

'That's a big call – the most wonderful story ever told. I might have to download it then. I'm stuck at home with this stupid foot anyway. That's as good an excuse as any to read the most wonderful story ever told.'

'No, you do not need to download it. Wait.'

She raced off to the back of the café and disappeared through the plastic swing door. A few moments later she reappeared holding a book in her hand.

She gave it to me with a flourish. 'You can borrow it.'

'Thanks.' I inspected the tattered copy of *The Philosopher's Stone*. 'So if I read this, I'll understand what your T-shirt says?'

'You will indeed. And if you enjoy it, I have the whole series here that you can borrow.' She pulled her shoulders back proudly.

I leaned back in the swing and had a swig of coffee. My body relaxed as the heat spread inside me. 'That's really sweet of you to offer. Thanks, Anna. Great coffee too.' I raised the cup. 'Just what I needed to pick me up today – a hit of good strong coffee.'

She laughed. 'Of course Gianni makes a very good coffee indeed. But Nick, this is a flat white – it is not a strong coffee. If you want a real coffee, then you must try Turkish coffee. It is the only way to have coffee when, as you say, you need something strong.'

'Is that a kind of espresso? I don't do espresso. That's not coffee, that's toxic tar.'

She put her hands on her hips. 'Espresso is not coffee? It is the *only* coffee. In Egypt, everyone will kill themselves with laughing if they see milk in coffee, and in such a big cup as this.' She pointed at my cup. 'But, you know, Turkish coffee is not just any espresso. It is pure velvet, Nick. If you truly want to drink coffee in the proper fashion, you must most definitely try a Turkish coffee. It is so thick, almost like a syrup. A velvet syrup.'

I pulled a face. 'Ugh, coffee syrup? I'm sorry, Anna, I'll read your book but I won't drink your coffee.'

'Very well, suit yourself. You can keep drinking this pretend coffee and telling yourself it is strong.' Her rolled 'r's made me smile. That accent was so damn sexy. Maybe she was my type.

She looked at her watch. 'I must be leaving now. It was very nice to meet you, Nick.'

I cleared my throat. 'Um, can I ask for your number, Anna?'

'Why?' She gave me a confused look.

'So I can call you and tell you what I think of the book. So we can perhaps go out together some time?'

Why was I so nervous?

She flicked her fringe back and looked up at the ceiling before making eye contact again. 'That is a very kind offer. Thank you, Nick, but no.'

I was taken aback. 'Oh, okay. Can I ask why not, Anna?'

'Because I am not a girl who gives her telephone number to somebody she does not know. A book? Yes. My telephone number? No.'

I felt the heat creep into my cheeks. 'Okay, so no phone number, but could I take you out for dinner tonight? Just dinner?'

She gave me a long look and then took a big breath in and out. 'I am working tonight.'

'But you just finished working.'

'I am not working here, of course. I am working at the restaurant that belongs to my Uncle Fariz.' She twisted one of the leather straps around her wrist.

'Oh, I see. Which restaurant?' I tried to make the question sound light, innocent.

'Masri's. It is Egyptian food, very wonderful food.' Her smile returned.

I spread my arms out. 'My favourite!'

She laughed that low husky laugh again.

A family walked into the café then. They stopped talking when they saw me. The father pulled out his phone and I sensed a photo session coming on.

'All right, Anna.' I pushed off on my hands and stood up. 'I'll let you go and I'd best be going too. But I'll come back and give you my verdict on Harry Potter, okay?'

'Hokay. I shall look forward to this . . . very much. Bye, Nick, have a nice day.' She tucked more strands of fringe behind her ear.

Our eyes locked together once again and neither of us smiled this time. I got a deep longing way down low. I looked away before I embarrassed myself.

'Bye, Anna.'

The family walked up with their expectant Rangers fan smiles on. I smiled back at them, gave a double thumbs up to each of the three gobsmacked kids and left quickly, hurting my foot even more in my rush to get out.

As I hobbled to the car the sky was a brilliant cloudless blue and the whole streetscape looked shiny. What a magnificent day it was!

I sent a group text to Joel and Bruce once I was in the driver's seat:

I know it's short notice but are you guys up for dinner out tonight? I've got a hankering for Egyptian food.